# THE WORLD HELD HOSTAGE

**Dr. Rachel Lesage.** A brilliant and powerful scientist, she commands total control over every aspect of her life. But her genius has turned deadly, love has corrupted into rage, and Rachel Lesage has become—the threat known only as Artemis . . .

**Tory Farr-Colwell.** Rachel's daughter, D.C.'s top lobbyist. When her mother asks her to save the world, Tory will do anything to help.

**Carson Colwell.** Tory's husband, the new FBI chief of counterterrorism. His first case will lead to unimaginable threats, unimaginable revelations . . . and inconceivable betrayals.

**Dr. Jack Hunt.** Renowned humanitarian with a troubled past, he has vowed to stop the terrorists who killed his wife—until he is trapped into helping Artemis, the woman he once loved.

**Laurel Hunt.** Jack Hunt's granddaughter. Her faith in Jack is absolute . . . until it's tested.

# BEYOND RECALL

## STEPHEN KYLE

**WARNER**
VISION
**BOOKS**

A Time Warner Company

WARNER BOOKS EDITION

Cover design by Diane Luger

Warner Vision is a trademark of Warner Books, Inc.

Warner Books, Inc.
1271 Avenue of the Americas
New York, NY 10020

Visit our Web site at
www.twbookmark.com

 A Time Warner Company

Printed in the United States of America

First Paperback Printing: January 2000

10 9 8 7 6 5 4 3 2 1

Thy god-like crime was to be kind,

To render with thy precepts less

The sum of human wretchedness.

—Lord Byron, from *Prometheus*

# ACKNOWLEDGMENTS

My special thanks to the following:

Graeme McRae, Chairman and CEO of Bioniche, Inc., for a tour in the biotechnology marketplace.

Eike Batiste, Chairman of TVX Gold, Inc., in Rio de Janeiro, for factual nuggets about gold mining in Brazil; and Jim Borland for the contact.

Dr. James Orbinski of Médecins Sans Frontières (Doctors Without Borders), whose work with this remarkable organization is an inspiration.

Dr. Jay Keystone of the Tropical Disease Unit at the Toronto Hospital and Professor of Medicine at the University of Toronto, for invaluable assistance with the medical background. (Any errors in the book are mine alone.)

Stephen Lewis, former Canadian ambassador to the United Nations, for a helpful, wide-ranging conversation during the planning of this book.

Readers of an early draft, whose comments were so useful: Sara Best, Dan Morast, Linda Bound, Nika Rylski, Bill Hunt, Anne Doncaster, David Doncaster, James MacMillan.

Barry Kent MacKay, for his ornithology expertise.

Peter and Marg-Anne Jones and family, for friendship and hospitality at their enchanting, real-life Swallow Point.

Susan Sandler, my editor at Warner Books, for her thoughtful and meticulous editorial fine-tuning and Jackie Joiner for shepherding the final edit.

Al Zuckerman, my agent, whose advice, guidance, and

judgment throughout the planning and writing of this book I deeply appreciate.

Simon Lipskar, my editor, whose spirited collaboration improved the book immeasurably; thanks, maestro, for drawing forth the best music I could make.

Stephen Best, whose clear-eyed view of the world inspired this story and remains a dynamic standard.

# 1

THE DEADLINE WAS UP. SHE WOULD HAVE TO KILL.

Rachel Lesage stopped on the dirt path, furious, and found herself in a no-man's-land between two worlds. The path from the ravine had brought her to the rear lawn of Lesage Laboratories, while behind her lay the woods. The peace there—the hush of the trees, dappled sunlight, shy birds—had given sanctuary from the decision she had to make, but now there was no more refuge. The lawn stretched before her with mono-green precision, purged of every nongrass species. No birdsong, no shade, no shelter. Nowhere for her soul to hide.

They had refused, ignored her warning. It enraged her. *I never wanted this.*

From the front of the building where a casino tent had been set up, the electric twang of a country band jarred her. It was Employee Appreciation Day here at her Bar Harbor facility, and families were picnicking on the front lawn. More were inside, piling up their plates in the cafeteria, line-dancing in the conference room, squealing over raffle prizes in the lobby. Their clamor had driven her to the ravine, though as Lesage Laboratories' founder and CEO she should be among them, playing host. Tonight, at the lobster dinner, she must make a speech; tomorrow, in Dallas, the keynote address at an industry conference. As a Nobel laureate she was a speaker much in demand. But here, now, the deadline was up . . . she must act.

She started along the concrete walkway, moving mechanically, feeling cold despite the glaring sun. *Like an accident victim in shock,* was her detached thought. She'd always been able to focus her mind clinically, to analyze phenomena, even her own reactions.

Suddenly, she wasn't sure she could go through with it.

The casino tent rose before her, garish yellow, a fool's idea of gold. Whoops from people playing blackjack drifted over the parking lot with a fairground giddiness, and the country singer went on whining out his heartbreak, his loss. False emotion. Rachel knew, because the anguish chilling her was so profoundly real.

She heard a child's wail. A little boy, all alone, was squatting in the parking lot, crying wildly, face red, eyes big with fear. Rachel felt a wave of sympathy, surprised by the force of this maternal response. It was over thirty years, yet she vividly recalled how her baby daughter's cry, even from another room, would tug milk beads to her nipples. She thought, Our primitive nervous system is hardwired for only two types of stimuli: biological needs demanding instant gratification, or immediate dangers demanding "fight or flight." Nothing else penetrates.

She crouched before the boy. "Where's your mother?"

He gaped at her, instantly silent, though fear and confusion still swam in his eyes, and his breath came in spasms. He pointed to the tent. "Daddy."

Gambling regulations barred children from the premises, so his father had simply left him outside. Rachel imagined the young man drawn to the bright tent as instinctively as a moth, as mindlessly as an addict. Instant gratification. Hard-wired.

An engine revved and a station wagon suddenly reversed toward them. Rachel snatched the boy up and stepped clear with him as the car lurched past. Not noticing them, the driver shunted gears and drove off, tires squealing. The boy squirmed in Rachel's unfamiliar arms, and the moment she set him down he tore away, crying again, running blindly toward a patch of tall ornamental grass.

Her eyes locked on the high stalks. The chill snaked out from deep in her heart as she saw again the tall sorghum grass in the hills above Kigali. Saw a wounded boy crawling, bleeding. Saw herself clawing over the stony ground, trying to reach him . . . her son . . . Paul . . .

"Dr. Lesage!"

Her public relations manager was hurrying across the asphalt. "Doctor, could we get pictures of you inside the casino? Maybe playing the—"

"No." She was staring at the boy. He was sobbing hysterically, hands on his head in a pathetic surrender to panic. He seemed to stand for all the earth's children abandoned in humanity's greed. His desolation galvanized her. She was resolved. The deadline had passed.

"Find that child's father," she told the PR man. "He's in the tent." She started toward the lab.

In her office she picked up the phone. She was sickened by what she was about to set in motion. *But if I falter, I'm worse than the rest. Denying responsibility, bewailing that nothing can be done.*

Something can.

She depressed the numbers: it was done. The system was

activated, beyond recall. The day after delivery, thousands would be dead.

An immediate danger. A primitive stimulus.

*The world will take notice now.*

# 2

JACK HUNT THREW BACK HIS HEAD TO DRAIN a final glass of his wedding champagne, but since he was laughing, a lot of it was dribbling down his chin. Guests crowding the marble foyer clapped rhythmically, egging him on, and as he raised his empty glass with a flourish, they cheered. Grinning, he turned to Marisa. Gone. She'd been right beside him a minute ago. "Great start," he declared with a laugh. "Married three hours and already I've lost my wife."

The guests laughed in delight, and Jack played along with the joke on himself: the bridegroom stranded, though not exactly at the altar. Marisa's uncle, the senator for Amazonas, was hosting this reception at his elegant home in Manaus, the metropolis in the heart of the Amazon jungle, and it seemed as if half of Manaus society had squeezed into the foyer to see them off. Still, Jack found himself at the door alone.

It hit him, right there amid the party chatter, that he hated the idea. Being alone. He'd done that for too long. Made work his whole life for too long. At fifty-three he'd never expected to fall in love again. Maybe he didn't even deserve to. But when Marisa Almeida joined his medical team in the jungle five weeks ago, it happened. She'd stirred something in his heart he had trained himself, during his long self-imposed sentence, to live without. He still felt a quiet astonishment that she had made a new beginning seem possible.

"I believe," the senator said above the noise, "she went upstairs to make a call."

Jack couldn't believe it. "She's on the *phone*?"

More laughter from the guests. Jack threw up his hands in defeat, laughing again too.

Until he spotted Gerry Trowbridge's video camera focused on him. Gerry and his wife, Liz, documentary makers, had been following him for weeks from one jungle clinic to another. The three of them had been friends ever since they'd chronicled his work for One World Medics in Sudanese refugee camps eight years ago. The film had garnered prizes and made Jack a household name, and when Liz had recently suggested this follow-up project he'd been glad to cooperate. But that's work, he thought now. This is personal. And getting embarrassing. As the two of them were jostled closer to him by more people crowding in, he caught Gerry's wicked smile behind the lens, clearly enjoying recording his discomfort.

"Give me a break, Liz," Jack said under his breath. "The world doesn't need to see this."

"Oh, don't be such an arrogant son of a bitch," she said lightly. "Your public will eat it up. It's cute."

He winced. *Cute?*

She laughed, but she took pity and nudged Gerry's beefy arm. He finally lowered the camera, grinning.

"You're shameless, you two," Jack said. "You planning to follow us into the honeymoon suite, too?"

"Nah, boring," Gerry said. "Won't be up to much, old geezer like you."

"Don't kid yourself, Ger," Liz said. "Half the women here would kill for one night with this old geezer."

"You blue-eyed devil, you." Gerry did a parody of a love-struck matron. "Oooh, Doctor, *take* me!"

Jack chuckled. "Liz, what rock did you find this guy under?"

"Here's Marisa!" someone called.

Jack smiled at the sight of her. Running down the stair-case, with her eyes sparking and her hand hovering over her corsage as protectively as any girl at the prom, she looked a decade younger than her forty-two years.

"Sorry!" she said, breathless as she reached his side. "Jack, I just talked to Gilberto's mother. She's ecstatic. The antimony derivative worked and he's out of bed. She says you're a miracle worker."

He shook his head, marveling. Who but Marisa would stall her own honeymoon to check on an eight-year-old leishmaniasis patient in a jungle squatters' camp? He slipped his arm around her waist. "*You're* the miracle worker," he said. He'd been assisted by nurses more highly trained, more efficient, but none as compassionate, as purely empathetic, as Marisa. It was her gift, and not just to pa-tients. She had stopped his workaholic life in its tracks with just her gentleness. That was the real miracle: he'd been changed. Only once before had he known such a feeling, of being changed. Then, however, it was a devastation—com-ing upon his daughter's corpse. And her terrified child, so starved with need. In that moment he'd felt his selfish, he-donistic existence consuming him like rot. The only escape from its rankness was to step out of his skin. So he did. He had labored since to remake himself. Maybe, finally, he'd succeeded. Must have, he thought with a rush of happiness, or Marisa wouldn't be here beside me. He bent his head to kiss her.

The guests applauded. Gerry had the camera going.

Jack made a mock show of sternly marching his bride to the door. "There'll be no phones on the beach at Santarém."

The fifteen-seat Bandeirante was a rugged Brazilian-built government plane the senator had made available for their honeymoon. The pilot and copilot had the starboard engine roaring as Jack and Marisa climbed aboard, followed by Liz and Gerry and their Brazilian soundman, all lugging their equipment. The Bandeirante raced down the runway, lifted off, and bucked through the turbulence of the cloud cover, rain beading the windows. As they broke above the clouds into sunshine, Marisa snuggled against Jack's shoulder. "What a wonderful day."

"Damn near perfect." He squeezed her hand. "I only wish Laurel could have been there." His granddaughter—that terrified child he'd become guardian to—was dear to him. Eighteen now, and anything but terrified. Hard to believe she was in her first year at Boston University. "Hop a flight," he'd said when he called her from the senator's house. "I need you to give me away."

Laurel laughed, but he heard the surprise in her voice at the news. "Getting married, wow. That's so cool."

"And so sudden, I know. Sweetheart, you're going to love Marisa."

But she couldn't get away from her summer job. "I'll be thinking of you guys, though," she said. "Bring me back a piece of wedding cake, okay?"

Marisa was looking at him with an amused twinkle. "I still can't believe you have a granddaughter in college."

"He was trying to set a record," Gerry kidded from the

seat ahead of them, folding his arms to nap. "World's horniest twelve-year-old."

Jack smiled, but he let the joshing end there. He'd found marriage and fatherhood at the age of twenty a disaster, and his daughter's pregnancy when she was fifteen a horror. Which had led to worse horrors. The worst would be his secret to bear forever. The nightmare's one bright saving grace had been the outcome: Laurel.

"Excuse me, Dr. Hunt? Would you mind?" The young pilot was holding out a copy of Jack's autobiography, *One World Medic*. "You said you'd sign it."

"Sure thing." Jack fished in his pocket for a pen. "Who to?"

"Freddie, that's me. For Frederico." Turning to Marisa, he added in his flawless English, "By the way, Mrs. Hunt, thanks for the bottle of champagne."

She said with a wink, "I hope you have someone to share it with this evening in Santarém."

"No such luck. After we drop you off we've got to go back for a pickup."

"Back to Manaus?" Jack asked, scribbling his signature.

"No, about halfway. Place called Jazida, gold-mining settlement. I just got the call. Got to take someone there to the hospital in Santarém."

"Why you, back and forth? There must be other planes in the area. If it's an emergency, time's important."

"No, they said it's just a bad case of flu, but the guy's insisting on a hospital. Anyway, senator's orders."

"Ah, a patient with pull," Jack said, handing back the book.

Freddie shrugged stoically. "The senator has a lot of friends."

The plan bothered Jack. Bad medicine. He'd seen too many deaths in jungle towns—everything from ruptured appendixes to pneumonia—because the victims had waited too long for treatment, often after a self-diagnosis of "a bad case of flu." "Look, there's no reason why this patient should have to wait hours for you to come back. We should pick him up on our way." He looked at Marisa. After all, it was her wedding day too.

She nodded without hesitation. "We have plenty of room."

He loved her for that. "This is a medical decision," he told the pilot. "I'll take responsibility. We'll pick up the patient."

Freddie didn't need his arm twisted. "Yes, sir." He went back to the cockpit clutching his book.

Jack caught Marisa's sly smile. He knew what she was thinking: that he couldn't resist taking charge. True enough, he had to admit. For a decade he'd been leading One World Medics teams into hellholes from Tajikistan to Bosnia to the Congo. He hated the misery the powerful inflicted on the helpless. Hated what they got away with, the warlords and famine profiteers and despots. The helpless had taught him a lesson or two about fortitude, though. At one Angolan field hospital he'd worked all night with a local nurse assisting him silently but ably—then, in the morning, he was told that she'd seen two of her children killed by a land mine just days before. In country after country, as Jack faced the war-lords in negotiations, he took fierce satisfaction in forcing concessions: a halt in the shelling, an agreement to allow refugees access to clean water, the opening of a road to let medicine in. Each gain saved lives. People like that Angolan nurse and her family.

The great thing—the paradoxical thing—was that Marisa didn't want him to change; *he* did. For her. Not stop, of course, but slow down, enjoy life with her. He was excited about the plans they were making to build a chalet in Ver-mont, near Stowe. Already he could picture them between missions. They'd ski, take walks, cook, relax. Laurel could drive up to visit. He smiled to himself. Who said you couldn't have it all?

He took Marisa's hand. They'd still get to the Santarém resort around sunset, and then it would be just the two of them. These last weeks, living with the team in tents, they'd only managed twice to find a quiet spot to make love. He was looking forward to the hotel, and told her so.

"Mmm," she agreed. "It'll be nice to have sheets."

"Nice to have a *door*." He kissed her hand, feeling a surge of contentment. I am changed, and this is peace.

The engines altered pitch as the plane began its descent. Jack looked down at the open mine operation, a deep bowl the size of a couple of football fields hacked out of the jungle. Hundreds of small, staked claims at varying levels made a three-dimensional checkerboard, which men were laboring all over, moving up and down an intricate system of ladders. A sluggish stream snaked by the site. Probably contaminated, Jack thought. Throughout the Amazon basin, mercury and cyanide used in the mining process had poisoned the waters. He'd treated a lot of victims.

Beside the mine was a muddy shantytown, a huddled sprawl of black plastic lean-tos and wooden shacks in a warren of boggy streets. The main street was cratered with potholes, which Jack could plainly see because the street was lined up beneath the plane; Freddie the pilot was going to land on it. A moment later the Bandeirante banged down, bumping over the potholes.

"Where the hell are we?" Gerry asked, waking up.

Liz peered out. "Not in Kansas anymore."

As Jack was explaining the stop, Freddie came out of the cockpit. "Interesting landing," Jack commented.

Freddie grinned. "This shouldn't take long. You all might as well stay cool here in the air-conditioning."

Jack wanted to stretch his legs. "I'll come with you."

"Me too," Gerry said. "Maybe grab a quick beer."

Marisa was already busy organizing space for the patient. Unfastening her corsage, she pricked her finger on the pin. "Ouch."

"Need a doctor?" Jack asked with a mock leer.

She laughed, sucking her fingertip.

Jack, Gerry, and the pilot stepped out into the humid heat. "I was told to go to the hotel," Freddie said, looking around. "Wherever that is."

"There." Gerry pointed to a dilapidated two-story building a block away. Jack could just make out its faded sign: CASTELO DOS SONHOS—the Castle of Dreams—HOTEL AND BAR. Good old Ger. Liz had once said of him that through seventeen years of filming wars and disasters together he'd always been able to sniff out a bar.

They started down the street. It was littered with auto parts and rotting fruit and dog feces. Stalls displayed cowboy shirts, soda cans, comic books. A shed, the town's movie theater, bore a poster of Arnold Schwarzenegger nuzzling a revolver, and from a window across the street came the tinny sound of Rod Stewart wailing "Rebel Heart." Above it all was the pervasive third-world odor of urine. Mud-covered men slogged by, going to and from the mine site. *Garimpeiros,* pick and shovel miners. Grim work, Jack thought. He knew most of them would extract no more than a spoonful of gold a month, just enough to subsist on and keep their dreams alive.

One thing seemed odd. He didn't see any women.

In the dusty Castelo barroom a scatter of miners were playing cards and drinking *cachaca,* a barely refined cane liquor. Gerry ordered a shot at the bar. Jack declined. He'd experienced *cachaca*. Once was enough.

"You here for the whore?" the barman asked in Portuguese. He wore a Chicago Bulls T-shirt stretched over his beer belly, and stood eating a plate of beans. Freddie launched into an exchange with him. Jack's grasp of Portuguese was only rudimentary, but he noticed when Freddie looked mildly startled. "Problem?" Jack asked.

"This guy—name's Mendes—says it's one of the hotel girls who's sick. The owner's favorite. He's away, but he told Mendes to be sure we get her to the hospital."

Jack turned to the barman. "You speak English, Mendes?"

"Some."

"Has a doctor seen the girl?"

Mendes made a wry face that said "A doctor in this dump?"

"Where's the girl?" Jack asked.

The barman pointed down the hall with his fork. "First room this side. Name's Raimunda. Sick like a dog."

Jack went to have a look. Knocking on the door, he asked, "Raimunda?" No answer. He pushed it open. The room was dark, the heavy curtains closed. A reek of vomit and excrement hung in the stuffy air. In the gloom a girl lay unmoving on the sheets, her eyes closed. About eighteen, she wore a sleeveless blouse and panties. Jack came to the bedside and felt her forehead. Burning with fever. She didn't move as he felt along her throat. The lymph nodes were enlarged. He palpated her abdomen. The spleen was inflamed, as hard as wood. Classic symptoms of acute viremia. His mind flashed through a catalogue of likely viral infections: Oropouche virus disease, dengue fever, Micambo virus, Guared virus. Dengue seemed most probable—it was rampant throughout Latin America—but the other possibilities were legion. Over four hundred known viruses occurred in the Amazon.

He needed more light. He went to the window and opened the curtains. When he turned back, the girl's eyelids fluttered open and Jack sucked in a breath of surprise. The whites of her eyes were crimson, bright as rubies. Clumps of her hair had fallen out, and a rash covered her skin in florid, starlike speckles, even on her scalp. A thread of blood oozed from her closed lips, but she stared at the ceiling, utterly passive. Suddenly she cried out in a voice shrill with delirium. Then, just as suddenly, she slumped back into her stupor.

Jack's heart beat faster. Lassa fever, here? Or Marburg virus? Or . . . Ebola? Impossible. Nobody's seen those filoviruses in humans outside of Central Africa. But the symptoms were alarmingly similar. Memories flashed of Yambuku, Zaire, in '76. Dark huts, bloodied corpses, wailing villagers.

He heard a faint moan from the room across the hall. He went across and found two women lying on the large bed, both presenting the same symptoms as Raimunda, one moaning in delirium, the other comatose, blood trickling from her nose.

Gerry poked his head in, making a face. "Whew, what a stench."

"Don't come in!" Jack pushed him out and shut the door behind them.

Startled, Gerry said, "What's up?"

Some kind of hemorrhagic fever, Jack knew. Almost certainly infectious. Potentially lethal. Thank God Marisa and the others hadn't got off the plane. "Gerry," he said, "these women have something much worse than flu. We can't risk taking them to Santarém. It could spread the infection. In fact, no one in the town should leave." He added carefully, "Including us."

"You're kidding."

"Wish I was." If it was an airborne virus, he and Gerry and the pilot might already be infected. He added, "Marisa and Liz and your soundman and the copilot haven't come into contact with the town. I'm going to send them out right away."

"Jesus," Gerry muttered, absorbing the shock. Then he nodded soberly, accepting Jack's fiat. "How can I help?"

Jack slapped his shoulder, grateful for such a friend. "Stick with me. I'm going to need you."

Back in the bar Jack took Freddie aside and quietly asked if the copilot could handle taking the plane out.

"Why would he do that?" Freddie asked.

"*Can* he?"

"Not without me."

Shit. Jack rubbed the back of his neck, thinking. "Then everyone on board has to stay there, and the plane's got to be sealed," he said. He quickly gave Freddie the minimum facts of the situation.

The pilot looked stunned. "But . . . I'm supposed to transport the girl to the hospital. The senator said—"

"The girl's not going anywhere," Jack said. "Neither are we. I'm going to try to quarantine the town."

Freddie stared at him.

"It'll probably just be for a few days," Jack added to soften the blow, though he suspected there was little hope of such a short quarantine. In Yambuku, with Ebola, it had lasted a month.

Freddie's eyes had darkened with a mutinous cast, and Jack saw that he needed convincing. He said sternly, "How secure would your job with the senator be if you were responsible for spreading an epidemic after I'd warned you? Assuming, of course, you *survived* the trip with this victim."

That seemed to sink in. "Now get back to the plane," he

ordered. "Let my wife and the others know what's happening. Only don't open the door. Yell, or show them a note through the window, but don't get on the plane and don't let anyone off. Go!"

As Freddie left, Jack turned to Mendes. "Do you know if anyone else in town is sick?"

"Sure, plenty. Swamp chills. Comes and goes."

"Not malaria, I mean sick like Raimunda."

An Indian listening at the bar said, "Most of the whores in the Quarter have been bellyaching all day."

"The Quarter?" Jack asked.

"Mendes's competition, far end of town." He pushed away from the bar. "I'm going that way. Want a lift?"

The Quarter was the last building at the edge of the settlement, a two-story brothel of rough wood whose pink paint was blistered and flaking. The Indian's truck dropped off Jack and Gerry, then rumbled down a muddy side street. No other cars were in sight, though Jack noticed a teenager tinkering over a motorcycle. "Gerry," he said, "check out that bike."

"You need it?"

"I might."

He entered the Quarter alone. A scabby-mouthed little girl on the doorstep solemnly watched him pass. The hallway was quiet. Along it, small rooms were partitioned off by plywood walls that did not quite reach the tin roof. Curtains across the doorways, some of them plastic shower curtains, offered the only privacy. In one room Jack noticed a pretty girl, maybe sixteen, sitting on the edge of her bed. She was wincing slightly, and looked confused.

"Headache?" he asked from her doorway.

She looked up. "Hell of a headache."

*Ebola always starts with a headache.* Get a grip, he told himself. Lots of things start with a headache.

"What's your name?" he asked, glad that she spoke English. She was barefoot and wore a long yellow tank top and a baseball cap sporting the emblem of the Flamingos, the Rio soccer team. A scatter of cosmetics and glossy magazines lay around her on the bed, and she was idly toying with a makeup trinket, two plastic tubes the size of lipsticks, red and purple, connected by a piece of cheap chain.

"Pia," she answered wearily. "But no fucking today."

Jack almost smiled. "I'm a doctor. Tell me, Pia, are many of the girls here sick?"

"Lots. Teresinha's the worst. And she's about to pop." Dropping the trinket on the bed, she fingered a movie magazine and said dreamily, "I'm going to be a film star."

"Could you take me to Teresinha?"

"Sure." She slid off her bed and led him down the hall. Her walk was unsteady. She drew aside a curtain. "That's her."

A woman of about thirty lay on a bed mumbling incoherently. She was pregnant, and by the size of her abdomen Jack judged that Pia was right: Teresinha was due. On the floor, beside a bottle of *cachaca,* was a brimming chamber pot, the smell foul. A dirty little boy sat in the corner eating a candy bar and looking scared.

Babbling, Teresinha looked up as Jack came to the bedside. Her eyes were crimson. Red tears dripped in a blood-and-mascara sludge into her thinned hair. Between her legs blood stained her skirt, and there was a slime of red-brown excrement on the mattress. Jack's brain whispered a warning litany: Lassa, Marburg, Ebola . . . the deadliest viruses on the planet . . . no known treatment. *Stop it,* he ordered himself, *it's not possible. It's something else.* He felt her fevered forehead. Maybe a hundred and four.

"God, she's got worse," Pia said from the doorway.

Teresinha began to twitch in spasm. It became a convulsion so extreme she lurched to the bed's edge. Jack took hold of her shoulders. She vomited on his arm. He held her steady to keep her from pitching off the bed as bloody vomitus spewed over his sleeve.

"Sweet baby Jesus," Pia said in horror.

"Go back to your room," Jack told her. "And take this boy out."

Teresinha gagged violently. She was choking on her vomit. Jack needed to clear her mouth or she would suffocate. Suddenly, beside him, a hand reached down, fingers whisked inside the woman's mouth to clear it, and she gasped a breath.

Jack looked up. Marisa!

At the sight of her filthy hand his heart jumped to his throat. The vomitus would be loaded with virus, maybe lethally hot. He snatched her wrist, grabbed the *cachaca* bottle, and sloshed liquor over her hand to cleanse it. A brute reflex only: alcohol wouldn't kill virus. Furious, he heaved the bottle away. "Damn that pilot! Didn't he tell you?"

"I'd already got off. I met him on the way. I thought maybe I could help you."

Teresinha moaned, and bright blood oozed between her legs.

"Vaginal hemorrhage," Marisa said. Grabbing a dress from a pile of laundry, she stuffed it between the woman's legs to stanch the flow.

"Marisa, don't," Jack said, grabbing her arm.

As the cloth quickly became saturated she looked up. "Jack, what's happening here?"

"Some kind of hemorrhagic fever. Several cases. It's bad."

"How bad?"

He couldn't hide it from her. "Maybe as bad as Ebola."

She gave a small gasp. Then, silently, she took a towel

from the laundry pile, wiped her hand, and started to clean
off Jack's sleeve. He stared at her fingers streaked with
bloody residue and remembered that she'd pricked her finger on her corsage not half an hour ago. A microscopic por-
tal of entry. His mind blared statistics: Lassa fever, fifty
percent lethality in some nonimmune populations; Ebola,
eighty percent lethality, period. *It can't be Ebola. It's something else.* Something he couldn't handle alone, though. Get
help.

"Go outside," he told her. "I'm going to call the authorities, then see if there's any supplies. Have the kids outside
collect towels and sheets for you until I get back. Until then
don't touch any—"

"Jack," she said, looking behind him.

He turned. Liz Trowbridge stood focusing the video camera.

"Christ," he said, appalled. "Did *everybody* get off?"

"Where you go, I go," Liz said. "That was our deal."

"Mine too," Marisa murmured.

"Our soundman and the copilot stayed aboard," Liz added
as she panned the camera across the room, taking in Marisa.

"Outside, both of you!" Jack ordered, motioning them
away.

There was no point now in sending them back to the
plane. Gritting his teeth, he had to accept that. He herded
them down the hall, Liz walking backward and videotaping
him as he quickly looked into several rooms. In almost
every one, women lay on their beds in passive misery. Two
were shuffling around the communal kitchen in a stupor. As
Liz passed Pia's room the girl called, "Hey, come back!"

Liz swung the camera to her. Pia hopped on her bed and
began posing, thrusting out her breasts and hiking her top
above her panties like a *Playboy* centerfold. "You'll make

me a star!" she said gleefully. She flopped down on the bed, suddenly dizzy.

Jack pushed Marisa and Liz outside as the motorcycle across the street roared to life. He strode over to it.

"Just a clogged fuel line," Gerry told him, wiping his hands on an oily rag. "Works fine now." Suddenly noticing Liz and Marisa out front, he looked at Jack in alarm. "You told the pilot to—"

"They'd already got off the plane."

Gerry scowled, shaken. "Jesus."

The motorcycle's teenage owner was saying something in Portuguese, and Jack pulled some Brazilian bills from his wallet and handed them over. "I need to borrow the bike, kid." He'd learned to ride years ago; motorbikes were ubiquitous in the developing world. "Stay here, Gerry," he said, straddling the ripped leather seat, "and don't let anyone into the Quarter."

He gunned the bike back to the Castelo, his mind racing. He needed isolation equipment, bleach, dressings, masks, gloves—he'd be lucky to find even half these things here— masks and gloves were the bare minimum to protect against a level four virus. *It probably isn't level four. Just get a team in.*

"Mendes," he said, rushing into the Castelo barroom, "is there an infirmary? First-aid supplies?"

"Upstairs. But—"

"You've got to make a phone call," Jack said, starting for the stairs. "Most of the women in this town are sick."

"You want me to ask the boss to fly in some more?" Mendes asked helpfully.

"I want you to call the authorities in Belém. Department of Public Health. Ask for the chief medical officer." He was taking the stairs two at a time. "When you've got him on the line, call me."

"Who's paying for the call?"

"I am."

The infirmary was nothing but a corner cupboard in a storeroom. A dusty box of Band-Aids. A sausage-size roll of gauze. Some antihistamine. Aspirin. Jack plowed his hands through his hair. *Shit.*

Mendes yelled up, "Doctor!"

Jack ran downstairs and grabbed the phone. They'd put him on hold. He waited, pacing within the confines of the cord's length, trying not to think of Marisa's blood-smeared hand . . . of the pinprick on her finger . . . of how dangerously he'd exposed her . . .

When the medical officer came on the line Jack quickly gave his evaluation of a hemorrhagic fever of unknown etiology, asked that an epidemiological team be flown in immediately, and instructed the man to coordinate the effort with the Chagas Institute, the Tropical Disease Research Center in Belém, and the Pan American Health Organization, and to *hurry.*

Then, with Mendes translating, he made an announcement to the men in the bar: some women had a sickness that might be infectious, and until help came a quarantine was necessary. There was a murmur of anxiety, but Mendes said few of them ever left town anyway. Small mercies, Jack thought.

"Doctor! The baby comes!" Teresinha's little boy was calling from the doorway.

Jack raced on the bike to the Quarter. Gerry was standing guard outside, eyeing the few nervous miners who'd drifted over. "Don't let them in," Jack told him.

He found the pregnant Teresinha lying unconscious, bleeding from her gums and eyes, and Marisa wiping the blood with a cloth in her bare hands. He grabbed her elbow. "You've got to be more careful!"

"I know, but—" She looked at Teresinha. "Oh, God." Blood was gushing from Teresinha's nose. Jack thought: This is it, she's crashing. Blood suddenly hemorrhaged from every mucous-membrane orifice—mouth, nose, eyes, vagina, anus. Jack and Marisa scrambled for cloths, but it was hopeless. And Teresinha's baby was coming.

Jack heard a noise and twisted around. Liz was videotaping. "Get out!" he shouted.

"No, I want all I can get of you handling this."

"I *can't* handle it, he wanted to yell as he bent to deliver the baby. It slipped into his hands, a boy, and Marisa cut the cord. The child wasn't breathing. Jack gave mouth-to-mouth resuscitation, and as he caught breaths between giving breaths, Liz crouched nearer with the camera. The baby started to breathe on its own, and Jack spat out blood and laughed in a surge of elation. One small victory!

Marisa stared at Jack's bloody mouth, appalled. She quickly wiped his face, then took the baby.

There was a sound like a sheet being ripped as Teresinha's bowels opened and vented blood, flooding the mattress. Liz lowered the camera in horror and backed away. Teresinha was dead.

A scream of engines sounded down the street. Jack whirled around. The plane! He ran out.

"Fucking pilot," Gerry growled.

Jack watched, aghast, as the Bandeirante lifted off above the trees.

He worked nonstop, going from room to room in the Quarter, then on the bike over to the girls in the Castelo, then back to the Quarter, trying to do what he could for the victims, which was almost nothing. A girl in the Castelo crashed and died. Raimunda fell into a coma. Pia was delirious. More women fell sick every hour . . . forty-six, forty-seven . . . Jack finally lost count. Three little girls were stricken, too: it tore him apart to watch their suffering. The victims' condition deteriorated with a speed he'd never seen before. He'd witnessed many diseases in which a virus had undergone extreme amplification, but over several *days*. *What in God's name is this thing?*

His worst fears were for Marisa. She was assisting him continuously. He couldn't stop her. She changed makeshift dressings, cleaned up messes of blood and vomit, did what she could to make the women comfortable, forced Jack to pause to drink water, found him clean shirts. He cursed himself for bringing her to this place . . . for exposing her. *Where's the fucking help from Belém?*

Night fell. Tree frogs sent up a frantic dirge from the black jungle. Miners came with kerosene lamps and hung around outside the Quarter, murmuring, fearful.

Inexplicably, none of the men had fallen sick.

Around midnight Marisa handed Jack a tin cup of cold beans at a woman's bedside. "Eat."

Wiping sweat from his forehead, he took the cup.

Marisa winced in pain.

Jack froze. "What's wrong?"

"Stomach cramps," she said. He saw her fear as she added, "A headache, too."

His legs went weak in dread. An incubation period of just eight hours? *It's not possible!* He grabbed her hand, panic crawling over him. "Marisa—"

"Maybe it's just exhaustion," she said quickly. "I've been doing too much. I'll rest." She looked at him anxiously. "How are *you*? You've been up to your elbows in blood for—"

"Sit down. Here, you take this food. Where's some water? Liz, get her some water! Marisa, you need—"

A shout came from outside, the men's voices yelling.

"Gerry can't control them," Liz said. She ran down the hall. Marisa and Jack followed.

Outside, someone said, "It's Silva," as a wiry man jumped out of a jeep, yelling, "Where's this bastard doctor? He's got to help my Raimunda!" He barged toward the building, but Gerry blocked his way. Silva lunged for him, and they wrestled on the muddy ground. Men gathered in a circle, shouting, their lanterns swaying. Gerry struggled to his feet and hauled Silva up with him. Silva's fist smashed his jaw, and Gerry staggered backward, spitting blood. Then, rallying, he lunged for Silva. Silva pulled a gun.

"No!" Liz cried.

Silva fired. Gerry fell backward, clutching his thigh.

"Gerry!" Liz ran to him.

Three miners overpowered Silva, and his gun thudded on the ground. Liz grabbed it and shoved it in her pocket.

Jack and Liz dragged Gerry inside to the kitchen, where Jack had only a paring knife to gouge the bullet from Gerry's thigh. Gerry's face turned white at the pain, and he passed out. Marisa found a needle and thread to assist Jack with the sutures, but she mumbled that she felt dizzy, and wandered away. Shakily, Jack sutured the wound, then ran after her.

Dawn. Panic in the Quarter. Women and children shrieking. Twenty-seven women and two girls dead, the rest all sick. The place looked like an abattoir. In a kitchen corner Gerry moaned from his wound, weaving in and out of consciousness. Obsessively, Liz kept videotaping, muttering she had a headache. Jack blocked it all out. All except Marisa.

She lay on the kitchen table, mumbling. He bent over her, smoothing back her sweat-soaked hair. His eyes burned, and his hands were shaking—from despair, from exhaustion, from rage. Where in God's name was the help he'd called for? He might still be able to save her—IV replacement of electrolytes . . . massive doses of human interferon . . . if only he had the supplies!

He lifted her head for a drink of water. Fear swam in her crimson eyes. It reamed Jack's heart. "Jack . . . don't go—"

"I'm here," he said hoarsely. "I won't leave you."

Her gums began to bleed. She staggered to her feet, delirious. "Jack!"

He threw his arms around her to stop her . . . to hold her . . . to keep himself from howling in despair. Her burst of strength ebbed and she slid down his body to the floor. Jack thudded to his knees beside her.

She crashed.

"Marisa!" He stripped off his shirt to try to stanch the hemorrhage from her nose and eyes and vagina. He worked over her wildly, desperately, mopping her body, his chest and arms smeared with blood.

"Not for me," Liz said dully. The camera slipped from her hands. She pulled the gun from her pocket, aimed it at her own face, and cocked it.

Gerry shouted, "No!"

Liz stuck the barrel in her mouth and fired.

# 3

TORY FARR-COLWELL SHIVERED WITH PLEASURE as her husband slid his hand over her knee and under her skirt. The black silk shimmered under the Washington streetlights gliding by outside her limousine's tinted windows. Carson squeezed her thigh and murmured in her ear, "Roasted to perfection."

Tory laughed a throaty laugh, slightly drunk, and slid farther down in the seat to let his hand ease higher between her legs. If he was thinking this was his reward for enduring the banquet with a crowd of lobbyists and congressional insiders, she was more than willing to bestow it. God knew he deserved it.

They'd gathered to roast her: Victoria Farr-Colwell, "Political Consultant of the Year"—at thirty-three, one of the youngest ever to accept the award. MC Senator Frank Owen's quips about her and Carson working different sides of the D.C. power streets had been a big hit, Tory being well known for her liberal causes while Carson, an ex-marine, was an FBI man. The senator's jokes casting her as a communist Mata Hari wheedling pillow secrets from her dull-witted leatherneck husband had drawn raucous laughter, even coaxed a few grins from Carson as he nursed his single beer. His indulgence had softened Tory's guilt at her own delight in the evening's fun, including some decidedly sophomoric whistling and table-thumping from her associates in her firm. Damn it, it *had* been a good year. She'd worked her ass off for it, though; she'd earned the night of glory. And she would have unreservedly enjoyed the whole rambunctious affair if it hadn't been for that little voice inside nagging: Earned it, but at what cost? She had to think hard to remember the last time she and Carson had spent a whole evening together alone.

Her fault, she knew that. Always so busy. Right now she was juggling three campaigns: one to reelect the aging governor of Ohio, another to squeak a liberal candidate into a North Dakota Senate seat, a third to head off a raid by Congress on the pension fund of the teachers' union, her client. The strategies involved complex tactics that she didn't have the time or inclination to explain to her husband.

That, she knew too, was the root of the problem. No one outside the back rooms of politics really understood what went on there, including Carson, despite his advanced degree in international relations. At the beginning of their marriage she'd tried to keep him abreast, but he wasn't all that interested. She knew he felt something like disdain for lobbyists' work. A common response, of course. Ask just about any person in the street these days and they'd give you an outraged earful about lobbyists and politicians being crooks and liars, all. Lately, Tory had less and less patience with this adolescent brush-off. It reminded her of herself at thirteen smugly declaring the world would run better without adults. Nobody likes a lobbyist until their *own* group's interests are threatened; then they can't beat down your door fast enough. Lobbying's just free speech in action, and politicians are just using the system, and that's democracy, my friends.

*Okay, enough soap-boxing. Speeches ended at midnight.*

Anyway, she reminded herself, Carson was no knee-jerk teenager. He kept his reservations about her work to himself, and she respected him too much to hold his prejudice against him. So the topic had become a no-man's-land between them. The trouble was, because his FBI counterterrorism work was also a prohibited subject, it didn't leave them much. That barren terrain separating them seemed to keep growing, forcing them to take ever more steps apart. She remembered a phrase her celebrated scientist mother, who was French-Canadian, once used to describe the divided French and English worlds in Canada: "two solitudes." Is that what Carson and I are becoming? Tory wondered. Sometimes they'd go for days without even speaking, she slipping into bed after working past midnight, Carson asleep; he slipping out most mornings around five before she awoke. And she wasn't sure which was more ominous: that for days she hadn't even noticed the silence, or that Carson didn't really seem to mind. Sometimes, she thought that if it weren't for Chris . . .

She put a brake on that train of thought. Their marriage had been through strained periods before and she'd always heeded the warning whisper in time: Get home before you become strangers. She'd always found a way to make it right again. It was just like devising a schedule to be with Chris, their four-year-old; she'd often nip home while her staff broke for lunch or dinner, spend an hour reading to Chris or putting him to bed, then head back to work. Their son was the one common subject she and Carson cared passionately about. Carson was marvelous with him, the best father in the world. Whenever she had doubts about the marriage, she only had to think of their child growing up in the love they both had for him. That warning whisper, sometimes so annoying, could also be very wise: Get home, because of all the good that's there.

That was why, tonight, she was grateful that Carson had come to the banquet and sat by her side. Pleased that he'd taken the jokes with good humor. Most of all, she was glad—relieved—that now, alone, they could come together on this familiar territory. *This,* she thought with a small gasp of pleasure as his hand moved higher between her thighs, *has always been sure ground.*

"If I'm hot," she breathed, her lips brushing his ear, "it ain't from being roasted." She threw her arm around his neck and kissed him hard.

He unfastened the two buttons of her silk cocktail jacket, slipped her black bra strap off her shoulder, and fondled her breast. She started to yank his tux jacket off him. He tugged the bra down and licked her nipple. She fumbled to undo his pants and he wrenched her skirt up to her hips. She pulled him down on top of her.

His pager beeped.

"Shit." He struggled to sit up.

Tory groaned. She pressed the intercom and told her driver, "Brent, pull over at the next phone booth."

She watched him punch numbers inside the booth; he wouldn't use her car phone, not secure enough. Damn, he looked good in that tux. Okay, maybe the Bureau needed him to save the world, but couldn't they have waited just fifteen minutes more? She sighed, accepting her fate, and did up her jacket, then lowered the car window and took a deep breath of the night air, enjoying its sultry summer promise with her eyes closed ... until a whiff of an alley's garbage brought her to her senses.

She checked her watch. Two A.M. Already an hour later than they'd told the baby-sitter they would be. What a headache, losing the live-in nanny. She reminded herself that she had only herself to blame, since she'd wangled a college scholarship for the Filipina girl. Nanny-hunting was again top of the agenda. Matching someone to the little four-year-old whirlwind at home was going to be a challenge.

She smoothed her skirt, smiling as she remembered. This year-old cocktail suit hadn't been her first choice. Horsing around with Chris minutes before she had to leave the house, with her car waiting, she'd been wearing the gown she'd bought for the occasion. Cost a small fortune, a slinky sleeveless number held up by spaghetti-thin straps and a prayer. It was a knockout. She'd starved herself for two weeks to look her best in it, and the effect in her mirror was impressive, even if she did say so. Then she'd gone in to say goodnight to Chris. He'd been wound up all evening, maybe to get a rise from the sour-faced baby-sitter, or maybe he'd just caught Tory's gay mood, she wasn't sure which, but when she came into his room he was flying, literally: on tiptoes up on his dresser in his pajamas, about to take off onto his bed. Seeing her, he flashed an impish smile and launched himself at her, sailing through the air with total trust that she'd catch him. She did, lunging with a laugh, then fell back on the bed, holding him tight. It was an ongoing game with them that whichever one landed underneath was fair game for tickling. Chris, on top now, set to his task with a giggling vengeance, his small fingers tickling her so devilishly that Tory couldn't help laughing. She flipped him on his back and got even. He squealed with helpless laughter, kicking and squirming, and snatched the top of her gown and yanked. One of the narrow straps snapped, *pop* Tory gaped at the dangling worm of fabric. Her lovely gown! *Damn it.* Chris froze, eyes wide. Tory knew he didn't really understand the problem—no time to fix the thing—he just sensed the abrupt change in her, that she was on the brink of anger, and it made him anxious. She felt a sharp stitch in her heart. Nothing was worth making him apprehensive like that. Certainly not a *dress.* She said, "You're right, I hate these silly things," and she grabbed the other strap and theatrically ripped it off too. "That's better," she said with a grin. Chris doubled up laughing. And Tory was chuckling too as she kissed him good night while clutching the ruined gown to her chest, then hobbled out to change.

Carson walked back to the car, and Tory knew from the closed look on his face that the call had been important. The Marine Stoneface, she called it. She'd seen it on their first date seven years ago. He was then the assistant special agent in charge of the FBI's Washington Metropolitan field office; Tory was running a mayoralty campaign in nearby Baltimore. Their conversation over dinner had been lively, until she'd asked a question—a harmlessly neutral one, she'd thought—about a current high-echelon spy scandal. He'd clammed up as though she were a CNN reporter ambushing him on live TV. It took dessert and coffee before she sensed he'd relaxed again, accepting she wasn't there to pump him.

He bent beside the car window. The tiny muscles at the sides of his eyes had tightened in worry, though only Tory could have read that. "Got to go," he said. He dug into his pocket and pulled out one of the cocktail napkins printed with her face in caricature from the roast. "Give this to Chris," he said.

"You mean in the morning?"

He nodded.

"So, an all-nighter, huh?" She imagined an airliner hijacked over the Middle East, and Carson at the FBI command center for the next twelve hours drinking coffee like sludge. "Can I give you a lift at least?" She gave him her best lewd smile. "We could kiss good-bye."

He'd already straightened up, his mind elsewhere. "It's just three blocks. Go on home."

The Marine Stoneface, fully operational. Tory wasn't surprised. Now that he was the FBI's new chief of counterterrorism she expected she would see The Face more often. When it came to closed shops, her world couldn't touch the Bureau.

Then he *did* surprise her. As she pushed the button to raise the window he motioned her to stop, and asked with concern, "Is your mother still in town?"

*A biological device.*

The words thudded like a battering ram at the barrier of Jack's consciousness but could not break in.

He sat in the Wardroom, a windowless room near the White House mess, watching a drop of condensation weep down the water pitcher on the table . . . struggling to take in what he'd just been told.

*Terrorists.*

Two FBI men stood in front of him. The leader—sober-faced, fit, fortyish—had tried to break it to him calmly, kindly: "Dr. Hunt, my name is Carson Colwell, chief of counterterrorism, FBI. Please, take a seat." The restrained voice had not masked the tension Jack sensed coiled inside the man.

"Doctor," Colwell had begun, "the tragic events you witnessed in Brazil the day before yesterday have just occurred at two other sites. Yesterday in a fishing village in Pakistan. Tonight, right here at home. Stoney Creek, Oregon. It's an isolated logging town in the Blue Mountains. Population two thousand and sixty. As of eleven o'clock tonight, Pacific Standard Time—an hour ago—virtually every female in Stoney Creek was dead. Eight hundred and seven women and girls. It appears only a handful have survived, apparently because of their isolation—shut-ins, a widow living on her own, two teens camping on the outskirts. The CDC's man on the ground says the victims died of a hemorrhagic disease, probably caused by a virus. It affects only females, and it looks like it killed them within twenty-four hours of exposure. Evidently, it's the same pathogen you witnessed in Brazil. The public health people went onto an emergency footing, figuring it was some new epidemic. I know that's why they called you here for their meeting. However, a little over an hour ago the White House received a communication claiming responsibility."

Jack hadn't grasped the connection. "Responsibility?"

"For a biological device. Doctor, this is the work of terrorists."

Jack stared at the world of water in the pitcher. Marisa . . . hemorrhaging . . . writhing . . . The battering ram finally broached his consciousness and the truth stormed in: *Marisa was murdered.*

The pitcher lifted. Colwell poured him a glass of water. "Here, drink this."

Jack downed it. So thirsty.

Colwell leaned straight-armed on the table, and said quietly, "Doctor, I'm sorry to have to put you through this, but I need to hear exactly what you witnessed in Jazida. Your input might help us."

Jack blinked, grit grinding his eyes. "Help. . . ?"

"To find these people."

*Find these people.* He hung on to the words, the only ones that made real sense. He heard himself say, "Do you know who they are?"

Colwell's face seemed to close. "We have very little information at this point."

"Not even why they've done it?"

"I prefer not to speculate."

*Meaning you don't know shit.* The crudeness of the thought tripped him. The man's only human, he told himself; only doing his job. He noticed Colwell was wearing a tuxedo. Called away from a party to do his job. And Me? Couldn't do my job . . . couldn't save even one . . . Marisa . . .

Roughly, he rubbed his stinging eyes, forcing himself to push past the miasma of exhaustion. No sleep in two days, just a blur of planes and airports as he'd rushed here at the CDC's request. Then the media vultures circling at National Airport, taking pictures, yelling questions about his ordeal, his grief. Now this. Marisa, *murdered.* And all those others. In Pakistan, too . . . in *Oregon.* Dear God.

"Dr. Hunt, we need information," Colwell was saying. "We've begun interviewing the male residents in Stoney Creek about any suspicious recent activity there, strangers in town, unusual occurrences. Naturally, though, they're in shock and, well, somewhat unreliable. You're an expert virologist and a physician. You're trained to observe and to read people. We need your statement about what you saw in Jazida. There may be clues, parallels between the target sites. I realize it's asking a lot of you after—"

"Statement . . . yes, of course." Jack's heart was slamming in his chest. Colwell needed details, precise, unemotionally presented, but remembering was . . . difficult. There were blank, black patches. No memory at all of leaving the place. He hazily recalled two Brazilian medics pulling him outside, away from the horrors of the Quarter. He'd seen Gerry, out of his head, hobbling to a miner's jeep and driving off crazily into the jungle . . . where had he gone? Jack had stood unsteadily as the two medics held him up in a miner's rough outdoor shower stall, washing blood off his body . . . pink water swirling over his feet, over the concrete floor, pooling in the mud . . . Marisa's blood.

He gripped the pitcher handle to stop his hand from shaking. *Mass murderers . . . no apparent purpose for their butchery.* When he tried to think of people deliberately unleashing such a thing—and just on women—his reasoning faltered.

But rage didn't require reason, and rage was what he was beginning to feel now. A hot surge of fury. He welcomed it, seized hold of it. Because now, where there had been only impotent grief, no target, now there was an enemy. An enemy meant you could fight back.

He got to his feet. "I'll tell you everything I can. But I want to do more."

Colwell looked mildly startled. "More?"

*Find these people.* "Let me go to the Oregon town. As you said, I'm an expert eyewitness to an identical attack. If I can detect any similarities, any patterns, that would help you, wouldn't it? More than you trying to sift through my information here?"

It took Colwell only a split second to grab at the offer. "Could you leave immediately?"

"I have to meet with the public health people here first. They're waiting for my report. As soon as that's done, I'm ready."

Colwell nodded. "I'll arrange transport. You'll leave from Andrews Air Force Base. Agent Ramirez here will escort you."

"Fine."

Colwell extended his hand. "Dr. Hunt, thank you. I know this can't be easy for you. I appreciate the assistance you're offering, and I promise you I'm going to do everything in my power to bring to justice the people responsible for your wife's death."

Jack fought down the painful lump in his throat. He shook Colwell's hand. He recognized, in the steady gaze that met his, a hunger for action almost as consuming as his own. Almost.

He thought: When you find her killers, death will not be punishment enough.

"Agent Ramirez will take your preliminary statement on the way," Colwell said, then handed Jack a card. "My private line. If you think of anything, call me, anytime. Now, please excuse me. I have a meeting with the president, and there's someone else I must first call in."

Rachel Lesage lay awake in her hotel room. Silence. Emptiness. Except inside her head. There, multitudes were screaming.

She flinched when the phone rang. She answered, and at the familiar voice her mind froze. Carson.

*He's discovered me.*

But he wasn't saying that. Dumb while he spoke, she listened. Deaf to her own voice, she agreed to his request. She hung up and sat on the bed's edge, her fingers digging into her knees.

*It's a trap.*

*It's over.*

No, stop, think! He hadn't given the slightest hint of suspicion, or even said what the summons was about—ony that a critical situation had arisen that required her input. "I've just cleared you with the president's chief of staff. We need you, Rachel. Now."

Calm down . . . step back . . . examine. She had long observed that the simplest explanations were usually correct. People projected their own hopes and fears onto the words

and actions of others, but such fantasies were usually base-
less. So what did that mean with Carson? The logical conclusion was that he did simply want her help. A face-value
request. No hidden agenda. She doubted he was even capable of such a subtly deceptive ploy. Not incapable of formu-
lating it; she had a high regard for her son-in-law's
intelligence and skill. But incapable of masking it so completely to her.

Hope shot through her, intense as pain. If they know nothing, it isn't over, it's just beginning. The terrible triage can
still yield success. This summons may be a bizarre stroke of
luck: I might influence their response from right there
among them.

He'd said he was sending a car. Must get dressed, she told
herself, organize my thoughts. Carson hadn't been in the top
counterterrorism post when she'd begun this, so she'd have
to prepare herself for—

For what? What is there to fear? Carson is simply doing
his job. So will I.

But as she sat in the backseat on the way to the White
House, her mouth was dry and her hands were cold. The
night streets and night people glided past. A teenager with
dreadlocks, shuffling in a narcotic haze, stepped in front of
the car. The driver swerved and Rachel was thrown against
the door. The car beside her blasted its horn. She stared out
the window, remembering Africa, the twisting road in the
hills, the guns, the knives. Almost two years since it happened, yet her black nightmares still flashed with those
knives.

*The car fishtails on the mountain road above Kigali,
throwing her and her son against the door. She holds him
tightly. He is tall for nine, but so slight he feels all bones.
Everyone who can is fleeing the capital. Back in the hotel
she grabbed him and they ran through dark halls amid the*

*screams of Tutsi people being hacked to death. The Hutu attackers ignored her because she is white. But her son . . .*

*Paul. He doesn't panic when bullets pepper the car up in the hills, killing the driver, nor when he and Rachel stumble out and run. He doesn't cry when they spend the night shivering on the dank ground of a banana plantation. When they get a lift in a truck carrying orphans he doesn't complain of hunger or fear, though Rachel knows he feels both.*

*Then soldiers stop the truck. Order the children out. Paul looks back at her with such trust. She claws at the soldiers to get to him, but their machetes flail at the children, hacking shoulders, ankles, backs. Children scream and fall. Some break through and run. Paul! He does not cry out. He just begins to run.*

"Dr. Lesage?"

She blinked. The driver was looking around at her, puzzled by her stillness. "We're here, ma'am."

She looked out beyond the security booth. The White House north portico. Floodlights. Ficus trees flanking the door, their glossy leaves gentled by the sultry breeze . . . not the cold night wind that would chill her soul forever . . .

Nothing can be accomplished with emotion. Override it. Focus. *The ghosts of Rwanda have no place where I am going.*

Rwanda, one of the most densely populated places on earth. Overcrowded to madness. Rwanda, where her life had ended.

But the agony had given birth to a vision of terrible beauty. Now she would make it real.

# 4

AN AIDE USHERED RACHEL INTO A WAITING ROOM in the White House basement. She stared across the corridor at the closed doors of the Situation Room where the president was meeting with his advisors, and tried to compose herself. Were they discussing her demand, her terms? Would they agree immediately? Or would it take endless days?

The doors opened and people walked out talking in tense undertones, Carson among them. He strode toward her, his face implacable. She held her breath. *A trap after all?*

"Rachel, thanks for coming," he said, guiding her toward the meeting breaking up. "The president wants to see you right away, so let me bring you up to speed."

*He doesn't suspect.* She breathed again.

Carson told her about the three biological attacks—the work of terrorists, he said, the perpetrators unknown—then briefly outlined the victims' symptoms and told her of the deployment of the National Guard to quarantine Stoney Creek. Rachel stifled a shiver of caution. *Perpetrators un-*

*known?* Why hadn't he mentioned Artemis? Or the demand? When he finished, she forced herself to display the reactions he would expect: surprise and shock, then a studied professional calm. She was acutely aware that he had divulged no information beyond the facts relating to her expertise. She warned herself of the pitfall here, subtle yet treacherous: she must not appear to know more than she'd been told.

In the Situation Room about a dozen people were talking in small groups or gathering papers from the conference table, preparing to leave. Rachel knew some of them because of her position on presidential councils advising on the biotech industry. The health secretary and his deputy. The chief of staff. Others, such as the attorney general and the FBI director, she recognized only from TV. On all the faces she read fear.

Good. Fear is the first objective.

Then she saw President Lowell. He sat at the table's far end huddled with a couple of advisors, his elbows on his knees. He looked disheveled—he'd thrown on a gray track suit and hadn't shaved—as though overwhelmed by the crisis. Rachel felt no sympathy, only anger. *If he'd submitted to my warning I wouldn't have been forced to act!* However, the demonstration had changed all the parameters, and he appeared aware of that. He must submit now.

"Rachel, one thing I need to know," Carson was saying as he led her through the room. "In your opinion, could the disease, the virus, have already spread beyond Stoney Creek?"

"If the town is as isolated as you say, and every victim is dead, the outbreak is likely contained."

"Really? The epidemiologists on-site advise us the thing is highly infectious."

"Exactly. So virulent, it's too successful." When he shot her a questioning look, she explained, "It kills its host, and therefore itself, before it can spread beyond the first leap."

Carson nodded gravely and said no more.

They reached President Lowell. Frowning at something in his advisors' conversation, he looked up and met her eyes. "Dr. Lesage, good to have you with us."

She forced calmness into her voice. "I hope I can help, Mr. President."

"So do I." Getting up, he led her to a sideboard where the stewards had left coffee thermoses, china cups, and cans of soda and juice. "Coffee?" he offered.

Face-to-face now, seeing the deep anxiety in his eyes, Rachel felt buoyed with hope. Was this going to be resolved even more quickly than she'd dared believe? "No, thank you," she answered.

He ripped the tab off a can of Coke, then gave her a rueful smile. "Sorry, no smoked salmon."

She managed a smile in return. The first time they'd met had been over an informal White House lunch, just the two of them, soon after his inauguration. He'd invited her to brief him about a scientific mission to Russia she'd undertaken for a previous administration to assess an infraction of the Biochemical Weapons Convention. He had not only impressed her by proving to be a quick study, he had also disarmed her by serving smoked salmon flown in from her hometown in Nova Scotia. She'd found it hard not to like Andrew Lowell.

"Doctor," he said now, "can you give me any handle on the bug these psychotic Artemis people are fooling with? How in God's name could anyone unleash such a thing?"

She asked carefully, "Artemis?"

"Didn't your son-in-law brief you?"

She glanced at Carson who stood across the room talking with the FBI director and the chairman of the Joint Chiefs. "Barely," she replied. "He's cautious about security."

The president scowled. "Well, hell, I can't tap you if

you're being kept in the dark." He grabbed a sheet of paper from the conference table. "Here's their manifesto," he said, handing it to her. "Top secret, of course. Have a look."

She scanned the document, a photocopy, feeling trapped under Lowell's scrutiny, aware that she must betray no recognition of the text she knew by heart.

## ARTEMIS DECLARATION
### Concerning Human Overpopulation

ARTEMIS,

CONVINCED that, due to the growth of the human population, its accelerating consumption of natural resources, and its increasing discharge of pollutants into the world's ecosystems, the ecological foundation for all life is threatened with imminent catastrophic failure;

MINDFUL that human population levels, as with all mammalian populations, are primarily determined by the number of fecund females;

ENCOURAGED that a proven method of reducing population levels lies in increasing the general education levels of girls and women;

DECLARES THAT

The developed world, beginning with the United States, shall establish within thirty days a Survival Education Fund equaling one percent of the U.S. gross national product, to be used exclusively to educate girls and women in less developed countries and regions experiencing rapid population growth;

AND FURTHER DECLARES THAT

In the event that the United States government fails to implement the Survival Education Fund— as it failed to do after being forewarned of the present demonstration of the biological device— extreme measures will be taken employing the biological device to directly reduce female population levels, beginning, in thirty days, in a major American city, and subsequently including, as necessary, selected cities worldwide.

"In other words," the president said, "either I authorize this global education fund or Artemis will release their weapon on one of our cities. In thirty days."

Rachel's anger surged. *I never wanted it to come to this!* "This document says you were forewarned," she said tightly. "What happened?"

"Actually, I wasn't." He shot a dark glance across the room at Carson. "Your son-in-law decided the threat was not—" He raised his voice, now tinged with anger. "How did you put it, Mr. Colwell? The Artemis threat wasn't *significant*?"

A half-dozen people turned, including Carson. He answered evenly, "That was my evaluation at the time, sir."

"Well, Mr. Colwell, your evaluation was a fuckup."

The room went silent.

Carson said steadily, "Yes, Mr. President."

Rachel stared at Carson. So *he* had been the stumbling block! The original notice had never even reached the president! She had to look away to mask her fury.

"With all due respect, sir," the FBI director said to the president, "Colwell took over as chief of CT only four weeks ago, and Artemis's demonstration threat was almost the first thing that crossed his desk. I know he moved on it right away. I read his report. Our people found nothing. I mean *nothing*. Artemis has no history, no one's heard of them—not one field office, not one foreign security agency—and they didn't make contact again. So Colwell's call was not out of line." He shrugged. "Can't launch a multi-million-dollar investigation into every threatening piece of paper that arrives at the White House. Congress would howl."

Lowell, clearly unmoved, took a swig of Coke. "How do you rate the threat *now,* Mr. Colwell?"

Carson looked the president in the eye. "Critical, sir."

A grim smile escaped Lowell. "At least you learn from your mistakes."

The president turned back to Rachel. "He's right. Artemis has proved they can convey their weapon into diverse remote locales and contain it there, which requires a high degree of organization and a sophisticated delivery system. They probably hit Pakistan and Brazil just to make that point, though they're only demanding action from *us*. The very fact they carried out their threatened demonstration proves a formidable strength of purpose, and since they produced it exactly when they said they would, I'm assuming the deadline in this second ultimatum is firm. Although we've been studying the possibility of a biological attack for some years, we have no real defense. Our vulnerability is maximum."

Rachel's anger evaporated. Lowell had outlined the danger impeccably. He knew he had no choice.

"Dr. Lesage," he went on gravely, "I've got to be certain of what I'm dealing with. Have these people truly engineered a female-specific virus, or are they just claiming ownership of some horrific natural phenomenon? Is biotech precision targeting like this really possible?"

"Yesterday I'd have said such a capability was only theoretical. Now it would seem the facts speak for themselves."

He heaved a troubled sigh. "No question it's an effective weapon," he conceded. "But I'm still mystified by their *demand*. So bizarre. Some of my people believe it's a front. Saddam jerking us around, or Qaddafi maybe. Could be they're right. I mean, a 'survival education fund'? What the hell is that?"

She couldn't let him continue this way. "Some experts would say it's a viable way to reduce global overpopulation."

"That's what I don't get. How?"

"It's not my field, but I understand that wherever women receive even a rudimentary general education, birth rates drop. In most developing nations girls aren't sent to school at all, but when they are, and they remain through primary school, their living standards eventually rise and birth rates fall." She added as noncommittally as she could, "It's well documented."

"But Artemis wants a hefty chunk of our GNP to do it. And what about their sadistic alternative, to *kill* women. That's not only bizarre, it's schizophrenic."

"It's biology," Rachel said evenly. "The fastest way to reduce any mammalian population is to reduce the number of breeding females."

"Why? It's men who get the women pregnant. And every man can sow an awful lot of wild oats."

"Males don't control the *rate* of reproduction." Did he really not grasp this fundamental principle? "Mr. President, imagine a village of a hundred men and one woman. They can only increase their number every nine months by one. Now imagine a village of a hundred women and one man. In a year that village can double to *two hundred* and one. The number of females determines the rate of reproduction."

He still looked skeptical, and now uneasy. His obtuseness astonished her. To her analytical mind the paradigm was clear: problem and solution. The problem was a lethally overcrowded planet, resulting in environmental devastation and vicious civil-war competition for life-sustaining resources. The solution was the general education of women; failing that, a large-scale removal of women. Did she really have to spell this out for him? She said carefully, "Mr. President, you've asked me here for a dispassionate scientific overview, correct?"

"Absolutely."

"Then, in my opinion—dispassionately—the point of this document seems to be that the global education of women is a benign solution to the crisis of overpopulation, and the preferred one, but, failing that, a partial cull of females is an equally viable solution. Limiting the cull to females could logically be seen as humane, since it requires the minimum reduction of overall population."

"Logical maybe, Doctor, but humane it is not."

Rachel felt herself losing patience. She struggled to maintain her mask of scientific detachment. "The planet itself may eventually kill off the surplus population through famine, pestilence, and war. Is *that* humane?"

"Surplus? Culls?" he muttered, uncomfortable with her terminology. "Dr. Lesage, I don't think you understand. We're not debating *alternatives*. This country has never yet given in to terrorist extortion and we're certainly not going to do it now. The day we let terror rule is the day we abdicate to anarchy."

She stared at him. Hadn't he comprehended one thing she'd said? "But when the public hears of the threat—"

"The public will hear what I judge is appropriate in the interest of national security," he said sternly. "I assure you that does *not* include divulging Artemis's insane ultimatum. It would only create hysteria. No, their threat does not go beyond this room."

He made a gesture of irritation, clearly finished with this discussion. "We're focusing on two offensives. The first, of course, is tracking down the terrorists, and I've just signed a finding to give the FBI and CIA unprecedented scope. The second is equally essential, and that's why you're here. I want an all-out push to develop a medical treatment in the event of another attack. After all, a cure would entirely defuse the weapon. So I need results, and fast. However, Health Secretary Takesaki warns me the challenge is almost impossible in thirty days, especially given the maze of bureaucratic jurisdiction, what with the CDC, the National Institutes of Health, the World Health Organization . . ." His voice trailed, attesting to the quagmire. "Doctor, what I need is a Manhattan Project approach. I want you to spearhead it. I'd like you to assemble an elite team in a top-priority research undertaking. It would parallel the CDC's effort, but would be an independent project."

Rachel was stunned.

"You'd have my authority to second any scientists you want from any government facility," he assured her. "You'd have complete autonomy, and all the funding you require. You'd answer to me alone."

She could only stare at him, dumbfounded.

He was waiting for a reply. "Can you do that for me?"

"I . . . I could, but—"

"Then begin immediately. Discuss the details with Secretary Takesaki. And now, you'll have to excuse me." He moved to the conference table and gathered up his slim file of notes, preparing to leave.

Rachel's heart thudded. *This can't be happening.* He didn't even consider the terms! Terms so rational, so beneficial, so *minimal*—no environmental revolution, just the rock-bottom condition, because it's *achievable*. He'd rather risk the lives of millions. The chart to a sustainable future is right here! I forced it under his nose! But he's tossed it aside as though—

He was almost at the door. People were falling in behind him. She had to stop him . . . make him see . . . "Mr. President," she called, "you're making a terrible mistake."

He halted. People turned in surprise. Rachel felt herself trembling and clamped control on her muscles. "You don't understand," she said. "Even if I could develop a therapy, it could be made ineffective in a moment with a variant strain. As for a cure, no cures for viruses exist. The best we have is vaccines, preventatives. We cannot *fight* this thing. The response you've outlined could destroy us all."

People looked shocked. The president's face clouded. Rachel went on. "When a virus as ferocious as this invades us, it overwhelms the immune system, and when it spreads through a population, it overwhelms whole societies. In the Middle Ages bubonic plague killed half of Europe. Here, native Americans died in the thousands when the Europeans brought smallpox. Their societies imploded. That's what we're facing here, only on a global scale. If there's a large urban release, a global plague is almost inevitable. You *must* reconsider."

The room was silent.

When the president finally spoke his voice was cold steel. "Thank you for your thoughts, Dr. Lesage, but let's get one thing clear. Delivering control of this nation into the hands of mass-murdering terrorists is not an option. Not now, not ever."

She walked stiffly down the corridor, fury immobilizing her thoughts, nothing registering past Lowell's appalling intransigence, his stupidity!

"Can I help you, ma'am?" a Secret Service agent asked.

"Yes, I have a car waiting."

The agent pointed the way. As Rachel walked on, she commanded her mind to move, to shunt her thinking onto another track. A way to *coerce* him, that's what I must find. But how?

Focus. Think!

Goal and obstacle. The goal has not changed. Lowell has my demand and I will settle for nothing less. But the obstacle—not only the president now, but their search for me as well. Carson and his security forces in the tens of thousands.

It didn't matter. She was ready. She had engineered a system whereby her incapacitation by arrest or death would activate delivery of the virus to a half-dozen cities worldwide. Now, she held it all back through a simple computer command, initiated by a phone call. Unless she input the command at regular intervals, however, the deliveries would go out automatically. A dead man's switch. She'd considered a fail-safe measure in case she was inadvertently detained from inputting the command, but had rejected that. It was prison or a bullet she was planning against, not sleeping late.

Damn Lowell, she thought. How could such horror mean so little to him? His top priority wasn't to do the right thing but the *political* thing. "Standing firm"—the entrenched U.S. antiterrorist policy, meant to outface fundamentalist fanatics and extortionist thugs. Well, I am neither, Mr. President. I'm trying to humanely save our world. Female education is the easy way, but if you reject that, I'll do it the hard way. Your policy is as obsolete against me as a suit of armor against radioactive fallout.

But damn me, too, for misjudging him. Politically naive, Tory once called me. It's true.

Wait. *Tory.*

*She moves in that world every day.*

\* \* \*

Dawn was breaking as the two dozen public health authorities at the table in the White House's Roosevelt Room went on talking around Jack—and about him. They'd been briefed by the health secretary with the same scanty details Jack had heard from Colwell: anonymous terrorists, no reason given for their attacks. After their initial shock, the group had carried on a heated discussion about how best to coordinate a massive international research investigation. Jack had listened silently with one thought crystallizing: he wanted in. The research blitz offered his best chance of bringing down the people who'd done this. He'd made a statement to that effect, and the discussion had immediately zeroed in on him.

"He'll be coming to *us*." Hank Vorhees, the bearlike director of the CDC, said with belligerent possessiveness. Vorhees was a beefy former college football star. Jack, sitting next to him, remembered how, when they were CDC colleagues, Vorhees had always used his size to great effect, smothering people either in bonhomie or aggression, depending on his objective. "Hell, it's obvious," Vorhees went on. "He used to be head of our special pathogens branch, and our people know him. For years I've been asking him to come back." Affectionately, he rested a slab of a hand on Jack's back. "Best team chief I ever had. Jack gets results."

"But NIH must have his input first for our viral data banks," a woman from the National Institutes of Health said anxiously. "As a virologist with firsthand clinical experience with this pathogen, he has information we must access immediately."

Jack poured himself another glass of water. He couldn't seem to get enough. He remembered, in Brazil, waiting in the Belém airport, unable to eat but feeling desiccated. Someone had brought him a beer. It tasted so good, alive in his throat. The intense pleasure seemed a betrayal of Marisa.

He'd downed the beer, every swallow, all the while hating the treachery of his body as it took gratification against his will.

"Look, people, this is *our* specialty," a bureaucrat from USAMRIID objected—the U.S. Army Medical Research Institute of Infectious Disease. "Dr. Hunt, out at Fort Detrick we could offer you state-of-the-art—"

"Oh, please," Vorhees cut in. "You think that's going to set the public's mind at rest? The grieving Dr. Hunt hustled away to toil inside the military's biological warfare laboratory? No, the natural spot for him in this crisis is with the CDC, the public's health protector."

"*Mon Dieu*, he left the CDC a decade ago," Marcel Thierault, the World Health Organization's representative, responded. "He's known everywhere *else* for his work with One World Medics. You Americans seem to forget the rest of the world exists, but the terrorists struck in Brazil and Pakistan too. This is an *international* crisis. Dr. Hunt can do the most good in Geneva, helping us."

Jack didn't miss the Frenchman's dig at his long inactivity in research. He also knew it was a tactic; each of them was eager to get him to their facility because of his celebrity profile, a fund-raising magnet. None of this mattered. He'd already made up his mind. He wanted to be on the front line. As for helping the FBI, that was going to be a long shot; tracking terrorists wasn't his expertise, it was Colwell's. *This* was his: the lab. "Marcel," he said to the WHO man, "I may have been out of the loop for a while but I haven't forgotten how to run a research team."

At the sudden command in his voice there was a rustle of fresh interest around the table.

Jack turned to Vorhees. "Hank, I'm with you. I'm coming to Atlanta. I have to go to Oregon first, to help the FBI, but immediately after that I want to meet with your senior scientists. Epidemiology and molecular biology department heads first. I'll call you from Oregon when I have a better idea of a timetable, and you can schedule your people for me. All right?" He thought: Believe me, I'll be taking control.

Vorhees sat back smiling, benevolent in triumph. "I'll get right on it, Jack."

An aide poked her head in. "Message for Dr. Hunt." An Agent Ramirez, she said, was waiting in the West Lobby and sent word that the helicopter to Andrews was standing by.

"On my way," Jack said, chair legs gouging carpet as he pushed from the table. He stood and dizziness rocked him. He grabbed the back of Vorhees's chair.

"You all right?" Vorhees touched his elbow solicitously. "Good Lord, Jack, I'm sorry. This situation has made all of us a little crazy, but none of us is forgetting about your . . . I mean, the hell you've been through. Your poor wife."

Jack was unnerved by a prick of tears. *Got to get out.* He blinked hard. The door . . . where's the fucking door?

"Jack?" Vorhees said.

He was already striding into the hall. Stoney Creek, he told himself. Help Colwell, then get down to work.

Tory set down the Artemis declaration on her desk and stared across at her mother in shock. Who *were* these monsters?

The early morning bustle beyond her closed door—the ringing phones, the intern calling for someone to hold the elevator, the sound track from the editing suite—all of it sounded eerily normal. Even Chris, on his knees under the window playing with a plane he'd made from Lego pieces, was oblivious to the crisis Rachel had brought into the room. When the stand-in baby-sitter had canceled at the last moment, Tory had brought Chris with her, and when her mother had walked in soon after, he'd run to her, calling, "Nana, see my plane!" as if Rachel dropping by was the most natural thing in the world. To Tory, nothing seemed natural this morning.

"Marcia," she said, hitting the intercom, "hold my calls." The composure in her voice was a lie.

She hit the mute button for the CNN broadcast on the TV in the bookcase. The seven A.M. news reports about Stoney Creek that she'd heard in the car had been devastating enough. Anonymous terrorists, a biological attack, almost every female dead. Unbelievable. She remembered the look on Carson's face in the phone booth last night. And he hadn't come home.

When she and Chris reached the office her whole staff was buzzing about it, CNN droning down every corridor. The *Washington Post* on her desk had a harrowing story about Dr. Jack Hunt, whose Brazilian wife had been a victim in a similar epidemic. CNN reported that the attacks were now known to be connected. Poor guy, Tory had thought, arrested by Hunt's striking page-one photo.

But none of the breaking news reports had mentioned a *demand* from the terrorists, so her staff's eventual response was relief that the virus appeared to have been contained and the horror was over: a thank-God-it-wasn't-me syndrome. Tory had to admit she'd shared it, along with the general trust that the FBI would soon be making arrests. Carson was in charge.

Now her mother had shattered that fantasy. She'd told Tory about the ultimatum and the president's response.

"A White House cover-up," Tory said, still stunned. "How can they think they'll get away with it?"

"They have no comprehension of what they're dealing with," Rachel said. "The release of this pathogen on a biologically defenseless urban population would bring devastation on an unimaginable scale. They cannot grasp it."

Tory couldn't remember ever seeing her mother so shaken. Except once, when she'd come back from Rwanda after losing Paul. She'd hoped that she would never again see such anguish on her mother's face. But her confrontation at the White House had done it. They hadn't listened to her.

Tory was listening. This was her mother's field. If she said it was so, it was so. Terrifying.

And yet . . . the Artemis demand gripped her. Female education to reduce overpopulation and prevent ecological collapse. An astonishingly progressive concept. These people, however, had gone far beyond concepts. They were willing to kill, and on a global scale. They *had* killed. The thought made her faintly sick. Who would actually execute such a savage scheme? She pulled herself together to ask, "When you saw Carson, did he have any idea who Artemis might be?"

"It's irrelevant."

"Not if he finds them."

Rachel's eyes flashed. "The crude apparatus of law enforcement is utterly unequal to this situation."

"Crude apparatus, the FBI? Not the last time I looked."

"Tory, all it takes is one person uncorking a test tube!"

Maybe it was the wild look in her mother's eyes, or maybe the stark image she'd just invoked: the deranged scientist unloosing Armageddon. Tory suddenly glimpsed the full, horrifying ramifications and knew that her mother was right. Carson could not possibly track down these people in thirty days. They would strike again. New York? Los Angeles? Right here in Washington. The question again overwhelmed her: Who *were* these monsters?

Her face must have changed, because her mother said, "You see it, don't you?"

Tory nodded, unnerved.

"I told the president that *no* price is too high," Rachel said, "but he is immovable." She threw up her hands, incredulous. "He's actually asked me to pull together a team to devise a therapy. Of course, I'll do what I can, but in thirty days? Produce a miracle in a test tube like in some bad Hollywood movie? It's *madness*." She seemed to regain self-control, then said earnestly, "Tory, it's your business to know what politicians respond to. Is there some way to *force* the president?"

She said wryly, "Sure, tell the public the truth. *They'll* force him."

Rachel nodded as though assimilating the concept, but with difficulty. "I see, yes. All right." Abruptly, she started to leave.

"Hey, hold on," Tory said. "Where are you going?"

"To do what you suggest."

"What are you talking about?"

Rachel was opening the door. "I'm not quite sure. Call someone in the media, I suppose. Give an interview about—"

"Good God, Mother, absolutely not!" Tory hurried to her, closed the door, and pulled her back into the room. Chris had looked up in surprise at her tone. Tory bit back her exasperation. She hadn't meant to speak so harshly, but her mother's political ignorance appalled her. "I know you mean well, but you can't just barge out there and declare the truth."

"Why not?"

"For one thing you'd probably be arrested for leaking a top-secret classified document. At the very least, face charges. Possibly jail. Is that what you want?"

Rachel turned pale. "No."

"For another, it's plain wrong. You'd be undermining your country's stand against terrorism."

Rachel said evenly, "Is it wrong if it's the only way to do right?"

The bald truth of it startled Tory. Did antiterrorist dogma apply if yielding would bring universal good? Besides, could dogma fend off the horrific alternative?

She was suddenly aware of Chris at her side. "Mommy, what's wrong?"

Tory gently took his face in her hands. "Nothing, sweet pea. Nana has a problem and we're trying to fix it." She kissed the top of his head, and the scent of his hair filled her with a warmth she found comforting beyond all proportion. She pulled him to her.

He looked up at her anxiously. "Do you have to go away?"

"Why would you think that?"

"You always have that sad look when you're going away."

As he gazed up at her for reassurance, it struck her. Dear God, it could happen. I could be gone forever. *Artemis could kill me.*

It hadn't hit home until this moment, the possibility of being a victim herself. Holding Chris, seeing his need, she suddenly knew in her bones what was at stake. Her life. Her death. The reality that she might not be here for her child.

How far would she go to prevent that? If she didn't believe Carson could catch Artemis in time—and she knew he couldn't—was her mother's idea the only way: blowing the whistle to force the government's capitulation? If so, was that sedition . . . or self-defense?

"I'm going, Tory," Rachel said. "Thank you for your advice."

"No, come back. Let's think this through."

"I have."

Tory saw her mother was going to do it. Going to stumble out onto the battlefield unarmed, trusting that "the truth" would smite the foe. Tory knew all about the truth's elusive smiting power: it existed, but only when a very large army backed it up. Could she let her mother walk out there alone and be crucified? "Mother, wait."

Rachel turned.

Tory hesitated. *How far am I prepared to go?* Her eye was caught by the plaque on the wall behind Rachel's shoulder. "No permanent friends, no permanent enemies." In the shifting sands of politics that statement was axiomatic, but one permanent friend had always been her mother. Growing up, she knew what a gift she'd been given as Rachel Lesage's daughter. It went far beyond love and support. The priceless inheritance had been Rachel's example. Her active mind. Her belief that every challenge was an opportunity. Her sense of limitlessness. Tory admired no one more. Now, for the first time, her mother had come to her for help. *Am I going to let her fight this alone? Fight to keep my world with Chris safe?* The question terrified her—the answer even more, because when she came right down to it, repulsive as it was to endorse a terrorist demand, what choice was there? She wouldn't sit still and wait for the plague.

"Mother," she said, "sit down." She sent Chris back to his scatter of Legos under the window. Rachel stood waiting. Tory took a steadying breath, aware that her whole life was about to change. *Am I taking on something impossible?* A memory surfaced—a South African anti-apartheid activist she'd done some lobbying for. He was a white middle-class journalist who, after a black friend was tortured and killed, left his comfortable life to fight the government, then spent years in prison for it. Tory had once asked him what had made him step over the line to activism. "I didn't step," he'd told her. "I woke up one morning and found the line had been drawn behind me."

She said to her mother, committed now, "Let me handle this."

Rachel looked aghast. "No. I only came for your *advice*. I don't want you involved."

"I'm already involved," Tory said grimly. An accomplice. I may be looking at jail too.

Rachel was adamant. "I have what I came for. Just forget I was here."

"*Listen* to me," Tory said. "You can't just go out and blurt the facts. The White House would demonize you, which would nullify the entire message and leave you broken. This requires *strategy*. A precise, orchestrated campaign. It isn't just about getting a shocking message out to the American people, letting them know the danger their government's putting them in. It's about making those people *act*. It's about withstanding devastating White House attacks for what we're going to advocate. It's about organizing a massive media blitz, plus intense national fund-raising to maintain an army of staff and to pay for that blitz. And the whole thing's got to be up and running overnight. I could go on, but you get the point. *You* can't run a full-scale campaign like this. I can. As you said, it's my business."

"Not you." Rachel spoke with a desperation Tory had never heard in her before. "This isn't what I want."

"Not what I want either, but who else can do it? Of the few people who have the experience and resources, who else *would*?"

Rachel kept shaking her head, but without conviction now, a painful acknowledgment that there was no alternative. "Forgive me . . . for dragging you into this."

The turmoil in Rachel's eyes tugged a string of tenderness

in Tory. She came closer and took her mother's hand. "It's okay. I'm glad you did."

It was true. Perverse of her, maybe, given the dangers ahead, but now that a plan of action was settled, she felt gratified that her mother's first impulse had been to come to her. "All my life," she said quietly, "I've taken the good stuff you've given. I'm glad to have a chance, finally, to give something back."

Rachel squeezed her daughter's hand.

*Settled.* Tory thought. Right. Now I just have to mobilize the country to get the president to cave in to a gang of murdering terrorists. Piece of cake.

Rachel collected herself. She lifted her chin and said, "You mentioned financing. I can help with that."

"I'll need millions just for seed money, and that's—"

"Would twenty million be enough?"

Tory was taken aback. Even for someone as wealthy as her mother it was an extraordinary offer. She seemed to be seeing this as some kind of private crusade, and Tory found it unsettling. Dangerous. "Mother, we're talking *war* here," she warned. "Against the government of the United States. It's going to be brutal, and people are going to get hurt. Probably you first, for leaking this information to me. Unless, that is, you do exactly what my lawyers tell you."

She was sorry to be so blunt. God knew she was going to need the funding, but her mother had to understand that what they were conspiring was enormous, and there were no guarantees. Tory had no concept yet of how to run with it, no strategy. To begin, she'd have to find a hook, something to grab the public by the throat. And find it fast.

She went to the window where Chris was playing and gazed out at the traffic on K Street, her thoughts skidding in all directions. So much to get moving on. She'd have to sub-contract out her other campaigns immediately, and educate herself about overpopulation issues, and find that *hook*. Chris had to be taken care of as well. She almost smiled. Save the world by all means, ma'am, but find that new nanny first!

Picturing home brought a jolt of dread. Carson. I'll be facing off against his world. Against him. No, Carson tracks terrorists, he doesn't make policy. This fight is with the president.

But if the FBI knows I'm planning a protest, they'll investigate. That would tip the White House. I can't risk confronting them until the campaign is solidly in place, so I'll have to keep all of this secret from Carson.

She felt a flush of shame. We may have our problems, but I'd trust him with my life. How can I deceive him?

Only, this is about trusting him with *millions* of lives. He'll never see it the way my mother and I do: victory through surrender. It goes against everything he stands for.

When he finds out, will he recognize what *I'm* standing for?

She shivered. *The line's been drawn behind me.*

"Artemis," she said uneasily, watching a bird fly into the morning sun. "Wasn't that some Greek deity?"

No answer. She turned. Rachel looked so pale.

*She's done all she can. Now it's up to me.* "Don't worry, Mother," she said quietly. "We're going to make this work."

Tory's eyes were drawn to the newspaper on the desk, to the page-one photo. An idea fell into her mind. *The hook.* It was so bold, she had to pull herself back for a reality check. Was she crazy to think she could persuade a victim to come on their side?

Well, you never know until you try.

She hit the phone line to her assistant. "Eric, find out where I can reach Dr. Jack Hunt. The One World Medics hero. Today's *Washington Post* says he's in town."

As she hung up she noticed her mother's look of dismay. "Jack?" Rachel asked.

Tory caught the familiarity. "You know him?"

Rachel hesitated. "Yes."

"Well enough to approach him?"

"Why?"

"I want him as our spokesman."

Rachel gaped. "Spokesman? Why *him*?"

"Because he's famous and attractive and Artemis killed his wife." She handed over the *Post* story with Hunt's photo.

Her mother gasped as though in pain, and for a moment Tory was afraid she was ill. It must be a blow, she realized, finding out this way about a colleague's tragic loss. Disturbing as it was, however, they were both going to have to harden themselves if this campaign was going to work. No place for squeamishness.

"Mother," she warned, "we *need* this man. Believe me, he's the key."

"Back to the Grand Hyatt, Doctor?"

Rachel sat unmoving in the government car idling outside Tory's building. She was still absorbing the shock. At Jack's photograph, her heart had seized. The same lean look of strength, same jut of his jaw, same direct gaze, with that enigmatic core of blue ice that made her tremble as she remembered. The morning sun broke into the car in a swell of radiance, and suddenly the bright void surrounding her was the sunlit English hotel room where she had stood naked in Jack's arms. Twelve years ago.

She'd had no idea, no knowledge that he had married, that he was even in South America.

A fist of sickness shot up inside her. *I killed Jack's wife.*

"Doctor?" the driver repeated. "Back to the hotel?"

"What? Yes . . . no. Just a moment."

She fought down the nausea and stared, unseeing, at the morning traffic rushing by, the glass muting its din to a whisper like the sea. Twelve years ago she'd thought she could not possibly have hurt him more. Now, I have.

That wasn't the only agony. Tory. Rachel's deepest fear, blocked from her consciousness for months, now menaced her: in the event of a pandemic Tory would be as much at risk as any female. At the outset—creating the virus, planning its delivery, sending the ultimatum—Rachel had faced this. But she had never truly believed she'd have to default to a large-scale release, so she'd never truly thought Tory was in danger. She'd been so certain the president would agree to her demand, so certain she could dismantle her threat. That plan had failed—her own miserable miscalculation.

Turning back was unthinkable. Thousands had been sacrificed for a grand vision. Aborting the vision now would reduce those deaths to plain murder.

But, sacrifice Tory?

An unbearable decision—and one Tory herself had just saved her from confronting. Her daughter was offering an extraordinary second chance. A national campaign. A popular revolution.

Could it work? Tory thought it could. Tory understood such things. Her daughter's energy left Rachel overwhelmed. Such trust in me! Such instant commitment! It moved her so deeply, she couldn't sort the tumult of emotions. Gratitude. Fear. Dismay at entangling Tory. Hope. She had never suffered such regret—nor loved her daughter more.

Given Tory's high resolve, how could she let her own determination waver for a moment, even over Jack?

"Not the hotel." She was operating on automatic pilot, thinking and speaking only on a level of brute necessity. She knew, on that level, what she had to do about Jack. Tory had made it clear.

Tory's assistant had traced him. Just missed him, an aide to the health secretary had reported: Dr. Hunt had just left a White House meeting convened by the CDC and was on his way to Oregon to assist the FBI. After that, he was scheduled for Atlanta to rejoin the CDC.

Jack helping Carson? It had thrown Rachel. What was going on?

She clutched at his absence, though, like a reprieve. I won't have to face him. Not yet. Clutched, too, at the news of his CDC enlistment, because that meant he was willing to work. All of it meant she might be able to arrange this privately with Hank Vorhees.

"Back to the White House," she told the driver.

She caught up with Vorhees outside the White House mess. Wolfing a ham sandwich as he walked, with two assistants at his right murmuring over notes, he apologized to Rachel for not being able to stop but he was hurrying to catch a flight back to Atlanta. She fell into step with him. They'd known each other professionally for years.

"Unbelievable, this situation, huh?" he said as they passed staffers in the hall. "Still, it's let me shake some serious funding out of these D.C. boys. You here to advise Secretary Takesaki?"

"Hank, I need to talk to you alone."

"Oh, sure thing." He motioned for his assistants to move ahead, and she and Vorhees walked on together. Rachel couldn't bring herself to begin. Couldn't drag her mind out of the smoking minefield of all that had gone wrong. The president's refusal. His directive that she create a team. Tory's abrupt involvement. Her insistence on recruiting Jack. Jack's dead wife. Rachel couldn't get her bearings beyond a panicky sense that things were spiraling out of her control. From this miasma one thought gripped like a hand at her throat: Don't hurt Jack again.

Yet that's exactly what she would have to do. Use him, exploit him. And lose him all over again. Could she bear it?

What other course was there? "Given this deadline," Tory had warned, "our only hope is to immediately seize control of the issue. We can only do that by launching with an instantly recognizable spokesman. Someone admired, sympathetic, irreproachable. In short, Jack Hunt. So this is the plan, Mother. You explain the situation to Hunt just as you have to me, so he sees there's no way out. You convince him and get him onto your research team. From that position of rock-solid credibility we'll have him denounce the government's stand, and tell the world why."

"Rachel, how do you stay in such great shape?" Vorhees was saying, eyeing her as he wiped mustard from his mouth with a paper napkin. "You work out? I tell you, you shame an old fart like me."

She said vaguely, still on autopilot, "Strange double standard. No one would call a woman that, though I'm fifty-two, easily your age."

He flashed a roguish smile. "I know what I'd call you. A damn fine-looking woman."

The idiocy of this banter snapped her back to reality. She was here for a mission. She said, "I hear you've signed Jack Hunt."

He nodded with satisfaction. "He's hot to join us. Poor guy," he added with appropriate sadness.

Rachel stopped walking. "Hank, I've been asked by the president to set up an independent research effort. Top priority. I'm here to second some of your people."

His eyes narrowed, on guard. "That so? Who'd you have in mind?"

She handed him a list of sixteen names she had written in the car. Top CDC epidemiologists, virologists, molecular biologists. Scanning it, Vorhees reddened. "Jesus, why don't you just shut the place down?"

"You can't operate without them?"

"Hell, no!"

"Then I'll make you a deal." She indicated the list. "I'll give you back half those names in exchange for Jack Hunt."

His stiffened at the trap. "No way, Rachel. I'm gearing up around Jack. He's mine."

"I have a directive, Hank."

"And I have Jack. He's dying to come to Atlanta."

"Don't make me pull rank," she said. "I've been given carte blanche by the president."

"Well, what does the fucking president know about science? Jesus Christ, I sweat year after year to stretch a budget over a thousand boiler-plate programs, all the boring vaccination outreach, the foot-slogging investigations and gagging paperwork, while you hotshot corporate types rake in the patents, the cash, the glory . . ."

Rachel wasn't listening. In fighting to get Jack she was flooded with memories of him. Memories she'd tried for years to dam up. The first time they'd made love, in the dark garden. The first time she'd taken him in her mouth. The first time he'd entered her from behind, and she'd felt primitive fire shoot through her. The only man who'd ever excited her so much she had begged for it.

Twelve years since she'd walked out on him and broken all her promises. Now, she was going to have to beg for his help.

Panic swamped her. He'll never agree!

But Tory had been adamant. *"We need this man. Believe me, he's the key."*

Rachel saw, in a shudder of insight, what she would have

to do if Jack refused. There was only one sure way to force him: tell him the truth. Tell him that she was Artemis, that she'd rigged a dead man's switch, that if he turned her in the switch would close, condemning millions to death, so the only way to prevent that pandemic was to do what Tory told him. The jangling overload in her brain reached the pitch of a screeching siren: *extortion.*

If she could believe in a god, she would have implored him now, Please, don't let it come to that. Telling Jack would kill me.

The shrill siren quieted. A calmness settled over her. An acceptance of death. Her death. Her life had ended in that Rwandan village, in the silence of the Church of Our Lady. She'd known it for a long time. The surge of feeling for Jack was just an illusion. *I'm already dead.* All that's left is this final duty to discharge.

She said firmly to Vorhees, "I'm only here as a courtesy. My mandate from the president is clear, and I will exercise it."

"You do this, and I promise you I'll be putting my resignation on Takesaki's desk."

"Put your resignation wherever you want, Hank. Just put your signature on a directive transferring Jack Hunt to me first."

# 5

WIND WAS TOSSING THE JACK PINES IN THE FOREST around Stoney Creek, and Jack sensed the pilot's concentration as he prepared to land the Jet Ranger helicopter in the gusts. Jack scanned the scene below, his heart thudding. His offer to Colwell in Washington had been on impulse, an adrenaline rush to act. Now, hours later, here he was about to step into a place that had been savaged just like Jazida, and he wasn't sure he could take it. The quarantined town below looked like a prison camp. Razor wire looped the perimeter, barricades choked every exit, army trucks crawled the streets, and in the riverside campground outside the town platoons were struggling to erect a burgeoning tent city. For all the imposed order, sanitized by this aerial view, Jack knew what horrors had gone on in these homes. He saw again the blood-slick floors of the brothel, heard the women screaming, smelled the stench of excrement and terror, saw Marisa's blood-engorged eyes, her agony. He had to rest his forehead against the shuddering window, his mouth dry.

As the pilot landed on the campground, a dusty Chevy pickup pulled up. Colwell got out and strode forward, stooping under the rotors. "Dr. Hunt," he called above the engine din, "thanks again for coming." Jack followed him to the pickup, but, still shaky, had to brace himself against the door, head down, to get his breath, his balance.

"Doctor? You all right?"

Jack looked up. Colwell was watching him in concern. Got to pull myself together. I'm here to *help*, damn it.

An army Humvee was racing toward them. The grizzled officer at the wheel braked beside them and called above the rotors' noise, "Colwell, no way I can make your deadline to move all the residents to the campground by midnight. A lot of them are too freaked to budge. I've got to let some stay put until morning."

"Negative, Colonel," Colwell called back. "I need the entire town cleared. Now."

"It's not that simple. I've evacuated disaster sites before, and I'm telling you these people are traumatized."

"This is not a disaster, Colonel. This is a crime. Criminals leave evidence. Any disturbance of the crime site compromises that evidence. So you get the survivors out of their houses by midnight, even if you have to truss them and drag them."

Jack winced. Survivors. He knew how they felt.

Colwell shot him a glance. "Sorry, Doctor."

Jack couldn't let this go on. "Listen," he said to Colwell as the colonel took off, "I don't want my hand held, I want results. Looks like you do too. So let's get started. I'd like to talk to the state epidemiologists who were first to arrive. Then I want to see as much of the town as possible before dark. I'm due at the CDC in Atlanta as soon as we're done, so what can you show me first?"

A quick reappraisal registered in Colwell's eyes, a gleam

of respect. "The scientists are setting up at the church," he said as they climbed into the pickup, then added, throwing an arm over the seat as he reversed, "I've got to head back to Washington in a few hours, but my CIRG commander will finish taking you around. Until then, I'd like to walk you through some of the houses myself. Get your feedback."

"Fine."

Colwell shifted and gunned the engine, and they bumped over the chewed-up campground turf. "Our first priority is to discover how the virus was delivered," he said.

Jack was thinking of epidemiology. "We call it the vector."

Colwell was grim. "I call it hard evidence."

They exchanged a glance. Their work wasn't all that different.

"One request, Doctor," Colwell said. "I must ask that everything you see here remain confidential. The media will be hounding you once you leave, but I'm sure you appreciate that this investigation cannot be carried on in the public eye."

"I agree," Jack said. He had no desire to let the media vultures pick at these people's misery.

And misery was what he saw. Hundreds of blank-eyed men and boys stared out from open tent flaps or sat on the ground watching the soldiers and FBI agents work. Jack had seen this dazed look on countless third-world refugees, but this was *America*. It shook him. He could feel their desolation. It went beyond grief, shock, homelessness. It was a bone-cold certainty of aloneness. He shared it. Like them, he had seen something so terrible he sensed that nowhere in the world would he ever feel at home again.

He'd be glad to leave this place. The quarantine had been imposed immediately in the fear that men, although unaffected by the disease, might be carriers. Blood tests, however, had ruled that out, and the quarantine was now being maintained for the purposes of the FBI's investigation. Jack could leave; for now, these people could not.

He glimpsed a dirty-faced little boy crying, and a bleary-eyed young father, his endurance sapped, twist around and shake the boy. Jack ached to help. He forced himself to look away, block it out, focus on what he'd come for. Evidence. He turned to Colwell. "Any news on the identity of the terrorists?"

"Sorry, Doctor, I'm not at liberty to discuss our investigation."

Jack studied the closed face. Did Colwell really have nothing yet to go on, or was he just very disciplined? Probably both. The hard-nosed act seemed genuine, whatever its source. Somehow it inspired confidence. Though Colwell appeared at least a decade younger than Jack, Jack felt the man's authority. If anyone could track these killers, he decided, Colwell could.

They reached town, where Colwell had to maneuver through the traffic of army vehicles. Jack felt a coldness in the pit of his stomach as he watched soldiers rounding up the holdout residents and herding them into open trucks. He caught heartrending glimpses in driveways and backyards. What agony had there been for the kid who'd pedaled that overturned pink tricycle? Or the owner of the hungry cat scratching at that kitchen door? Or the family whose laundry was left out on that clothesline?

"We're sorting the household garbage here," Colwell said, pulling up at a stone church where a huge awning had been erected over the front yard. Scores of people were at work milling around industrial-sized bins: FBI agents, army technicians, state and CDC epidemiologists, pathologists, forensic scientists. All men, Jack noted. No women were allowed into Stoney Creek. He watched a group cataloguing bins of soiled food containers, and felt awed by the sheer scale of the operation: an entire town as a crime scene. "The scientists are set up inside," Colwell said.

Jack spent a half hour talking to the epidemiologists. Overwhelmed, they had completed only the most preliminary tests. "Water supply checked out clean," a Dr. Chaudhury, the weary team leader, told him. "None of the residents we've interviewed so far remember anything that suggests an obvious airborne release."

Jack wasn't surprised. In Jazida, too, nothing had seemed abnormal to the miners. Yet somehow, someone had brought in enough deadly virus to kill almost every female here. How? In what?

Colwell drove him to a side street where working-class bungalows sat on small but tidy lots. "We've divided the town into sectors, A to J," Colwell explained. "This block's in A. We'll start here." This was what Jack had been dreading, though it was why he'd come: going through homes where victims had died. In house after house he and Colwell sidestepped FBI people who were videotaping and dusting for fingerprints and gathering scraps: food, clothing, soiled carpet. Jack couldn't avoid dry bloodstains everywhere—on beds, chairs, floors, steps, from corpses hastily dragged away. As they looked through house after house, a crew-cut young agent accompanied him and Colwell, reading them stats about the victims who'd died on the premises. Jack tried to take it all in while battling an overpowering sense of emptiness, of loss. House after house, bleak with death.

What was he looking for anyway? Superficially, *nothing* here was like Jazida. *TV Guides* and half-eaten pizzas. Sideboards with wedding china behind glass doors. Cling-wrapped leftovers in fridges. Freezers stocked with sides of beef. Computer games, sneakers in the back hall, backyard barbecues, toddlers' paddling pools. Humble as this logging community was, it was Beverly Hills compared to the poverty of the Brazilian shantytown.

Laundry rooms, cellars, bathrooms, bedrooms. Jack moved through them slowly, eyeing a thousand familiar household objects, feeling a disorienting sense of being surrounded by the dead who'd used them. Colwell stuck by his side, watching him as if he were a dog trained to sniff out narcotics. Jack couldn't see anything that tripped any memory. *What the hell am I looking for?*

"Reynolds, thirty-four, single mother, and her daughter, twelve," the young agent read from his clipboard as they moved down a hall toward two small bedrooms. "Lived alone. Died together on the living-room couch." Jack stopped, the sorrowful litany weighting him like heavy shackles. They'd reached a bedroom, walls plastered with magazine photos of horses—obviously the twelve-year-old's room. Even Colwell silently shook his head. The young agent fidgeted with his clipboard.

"Sir," an agent called, coming down the hall with a cell phone, "it's the command center."

As Colwell took the phone, Jack moved slowly into the bedroom. The bed had a rumpled yellow nylon coverlet, the frilly border frayed from many washings. He edged toward it, thinking: A child slept here until last night. His knee brushed the bedside table, faintly jostling the objects on it: a lamp with ponies prancing on the shade, a ceramic palomino pawing the air, an open diary with pink shooting stars on the page borders, the pages crammed with a childish but determined handwriting. He couldn't help thinking of Laurel at that age, full of secrets, gangly as a filly. It had been torture phoning her early this morning before he'd left Washington. He'd woken her—it was before the news of Stoney Creek had broken on TV—and she'd thought he was calling from Brazil.

"Jack?" she'd asked in surprise. Then, instantly cheerful, "Hey, how's the honeymoon? And when can I meet Marisa? I can't wait."

His own voice had sounded hollow in his ears. "Sweetheart, something's happened."

He sat down on the girl's yellow bedspread, overwhelmed with the futility of this exercise. What did I think I was going to find?"

His gaze drifted over the open diary entry, but a well-honed habit of life with Laurel kicked in: not right to read a kid's private thoughts. So, making a mental note to have Colwell get a specialist to check it out—maybe they'd find a mention of some stranger?—he closed the pink plastic cover.

That's when he saw it. The trinket. It had been beneath the diary cover. Two plastic tubes the size of lipsticks, one red, one purple, joined by an inch-long length of chain like on a cheap key ring.

His pulse quickened. He'd seen this thing in Jazida.

But where? The images of the place were a blur.

The brothel? Yes, that pretty teenager, what was her name? Pia. She'd been sitting on her bed in a nest of movie magazines and makeup. She'd been fingering a trinket just like this. Two joined vials, red and purple.

He shook the pillow out of its case and, using the fabric to avoid leaving prints, picked up the vials. He saw that each one bore a thin, glued-on strip of printed paper.

Jesus. "Colwell!"

He bolted out. Colwell, down the hall, was just handing back the phone. Jack pushed past agents and showed him the vials. "I saw this in Jazida," he said, trying to hold his excitement in check. "And look." He pointed to the narrow labels. "Instructions."

Colwell inclined his head to make out the printing. Jack

had already read it. "Create an irresistibly personal perfume, as potent as you dare," it said, then specified that the red vial contained "the base" and the purple one "a concentrated essence," several drops of which, mixed with the base, would produce "the scent of passion."

Colwell looked up. "Perfume?"

"Perfect medium for a virus," Jack said. "Ever seen a woman test scent? They put it on the pulse point at their wrist and sniff. The stuff goes directly into the lungs and bloodstream."

Colwell's eyes widened. Now they were both excited. Jack felt a surge of energy that was almost vicious. Now we'll nail the bastards!

A voice crackled over the portable VHF clipped to Colwell's belt: "Situation at the morgue, sir. A resident's inside one of the trucks and won't come out. He's got a shotgun. Says he's looking for his wife."

"Christ." Colwell answered over the radio that he was on his way, then handed the vials to a gloved agent. "Get this to the CDC immediately. Tell them top priority." He turned back to Jack. "Doctor, you're with me. On the way, give me your theory about this stuff."

In the pickup they headed for the main street, Jack giving Colwell a rundown on the viral investigation the CDC would do, beginning with electron microscopy. Because of the hemorrhagic pathogenesis, they'd be looking first for viruses that caused known lethal hemorrhagic fevers such as Machupo, Hantavirus, Lassa fever, Marburg, Ebola. The last two, Jack explained, were in a class called filoviruses, named for the microbe's threadlike shape. Under extreme magnification Ebola showed distinctive loops, like shepherd's crooks, at the end of some particles. Marburg virus took two different forms. One looked like a caterpillar, a thin tubular shape coated with "fuzz." In the more dangerous form the viral tube was rolled into a tight coil, impenetrable by the antibodies of a victim's immune system. Besides microscopy, investigators would simultaneously be testing victims' blood against antibodies for known viruses, and using victims' tissue to try to grow the virus in flasks of monkey cells. They'd also observe whether the perfume fluid killed monkey cells.

"Cells die, like the victims?" Colwell asked.

"With Ebola, cells literally burst." The wild card in all of this, however, Jack explained, was the disease's female-specific manifestation. No known virus exhibited that characteristic.

Colwell was turning sharply into the high school parking lot. "Our command post's in the school," he explained. "Morgue's here in the lot."

Jack saw a long line of parked refrigerator trucks, several with lettering that read BRYDON'S MEAT PACKERS. Despite all his years in war zones and refugee camps, with death a constant presence, the sight of this makeshift morgue lanced his heart.

The lot entrance was blocked with vehicles and people—military, FBI, CDC, and surprising number of civilians. Holdouts the army hadn't yet got to? Colwell pulled over, and he and Jack jumped out. Jack saw that the crowd was focused on one truck, its rear door rolled up, open. He couldn't see anyone moving inside the cavernous space. Just shadowy tiers stacked with body bags.

"Any info on the guy inside?" Colwell asked the agent who met them.

"Local sheriff, sir. Name's Roy Hodge."

Colwell strode off to issue orders.

Jack looked around with growing uneasiness. Along with the dozens of milling FBI forensic personnel and CDC scientists interrupted in their morgue work, more civilians were

running in from all directions, and soldiers were trying to restrain them. Jack saw the grizzled army colonel stop Colwell. They seemed to be arguing, the colonel irritably
pointing. A dispute about jurisdiction? It looked like a standoff. Nobody seemed to be approaching the man inside the
truck. The townsmen out here looked tense, unruly. Jack had
a bad feeling. No doubt Colwell was an experienced hostage
negotiator, but did he really know how these men felt, with
their loved ones stacked like cordwood inside those trucks?
Wives, daughters, mothers, sisters.

He longed to help. Maybe it was the bond he felt with the
men, maybe it was the gnawing anguish that he hadn't been
able to do a single thing to help in Jazida. Whatever, he
shouldered through. "Colwell, let me try talking to the guy."

"No," Colwell said, preoccupied. "We'll handle it."

"Without loss of life?" Jack gestured at the weapon-
bristling soldiers. Many looked exhausted; they'd had the
grisly job of labeling and piling the corpses. A few looked as
strung out as the townsmen.

Colwell considered his offer. "Too dangerous. He's
armed."

"Look, I've negotiated with warlords toting Kalashnikovs," Jack said. He added more quietly, "Besides, this
sheriff and I have something in common."

Colwell seemed affected by this. He conferred for a moment with the colonel, then nodded to Jack. "All right, but
just get him to come out if you can. We'll take it from there."

Jack pushed through the crowd. When he was close
enough to the truck's rear he called into its darkness, "Sheriff Hodge, my name's Hunt. Jack Hunt. I'd like to talk."

"You FBI?" a deep voice inside answered.

"No, a civilian. I'm a doctor. I hear you have a problem.
Let's discuss it. Can I come in? I'm unarmed."

There was a pause. "Deal."

When Jack stepped up on the truck's metal platform he had to look down for his footing. A strong hand clamped his elbow and yanked him inside. The door slammed down, cutting off the daylight. Jack stood still, blind in the dark. His sinuses pricked at the reek of disinfectant and death.

"Good idea, a hostage," the deep voice said. "I should've took one right off."

A work bulb clicked on. Jack saw a silver-haired man in jeans and a windbreaker move backward down the aisle, apparently searching the crowded tiers. He was maybe in his late sixties, although his lumberjack build still looked powerful. Even as he searched he held his shotgun trained on Jack, like a pro.

"I mean no harm," he said gruffly. "Just came to find my wife. Those FBI boys turned me back. So I got my gun."

Hodge had zipped open some of the body bags, uncovering naked corpses. Near Jack's knee a cadaver stared sightlessly up at him, the eyes black clots of blood, the lips stretched in rictus over blood-caked teeth. He saw Marisa's face. Sickness boiled up to his throat.

He fought it and dragged his mind back. "Let it go, Sheriff," he said. "Leave your wife in peace."

"That's the idea. I'm going to bury her."

Jack's heart lurched. He'd never got a chance to bury Marisa.

Still, Hodge's wish was impossible. The FBI needed these corpses for autopsies. The CDC needed them for tissue samples. He'd be relying on such samples himself once he got to Atlanta. "Sheriff," he said, "you're a law enforcement officer, so you know there could be vital evidence here. I can't let you do this."

Hodge regarded him. "You married, Doc?"

Jack groped for an answer. "I was, for a few hours. My

wife's dead. Believe me, I know what you're going through."

Hodge looked skeptical. "That so?"

"She died the same way your wife did. An attack in Brazil."

Surprise spread over Hodge's craggy features. He gave a curt nod, sympathetic. Then he lifted the gun ominously. "No offense, Doc, but about spending a lifetime with a woman, you don't know shit." His eyes became hard. "I'm taking her out. And no goddamn FBI or army's gonna stop me."

Jack raised his hands in a conciliatory gesture. Just get him outside, he told himself, then Colwell's people can overpower him.

Hodge was moving down the truck, unzipping bag after bag. Suddenly he halted at the last one he'd uncovered and heaved a strangled moan. "Aw, honey."

Jack saw a small woman, delicate, silver-haired like Hodge. Passing the shotgun from hand to hand, Hodge tugged off his windbreaker and covered his wife's nakedness as tenderly as though he were tucking in a child to sleep. He looked at Jack, tears brimming. "My Rita. Forty-three years we been together. She ain't evidence, Doc, she's my wife."

Jack had no heart to argue. It would only prolong the man's pain. *Just get him outside and get this over with.*

Hodge roughly swiped away his tears, then tossed Jack a shovel. "Join the work party." He lifted his wife in his arms, but beneath her he still pointed the shotgun at Jack. "Let's go."

Jack rolled up the door. The lot was now swarming with many more civilians, though soldiers had scrambled to form a line to block them. Jack stepped down with the shovel. Hodge, carrying the body, was right behind him.

Colwell shouted over a megaphone, "Stop there, Mr. Hodge! Put down your weapon!"

"I mean to bury my wife," Hodge yelled. "I'm heading yonder to the football field and I'm gonna dig her grave. You want to stop me, you'll have to kill me."

"Stop now, or we'll fire!"

Hodge told Jack, "Keep going."

A warning shot cracked above Jack's head. Hodge said, "Steady, now. Straight on."

Another shot. Hodge gasped. Jack twisted around. Hodge was hit in the shoulder. His shotgun clattered on the asphalt, but still he held his wife. Jack threw down the shovel, shouting, "Medic!" and started for Hodge.

Hodge staggered past him, blood soaking his sleeve, breaths wheezing form his throat. Jack said, "Sheriff, stop, let me see to your wound."

"Fuck you," Hodge said through teeth clenched in pain. He shuffled on. Suddenly his legs buckled and he thudded to his knees. Still, he held is wife. The crowd watched in silence. The soldiers lowered their weapons a fraction.

Hodge tried to stand but couldn't get a footing beneath his burden. His strength was ebbing, his arms lowering inch by inch, his muscles trembling, but he held his wife that last foot above ground, unyielding.

Jack watched in awe. He understood, in the deepest part of himself—the part that would always remain in Jazida—Hodge's need to lay his wife to rest.

A man in coveralls broke through the soldiers' line, dashed forward, and lifted the body, saying, "I got her, Roy." Unburdened, Hodge sagged to the ground. The man started toward the field, carrying the sheriff's wife. An FBI agent rushed him from behind, restraining him, but the man held the body as fiercely as Hodge had. Then two young men ran out and together they lifted the woman and started forward.

Someone shouted, "I want my daughter!" and ran toward the truck. Soldiers barred his way. Two more men tried, and were stopped as well. Then four broke through. And three more. The soldiers went after them all, but for every one they stopped, more burst through.

Jack heard Colwell's raised voice: "Colonel, have your men stop these people!" The trickle became a flood. The men charged the trucks. They hauled open all the doors and poured inside. They didn't search, just picked up the first bodies they reached, carried them out, and started across the lot. More came running from town with shovels and pick-axes. Old men, young men. Teenagers. Boys. They swarmed past Colwell, heading for the football field. Nobody stopped them. Nobody could. They were going to bury their dead.

Colwell looked at Jack in disbelief, as if to ask: This chaos, this breakdown of all authority, just to bury a corpse?

Jack couldn't explain. He walked over to Chaudhury, the CDC man. "Have you got tissue samples? I mean, enough?"

"Certainly, hundreds. But—"

It was all Jack needed to know. He walked back to where he'd dropped the shovel. Though army medics were helping Hodge now, he was obstinately trying to stand. Jack picked up the shovel, and with a silent nod of respect to the sheriff, headed for the football field, to dig.

# 6

"No, Mr. Trowbridge hasn't called in. My God, Dr. Hunt, it must be so terrible for you after—"

"Just give him my message if he does. Thanks."

Jack hung up. Since he'd got home to New York an hour ago he'd been trying to track down Gerry. The receptionist at his agent's office didn't know where he was, and nobody Jack had called in Brazil knew either. A while ago he'd tried Gerry's SoHo number, a loft that was both home and studio. Gerry hadn't answered. Jack tried again now, steeling himself for the recording.

Liz's voice: "Hello, you've reached Trowbridge Productions, but at the moment—"

He hung up.

The Manhattan apartment was silent. Eleven floors below, car horns blared and tires were splashing through the afternoon rain, though only a whisper of it penetrated up here. Like some high-rise prison cell, he thought. In solitary.

He rubbed the back of his stiff neck, his shoulders sore

from the digging last night. He'd helped with the burials, believing the men's zeal would soon be softened by the hard work. It hadn't taken long. Once thirty or so women were laid to rest, Colwell and the soldiers had been able to impose order again. Thirty graves. Small price, Jack thought, for easing the troubled minds of those men.

His own mind had been restless all night and during the morning flight here, chafing to know what the CDC had found in the perfume vials. He'd put in several calls to Hank Vorhees from Oregon, and the moment he'd walked through the door he'd checked his messages. Vorhees hadn't called. It bothered Jack. This runaround was no way to begin working together.

He pulled Colwell's card from his wallet, called the Washington number, and was put straight through.

"I was about to call *you*, Doctor. Yes, I got the CDC's report this morning."

Jack didn't miss the coolness in Colwell's voice. They hadn't seen eye to eye on Sheriff Hodge. "And?" he asked.

"Not just one virus—several. Apparently a real soup. So far, none of the hemorrhagic ones you mentioned, though. I'm told it'll take some time for you scientists to disentangle them all."

Jack was itching to get started.

"However," Colwell went on, "we've nailed the delivery system. The U.S. Postal Service—an unwitting accomplice. Free, direct-mail samples of mix-your-own perfume, delivered door to door. Our videotapes confirm the vials in over thirty homes so far, in bathrooms, bedrooms, kitchen garbage. Our computers didn't flag the proliferation earlier because our sector people were cataloging the vials under different descriptions—cosmetics, perfume, makeup, samples. A mess."

Besides, the trinket looked so ordinary, Jack thought. "What about in Jazida?"

"The Brazilian authorities are still sifting through the place but, yes, now that we've alerted them they've begun to turn up some vials."

Jack felt a wave of loathing at the sick irony of the terrorists' weapon. They'd murdered Marisa with *perfume*.

"Doctor, there's one thing I don't understand," Colwell said. "I find it hard to believe that virtually every female in these towns used this stuff. Some were preschoolers, some were over eighty."

"Every one of them wouldn't have to," Jack said. "Just a few dozen trying it would create the epidemic. They'd sniff it and become infected, and then, while the virus was in its most highly contagious stage, each one who came into contact with another female would breathe particles of virus at her. Friends would kill friends. Mothers would kill their own daughters."

Marisa's patients in the brothel killed her.

"Well, Doctor, I owe you," Colwell said. "Thanks to you we now have a hard-evidence trail."

When Jack asked if it had led them to any suspects, Colwell replied there was nothing more he could discuss at this point, thanked him again, and hung up. The usual pattern with Colwell, Jack noted. Nothing volunteered. He doubted he'd ever get more than the rest of the public would: TV statements from some wooden FBI spokesman.

He glanced at his bags outside the bedroom door. When he'd arrived stale-mouthed after the flight, he'd dropped them there. He couldn't go in. Over the last four days he'd only napped fitfully in airplane seats and hotel armchairs. Hadn't been in a bed since Marisa died.

Just tonight to get through, he told himself. He'd come home only to get organized and pack. In the morning, he'd be on his way. In Atlanta he'd get some answers from Vorhees.

The phone rang. He held back, hoping it was Vorhees or Gerry, but suspecting another reporter. He'd already erased a slew of their damn messages. He waited for the recording to kick in, ready to grab it if it was Gerry or Vorhees.

Just another reporter.

He went to the kitchen, drank some water, walked back to the living room. Such a cold place. Utilitarian. It was like this when he'd taken it ten years ago and he'd never bothered to change it. Too busy. Besides, it had been what he'd wanted then, the antithesis of the way he'd once lived in Atlanta. Hard even to remember all that now. The plantation-style house, the pool and tennis court. The sleek, silver Porsche. The sleek, smart women. Then Laurel had been thrust into his life, making it all seem obscene. He'd walked away from the fancy house and the choice CDC job, joined One World Medics and hadn't looked back. With Laurel either away at school or staying with him in cities near his assignments, he'd only needed this apartment as a base between missions, and he'd never really noticed how sterile it was until now, remembering the Vermont chalet he and Marisa had been planning.

He switched on CNN, hungry for an update. They were covering some conference in Japan. He hit the mute button. There'd be an update soon.

He flipped through the stack of mail the super had left on the dining-room table. There was a handwritten card from Rio de Janeiro: Marisa's brother sending congratulations on the wedding and "hoping we will meet soon." Jack set down the card, shaken. He hadn't known she had a brother. Knew her parents were dead, that she'd been a senior nurse at a Rio hospital, but so little else. He'd been looking forward to learning. He thought of Sheriff Hodge's words: *"About spending a lifetime with a woman, you don't know shit."*

I never really knew her.

He listened to the room, the silence pressing in on him. How was he going to get through the night? His body craved rest, but every time he'd tried to drift to sleep, he was back there—Marisa writhing, hemorrhaging, crashing. *I brought her to that place.*

A key clicked and the door opened. Jack turned in surprise. Laurel.

She dropped her bags, ran to him, and threw her arms around his neck. Her curly hair and denim jacket were damp from the rain. His arms tightened around her slight body. When he'd called her in Boston yesterday he hadn't asked her to come, but now he was filled with relief to have her near. "What about your job?" he said, gently drawing her away. He'd pulled strings to get her a data entry position for the summer at a municipal lab.

"I quit. They understood. I didn't want you to be alone." She searched his face. "Are you all right?"

No. "Yeah."

She frowned in concern. "Have you eaten today?"

He tried to remember.

"That's what I figured," she said, "so I had the taxi stop at a deli."

She made him sit on the sofa while she got plates and cutlery and set everything on the coffee table, then kicked off her sandals and sat beside him cross-legged in her skimpy skirt, unpacking croissants and salad containers. She didn't ask any questions. He was grateful for that. He did tell her he was leaving in the morning for Atlanta.

"I'll come with you," she said simply.

"It'll just be a hotel," he warned. "I'll be at the lab all day."

"Then you'll want to come home to someone who doesn't talk science. Anyway, I like room service."

He was touched. No tears, no sentimentality; that wasn't Laurel's way. He watched her spooning chicken salad onto a plate for him, her punk-orange hair and black bat earrings such a contrast to her bustling solicitousness. He'd often marveled at the hardy exterior she'd developed to deflect life's blows. Since becoming her guardian he'd been in awe that her thin young shoulders could bear the weight they had. He worried about it sometimes. Laurel had seen too much. It was why he'd never told her the truth about her mother's death. And never would.

She was picking up the remote with a glance at the mute TV. "You don't want to watch that," she said, about to click it off.

"No, turn it up," he said quickly. It was Stoney Creek. The CNN reporter was standing beside soldiers at a high gate bristling with razor wire at the campground's edge.

"The quarantine has made this town a virtual prison. Nothing seems to be known yet about the anonymous terrorist group that has claimed responsibility. For now, the dazed men and boys behind this fencing are simply struggling, like the rest of the nation, to comprehend the unspeakable tragedy. Mike McIvar, Stoney Creek, Oregon."

*"Nothing known yet."* Was that true? Jack wondered. Or just the official line?

CNN cut to a replay of a press statement from the attorney general. She spoke in a calm monotone: "The investigation is proceeding in a comprehensive and orderly fashion. Every available resource has been dedicated to the FBI, and the governments of foreign nations are fully cooperating with our efforts. Make no mistake, the perpetrators of this crime against humanity will be brought to justice." Reporters shouted questions as she started to leave the podium.

One yelled, "Have the terrorists threatened another attack?" She was already moving away.

Laurel looked at Jack. "That's the same thing that killed Marisa?"

Killed. *Murdered.* He nodded.

"My God," she whispered, shaking her head.

CNN cut to an interview with a senator. Laurel clicked off the TV. They sat in silence.

"I'm going to call for a ticket to Atlanta," she said briskly, starting for the kitchen. She came back with the portable phone and the yellow pages, and sat beside him again, flipping pages. "What are you booked on?"

"American. Seven-fifteen. Flight—" His throat caught with a sudden tightness, a choke of tenderness. This little punk girl, this once-bewildered street kid, wary as a wild cub, had become the rock of his life. The world would say he'd taken her in and looked after her, but he knew better. For ten years they'd looked after each other. At this moment, it was she who was keeping him sane. "Sweetheart," he managed, "I'm so glad you're here."

Her businesslike face seemed to crumple. "Oh, Jack," she said, her voice catching too. She sank back against him and pressed her head on his shoulder, as though to infuse her young strength into him. He put his arm around her shoulders and squeezed.

She sniffed, then sat up, suddenly brisk again. "*You,*" she said with mock strictness, "need to sleep." She nodded toward his bedroom. "Go on, lie down. I'll hold down the fort."

He didn't move.

She seemed to understand. She brought out a blanket and pillow, tucked the blanket around him, and slid the pillow under his head on the sofa back.

Jack finally allowed his eyes to close. A siren was wailing

down on Riverside Drive. He listened as it faded like a dying scream.

She would have rocked him in her arms if he'd let her. But, being Jack, no way would he let on how broken up he was. She'd seen it, though. In his eyes. In the way he was just standing there in the middle of the room when she'd arrived, as if he were lost. She'd do anything to make him feel better, anything. People always said that, in movies, in books, "I'd do anything. I'd die for you." It sounded so dumb, but she knew it was true. She really would give up her life for Jack.

Hey, dying isn't exactly the job description here, she reminded herself before she got carried away. More like: fix a hot meal, answer the phone, see his laundry's done. Guess I can handle that.

As he slept she quietly cleaned up the deli garbage and put the leftovers in the fridge. He'd eaten almost nothing. She'd nip out to the market later, she decided, and get stuff to make a nice mushroom risotto. He liked that. Maybe with some fresh green peas. She hefted his bags into his bedroom and unzipped them on the bed, wondering, for the hundredth time, what Marisa had been like. From Jack's description before the wedding she sounded pretty cool. Well, she'd have to be if he'd fallen in love with her. God, she thought with a shiver, it must have been so disgusting, the way she died. I couldn't have handled seeing it. Then it struck her: being female too, I wouldn't have lasted long enough for wimpiness to matter. Just as well. Sometimes it seemed as though she couldn't handle *anything*. She'd fooled Jack there. He had some idea that she actually knew what she was doing with her life. He didn't know what went on inside her head. He didn't know about the nightmare.

It was always the same. She was too late getting home,

she couldn't get inside because the door was locked, and by the time she did they were all dead. When she was conscious, awake, she realized there was probably no way she could have stopped it. She was only eight. What could she have done? Still, it haunted her—there might have been *something*.

What actually happened had been nightmare enough. It had been a Friday in February, the ugliest month in Detroit, and she was supposed to come home from school to look after her little sister and brother, because on most Friday mornings her mother's boyfriend brought over more junk, either crack cocaine or heroin, and they smoked or shot up, and by the afternoon her mother didn't much notice what the two little kids were up to. So Laurel knew she should get home. That day she didn't. She goofed off with a friend, fooling around outside the corner 7-Eleven, throwing snowballs and working up a plan to swipe a couple of Cokes, which they did. They ran down the block and drank the Cokes as they horsed around on a snowbank. It was getting dark when she tossed her can in the slush and headed home.

She got out her key to the basement apartment but found the door unlocked. Nothing weird there, her mother sometimes forgot even to *close* it. The stairwell was dark—her mother never thought to turn on the light for her—and she felt her way down in the gloom. The air was cold and stank of cat piss. The smell was always worst in winter. At the bottom she switched on the light. She found them sprawled on the ratty sofa and the floor. Each one shot. All dead. Her mother, mother's boyfriend, little sister, baby brother. She sat stiffly on a kitchen chair, refusing to look at the blood, wondering what to do.

Later—she didn't know if it was minutes or hours—a man she'd never seen before came down the stairs. He said he was her grandfather, Jack. He called the police, and when they arrived they asked him questions. She felt sorry for him because his face was the color of the slush outside as he told how he'd found them, how it looked like an addict had broken in and done it. The police asked her questions, too. Jack told them to let her alone, for God's sake, she was only a child, and she wasn't even home when it happened. The cops finished their questions anyway. Then, Jack took her away. Jack made her safe. Jack gave her a wonderful new life. She loved him so much, she couldn't bear to think he might find out what she was really like: useless. So she'd never told him she was supposed to come home early that day, never told him that if she'd been there she might have stopped the man with the gun. She knew the truth in her nightmares, and she knew it in her heart. She should have come home, and kept the killer out.

A ringing startled her. The fax line. She left Jack's bedroom and headed for the small office across the hall where she lifted off the one-page fax. From the CDC. She was reading it when Jack came to the doorway. He leaned against the frame, still groggily waking up. "What is it?" he asked, rubbing the back of his neck.

"What does 'seconded' mean?"

"Transferred. Like being traded."

"Well," she said, "you've been traded." She scanned the last paragraph. "To a Dr. Rachel Lesage."

His face looked like she'd thrown ice water at him. "Rachel?" He came and grabbed the fax.

Laurel couldn't tell if it was good news or bad, but she'd never seen anybody wake up so fast.

## 7

"YOU WON'T BE NEEDED AT THE LAB TODAY, Dr. Hunt," the young chauffeur said with a glance back at Jack and Laurel. Pulling out of the Bar Harbor airport, he merged Rachel's blue Mercedes with the summer traffic. "Dr. Lesage's team won't have all arrived until tomorrow."

This was news. Jack didn't like it. On the phone Rachel's executive assistant had assured him that all arrangements had been made. Apparently not too well, he thought with some irritation. It had been enough of a shock yesterday just to know he'd be seeing Rachel, though he'd gotten his mind around that now, he hoped. Anyway, being pulled from the CDC to her facility wasn't what bothered him—far from it. He knew all about her cutting-edge work with biotech therapies in the state-of-the-art labs she owned, not only here in Maine but also in Virginia and Puerto Rico as well as a couple in Europe. The president's request that she pull together an elite team was an inspired move—she'd have no bureaucracy to slow her down—and if Lesage Laboratories instead of the CDC was going to be the front line of the research attack, this was where Jack wanted to be. When her Learjet had met him and Laurel in New York this morning he'd assumed he was going to brief her team immediately about Jazida and get rolling. Instead, it now seemed he'd be hanging around a hotel for a day and night waiting. He didn't like the idea and said so to the chauffeur.

"Oh, not a hotel, sir," he replied. "You'd never get decent rooms at the height of the season, especially with the other scientists and their staffs arriving too, plus all the media. No, Dr. Lesage wants you to stay at her home."

Jack liked this even less. Still, it was true that at a private home he could avoid the damn media. Anyway, it would only be temporary. He'd soon arrange a hotel.

"You'll like it out there," the chauffeur added, smiling in the rearview mirror. "It's on the ocean."

Laurel murmured, "I think this lady's used to getting her way."

Always could, Jack thought. Get her way, and make you glad you were part of it. He couldn't deny that's what really disturbed him. Yesterday, just knowing he was going to see her, he'd felt it again. An instant sexual charge. How could she still do that to him after all these years? And after these last days of horror. It shamed him.

Yet it had been the same the very first evening they'd met.

It happened in England, twelve years ago. East Sussex, in spring. He was head of the CDC's Special Pathogens Branch in Atlanta then, and was finishing a series of guest lectures at England's Porton Down virology lab when he heard that Rachel Lesage was in the country. She had just accepted her Nobel prize in Stockholm and was visiting English friends on her way home. He'd never met her, but one of her early bacteriophage experiments had been in collaboration with him, and others, long distance. It had been years before, his input had been slight, and they hadn't corresponded since. Nevertheless, in her Nobel acceptance speech she had acknowledged his contribution. That was a class act, he thought, and he wanted to thank her. He heard that her hosts were planning a party in her honor at their Sussex country home, so he finessed an invitation.

That was the first time he'd felt the pull of Rachel's gaze. During the party he noticed that she did not gladly suffer fools. If she found a person's conversation dull she barely acknowledged them, but anyone who interested her drew that almost brazen stare, intense yet nearly expressionless. He'd been struck by how unfeminine it seemed. Most women were animated, advertising charm, especially women who were attractive. And Rachel Lesage was very attractive. It seemed she found him interesting, and the cool beam of her eyes fixed him with frank appraisal, womanly in a primal way. Just meeting her gaze, he got an erection.

She left the crowded drawing room first. He watched her go out the French doors to the back garden and into the darkness. He followed her, more excited than he could ever remember being. He moved among shadowy fruit trees faintly lit by fairy lights, trying to find her. There was only silence and shadows. He turned, and there she was, standing by a potting shed, watching him. He went to her, and for a moment, unsure, they searched each other's eyes. Then she touched his mouth. He kicked open the shed door and pulled her inside and pressed her against the wall. Her mouth was already open when he kissed her. He went to his knees and shoved up her skirt, the smell of her as pungent as the spring earth. She climaxed in his mouth, and he almost came himself before he stood and had her against the wall.

That was the first time. For the next five days, he couldn't get enough of her.

Then she'd disappeared from his life. Until today.

"Here we are." The chauffeur pulled into a private road canopied with the boughs of maples and beeches. At a gatehouse he opened the barrier by remote control and they continued deeper into the woods. Jack reflected that such cocooned privacy was available only to the very rich. He knew Rachel had earned her success. She had won the Nobel prize in medicine for her early work with bacteriophages to alter cellular DNA: twenty years ago she'd used monkey virus SV40 to carry genes inside *E. coli* bacteria, demonstrating how viruses that infect bacteria might be used to treat genetic deficiency diseases. A stunning piece of work. On the strength of that achievement she had built Lesage Laboratories, starting with this lab in Bar Harbor, which remained her flagship operation, and subsequently expanding; he believed her Puerto Rico lab was the latest addition. Her company now carried on a worldwide trade in genetic diagnostic systems for clinical microbiology and was involved in very creative biomedical research, using recombinant DNA techniques with genetically altered retroviruses to treat inherited diseases like cystic fibrosis. Rachel had become a biotechnology magnate.

They emerged from the woods and skirted a lawn that led up an incline to a three-storied white house. It wasn't what Jack had expected—a rambling, old-fashioned place, maybe turn-of-the-century, with gables and dormers and wooden shutters. Imposing, yes, but obviously a lived-in family home. Broad green verandahs were footed by a white froth of hydrangea bushes. Birdhouses nestled in the trees, and wind chimes glinted from the verandah eaves. He caught glimpses of a kitchen garden, a raspberry patch, a stone sundial, an ivy-covered woodshed. From a third-story window a white cotton curtain billowed out in the breeze. Rachel could have centered her business in any of the country's busy biomedical communities, so Jack wondered if she maintained this pastoral retreat to guard her privacy. He knew almost nothing about her private life.

"I don't think Dr. Lesage is back yet," the chauffeur said, stopping the car, "but I'll leave you with Doris, the house-keeper. She'll show you your rooms."

Jack stepped out and immediately smelled the sea. He turned. The lawn sloped down to an ocean bay. A sheltering line of pines masked part of it, but he could make out a stony beach and a dock, and a gleaming white sailboat bobbing at the mooring.

"Nice work if you can get it," Laurel said, taking it all in.

As she dragged her knapsack from the seat Jack helped the chauffeur get their bags, then followed him up the ve-randah steps. Pausing to wait for Laurel, he noticed a man in a chair inside a screened porch at the far end of the veran-dah, the screen obscuring his features. He was talking qui-etly, though he seemed to be alone; Jack realized he was dictating into a microphone. Rachel's husband? He'd never met the man, but he'd always pictured a hard-driving ty-coon, an integral part of her biotech empire. A man she would not leave.

He suddenly wished he hadn't agreed to stay here.

A gangly Irish setter bounded across the verandah to meet them. "Hello there, you," Laurel said, bending to stroke the dog's head.

"His name is Liam," a voice informed them.

Jack turned. The screened door at the far end had opened, revealing the speaker as the man in the chair. A wheelchair, Jack now saw. The man, about seventy, looked very frail.

"And this must be Dr. Hunt." His words were slurred. The wheelchair motor hummed as he glided forward. "Welcome to Swallow Point. I am Dr. Lesage's husband."

"Professor Delbert Farr," the chauffeur informed Jack.

"Del," he insisted, and held out his left hand in greeting.

His right lay useless in his lap, and Jack realized—the impaired speech, the unilateral paralysis: a stroke. Blankly, he shook the bony hand. The firmness of the grip surprised him.

"I am a great admirer of yours, Doctor," Del said. "It is an honor to meet you." He spoke carefully to counteract the slurring. "Though I deeply regret the circumstances that bring you here. Please," he added warmly, "accept my condolences on the death of your wife. A tragedy that is difficult to comprehend."

Jack mumbled his thanks and introduced Laurel. Del asked the chauffeur to take their bags to their rooms. "I am sorry to report that Rachel has been delayed at the lab. Perhaps she'll make it home in time to join us for luncheon. In the meantime, Laurel, may I offer you a soda? And for you, Doctor," he added, the left side of his mouth curling in a smile, "my guess is scotch, correct?"

Jack roused himself to stop staring at this age-spotted man, so ill, so gray, so totally unlike the husband his mind had created for Rachel. "Scotch is fine. And, please, it's Jack."

They had drinks inside the screened porch where Jack had heard Del dictating. Dredging for conversation, he noticed the tape recorder beside a stack of pages like a manuscript. "Are you working on a book?"

"Yes, for several years now. Essays on demographics shaping the environment. Shocking how long these things take to complete."

As Laurel lifted a pair of binoculars from the table, Del said, "Ah, you've discovered how I *really* spend my time. Watching the birds."

Laurel smiled. "Hobby?" she asked, training the binoculars on the beach.

"All my life. For several days I have been following a

gyrfalcon over at the rocks on the point," he said, indicating the direction for her. "Did you know the gyrfalcon is the world's largest falcon? It is an arctic species that breeds no farther south than Labrador, so it's very rare to see one here. Oh, some winters a few have ventured this far south, but never in summer, so I fear this vagrant out at our point has stayed behind because it is sick. Sadly, they often suffer from environmental ills. The gyrfalcon is a raptor, you see. Its prey is smaller birds, ducks for example. Such birds often have ingested heavy metal these days, and the contamination can pass directly into the raptor. I have concluded that civilization is not good for them." He added quietly, "Perhaps not good for any of us."

He rearranged his useless right hand on his lap, and went on, "The female gyrfalcon is bigger and stronger than the male. Arab countries have trouble captive breeding the species because the Arabs resist accepting that the male is the smaller of the pair. Interesting, isn't it? How human biases mar our ability to see clearly." He looked up at Jack. "Naturally, for the male gyrfalcon, the fact that his mate is more powerful presents no problem at all."

Jack felt a shiver. Did Del know about him and Rachel? Jesus, he thought as Del and Laurel kept talking, how could she have brought me here?

"Three weeks," she had promised that last morning in England, in their country hotel. She'd said she must go home first, must tell her husband face-to-face. She owed him that much, she said, but then she would meet Jack in New York and they would start a new life together. She stood naked in his arms in the morning sunlight and promised. Heady with the wonder of her, he said he'd leave the CDC and move wherever was best for her. Maybe they could come back to England, he said. Maybe she could build a lab there and they could work together. "Three weeks," she said again, smiling, her eyes shining with tears. "Jack, how can I wait that long?" He'd never known anyone like her, electric with contrasts. Fearless, but so impressionable. Voracious in her passion, but so generous. They'd only known each other for six days, but he felt he could not live, could not breathe, without her.

Within one week, back in Atlanta, he got her note. Two lines. Three if you counted the Dear Dr. Hunt. "Regarding our meeting, my plans have changed. I am canceling my New York trip." No explanation. A Dear John if ever there was one. Reading it, he'd felt a pain like a scalpel in his breastbone.

Days went by. He left messages with her assistant and her housekeeper, but Rachel returned none of his calls. He kept expecting he'd hear from her somehow, a letter, a card, saying work had delayed her, and suggesting a fresh plan. Or maybe she would just show up on his doorstep. He heard nothing. He felt confused, angry, cheated. After a few weeks the painful wound scarred over and subsided to a dull ache, a bruise. He saw that Rachel hadn't felt what he had. Not a new story, he told himself. Happened all the time. Two people meet, share a passionate week, then say good-bye. For him, however, Rachel had meant far more.

Months passed, filled with long days of work at the CDC. The scar hardened. He got on with his life. One morning, driving to work in a gray drizzle, he recalled the Greek myth about Icarus, who had crashed to earth after flying too close to the sun. Rachel was like the sun. He had entered her aura for six shining days. In public he'd discreetly waited for her during the London parties and receptions where the international science community wooed her and the press fawned over her, the new Nobel laureate. In private they made love every night and every morning at the Pear Tree Inn, where the daffodils and the spring sunshine and the thrill of her dazzled him and blinded him. Then, suddenly, she was gone. And he had tumbled to earth.

Lunch was a trial. Del had waited as long as he could for Rachel, but by two o'clock, conceding she was not coming, he asked the housekeeper to serve them on the verandah. Over the cold salmon and asparagus Del soldiered on, commenting on the history of the house, the flora and fauna of the area. Jack managed a few remarks. Laurel cheerily kept the conversation going. Thank God for her, Jack thought.

"Nice sailboat," she said, nodding toward the water.

"Yes, a J-35. She's Rachel's. Do you sail, Laurel?"

"Never."

"Would you like to?"

"I'd love to."

"Then you timed your visit well," Del said. "Rachel had the boat out for repairs until yesterday. What with mounting a new propeller shaft and sacrificial anode, then fairing the rudder, it took weeks."

"Sacrificial what?" Laurel asked.

"Anode. A zinc bulb on the propeller shaft." Del explained, in his patient professorial style, about corrosion in underwater metals. "But if a zinc anode is mounted near the metal you want to preserve, like the bronze propeller, the zinc corrodes first, protecting the bronze. It's sacrificed."

Laurel said, "Sounds like part science and part black magic."

"Sailing is, you know. Even in my dinghy, Sandpiper, I try to apply scientific principles, but I sometimes wish I could cast a spell to tame the wind and waves."

"You sail?" Laurel asked in amazement, then blushed, aware of her faux pas.

Del smiled. "My dinghy is rigged for challenged sailors. Of course, I don't go far." He added with a twinkle, "The sandpiper is a shore bird." He laughed softly as he spoke about his nurse, Ron. He and his wife, Doris, the house-keeper, lived upstairs. "Each time Ron lowers me into the cockpit he asks with a frown, 'You *sure* you want to go out today, Professor Farr?' If you'll fetch the binoculars from the porch, Laurel, you can see my boat at the dock."

Jack was nearest. "I'll go," he said.

He'd taken only a few steps when he heard behind him, from the far end of the verandah, "Hello, Jack."

He turned. Rachel stood on the top step, looking just as he remembered. The wide mouth, the thick dark hair, the brilliant brown eyes, the penetrating gaze. The sun behind her silhouetted her body, slim in white linen slacks and silk shirt. He could see that it was still an athlete's body, radiating focused energy. "Hello, Rachel," he said.

Neither moved. In the silence, Del and Laurel, between them, waited.

Rachel finally came forward. Jack was acutely conscious that her eyes hadn't left him. "I hope the flight was all right?"

A blade of anger entered him. "I could have caught a commercial flight tomorrow, since that's when the first meeting is."

"Forgive me. I just thought some quiet out here first might do you good."

"No, it's okay," Laurel said with a mollifying glance at him. "He's just really tired."

Jack sensed the pall he'd cast. As Del introduced Laurel, he groaned inside, knowing he should have done that. Why was he standing here so stiffly, like some fool teenager?

Del broke the silence by telling Rachel they'd been discussing her boat.

"Care to go for a sail?" she asked.

"Now?" Laurel said eagerly. "Cool."

Rachel's eyes snapped to her in annoyance, and Jack realized she'd meant the invitation for him alone. She said, again to him, "There's a lovely breeze, and it may be the last chance, with all the work ahead. What do you say, Jack?"

It wouldn't have been his first choice. That would be getting to the lab. But he saw Laurel's enthusiasm, and after bearing his heavy moods she deserved a break. So did he, for that matter—any activity was better than straining at polite conversation here. "Why not."

"Then I shall see you after your adventures on the water," Del said pleasantly, and backed his wheelchair from the table.

"I'll just get changed," Rachel said.

Jack watched as she went with Del through the open French doors to the living room and as far as the hall staircase, where a corridor led to a modern addition. Stopping at this crossroads, she bent and kissed Del gently on the mouth. His hand cupped the back of her head, and his gray fingers disappeared into her thick dark hair. Forehead to forehead, they spoke quietly for a few moments. Then Rachel straightened, Del turned his wheelchair and glided down the corridor, and Rachel started up the stairs.

"You okay?" Laurel asked Jack.

He quickly turned back. "Of course."

Closing her bedroom door, she had to lean against it for strength. Her knees had gone weak at the sight of him. Twelve years since she'd been with him, but it might as well be twelve hours.

The way he'd looked at her—such wariness. He'd never forgiven her. It was so clear, etched in his eyes, in the tightness of every muscle. Panic rocked her. How can I broach the campaign to him if I can't even break through his mistrust?

And the girl, she thought desperately as she pulled off her clothes, grabbing shorts, a sweatshirt. She'd never anticipated him bringing his granddaughter. She'd hoped to get him alone on the boat, gain his confidence, bring him around, somehow. She had to do it today. Tory would be arriving in the morning, expecting to have it arranged. *There's so little time.*

She forced a mask of calmness as she reached them downstairs. At the dock they took the inflatable tender and motored to the boat at its mooring. "*Curious.*" Laurel said, reading the red lettering on the hull as they came alongside. "Good name for a scientist's boat."

They climbed aboard. As Rachel hoisted the mainsail, Laurel asked, "You usually handle this big boat all alone?"

"It's rigged for solo sailing. All lines lead to the cockpit." As she took the helm she asked Jack, "Ever sailed?"

"One summer, long ago," he said, glancing around at the rigging. "You'll have to remind me what to do."

"Like riding a bicycle, it'll all come back." She asked him to cast off from the bow. She hardened the mainsheet, unfurled the head sail, and they were under way.

Laurel perched on the hatch and gazed out while Jack came back to the cockpit and sat across from Rachel. She sensed him avoiding her eyes, and she felt the space between them was a chasm. The silence of those dozen years. How can I reach him?

With some of the truth in my heart?

She said haltingly, "Jack, I'm so sorry for your loss. More sorry than I can say."

In his haggard eyes she saw a shield go up. Armor against condolences, or just against her? He looked away, and she gritted her teeth. What a clumsy way to begin!

But she'd forbidden herself more remorse about his wife. She had a mission: get him to do the campaign. Nothing else mattered. She wanted his *willing* agreement. If he refused, her only option was to force him by telling him the truth, and that would be a torture for them both. But to get his willing agreement, she first had to get his trust. *Nothing can happen until I have that.*

They were making a smooth six knots in placid seas. She asked Laurel to go to the foredeck to keep a lookout for a flagged rock, awash now at high tide. She'd navigated around it a hundred times, but it was a good pretext to send the girl out of earshot. She watched Laurel go forward and sit cross-legged on the bow, her back to them.

Rachel and Jack were alone. She felt his eyes slide to her as she manipulated the sheets and tiller. He finally asked with grudging interest, "How long have you been doing this?"

"Since I was about seven, growing up in a little French port in Nova Scotia. My father taught me. He was a navigator in the Canadian navy."

"Oh?"

She understood his surprise. Few people knew of her French-Canadian background. She'd purged her accent years ago.

Rocky little Lone Pine Island was dead ahead. Preparing to tack, Rachel told Laurel to move to the mast and asked Jack to handle the jib sheets. As she brought the bow through the wind, he stood grinding the winch. He cleated off the sheet, then straightened, keenly watching their progress, the wind rippling his shirt. Rachel saw, with a glimmer of hope, that he'd enjoyed the bit of exercise. *One step forward,* she thought.

Close-hauled now, they were heeled more, and Jack settled near her on the high side. He closed his eyes and drew in a deep breath. She read intense relief on his face, as though that breath had been the first clean one he'd drawn in days, and this was the first moment of peace. Opening his eyes, he turned to her and said quietly. "This is nice."

It was his apology. Her hope surged. *Not too fast,* she warned herself. She said, "My father used to say that when he was in church he thought about sailing, and when he was sailing he thought about God."

Jack smiled.

*Two steps forward.* Her heart crammed up in her throat. Now's the time. "Jack, about the situation. There's been a development."

His smile evaporated and he asked, suddenly keen, "What is it?"

In watching him her concentration on the gusts had wavered, and one hit them now, heeling them violently. Rachel stood and eased the mainsheet, instantly leveling the boat. Jack twisted around to check on Laurel, who'd tumbled onto her side. "You okay?" he called to her.

"Sure." She laughed, holding on to the lifeline she'd grabbed for support. "What a rush!"

"Come on back here where it's safe," he told her. "I can see the rock now. Over there." He pointed to show Rachel.

"Good, thanks," Rachel said. She could only watch in frustration as Laurel joined them in the cockpit.

Standing to make room, Jack said to Rachel, "We can't talk here. Let's head back." At that moment another gust hit, and he grabbed her elbow to steady her. Her breath caught at the sensation of his grip. He quickly drew his hand away, but she saw he'd felt the shock of it too. She tried to compose herself. He'd been so close she'd smelled his skin, that trace of male sweat, and it instantly ignited the old ache, as sharp as that first night with him at the inn.

He strode into her room and they laughed at how they'd given the London reporters the slip.

It had been her idea. At the evening's Barbican media reception she was quietly telling him that she'd moved to a country inn, and was about to tell him its name when she noticed a reporter trying to overhear. Boldly, loudly, she recited the inn's phone number instead. As she brushed past Jack, she whispered, "Deduct one numeral." He'll get it, she thought, confident that the reporter, on the other hand, would give up after the original number proved wrong. He'd get no story.

She didn't know what she'd do if *Jack* gave up. She wanted him so much after last night in the garden shed. It was all she could think of during the day's string of press conferences. She'd answered questions about Stockholm and the Nobel committee, bacteriophages and DNA, all the while remembering Jack's hands shoving up her skirt in the darkness, his tongue between her legs, his cock driving into her against the wall.

She'd never done anything like this before. She'd been a faithful wife to a husband who was gentle, companionable, an undemanding lover.

But Jack *was* demanding, and he hadn't given up. He'd got the right number, and now he was here.

They pulled off their clothes and fell together on the bed. He rolled her on her back and spread her legs. He teased her, with his fingers, his tongue, until she gasped. Then he waited. She groaned, frantic for him to go on. She groped at his shoulders where his muscles bunched as he held himself above her. She begged, "Oh, please . . . fuck me! *Please!*"

Twelve years. Nothing had changed.

Except, everything had changed. And she was running out of time. Would she have to tell him the truth after all? *There's a dead man's switch, Jack. If you turn me in—if I'm arrested—it will close, unleashing a pandemic. Only you can prevent that. Only you can save us all, by leading Tory's campaign.* How could she get him on her side without resorting to that? She didn't think she could bear to exploit him so brutally.

Suddenly, the memories that had ambushed her spawned an idea. Is *that* the way to bring him to me?

The thought made her tremble. Seduce him? If she could, maybe she wouldn't have to use the truth to extort his compliance, maybe he'd do the campaign of his own free will, to be with her again. Could it work? Was it wise . . . or just what she wanted?

*Whatever,* she thought, homing in on the decision, *tonight is all I have.*

The sun was setting by the time they got back to the dock, and Jack was restless to ask what she'd meant by a "development." He didn't want to alarm Laurel with talk of autopsies and pathogens, so he sent her on ahead to the house, saying he and Rachel had business to discuss. He watched her start up the slope, the dog bounding down to greet her, then he turned to Rachel and asked, "So, what's happened?"

She hesitated. "Let's walk. Come, I'll show you the beach." They started across the stony patch beside the dock. "I just wasn't sure if you'd heard, about Oregon. The FBI found virus in vials of perfume."

He stifled a groan of disappointment. Was that all? "I know. I was there."

"Oh, of course. Well, that's what we'll be working on. The CDC is couriering me samples tonight."

As they walked he questioned her about the team—who was on it, how she intended to direct the effort, what further liaison she planned with the CDC—but her answers were brief, indefinite. She seemed preoccupied, or reluctant to go into detail, or both. Anyway, he told himself, there wasn't a whole lot to discuss until they could get a good look at the stuff in the vials.

An osprey whistled shrilly overhead. Jack watched it glide toward the pines at the point. The light was fading quickly. Across the bay to the east the woods were already dark against the purple sky, and the far-off cries of birds sounded as they flew to safety for the night. The air held a faint chill, Jack thought. The first threat of fall.

Or maybe it was just him. That moment on the boat had thrown him. Touching Rachel. All the old sensations. Abruptly, he stopped walking. "Think I'll head in, get cleaned up."

"Oh, not yet," she urged. "I do want to talk, Jack. About the work, I mean. Let's enjoy the sunset first. Come on, a bit of a walk will help you sleep." She added quietly, "You look like you need it."

True enough, he thought. He hadn't slept properly since Jazida. Anyway, it was time he got over this unease at being with her; they were going to be working together. Deal with it, he told himself. "Maybe you're right."

They walked on. Rachel was gazing out at the sunset-reddened sea. "I've always loved the beach," she said, her voice vibrant, serious. "It's like a frontier—between what we know and what we can only imagine."

He looked at her. What an original she was. Her intellect, her drive. Handling that boat, running her empire. She didn't need anyone. Did that really still bother him?

As they picked their way over the stones and broken driftwood, she slipped her arm through his. She'd done it casually, easily, as though they were old friends who walked on the beach every evening, but his blood leaped at the touch of her, again. He glanced at her bent head. Even in the fading light he saw that the back of her neck was tanned. He thought he could smell the tang of sea salt on her skin, almost like tasting it. He concentrated again on making his way over the stones.

A few minutes later she stopped. "I usually go for a swim at this hour. Join me if you like." She left his side.

He saw that they'd stopped in front of a small beach house faced with weathered gray shingles. On the open deck, clothes were draped over the railing: a woman's white bathing suit, track pants, a sweater. Tall grasses grew in clumps from the sand at the deck's edge, the stalks nodding in the breeze.

Rachel opened the door and Jack followed her in. It was basically one room. Crammed bookshelves lined the walls. A desk at the window was messy with books, papers, a computer. A futon was strewn with newspapers and more books: he glimpsed a volume of French poems and a book of Escher drawings. In front of the fireplace a rocking chair sat on a rough-woven rug.

"This is where I come to think," she said. She hadn't closed the door, and the blue, liquidlike twilight from the doorway and window filled the room. "The French call this time of day *entre chien et loup*. Between dog and wolf."

The blue glow caught a photograph on the desk, a picture of a black child about seven or eight years old. He wore a Superman bathing suit and an orange life jacket as he sat at the helm of a sailing dinghy. His shoulders were hunched as he giggled, making a mock salute to the camera.

"Who's this?" Jack asked.

Rachel's face went blank. "My son."

He looked at her, astonished.

"Adopted." She turned abruptly from the photograph. "He's dead."

She went to a deep wicker basket and rummaged inside. "There are some guests' things here." She pulled out a pair of men's bathing trunks and handed them to him. "My suit's on the railing," she said, and went back out.

He stared after her. An adopted son, dead. He hadn't known. But then, he knew nothing about her life since they'd parted.

He changed into the trunks. When he got outside, she was walking into the water, already knee-deep. He reached her and they stood together looking out at the sea and sky. A heavy cloud bank was turning the twilight to darkness, and the strengthening wind was pushing up waves out on the deep water. Far to the west, dry lightning flashed.

"I married Del when I was a freshman at Yale on scholarship," Rachel said. She was watching the cloud bank as water lapped at her legs. "He was thirty-four, my sociology professor. I was eighteen, a bundle of raw ambition, out to demystify the universe." A slight smile crept into her voice as she added, "Del civilized me." then, very seriously, "He's always been my best friend."

The wind fanned her hair along the side of her face. Jack couldn't see her eyes.

"I left you in England on a Monday morning," she went on. "When I got home that evening Del had just suffered a massive stroke." She picked up a floating stick of driftwood and turned it in her hands as though studying it. "I didn't tell him about us. He was so sick. He needed so much care." Her hands stilled. "I've only loved two men in my life. When it came to a choice, I knew you could live without me. Del couldn't."

She added quietly, "But I've never stopped loving you, Jack."

It was a jolt straight to his heart.

She looked up at him. "I sent you that terrible letter because I believed that if I didn't turn you against me you'd come after me. I was afraid that if you did come, if I even heard your voice on the phone, I wouldn't have the strength to stay with Del." She gave a slight shrug. "I suppose no one uses the word duty anymore . . . but there are some people one simply cannot desert."

Jack couldn't speak. All those years ago he'd never thought past the coldness of her rejection, her cruelty to *him*. Never had he imagined she'd been acting out of love for someone else. Acting in honor.

She said softly, "I'm glad to be able to explain, now."

Why? Did she think he was feeling so little? Not so. Every nerve end felt exposed. He could touch her, smell her, taste her in the air between them.

He knew she felt the same, not calm as she'd tried to look when she started this. He knew because he heard the unsteadiness in her voice as she went on. "I suppose I should tell you I'm sorry for the way I hurt you all those years ago," she said, "but you don't need my apologies. You recovered. I'm the one who paid. Every day since England, I've wished I could be with you."

She dropped the driftwood and it floated away. She walked forward and dove in. Jack stood looking after her as she swam out doing a brisk crawl. He could see her arms flash above the water. The wind was chilly with the threat of rain, but he was inflamed by what she'd said. And ashamed at how much it pleased him.

He dove in, the cold water a shock. He welcomed it. He swam hard for about ten minutes, then checked Rachel again. She had swum out so far it was difficult to follow her shape in the dark waves, but she appeared to be turning back. He swam to shore and walked up to the deck, where he found an overhead spigot and washed off the salt. When he turned the tap off the evening was quiet, except for the tall grasses rustling beside him in the dusk. Rachel's clothes fluttered on the railing.

He went inside and turned on the brass desk lamp. He found a towel and dried off, and put on his pants. As he picked up his shirt he checked out the window again. Rachel was walking out of the water.

He was buttoning his shirt when he heard a soft thud under the deck, and a minute later she came in carrying a canvas bag with some logs. "It's cold," she said, moving to the fireplace, "and I'm staying here tonight." Water from her suit dripped down her bare legs. Water from her slicked-back hair dripped down her back.

"I'll do that," he said, taking the logs. "Go get dry." She went outside.

He squatted at the fireplace and started to build up the logs. He'd make the fire for her, he told himself, then go back up to the house. They could talk in the morning. When he'd cooled off.

He looked around for kindling. A basket held some twigs and old newspapers. He was gathering some of this together when he looked out the window. Rachel stood naked under the spigot. She was facing him, head tilted back, eyes closed to let the water rinse her face. Her arms were bent as she ran her fingers through her wet hair. The spill of light from the lamp glowed on her taut body as water sluiced over her shoulders, around her breasts, the nipples hard, over the slight mound of her belly, into the dark triangle thicket, down her thighs. She opened her eyes and saw him. Arms still raised, she didn't move.

Jack stepped back. He dumped the kindling at the fireplace and looked for his shoes. He couldn't remember where he'd put them.

She came in toweling her hair, wearing only a man-sized white pullover that came halfway down her thighs. "There's brandy there in the bookcase, and glasses. Help yourself."

She added quietly, "I know I could use some." She tossed

the towel onto the futon and knelt at the fireplace to finish building up the logs.

Jack poured the brandy. He took a big swallow and its heat shot through him. He set Rachel's glass on the hearthstone beside her, then stood behind her, watching. She struck a long match and bent to light the fire, her buttocks rising. He couldn't turn away. He was hard for her, his body remembering hers, his heart pumping, his mind stalled.

He forced himself to move, put down the brandy. When he turned back she was standing, leaning back against the desk, watching him. She held her glass between her breasts, and with the other hand nervously fingered the bottom of the sweater, making the hem lift a little up her thigh. As she looked into her brandy Jack tried not to watch the sweater's twitching hem. Tried to ignore the fire in his blood.

Her breathing was uneven now, like his. She said, "I've been faithful to Del, but I sleep alone." Her lips curved in a half smile. "In a way, it was like being faithful to you." The smile vanished. "But twelve years is a long time without a man in my bed."

She looked at him, eye to eye. There was no artifice, no pretending. A tremor shivered over her body. "God, Jack, all these years alone. Every time my hand lingers between my legs, my fantasy is you."

She put down her glass and moved so close he could feel her heat. She touched his mouth with her fingertip, then whispered, "Please." It was more than he could bear.

He caught her wrist to stop her. "Rachel, this is—" He'd been about to say *all wrong*, but he craved it to be right, craved her, craved to drag her back with him into the past. He pulled her hard against him, and he would have tried to enter that past again, force himself in, if she hadn't breathed, "Jack, stay with me—" and he hadn't heard an echo of Marisa pleading, "Jack, don't go!"

Marisa. Dear God. The gentlest, the kindest . . .

*What am I doing?*

He had to get air. He pulled open the door and stopped on the deck, unsteady from the brandy, and took deep breaths. Rachel's clothes had blown off the railing. Rain was spattering the stones of the beach. It spattered him too.

He heard her come up behind him. Felt her hand on his shoulder, her touch like a spark in the rain. He twisted around, stepped back, sat down heavily on the railing. Rain was pounding them now. He found it hard to breathe. "This was supposed to be my honeymoon." He couldn't stop the sting of tears, nor the sob that ripped through his chest. He gripped the railing on either side as he sat there.

"Don't," she whispered. She stroked his wet face. She softly kissed his cheek. "You need to forget."

But he knew he would never forget. Knew, as he fought to master the sobs, that he *must* not forget.

She squeezed between his legs. Her hands were hot on his thighs. Her wet sweater clung to her breasts. Her wet mouth pressed on his.

He gripped her arms—to stop this, to steady himself. He stood up, holding her away from him. "Rachel," he managed. "No."

"I *know* you want it. Just as I do. Jack, please, we can be together again, if you'd just—"

"Listen to me," he said, dragging himself back down to reality. "Twelve years ago you made a choice. The right choice. You belong here with Del. And I—" He looked into her eyes. *I have a murder to avenge.*

He strode up toward the house, his thoughts in turmoil. How had he allowed it to go so far? His fault, he knew. Rachel was in such a volatile state, faithful to Del all these years, but celibate. He had nothing but admiration for her, but there was no excuse for him. He'd so hungrily listened to her, encouraged the temptation. Remorse alone had finally stopped him.

The rain was over; the squall had passed as suddenly as it had come. The wind had died and the clouds had moved on, bringing an unexpected reprise of rosy evening light, like the day's final benediction. But Jack felt no solace. Besides the bite of guilt, something else was nagging, something he'd seen in Rachel, indefinable but almost more disturbing. Some fierce struggle seemed to be going on inside her. He couldn't believe he was the source of all that. What was? She'd said she wanted to talk about the work, yet her reluctance had been clear. Did she have some suspicion about the terrorists' viral creation, something that alarmed her? Should he go back, press her about it? Halfway up to the house he stopped. Going back was the last thing he wanted.

He noticed someone on the verandah. Two people actually—a woman holding a little boy of about four who straddled her hip. Apparently, she hadn't seen Jack. She and the boy were both still, their heads lifted as if to better take in the view: together they looked like some fine sculpture. Jack felt oddly stirred by the purity of the image: mother and child caught in this last radiant glow of sunset. Such a contrast to the murkiness in his own soul. The sculpture sprang to life as the woman set the boy down and he skipped into the house. Jack's eyes stayed on the woman. She was striking. Early thirties, he guessed; trim jeans and blazer, sleek dark hair, fine-boned beauty. But it wasn't her good looks that made him watch as she stood smoothing back her hair with both hands and looking around as if she owned the place. Something in that gesture was familiar. And in her air. It hit him. This could only be Rachel's daughter.

\* \* \*

Tory reached up to touch the wind chime. It was a new one, of white shells tinkling against slim nickel cylinders: a chime of some kind had been hanging here for as long as she could remember. As a kid it was her ritual every time she passed to jump up and touch it. Soon after her twelfth birthday she'd managed without even jumping.

I love this place, she thought, watching droplets dribble from the verandah eaves. I don't get back here often enough.

The departing airport limousine was crunching down the gravel drive. She'd come early—her mother wasn't expecting her until tomorrow morning—but her mother had had all day with Hunt, and there'd been no phone call from her to say he'd refused. Anyway, Tory couldn't afford to waste another night, even another hour. It was time to meet the famous doctor and get things rolling.

She could faintly hear Chris chattering to Doris in the kitchen. He'd run in hoping for a cookie. Thank God Doris had agreed to keep an eye on him until the new nanny arrived. Tory didn't want him hurt by the tension at home, which she knew was going to be extreme the moment Carson learned what she was organizing. He'd been camping at the FBI command center—hadn't come home in three days—so at least she hadn't had to lie to his face, but she'd found deceiving him with silence, even at a distance, almost as painful. She and Carson had drifted apart, it was true, but in seven years of marriage she'd never lied to him.

Am I doing the right thing? Is my mother?

Academic. What's the alternative? Global plague.

She took a deep breath of the clean air, rich with the elementary smells of earth and sea after the sudden downpour, and willed back memories of more carefree days.

Her seventh birthday. She'd been longing for a Barbie doll, and she'd started her campaign for it weeks before. Her mother had looked horrified, as if she'd asked for a machine gun. Tory still coveted the doll, though, so she methodically petitioned every other potential gift source. On the day, her aunt in California came through: a stunning Skating Barbie arrived, complete with flimsy pink micro-skirt, fur-trimmed cuffs, and her own removable skates. Tory was ecstatic. Her mother didn't say a word.

About a week later, as she was combing her heroine's plastic hair, her mother asked if she'd join her on the beach, saying she'd like her help with an experiment. Her mother's undivided attention being a rare treat, Tory eagerly went with her, the Barbie clutched lovingly in her hand.

The experiment was a study of starfish changing colors in a tidal pool. Her mother explained the investigation's parameters, gave her colored pencils and a notebook, and left her to observe and make notes, while she sat on a nearby rock and began reading a stack of lab paperwork. Tory set to work, enthralled. For hours she filled pages with notes and drawings, enchanted by the living creatures and, even more, loving the afternoon-long intimacy with her mother, who quietly answered her questions. Years later, of course, she understood that Rachel's papers that day had been completely unconnected to starfish, but she didn't know that at the time, or care. Her mother had asked for her help and they were working together. That was all that mattered.

When they were called in for dinner they started hand in hand up to the house, Tory chattering about starfish, an expert now. "Oh, my Barbie," she said suddenly. She'd forgotten it. She found it lying soggy and bedraggled on the beach—inert, lifeless, boring. Grabbing it carelessly by its hair, she ran back to her mother, and as they came in the kitchen door she dropped the doll in a corner box of old hats. Her mother didn't say a word, but her smile was one of satisfaction. Tory never played with the doll again.

Remembering, Tory smiled too. Somehow the memory gave her courage. Together, they just might pull this off.

So get your ass in gear, she told herself. Let's meet the good Dr. Hunt.

Suddenly, she saw him. He was coming straight toward her from the beach, wet from the rain. He was even more impressive than in his photos. Stronger, both in build and in aura, but with a shadow of suffering deep in his eyes. Her first thought was: Poor man, what he's lived through. Her second was: He's perfect.

Rachel, hurrying after Jack, was appalled to see Tory move across the verandah toward him. *She's come too soon.*

"Jack," she said, reaching him first at the foot of the stairs. He turned to her with a wariness that cut her heart, the pain of his rebuff still fresh. *No time for such feelings.* "I must talk to you, alone. There's—"

"Nana!" Chris came flying out of the house and down the steps and threw his arms around her waist.

She looked distractedly at her grandson as he clung to her. "Hello, darling," she said. She gave him a quick hug, then gently freed herself. He offered up his stuffed rabbit for her blessing. "Yes, hello Bunny, too," she said. "Now run along and see Grampa. I have to talk to—"

"But I want to go on your ship. Mommy said—"

"I said maybe tomorrow. It's almost bedtime," Tory told him, reaching them. She smiled. "Hello, Dr. Hunt."

Rachel gripped Chris's shoulders, steeling herself. She couldn't prevent what was coming. "Jack, this is my daughter, Victoria Farr-Colwell."

His eyes snapped to her. "Colwell?"

"Tory," she said blithely, extending her hand.

Something in her daughter's buoyant confidence as she and Jack shook hands made Rachel dare to hope. Could *Tory* persuade him? She felt desperate. Her seduction gamble had failed, humiliatingly, miserably. Still, she recoiled from the only sure way to force him to act—with the truth. Tory offered a last chance. *If she can persuade him, I won't have to tell him.*

Laurel came out with the dog at her heels. "Liam!" Chris cried in delight, and threw his arms around the dog's neck.

"Chris, go get ready for bed. I'll be up soon," Tory said.

"Nana, will you come and read to me?"

When Rachel looked at him blankly, Laurel offered, "Want me to?"

Tory said, "And you are. . . ?"

"Laurel Hunt."

"Oh, the granddaughter. All right. Thanks."

"No problem." Laurel took Chris's hand. "Got a favorite story?"

"Hamilton Duck," he answered as the two of them went in.

Tory turned to Jack. "Well, that's about it for the social niceties, Doctor," she said dryly. "It goes without saying that you have my sincerest sympathy, but, sadly, time is not on our side here, as I'm sure you'll agree. Now, I've outlined a preliminary strategy that I'd like to run by you, so how about you get changed, you look soaked—you too, Mother. I'll ask Doris to bring sandwiches and coffee into the living room, and we'll pull up some chairs and get started."

Jack looked puzzled. "Get started?"

They were climbing the stairs. Rachel followed, holding her breath.

"Details about your time in third-world countries are what I need immediately," Tory answered as they crossed the verandah. "Personal stuff, not stats. Like the *Newsweek* interview last year where you described how you handled the Somali warlord. Your team wanted access to his camp to treat wounded prisoners, and he wanted diesel fuel, which you had. So you made him a deal. A gallon of diesel every time he let one of your doctors in. Stories like that are exactly what I need."

They had come through the French doors into the living room, and Jack stopped, throwing Tory a suspicious look. "Are you a reporter?"

Taken aback, Tory shot Rachel a frown. "Haven't you told him?"

"Told me what?" Jack demanded. "Rachel, what the hell is going on?" He turned on Tory. "Is this something to do with the terrorists?"

Rachel felt dread prickle beneath her clammy clothes. No turning back now. "Tory's right. Get changed first, Jack. There's news."

When they met in the living room fifteen minutes later, Rachel had the worst of her nerves under control. She would just listen, and leave the opening to Tory.

"The terrorists have a name, Doctor," Tory began briskly. "Artemis. They've presented an ultimatum. My mother was told about it at the president's emergency meeting three days ago. If the government doesn't meet Artemis's demand, they've threatened to release the virus again, this time in a major American city, in twenty-seven days."

Jack stiffened. "Demand?"

"One percent of GNP to go into a global fund for general female education through primary school, as a strategy to lower population levels. Otherwise, Artemis will lower those levels directly, with the virus."

Rachel flinched as Jack twisted to her. It wasn't suspicion on his face, but amazed revelation. "*That's* why it's female-specific," he said. "Overpopulation."

She managed to answer, "Yes."

"Hank Vorhees told me none of this."

"Only those of us at the president's meeting were informed."

Fury leaped into his eyes. "Who *are* these people?"

Rachel gripped a chair-back, willing steadiness into her voice. "The authorities don't know. In any case, the president has categorically refused the demand. That's—"

"My God, this virus let loose on a *city*? It's unthinkable."

"I know that. *You* know that. It's obvious the president must agree to the demand." She heard her own desperation, and stifled it. "Jack, there may be a solution. That's why Tory's here. She's a political strategist, and she believes an aggressive campaign to mobilize public opinion might force the president to yield. She's agreed to undertake the campaign. Given the deadline, however, she says success will depend on launching it with an instantly recognizable spokesman, and that"—she made herself plow on—"that spokesman must be you."

He looked at her as though she were mad.

"Jack, hear me out. It's a question of credibility. People admire you. They trust you. And they sympathize with you after—" She didn't finish. "The point is, they might accept the hard facts about what has to be done if they hear them from Jack Hunt."

His face hardened. "Is this the reason you dragged me out here? To talk me into this crazy scheme? Jesus, Rachel, why weren't you just straight with me?" His anger showed her that he saw the full betrayal. "That . . . conversation, out there." He nodded toward the beach house. "Was that just to bring me around, in whatever way you could?" Revulsion crept into his voice. "That was beneath you."

A knot cramped Rachel's stomach. She had to look away.

"Dr. Hunt," Tory intervened sharply, "my mother has

taken a courageous personal risk here, so please, leave her out of your judgments."

He turned on Tory. "I gather this was *your* idea. Recruiting me. Well the answer's no. Get someone else."

"There *is* no one else," Tory said. "Or if there is I don't have time to find him. Twenty-seven days is all we have. You're it." She stopped, as though to cool down, then went on more reasonably, "Look, Doctor, this campaign requires two elements: a clear message and an exceptional spokesman. The first is my job, but people are going to find it a hard message to swallow, and that's why you're essential. The great humanitarian, leading the way. The grieving widower soldiering on, his bereavement tugging at the nation's heartstrings, yet a man tough enough to make a Somali warlord blink first. Unless we run with a spokesman as beloved and respected as you, we start with one hand tied behind our back."

He glared at her. "You make it sound like some kind of movie. God damn it, it's my *life.*"

"You're ideal *because* it's your life. You saw the horror. People will listen if you say the survival education fund is our only hope."

"Now you listen to me. The last thing in this world I'd do is plead the cause of my wife's murderers. I don't want Artemis appeased. I want them caught. I want them *dead.*"

Rachel shuddered. "What if that doesn't happen in time? Twenty-seven days, Jack. Devastation on a scale never seen before, a possible global pandemic. Are you prepared to take that risk? To let *others* take that risk? Maybe a third of the world's women will—"

"For God's sake, it's not up to me. This thing is beyond the capacity of just one person to change it. Only the government has the resources to stop this now. The intelligence agencies, the FBI, the—"

"There isn't time!" Rachel cried. "Good Lord, is the demand so unreasonable? Is improving the lot of the world's women such a terrible thing?"

"Mass murder is!"

They stared at each other. Panic flooded her. This was a disaster.

"Well," Tory said flatly. "I guess that's that. Looks like I've come a long way for nothing." She turned to Rachel. "I'll head back and start looking for another spokesman."

"No!" A switch clicked in Rachel's brain. No more time for persuasion. No more time at all. Only she could make Jack act. And there was only one way to do it: tell him. *That I am Artemis. That virus shipments—not perfume this time—are waiting to be triggered by a dead man's switch. That he can help me or turn me in, but his decision is the one by which we all will live or die.*

She said to Tory, "Leave us alone."

"I don't see the point of—"

"Go," Rachel said.

Tory shook her head in exasperation, but she left the room.

Rachel closed the living-room door. She gripped the handle, unable for a moment to face Jack.

When she did, he was watching her through eyes narrowed in anger. She heard the weary disgust in his voice as he said, "I should never have agreed to come here."

She fought the impulse to plead. Only one way was open, and it required cruelty. "You were right," she said. "The only reason I brought you out was to persuade you to do the campaign, however I could. This goes far beyond you and me. The world has to face facts. Overpopulation has brought us to the brink of catastrophe, and soon it will be too late to reverse it. So I acted—"

*No, these weren't the right words.* She was lying to herself if she thought she could ever be cruel to Jack. She must choose well—the last intimate words she would ever speak to this man she loved, before losing him forever.

"Jack, one thing you must believe. I never meant to harm your family. Your wife. For that I am more sorry than you will ever know."

He stiffened. "What are you talking about?"

She looked into his eyes and saw the terrible way ahead. For one last desperate moment she fought it.

Then she remembered. *I am already dead.*

She said, steady now, "I'm talking about Artemis."

His gaze bored into her. "What about them?"

"Not them, Jack. Me. I am Artemis."

# 8

"IT'S YOUR DECISION NOW."

Rachel's words echoed over and over in his head.

He sat in Tory's crowded limousine in Washington's afternoon traffic, watching raindrops splatter the window. The words had battered him for so many hours—throughout the endless night—that his mind now seemed anesthetized. He felt his body brutishly carrying on—stomach churning, skin squeezing out a clammy sweat, pulse drubbing against his skull—but his brain seemed shut off, dead. The last dynamic thought he could recall was at the sight of Rachel's face when he was leaving Swallow Point this morning. No, more primal than a thought, more primitive. An upswelling of hatred so intense, so consuming, it overpowered all the other motions of his mind: *I will stop you, somehow, and I will make you pay.*

The world outside passed by the car, eerily normal. A man leaving a restaurant picked his teeth. A woman scurried through the rain with her arm crooked over her head, as if that would protect her. A parked cabbie flicked his cigarette butt into a puddle. They seemed part of some other reality. Jack could feel no connection to them.

To the faces in the car, even less. Four of Tory's people had met them at the airport, the introductions still a blur in his mind. They were all crammed together now: him, Tory, her two associates, her assistant, and a girl—an under-ling?—with a platinum brush-cut, her nostril pierced with a ruby stud. As Jack stared at the red stone it became a bead of blood, Marisa's blood.

He was gripped by a dread that if he could not hang on to reality, the horror would pull him under. He fought to see, hear, smell what was real in the car, root himself in nor-malcy. Tory, across from him, was dictating to her young as-sistant—what had she called him? Eric? Her two associates, flanking Jack, were busily at work. He struggled to remember their names too. Vince Delvecchio was the one jabbering on the phone. The other, tapping at a laptop keyboard, was Noah Shapiro. The faces of these people—their workaday expressions—seemed unreadable. Their words didn't pene-trate his ears in patterns that made sense. He was sealed off, alone with his terrible knowledge.

*She murdered Marisa. She's planning to murder millions more. And no one knows but me.*

He stared at Tory, so busily concentrating on her notes. Her face was the most disorienting of all. Unaware of her own mother's crimes.

He flinched as a hand pressed two loose neckties to his chest. The girl with the ruby stud. She studied the ties as though judging them, and Jack vaguely recalled this was her job, to "dress" him for CNN. His fingers dug into his knees. How was he going to get through this nightmare?

"Striped or paisley?" the girl asked Tory.

The assistant, Eric, objected. "I thought we decided *no* tie."

"Absolutely a tie," the girl insisted. "Tory says he's got to look successful."

"I thought the idea was, like, the Noble Jungle Healer. What happened to the safari suit concept?"

"Striped tie," Tory cut in brusquely, settling it.

The limo pulled up at a glass and steel tower and they all hurried in through the downpour, then up to the ninth floor. The receptionist said to Tory as they passed, "The CNN crew can be here in twenty minutes, they're just waiting for your call. Mr. McIvar will come separately."

"Call them in," Tory said, "and get McIvar on the line."

"Twenty minutes?" Shapiro protested. "No way, Tory. These speech revisions—"

"I don't need a speech," Jack blurted. The others shot him anxious looks, which he ignored. Whatever he decided to say on CNN, he'd be out there on his own.

They reached Tory's office suite. Maplewood and chrome and a huge half-moon window. The desk phone was ringing. Tory answered it, standing, as the others spread out, dumping jackets, umbrellas, briefcases. Shapiro set up his laptop on the coffee table. Delvecchio was still on his cell phone. More staff people filed in, talking. As Jack stood still in the middle of it all, his eyes fell on a plaque behind Tory's desk: "No permanent friends, no permanent enemies."

*Wrong. Rachel is my enemy forever.*

The intercom: "Mr. McIvar, line two."

Tory punched the line. "Mike, hi. Dr. Hunt's here and your crew's on the way, so we're ready when you are . . . Hey, if I told you, it wouldn't be a surprise, would it? It's big, Mike, very big, so get on over." She hung up and again hit the line, buzzing the receptionist. "Marcia, when the crew arrives send them right in."

"Send in the clowns," Shapiro muttered as he typed.

The girl with the nose stud was pawing through a heap of newly purchased wardrobe choices for Jack, rejecting jackets and shirts one after another. "No, no, God no."

Delvecchio closed his cell phone. "Okay, Tory, things are wired pretty well, quote sluts standing by."

Jack winced. "Sluts?"

Tory, sorting message slips, explained. "We try to anticipate what experts the media will call for comment, then we reach them first to give our side, prime them." She called across the room, "Eric, where's the One World Medics video clip?"

"Rhonda's still doing the sound mix."

"Well, tell her I need it for McIvar. An hour, tops."

Jack watched Tory, his dread crawling back. A tone in her voice—sureness, focus—sounded so much like Rachel.

"I've created a dead man's switch," she had warned him. "Containers of virus are waiting in storage locations around the country, and other countries, with a standing order with commercial couriers for their pickup. I routinely send the couriers a computer instruction to delay that order. If I'm arrested, or dead, the shipments will be picked up automatically and delivered. Their form is unlike the containers sent to Stoney Creek, and they are addressed to outlets in public places—airports, malls—in major cities. Believe me, this is a course I would rather avoid, but humanity's overbreeding must be stopped. I'm offering solutions. One easy, one hard. Education or plague. Which will it be, Jack? It's your decision now."

His first thought—once he could think at all—had been: Call Colwell. The FBI has multimillion-dollar surveillance technology, and experts to crack computer codes. They'll find out how she's rigged her system, disarm it, and seize her.

But what if they couldn't figure it out in time? It took them twenty years to track the Unibomber. Or what if they panicked and rushed in on her? He thought of their botched shoot-out at Ruby Ridge. The fiery catastrophe at Waco. The FBI was a bureaucracy crawling with jumpy people who made mistakes. Rachel was a calm, formidable foe. To release the virus, she didn't even have to make a move that would alert them; just wait for her "switch" to close. Could he trust the FBI to discover her system and disarm it before she suspected they knew?

His vision pulsed red with rage. Had he actually once *loved* this woman? Once thought he *knew* her? Her extortion of him was barbaric . . . but flawless. She was holding half of humanity hostage. And she knew *him*.

"Charcoal suit, blue shirt, striped tie," the wardrobe girl declared, holding up the ensemble for Tory's approval. "Yes?"

"Fine. Ten minutes, Holly," Tory said, pointing to her en suite bathroom. "I want him ready when McIvar arrives."

Jack changed clothes, the girl fussing over him like a mother, buttoning and brushing, as he stared, his disorientation deepening, at the bloodred jewel in her nose. When he came out, the CNN crew were setting up lights, hauling cables, moving furniture. The girl flipped open a box of TV makeup. "Showtime," she said with a smile, and stuffed a tissue into Jack's collar like a bib.

"No," he said shakily, yanking it out.

"But you need—"

"Forget that," Tory said, coming between them. "He's a handsome man, Holly. No makeup."

"But he's got dark circles under his eyes."

"Well he's not here to spin the Miss America pageant!"

The intercom: "Mr. McIvar's here. I'm sending him in."

Jack's panic surged.

Shapiro handed him a page of speech revisions. Jack crumpled it and tossed it away. "Hey!" Shapiro protested, "we've got to review the main points on—"

"We've been *through* it," Jack said hoarsely.

Shapiro shot Tory a look of alarm and whispered, too loudly, "Fuck, Tory, can he handle this?"

"He's used to giving speeches."

"But not like—"

"Back off!" Jack snarled.

Shapiro and Tory exchanged glances. "Leave me alone with him, Noah," she said.

Jack was afraid he was going to be sick. He thudded into a chair and leaned over, elbows on his knees, and cupped his face in his hands. He remembered a patient he'd once treated in Sarajevo, a man whose forehead had been partially blown away by a grenade, though he remained conscious, even lucid. That was the image he had of himself now. A man walking and talking, but with part of his head blown off. *How will I get through this?*

"Have I made a mistake?" Tory asked him. Her voice had an anxious edge, but it was controlled. "Have I got the wrong man? If so, you'd better tell me now."

"Then what?"

"I'll cancel. Pick the next name. Reschedule."

"Reshuffle your quote sluts and spin doctors?"

"Look, I don't know what world you're living in but I'm living in *this* one."

He looked up at her. Anger flashed in her eyes. "You think the rest of us are enjoying this?" she said. "That we're looking forward to calling the president a liar? You think my mother *likes* risking her reputation, her entire career? You think we're not all as scared shitless as you are?"

He stared at her, the unreality of it knocking him back again. She had no idea. Rachel was using her own daughter, just as she was using him. But, Jesus, this was Colwell's *wife*. How long before such a web of family relationships netted Rachel, exposing her—forcing her to do the unthinkable?

Tory said, "The difference is that you can turn this thing around."

He swallowed. "Can I?"

"Yes. I'm building a top team around you, Jack. The best analysts, pollsters, ad people, film people. But you're our point man. Nothing will work unless you lead the way. Only you can turn terror into hope. Don't you see? You alone have the power."

There was a flutter of activity at the door. Delvecchio was leading the well-known CNN anchorman across the room. "Mike McIvar," he announced, "meet Dr. Hunt."

Tory said quietly, steadily, in Jack's ear, "What's it going to be? The choice is yours."

Carson Colwell stood staring at the TV screen, a foam coffee cup halted halfway to his lips. He couldn't believe what he was seeing—Jack Hunt giving an interview. *After he gave me his pledge he wouldn't speak to the media.*

He couldn't make out what Hunt was saying. OPS1 in the FBI command center was buzzing with people, phones, electronics, all drowning out the overhead bank of TVs tuned to CNN. Whatever the gist of the interview, Carson felt bitterly betrayed. He'd never pegged Hunt as a man to go against his word. And for what? More of the nation's pity? How much celebrity did this guy *need*?

*Just goes to show*, he thought uneasily, *you never can tell about people.*

Unease sharpened into alarm as he realized Hunt was now making some kind of direct pitch to the camera. Carson

strained to hear above the din of voices around him.
"Quiet!" he called.

OPS1 fell silent.

". . . facts are these," Hunt was saying somberly. "The terrorist organization behind the attacks is called Artemis.
They have made a demand, and a threat, but your government has kept all of this secret from you, the American
people."

In shock, Carson's hand crushed his foam cup, bursting it.
Black dregs dribbled over his fingers.

"The ultimatum is simple," Hunt went on. "Either this
country agrees to fund a female primary education program
globally, or Artemis will release the deadly virus in a major
American city. The deadline is in twenty-six days."

Carson's mind lunged at questions. How did Hunt know?
Where did he get the information? *Why is he doing this?*

"There is no treatment for the virus," Hunt went on, "and
we've seen the devastation it causes. All of you in Stoney
Creek have lost loved ones. So have I." When he paused,
apparently to get control of his voice, Carson flashed back
to their first meeting, at the White House. It was only two
days after Hunt's wife had died, yet how instantly Hunt had
offered to join the FBI's search in Stoney Creek, how
quickly he'd mastered his grief.

His mind clamped down on one answer like a sprung trap.
Maybe Hunt didn't "get" the information at all. Maybe he's
always known.

"Personal sorrow pales when the danger we face threatens
humanity's very survival," Hunt went on firmly. "Yes, survival. Because I believe that if our government continues to
refuse the education alternative Artemis demands, we are
courting an unimaginable disaster. I want to make that very
clear. An Artemis plague would be more devastating than a

thousand Hiroshimas. At the next strike, *millions* of American women and girls would die."

"My God," a female agent whispered near Carson. "Is this true?"

He looked around in dismay. All over the command center people had left workstations and were watching the TV monitors. He thought, stunned: Hunt's done it, he's got the ultimatum out to the whole country, the whole world. He quickly pulled himself together. *Move on this.* He dropped his mangled cup in a trash basket and reached for the nearest phone.

He froze, eyes locked again on the screen, not at Hunt now, but at a photograph on the wall behind him—a photo Carson had glanced past many times while standing right in front of it: the vice president shaking hands with Tory. This interview was coming from Tory's office.

Tory . . . backing Hunt.

Something collapsed the air in his lungs and sucked off the air around him. *Tory backing Artemis?*

He got control of himself enough to punch his deputy's line. "Stan," he said, "bring in Jack Hunt."

Tory had never seen anything like it.

McIvar was staring at Jack in shock on live TV. The CNN crew on the sidelines with her were staring too, as were all her staff, who had not known the facts. Everyone was staring at Jack in shock. No one moved.

Tory's eyes met Jack's. She felt something pass between them. Two leaders aware of the war to which they had just pledged their people, and themselves. She was full of misgivings, yet exhilarated.

She was more terrified than she'd ever been in her life.

From this moment on, there was no return.

*   *   *

Rachel was sitting with Del on the verandah. They'd come to watch the sun go down. Earlier, they'd both seen Jack on TV, she at the lab, Del here in his study. When she'd come home Del had said, his face white and drawn, "What kind of people . . . ?"

Now, she gazed distractedly at the shoreline where the familiar rocks and trees were shape-shifting in the bloodred sunset. She gazed, feeling the danger encroach, and remembered what had brought her to this terrible moment.

She is holding him tightly in the Volvo's ratty backseat on the twisting, mountainous road above Kigali. He is tall for nine but so slim he feels all bones. His eyes widen as a white Mercedes races past, automatic weapons jutting from every window. Its wealthy Tutsi owners are fleeing the capital, like Rachel and Paul and the Belgian shoe salesman she flagged down this morning in his Volvo. She dragged Paul from their Kigali hotel amid the screams of people being hacked with machetes in the dark halls. No electricity, no phones. In the streets, she saw Hutu gangs killing with machetes, knives, bats, screwdrivers. They ignore her because she is white, but she is terrified for her son. She must get him out of this country.

A whistle shrills. On the road ahead a stocky Hutu soldier stands at a checkpoint barrier, one hand raised, the other gripping a rifle. Rachel pushes Paul to the car floor and throws her raincoat over him, hissing, "Don't make a sound!"

The salesman stops the car. The soldier peers inside. He is wearing a Harris tweed jacket, even in the heat—booty from people he has murdered. Under Rachel's raincoat Paul's warm hand is clutching her ankle and she has to hold herself back from reaching for him.

The soldier studies her passport, frowning. She can hear,

far off, the dull popping of machine-gun fire. Oddly, it reminds her of the dull flapping sound of sails in fluky winds. Last week, in Maine, Paul won a sailing race, tops in his dinghy class. In a different universe.

The soldier is looking at her with vague suspicion. "Lesage. *C'est un nom français.*" He seems unable to reconcile the French name with her American citizenship.

Dry-mouthed, she is about to explain, when another soldier approaches with a half-full bottle of Cutty Sark. The first one, eyeing the scotch, loses interest in her and waves the car on.

She waits until they are far from the checkpoint before she lets Paul get up on the seat. She checks the map, her alarm rising. Still so far to the Tanzanian border!

They drive through a silent roadside huddle of thatched-roof huts. She can smell the death. A man lies facedown in a vegetable garden. By a latrine, a dog is snuffling at the corpse of a girl in a yellow blouse. Rachel gives Paul her scarf to block out the stench, and curses herself again for bringing him back to this country. It had seemed the right thing to do, a trip to let him meet his natural mother. Who could have known such savagery was about to erupt?

Gunfire explodes over the car. The salesman gasps, shot in the shoulder. As he stomps on the brakes the car spins and stalls. He opens his door and staggers out. A half-dozen men swarm from the trees with machetes and converge on him. He falls, and they hack at him with the long knives.

She pushes Paul out. Wildly, they run. She is holding his hand so tightly he gasps in pain. She sees a banana plantation and runs toward it, dragging Paul into the trees. They flail their way deep into the green cover. She stops and clamps her hand over his mouth, and they crouch, panting, sweating, listening to the whooping and laughter from the road as the attackers pile into the salesman's car and drive off. The road becomes quiet.

That night, Paul's sleep is fretful on the cold, dank earth. He asks her softly, "Mommy, can I have some water?"

She fishes in her bag for the plastic Evian bottle. In the moonlight she sees there are only a few swallows left. She gives it to him, and he falls into a fitful sleep. She holds him close, to give him her body warmth, to feel his warmth. Her tongue is thick from thirst. How will she get him to the border, to safety?

The rumble of a truck awakens her at dawn. She tells Paul to wait, and runs to the edge of the trees to look. A Red Cross transport truck is approaching like a floating mirage, its wheels invisible in the dust. She runs out and frantically waves. The truck squeals to a stop.

"*Où allez-vous?*" she asks the driver. In his ebony face, his eyes are bloodshot.

"*La frontière de la Tanzanie,*" he answers.

Hope surges. Tanzania!

"*Venez,*" he says. "Hop in.

She runs back for Paul, and they clamber into the huge truck's open rear. She is trembling, so filled with relief to get him aboard. As the truck takes off she sees, in the gloom, scores of children's eyes, staring. There are maybe thirty children, raggedly clothed, silent.

A nurse sits among them. "*Orphelins,*" she explains to Rachel. Orphans. She is a statuesque Tutsi woman, businesslike, talkative. She offers the newcomers cold rice in a pot and a canteen of water. Paul is shy as he uses the French that Rachel has taught him: "*Merci, madame. J'ai faim.*" Rachel is proud of him, for trying, for being so brave. He giggles nervously as he eats rice in handfuls, such gross manners forbidden at home. It almost makes her laugh.

She is listening to the nurse's harrowing stories when the

truck stops. The nurse groans about the checkpoints—every few miles, she says, *"Neuf depuis nous—"* Her words are cut off by a bullet in the throat. She falls over, dead. A Hutu soldier with a rifle stands at the back of the truck. Rachel yanks Paul to her. More shots from the front. The soldier yells at the children to get out.

Rachel grips Paul's hand as they all climb out. The dead driver lies bleeding in the dust, his hands hacked off. There are five soldiers with rifles and bloody machetes. They herd her and Paul and the other children into the road, and push the children into two groups, separating them by height. Rachel feels sick with dread, knowing why: Tutsis are generally taller than Hutus. Paul is wrenched from her and shoved in with the tall children. She fights to get back to him. A rifle butt cracks her temple and she staggers in pain, bleeding, and falls on her hands and knees, gasping dust.

Two soldiers lift their machetes above the tall children. "No!" Rachel shouts. They start to hack. Shoulders, elbows, ankles. The children scream. All the children, both groups, panic and run. The soldiers laugh and start shooting. Some children are hit and fall. The rest are running in all directions.

She sees Paul racing away. A soldier aims his rifle at him. She screams in French, "No! *He's not one of you!"* but the soldier hardens his aim. She sees Paul look for her over his shoulder, and she screams at him, "Run!"

Paul and three other fast children veer into a sorghum field and disappear in the five-foot grass. The soldiers shoot at the slower ones on the road. Most of them topple. The soldiers advance on them, machetes flashing.

She staggers to her feet and runs after Paul into the tall grass. Blood from her temple trickles into her eye and she trips. The children's screams behind her are terrible. She crawls through the sorghum, blindly searching. She dares not call his name or the soldiers will come. On her knees she claws aside the stalks, inching through the stony dirt, reaching out for him . . . reaching.

# 9

IT WAS DARK WHEN TORY'S LIMO DROPPED Jack at the Hay-Adams Hotel on Sixteenth Street, a block from the White House.

"The room's in my name, otherwise half the reporters in the country would be breaking down your door," she said as they pulled up. "Get some rest. In the morning you fly back to Bar Harbor. That's where we'll finally let the press get at you, highlighting you working at the lab." As he got out she handed him a stack of background papers—U.N. reports on overpopulation, female poverty, the environment. "Study these. You don't have to sound like an expert but you should know the basics. Your first press conference is tomorrow at two. Wear a lab coat."

In his room Jack didn't turn on a light, just dumped the papers on the bed, then thudded into an armchair. First moment he'd had alone. He'd been with Tory and her people nonstop, first making his CNN statement, then off to a video studio to tape an appeal, Tory managing the production while simultaneously conferring with her analysts and pollsters and schedulers.

In the end, of course, he'd had no choice. Rachel's dead man's switch had forced him to perform. Just as she knew it would.

Sitting in the darkness, looking across Lafayette Square at the lit-up White House, he willed back memories of the horror. Marisa drooling blood, brain-damaged, her organs disintegrating, the hemorrhage a flood. He *wanted* the agony of remembering, to fuel his hatred. He existed now only for the hatred. To stop Rachel. And more. His goal was to destroy her. *And to see in her eyes, when I do it, that she knows it's me.*

To get there meant going one step at a time. First, the campaign. He had to do everything in his power to make it succeed. For that he had to put himself in Tory's hands. Could he trust her? After the CNN broadcast, while he'd imagined shock waves rolling across the country, and agonized whether he'd done enough—made the danger clear enough—she'd sat coolly assessing his performance. Her showbiz approach unnerved him. *She* unnerved him, running this thing without any suspicion of the truth. Rachel's own daughter—Colwell's wife. But she was good, he saw that, and took what hope he could from it. He would need all her skill to make this work.

He tugged loose his tie and rested his throbbing head on the chair-back. Tory. The last ten minutes alone with her in her limo had been a trial.

"Any past indiscretions I should know about?" she'd asked. "Fraudulent dealings? Drug habit? Homosexual affairs?"

He'd groaned and looked away.

"Don't brush me off, Jack. I have to be prepared. So tell me the truth."

She was right. She knew her job. "A nasty divorce eighteen years ago, does that count?"

"Nasty? Why, were you unfaithful?"

To what? he wondered grimly. It had been a travesty of a marriage. He shook his head and said only, "The usual. Incompatibility."

"After it, I understand you took up a lifestyle that was more . . . hedonistic?"

"Look, it was a long time ago."

She let it pass. "What about money? How can you afford to do full-time volunteer work for One World Medics?"

"Investments. And my publisher paid a generous advance for my autobiography."

She jotted a note. "What about Laurel?"

"What about her?"

"Why has she spent the last ten years with you? What happened to your daughter?"

A warning flashed. He said carefully, "Your research staff must have those facts."

"Only that you've been Laurel's guardian since she lost her family. Fill me in. What happened?"

It was the last thing he'd talk to Tory about. "They were killed." The words were a simple statement, but his tone held an order: Drop it.

"How? Car accident?" She wasn't going to let this go.

It didn't matter. He'd had ten years to create a fable so durable it had become almost real to him. Like a pearl, the polished story hid the grain of grit that had begun it—his terrible failure with his daughter. That guilt would always scrape at his core, but it was a pain he wouldn't disclose to anyone.

Besides, he had Laurel to think about. And now, his credibility to this campaign too. He shuddered to think what would happen to its chances if the facts came out.

"They were murdered," he answered. "Senseless, random act. An addict looking for money, the police figured. They never caught the guy." How smoothly the old lie slid out. He was relieved to move on to the truth. "Laurel came home from school and discovered the bodies. I found her in shock." He added quietly, "I think some part of her still is."

"You too?"

He looked at her. She didn't miss much. "Me too."

"So that's when you gave up the playboy life and the big CDC job? Threw yourself into humanitarian work?"

He nodded grimly. More of the truth. "It put things in perspective. Laurel needed me. And with One World Medics I found I could do some real good."

She cocked her head at him. "You really *are* a hero."

It had thrown him, that look of hers. Cynical but curious, as though she somehow saw through him, yet didn't turn away.

He got up from the armchair. He needed a shower.

He turned on the water and was unbuttoning his shirt when there was a knock at the door. When he opened it two FBI agents flashed credentials. "Dr. Hunt, we'd like you to come to headquarters to answer some questions."

Adrenaline shot through him with a chill. Tory had briefed him on this, but Tory didn't know what he knew.

They took him downstairs by way of the service elevator—to avoid reporters?—then through the kitchens and out a rear door to a waiting car. In the back, he sat between the agents, his heart pounding. Yet the procedure was familiar enough. He'd once sat in the back of a jeep in south Sudan with a soldier's Kalashnikov pointed at his head. The Sudanese had been bombing refugee camps, scattering thousands of people into the bush, and he'd led a One World Medics team into the area. Nuer refugees were trapped in a school, surrounded by their enemies, the Dinka, and every night Dinka soldiers would kill some of the Nuer in a drawn-out show of terror. Jack asked for a meeting with the Dinka warlord. Soldiers picked him up and drove him to the thatch-roofed guerrilla command post. A barefoot attendant was shining the warlord's combat boots.

Before this meeting, Jack had already been through variations of it—in Afghanistan, Peru, Somalia. He knew that, despite the intimidation, the Dinka warlord wanted things he had: surgeons, medicine, a Western voice to carry his story to the world. Jack showed him a list of the trapped refugees and told him a copy had been sent to Western media outlets, letting him know that if he wanted Western aid, it cut both ways: the eyes of the world were on him.

The FBI agents weren't some warlord's henchmen, of course. Still, he knew this drill.

The car slowed over a potholed street of the ghetto that ran down to Buzzard Point. They passed an electrical substation, and spindly trees where windblown garbage hung in the branches, then bumped over railroad tracks where a trio of black teenagers sat passing a bottle. Buzzard Point was deserted except for a twelve-story government building overlooking the muddy Anacostia River. Bargain basement real estate, but the building was imposing enough.

They took him through a security check, then up to the tenth floor. Passing offices, he glimpsed men hunched over computer monitors, others talking in knots. A woman in the hallway stared at him nervously. She saw me on CNN, he thought.

They brought him into a windowless room brightly lit with fluorescent panels. It held a long table, a scatter of metal folding chairs, a wall clock beside a map of the country, a video camera suspended from the ceiling. A tape recorder sat on the table. Three men were waiting, two sitting, one standing. Which would be his interrogator? The agents who'd brought him leaned against the wall to watch. Jack thought of the Sudanese warlord's soldiers.

The door opened and Colwell walked in. Jack felt a warning shiver. He hadn't expected the top man.

Colwell's expression was as implacable as ever, but in the guarded eyes Jack read raw emotion: the bitterness of a man who felt betrayed. Still, his manner remained coolly professional. "Dr. Hunt, I have a few questions," he began. "We'll be taping the interview, with your permission, both on audio and video." He indicated the tape recorder and camera. "Of course, you have the right to call in an attorney at any time, or to remain silent, but I hope you won't feel either is necessary. Hopefully, this interview will simply help us eliminate you from our inquiries."

Jack said carefully, "I'll be glad to help you do that."

Colwell gave him a wintry smile. "Good, then we'll be helping each other." He gestured to a chair. "Have a seat?"

"I'm fine."

Colwell sat on the corner of the table and nodded to the man at the tape recorder, who started it, but Colwell's eyes hadn't left Jack's face. Jack, too, didn't break eye contact, but sweat prickled under his shirt. Tory's husband. Rachel's son-in-law. A minefield.

Colwell stated his own name and the date for the record, then asked Jack to identify himself also. The preliminaries finished, he said, "Dr. Hunt, you gave a CNN television interview today divulging the contents of a classified document issued by the organization known as Artemis. Where did you get that information?"

If only he could tell everything, have them drag Rachel in, force her to her knees! But that was impossible. He must not implicate her beyond the unavoidable minimum. He must make no mistakes.

"Where did you get it?" Colwell repeated.

"Dr. Rachel Lesage brought it to me." A startled look flickered over Colwell's face. Fleeting, but Jack hadn't missed the shock. He added with emphasis, "She did nothing more than show me the document. The decision to act was mine alone. I thought the country had a right to know."

"I see." Colwell made an almost imperceptible nod to one of the other agents, who immediately left the room. He went on, "Before Dr. Lesage approached you, had you ever been in contact with anyone representing the organization known as Artemis?"

"No."

"Or since?"

Jack said carefully, "The first and only time I heard of Artemis was when Dr. Lesage told me about the ultimatum."

Colwell regarded him, then stood. "Would you excuse me for a moment?" He walked out.

Jack looked at the other agents, but their faces told him nothing. Was Colwell checking on Rachel? He'd had to tell *that* much of the truth; Tory had made it clear it would be foolish to try to hide it, and he'd agreed. But what would Rachel do when they reached her? She was in meetings tonight with the health secretary in the EOB just a few blocks away, Tory had said. Would Colwell call her out of the meeting? Surely Rachel was prepared for this. She could confirm what he'd said without drawing suspicion on herself. She wouldn't buckle under such slight pressure, would she?

An agent offered to get him a glass of water. Or would he prefer coffee? He declined both, though his mouth was dry as canvas. He sat watching the clock's second hand creep through the next ten minutes.

Colwell came back. His face was hard, but he sat again on the edge of the table and went on as if there'd been no interruption. "I'd like to talk about Jazida."

Jack was relieved to have the focus back on him, off Rachel.

Colwell said, "I have a problem with it, Doctor. Last week you were passing through this remote mining town in the heart of the Brazilian jungle when the Artemis virus was released, killing every female there. Now, seven days later, you appear on national television to urge that the United States government agree to Artemis's extortion demand. Would I be wrong in calling the timing a remarkable coincidence?"

Jack tensed. "Call it what you want."

"What were you doing in Jazida?"

"I told your people all that four days ago."

"Please tell me."

"My wife and I were beginning our honeymoon. Our pilot got a message to stop at Jazida to pick up a patient. The woman was sick when I got there. Others, too."

"Sick with flu, the miners said. Yet women began dying soon after you arrived."

A bitter taste erupted in Jack's mouth. "Are you accusing me of having some part in—"

"I'm only trying to understand what happened, Doctor."

"Well, this is what happened. I tried to help, but there was nothing I could do."

"How long did you know Marisa Almeida before you married her?"

The sudden shift was disconcerting. "What?"

"How long had you known her?"

"We met about two months ago."

"Forty-seven days ago, in Rio de Janeiro. Is that correct?"

Jack wondered what he was getting at.

"Doctor, is that correct?"

"Yes."

"And how long were you actually married before she contracted the virus? A few hours?"

He swallowed. "Yes."

"Yet, even en route to your honeymoon you insisted on stopping in Jazida. The pilot says he'd arranged to drop you and your wife off in Santarém and then go back to Jazida for the patient, but that you insisted on stopping there. Is that, in fact, what happened? That you went out of your way to bring your wife to that spot?"

Jack stared at him, incredulous. "You think I married Marisa to get her killed?"

Colwell ignored the question and picked up a folder. "A video production company based in New York taped your wedding in Manaus and your subsequent stop in Jazida." He glanced at a document inside. "Trowbridge Productions. Were they, too, along at your personal request?"

"Liz Trowbridge suggested the documentary several months ago. I agreed. I hoped it would raise money for One World Medics. In Jazida, Liz died too."

"What other organizations do you belong to?"

Again, the shift threw him momentarily. "The American Medical Association. The National Academy of Sciences. Other professional societies."

"International Planned Parenthood? Friends of the Earth? Zero Population Growth?"

"None of those."

"You're on their mailing lists."

"So are thousands of people."

"You like to keep abreast of issues, is that it? Keep informed?"

"I get on lists because of the work I do."

"Yes, volunteering. You like to help, don't you? You offered to come out to Oregon, to Stoney Creek, and help my investigation. You helped the residents dig graves. You also brought the perfume vials there to my attention. Why?"

The vials. Jesus. I led him right to the trail that could lead him to Rachel. "Why?" he repeated shakily. "You said it yourself, it's evidence."

"Is it? The CDC has assessed seventeen viruses so far in one vial alone. How much time do you estimate they'll take to analyze this mess of viral material? Weeks? Months?"

"That depends on a variety of factors."

"Would you say you're an authority in the field of virology?"

"Years ago, when I was with the CDC."

"Not now?"

"I follow the research. At actual benchwork I'd be a little rusty."

"Yet you got Dr. Lesage to take you onto her elite team."

Caution pricked his scalp. "She requested my help."

"Oh? On Tuesday your name was not on the list of scientists Dr. Lesage submitted to the State Department. On Tuesday afternoon you made a phone call from New York to her office, and the following day, yesterday, you visited her home in Bar Harbor and stayed the night. This morning, at a news conference there, she announced you were part of her team. If you're not an expert, why did she include you?"

So they'd already checked his phone calls. The one to Rachel's office had only been to confirm arrangements with her assistant about Rachel's jet picking him up, but it was clear they were watching his every move. What else would they do? What else would they find?

"Doctor," Colwell repeated, "why would she include you?"

He was forming an answer when a voice came from the doorway: "Where to, sir?"

Jack turned. Two agents stood at the door. With Rachel. His heart kicked.

"Interrogation room two," Colwell said, and they led her away.

Jack twisted back to Colwell. Had they arrested her? Panic swamped him. *Her dead man's switch.* Got to tell him, warn him! "Colwell," he blurted, "you don't know—"

No, wait . . . Jesus, what can I say? "Let her go or the virus will be released, *because she's Artemis*"? Just shut up. He can't possibly suspect her or he wouldn't be wasting time on me. In fact, he probably brought her past me just to watch my reaction. It's *me* he's after. He'll just question her, then release her. She can handle it.

"Don't know what?" Colwell asked, alert to the change in him.

Only, the shock on her face when she saw me—my God, what if she thinks I've turned her in? Will that make her crack? If I could just warn her—

"Doctor," Colwell repeated, "what don't I know?"

Jack dragged his mind back. *She's on her own, and so am I.*

Colwell's voice became stern. "Dr. Hunt, let me remind you that you have made public a highly sensitive classified document. A thorough investigation could require detaining you indefinitely."

Jack saw again the Sudanese warlord and his men with their Kalashnikovs. Enraged by his interference, the warlord had threatened to blow his brains out. But Jack had been almost certain he wouldn't. He had things the warlord needed. Survival lay in bargaining.

I have what Colwell needs. Artemis's identity. Can't bargain with that, though, and I can only hope Rachel trusts I won't. So, he thought nervously, what else do I have?

Tory had briefed him: he had the eyes of the world.

He said firmly, "I'd like to make a call."

Rachel sat across from the two agents about to interrogate her. Beneath the table her hands involuntarily balled into fists, her nails digging into her palms. Tory had warned her they'd question her as soon as Jack told them how he'd got the declaration, and Rachel had felt prepared, but the glimpse she'd just had of Jack had shaken her. His face told her the worst: it was over.

I was insane to think he'd do what I want! He's told Carson everything. Now these two agents will try to pry out the details, to stop the switch from closing. Well, they won't succeed. Her eyes flicked to a wall clock above a mirror. Nine-forty. I must endure just an hour and twenty minutes. At eleven, if I haven't made the call, the switch will close and the virus, not in perfume this time, will be delivered.

The thought rocked her.

Step back! Is there something I've missed? Seeing me, Jack didn't look just distraught—he looked shocked. Why? If he's told them everything he would *expect* them to bring me in. Does his shock mean he *hasn't* told?

If so, I could still prevent delivery. I could ask to phone my attorney and instead make the call to keep the system open. Then finish this interrogation with Carson still in ignorance. Is it possible?

No, she thought in agony, I was right the first time. I saw beyond Jack's surprise. He despises me. He played along, went on CNN, all just to buy time, and now he's come and told Carson everything. It's over. Jack's compliance was too much to expect. Wisdom from the president was too much to expect. Rationality from humanity . . . too much to expect. I've failed. No more options. Just let the time play out. Let the switch close.

The voice of the interrogator, Agent Baker, broke her thoughts. "Before we begin, Dr. Lesage, would you like to make a phone call?"

*Yes*—but only under one condition: that I find Jack hasn't told you. Please, let me find out before eleven!

When she caught Baker's partner glancing at the mirror, she realized it must be a one-way window. Was Carson watching?

"Thank you," she replied steadily, "but I have no need at the moment." She fixed her eyes on the mirror. *One hour and twenty minutes, Carson. Let's see how much you've been told.*

And so they began.

"Your full name please."

"Rachel Helen Lesage."

Baker asked slowly, distinctly, "Did you pass along the Artemis declaration to Dr. Jack Hunt?"

She answered with mild disdain, "You could have asked me that on the phone, Agent Baker, and not pulled me out of the secretary's meeting. Yes, I gave him the document."

"Why?"

"It was the right thing to do."

"Who for?"

"I made my thoughts on this quite clear to the president at the emergency meeting four days ago. Surely you were briefed."

"Everyone at that meeting pledged their silence."

"No, I pledged my assistance. I never agreed to a cover-up."

Baker frowned slightly. "If you'd decided the declaration had to be made public, why not do it yourself? Why pass it on to Dr. Hunt?"

*Odd questions—odd waste of time—if you suspect I'm Artemis.* The thought gave her a jolt of hope. Her fists relaxed. No, not so fast! Don't *assume* they don't know. Be *sure.*

"First," she answered, "because I intend to carry out the task President Lowell entrusted to me, if he'll still allow me. It will require my total commitment and objectivity, both of which would be compromised by the media attention if I spoke out." She was watching Baker's face closely, and his partner's. *Be sure.* "More important, it required someone with a high public profile—a *popular* profile, which I lack. Dr. Hunt is not only well known and respected, he also has the public's affection. So I approached him hoping he'd be as appalled as I was about the government's stand. Enough to speak out. I found that he was."

Carson stared at her through the glass. He was so shaken he couldn't even look at Ed Liota beside him.

"Intellectuals," Liota muttered, slurping coffee as he

watched Rachel. Head of the Bureau's national security division, he was Carson's immediate superior. "Think they're above the law."

Carson hadn't taken his eyes off her. What did she think she was playing at? And how had *Tory* got involved? Questioning Hunt had taken all his concentration as the voice in his head had kept needling: How is Tory mixed up with this man?

"Dr. Hunt's representative." That was how the CNN anchorman, McIvar, had described her in the statement he'd given. "She offered me an exclusive live interview," McIvar had said anxiously. "I jumped at it, sure. I mean, Hunt's a legend, and Artemis killed his wife. I swear I had no idea about the bombshell he was going to drop."

The fact tearing at Carson was: Tory had known. She'd set up the McIvar interview. Why? In the terse statement she'd given his agents at her office she'd said only that any concerns the FBI had should be put to her with her attorney present.

Now Rachel! How could she *do* such a thing? Damaging the president, creating public hysteria, and jeopardizing my whole investigation, because I brought her in right at the start, I'm responsible, I'm . . .

*Too close,* he realized with a shock. *Family.*

Shakily, he said to Liota, "Look, if you need my resignation—"

Liota regarded him dispassionately. "I already checked with the director. He said no."

Liota's brusque candor brought Carson back, anchored him. Outranking all personal considerations was the objective: find Artemis. Appalled as he was by Rachel's act—and Tory's—all of that was eclipsed now by a hard, clear suspicion about Hunt. *The man is not what he seems.*

"Okay, Lesage's story matches Hunt's," Liota said, turning away from the window. "What does that tell us? Are they working together?"

Carson said, "She made an error in judgment. But she only passed on the document. Hunt's the one who went public."

Liota nodded. "Let's hold him. Get some answers."

"I doubt we will," Carson said. "He's too prepared. Since he's making his call now, he'll have a lawyer on the way. I'll question him further, but I'm not expecting much. In fact, I'd like to let him go."

"What?"

"I want to watch him. See where he takes us. We can pick him up anytime."

Liota considered this. "And Lesage?"

Carson hesitated. For years he'd known of her liberal opinions. Yes, she'd taken them much too far now, leaking the document to Hunt, but that wasn't a hanging offense. He'd heard all he needed. "I see no reason to keep her."

Liota gave a nervous snort. "White House might feel different." He went to the phone, muttering, "I better check."

Carson stiffened. Bureau collusion with the White House? That was breaking the law, a thing he'd never done.

Liota must have caught his expression. "You have a problem with that?"

Carson pulled himself together. "No, sir." War sometimes required bending the law, and this was definitely war.

He glanced at his watch as Liota lifted the phone. Nine-fifty. Baker was still questioning Rachel. Grimly, Carson folded his arms to wait. He doubted the president had planned an early night.

# 10

RANDALL QUINCY, CHIEF OF STAFF, PUNCHED the hold button on the Oval Office phone. Past milling advisors and aides, he could only see the president's back as Lowell stood stroking out phrases in the speech draft he'd just been given. Quincy raised his voice to him. "They've got Dr. Lesage at Buzzard Point. They're asking what we want to do about her."

Quincy had never felt so unstrung. He'd been through many tough times with Andrew Lowell, ever since they were both managers at Bromax Oil back in the early eighties when a stock fraud had shaken the company—and catapulted Andy to the CEO's chair. But this disaster with Hunt had caught them completely off guard. Quincy had been scrambling into full-scale damage control. He'd scheduled a live televised address by the president in fifteen minutes, but no one was ready, and Andy was spitting fire. And now, Christ, this. He repeated tensely, "What do we want to do, sir?"

"Shoot the bitch," Lowell said.

No one moved.

Quincy couldn't let this slide. Andy had to be made to see the downside of playing the heavy with Lesage. He wasn't sure he could push it, though, not with Andy in this mood; he'd felt the brunt of the president's vicious streak before. He hit the line reconnecting him to Buzzard Point and quietly told Liota, "Stand by." He hung up just as the FBI director hurried in.

The president glanced up. "You're late." He and Ian McAuliffe were old friends.

"Sorry." Out of breath and wan, McAuliffe explained that he'd just come from home. "Adele saw Hunt on CNN. She's upset."

"Who isn't?" the attorney general muttered as she took a fax from an aide.

"I mean she's . . . I had to give her a sedative to calm her down." McAuliffe looked haggard. "She's talking about leaving the country."

Holy shit, Quincy thought, that's all we need.

The president threw down his pen in anger. "Could we stick to the crisis *at hand*?" He wrenched off his reading glasses. "Ian, what the fuck are you doing about Hunt?"

McAuliffe pulled himself together. "Colwell wants to release him and initiate surveillance. I've agreed. If Hunt's an Artemis operative we have a better chance of him leading us to his handlers if he's at liberty."

Lowell's face clouded, then he nodded. "All right."

"Lesage is another matter," McAuliffe said. "She's claiming she gave Hunt the document as a matter of conscience, and there's no evidence to indicate that she—"

"Bullshit. Lock her up."

Quincy flinched. "Mr. President, that may not be a good idea."

"After what she's pulled? Jesus, she's blown this thing up right in my face. How the fuck am I going—" He stopped, aware that everyone was watching him. Under his breath he growled, "Cunt." He caught his wife's frown. "What is it?"

Susan Lowell said, "I'm thinking Adele McAuliffe isn't alone. In her fears, I mean."

"Adele's paranoid. Always has been. No offense, Ian."

"Maybe we're all paranoid," Susan replied coolly. "All of us who weren't told about the danger."

The room went silent. The president met his wife's gaze. He said flatly, "National security policy cannot be made in public."

"Of course," she said. "But the whole country knows everything now. Women are frightened. I think it would be wise to make a public show that we're not panicking, not . . ." She glanced at McAuliffe. "Not leaving." She looked back at her husband. "I mean me."

Bless her, Quincy thought. A trooper. He could see Andy had got the message, too, because he asked her, "Would you come and stand beside me for this address?"

An aide rushed in. "Please, Mr. President, the speech has got to go to the teleprompter *now*."

Lowell was waiting for his wife's reply.

She nodded. "Yes."

Quincy let out a breath of relief, then steeled himself. "Mr. President—"

"What?" Lowell snapped. Jutting his jaw, he tightened his tie in preparation for the camera.

"Please reconsider about Dr. Lesage. Susan's right. This is now a battle for hearts and minds. We've got to prevent public panic at all costs, and if we punish Lesage we're *inviting* panic. We've told the country that she has your trust, that she's on top of the biotech know-how to beat the virus, that she'll be able to prevent a plague. We've made a

huge deal of her and her team, and we've practically guaranteed that she'll find a cure. Now we're going to throw her
in jail? A Nobel laureate who says she was only doing her
civic duty and still wants to carry out your orders? We'd be
crucified. We must *not* appear spooked by this, sir. We've
just got to move on."

Her skin still damp, Tory strode naked to answer her bedside phone. She'd taken a moment amid the stream of calls
from the office to grab a shower. "Yes?"

It was Jack, saying he'd been brought in by the FBI. "And
the man asking the questions is your husband."

Tory groped for the edge of the bed and sat. The moment
had finally come: she and Carson pitted against each other.
It scared her. "Don't say anything more until my lawyer gets
there."

She called Pete Gowan, interrupting a party at his
Georgetown house, and asked him to get down to Buzzard
Point to handle it, and to call her the moment Jack's interro-
gation ended. She hung up.

All right, calm down. She'd known the FBI would question Jack, and she'd prepared him as best she could. She was
betting they'd go easy. "Grieving Hero Arrested for Warning
Country of Cover-up." The White House couldn't risk such
headlines.

Still, it was a gamble. Political priorities might not wash
with Carson. He could detain Jack, and she couldn't afford
that. If Jack was sidelined even for a few days the campaign
would be crippled. There was no latitude for change or error.

As for her mother, they'd discussed the ramifications of
her leak, and Rachel seemed prepared for the fallout. Anyway, her mother didn't matter to the campaign. Jack did.

As Tory made a note of the time of his call, the pen
bumped on something beneath: Carson's sports watch, the

one he used to time his morning run. Except he hadn't been home in four days. She slid it in the drawer and finished writing, but a chill tightened her skin. No, she didn't relish having to strategize against him.

It galled her. Grieved her. The injustice of it. The enemy wasn't Carson, it was Artemis. She cursed them for making her husband her adversary.

But she had chosen sides, eyes open, and had known she'd have to face him sometime. Would he bring her in tonight, too? Would she have to fight him for her own freedom? Without her there was no campaign. Shivering, she pulled on a track suit and went downstairs to wait for Gowan's call—or the FBI's knock on the door.

The living-room phone rang as she walked in. It was Vince. "You watching? The president's on, live."

She grabbed the remote.

". . . regrettable actions of a few individuals. I come before you tonight to assure you that our cities, towns, and communities remain safe and secure. The cowardice of a few will not shake our firm resolve. Make no mistake—we will not yield, now or ever, to terrorist extortion. On that steadfast principle our nation remains unified and unshakable. I promise you, just as surely as I pledge my commitment to your safety: justice shall prevail. Good night. God bless America."

Succinct, powerful, presidential. Not bad, Tory thought, except they were scrambling, Lowell on the defensive. Despite his calm defiance, she'd noticed his eyes flicker with rage at his impotence. However, this was just the first of their return fire. She knew it would get far worse.

Vince was still on the line. "What did I miss?" Tory asked.

"Quincy made a statement first. Looked like he'd swallowed battery acid, but he basically admitted everything Jack said was true. Shit, it was beautiful."

She asked him to send the tape over, then told him Jack was being questioned by the FBI.

"Oh?" He added quietly, "Sure hope you've called this right, Tory."

When she hung up, CNN was doing the postmortem on the president's address. They were scrambling, too: commentators wired across the country, with experts opining on the terrorist evil, warning against panic, dissecting the threat. On NBC the same, and CBS. "We'll bring you more details as they become available," the CBS anchorman intoned. There was a frantic edge to their voices. They were scared. Everybody was.

*Good*, Tory thought. *I can work with fear.*

She turned off the TV. The house was silent. She needed to keep busy. She read Noah's speech for Jack's press conference and cut some of it, then opened her laptop and worked on instructions to the ad people, then on memos about the grassroots organization she was creating around Jack. Vince's tape of the president's address arrived by cab and she watched it carefully, rewound it, watched it again. She glanced across the hallway at the antique grandfather clock, an heirloom from her mother's family in Nova Scotia. Almost eleven, and still no word from Gowan.

*Had* she called this right? Her strategy was built on two straight-to-the-heart principles: terror and hope. The twin emotional prods that propagandists had used from time immemorial. But it needed a leader, a man who could inspire a frightened mob. Tory had been certain, from the moment she'd met him, that man was Jack. She could stun people with the message of terror, but only he could excite them to action, through hope.

She couldn't let Carson kill that hope.

Kill hope? she thought with a shudder. Had her faith in their marriage eroded to such mistrust? For days she'd held a menacing thought chained at the back of her mind: *Why didn't he tell me about the danger?* If her mother hadn't leaked the Artemis ultimatum to her she wouldn't have known; Carson would have kept her in ignorance, along with the rest of the country. What kind of faith is that in *me*?

Stop it, she ordered herself; it's his job. Artemis has forced *everybody* to extreme positions, even me. *Especially* me. Anger surged again; Artemis was making her risk breaking up her family.

She suddenly longed to call Chris at Swallow Point, talk to him. Silly, of course; he'd be asleep, and she'd spoken to him just this morning.

"Mommy, are you coming swimming?"

"Not today, sweet pea, I've got work to do at my office. Are you having fun?"

"I can go in Grandpa's little boat with Orel!"

She'd had to smile at his difficulty with Laurel's name, but his voice told her he was happy with the arrangement: since Laurel was staying on at Swallow Point to be with Jack until her fall classes started, she had offered to baby-sit Chris until the new nanny arrived.

"How did the tattoos work out?" she'd asked.

"They didn't stick."

"Oh, too bad. We'll buy better ones next time."

"Are you and Daddy coming here?" he asked eagerly.

She'd felt a pang then, and a sharper one now. He was going to be out there for so many weeks, and he'd never been separated from them both for that long. Would anyone read to him, as she did? How would he manage without Carson's good-night kiss? It was always the last thing he asked for. Dread snaked into her heart. If Carson and I can't resolve this, what will happen to our son?

*Don't think negatives. If the campaign succeeds, I'll make everything normal again.*

So get back to work.

But when she found herself reading the same paragraph the third time she had to admit she couldn't concentrate, couldn't get her mind off Chris. She'd packed him off so quickly, without even his storybooks. She decided to send them out right now, with a note asking Laurel to read to him. It was better than doing nothing. She shoved the portable phone in her pocket, found a box, and carried it upstairs.

His bedroom was dark. It smelled faintly of Play-Doh. She switched on the Spiderman lamp on his bookcase, and its cartoon-covered shade created a small pool of circus-colored light. In the gloom beyond it, the Winnie-the-Pooh mobile over his bed stirred in the faint draft of air-conditioning, making Piglet and Pooh and Kanga sway in a dreamy dance.

She knelt by the bookcase, moving aside the scatter of toy boats and planes on the rug, and started pulling out his favorite stories. *The Vegetable Men. My Dog Rosie. Alligator Pie—her* favorite. However busy her days, she always loved reading to him at night. He was learning to read himself now, and picking it up so fast. Opening his alphabet book, she traced an oversize letter G with her fingertip, the way he did. What a joy to see discovery glow in his eyes as he connected a word. She hated to miss even a few weeks of watching and helping. Until this thing was over she might not see him again for . . .

*Not see him again.* She felt a stab of fear, just like on that morning her mother had brought her the news of Artemis. Fear that she herself could become a victim, leaving Chris forever.

She hugged his book against her stomach, trying to hold on to what was precious, aware that beyond the cone of lamplight darkness surrounded her. But her mother had instilled a lesson early, teaching her to sail in a squall: fear can draw out strength. Tory willed it forth now—strength to make the choice. Continuing this fight threatened to split her family apart, but abandoning the fight could leave Chris motherless. She realized the choice had already been made, in her blood. Every instinct compelled her, right or wrong, to survive for the sake of her son.

Headlights suddenly blazed through the window. She stiffened in the glare. Carson's agents? No, they wouldn't drive to the back of the house. As the lights struck Chris's mobile, throwing jagged shadows on the walls, she realized: Carson. His car stopped, and the headlights released her.

The car door slammed, and a moment later the kitchen door squealed faintly. She went on packing books, her hands moving mechanically, the titles barely registering. She heard his footsteps on the stairs. She knew what was coming. She'd known since the beginning.

*Whatever the cost, I must not fail.*

Two priorities now. Reveal nothing about the campaign, and get Jack free.

"Tory," he said darkly. "What's going on?"

He'd stopped in the doorway. She was still kneeling by the bookcase, her back to him, but she felt his concentrated anger like a laser. She smoothed her hand over the storybook in her lap, unable, for a moment, to face him.

"Why did you arrange that interview with Hunt?" he asked.

"You saw it?"

"The whole world has by now."

She finally turned to him. "That was the idea."

Disgust tightened his face. He walked in. "We're not talk- ing about one of your harmless pols here," he said, throwing his briefcase on Chris's bed. "Jack Hunt has made himself the spokesman for the most ruthless terrorists we've ever faced. Now what the hell is going on?"

She put down the book and stood. "Is this an interrogation? Should I be calling my lawyer?"

"Don't do this," he warned. "Don't shut me out."

"I need ground rules first. Who am I talking to? The FBI, or my husband?"

"Would your answers be different?"

"Of course. I can trust my husband."

A breath of surprise escaped him. Tory was glad she'd put him off balance. She was prepared to talk to him—but *only* him.

"All right," he conceded, "this is between us. Unofficial. It won't go beyond this room."

"Thank you," she said quietly, and kissed him. Not a come-on, just gratitude for this acknowledgment of trust. It moved her in spite of herself. There *was* still enough between them to build on.

Carson suddenly grasped her hand. "If Hunt has got you into something, let me help you get out of it. Now, before it's too late."

It was Tory's turn to feel off balance. She knew—as he surely did—that this offer could cost him his career.

"It's not like that," she said. "Don't worry, I know what I'm doing."

Disdain crept into his eyes. "Do you? How did you get involved? When did Hunt contact you? Tell me, Tory, and I mean everything."

She smiled faintly. "I learned long ago there's only one safe tactic with you—the truth."

He waited, watching her.

"It was my mother," Tory began. "She told me after your White House meeting that Artemis had presented their ultimatum but the president had refused and was keeping it secret. She said it was a disastrous decision and asked my advice about how to pressure him to consent. I suggested we break the story, but I warned her that a credible, sympathetic voice to carry the message was essential. Bingo, there was Jack Hunt and his tragedy already on the front pages."

Skepticism clouded his face. "Handy."

"Carson, you should have heard the plague scenario she painted. It's terrifying. And she knows what she's talking about, you know she does. Look, I wish you *could* catch Artemis. It would solve everything. But you can't, not in twenty-six days. It's impossible. That's why I—"

"Was Hunt at this meeting?"

"What? No."

"But he could have persuaded Rachel beforehand."

"No, it was my idea to recruit Jack. And it was a hard sell, believe me. It finally took my mother, privately, to convince him." She shook her head in irritation. *Don't get sidetracked.* "Anyway, that's not the issue."

"Then what is?"

She took a deep breath to steady herself. *Don't give away any more than necessary.* "You've got to release Jack."

He stiffened. "How did you know we'd brought him in?"

"He called me."

"Jesus," he said in dismay. "One call, and he made it to you?"

"Carson, people need to hear Jack to understand the danger. I know you could hold him, but I'm asking you not to. Let him go. Please."

"You can't have it both ways," he said harshly. "You're talking to your husband, remember? Not the FBI. Your rules."

*Moving too fast.* "Sorry."

"How long have you known Hunt?" he asked.

"I met him yesterday, at Swallow Point."

"Then you don't really know him at all."

"Everybody knows Jack Hunt. He's a legend."

"Or a terrorist."

"Good God, you can't believe that. Look at what he's just been through. A week ago he watched his wife die."

"He hardly knew her either."

Tory was shocked. "She was his wife."

"Barely." Before she could protest he said, "Tory, he's hiding something. I can't put my finger on what's wrong with his answers, but I've done enough interrogations to know when a subject is lying."

"That's absurd. Why would he lie?"

"I just look at *facts*," he said, exasperated. "Hunt's a medical man with a specialized knowledge of viruses. A man whose fame lets him travel the world with a medical carte blanche of access. He goes out of his way to stop at the Brazil epidemic site, bringing the woman he'd married just hours before, and she dies there from the Artemis disease. He becomes a figure of national sympathy, then goes public with the Artemis Declaration."

She stared at him. The facts *did* look bad. Anyone who didn't know Jack might find them damning. A needle of doubt pricked her. Jack was uncomfortably front-and-center in all of this. Do I really know him? She caught herself. What am I doing? Selected facts can be lined up to make *anybody* look bad. She wielded the technique all the time against opponents in election campaigns. Anyway, Jack has explained, and that's good enough for me. I know the *truth* here. She jumped on Carson's hypothesis with scorn. "So you suspect him of what? Killing his own wife? That's crazy."

"What's crazy is for you to be involved with him. You're helping a man who may be an operative for the most brutal terrorists the world has ever seen. What if they decide you're too close to the FBI? Or that you're just no longer useful. You think they'd hesitate to remove you? You're in danger, Tory, and I want you out."

She shook her head. "You've got this all wrong. Jack has absolutely no connection with Artemis."

"You don't know that!"

"Carson, he's in pain! He watched his wife die in his arms. In going public he's doing a brave and generous thing. All he wants is to prevent another Artemis attack."

"Bullshit!" He grabbed her by the shoulders. "Don't you understand? He's our prime suspect!"

She gaped at him.

He looked as shocked as she was, and she realized he'd revealed more than he'd intended.

Unnerved, she shrugged out of his grip. "Let's get something clear. I believe there's only one way we can survive Artemis. Compliance. I intend to go on helping Jack Hunt get that message out. I swear I'll have a gang of lawyers tie the Bureau in knots before I let you muzzle him. Or me." She added shakily, "Well, now we've both broken the rules. I think this conversation is over." She made a move to go.

He stopped her, forcing her to step back, and her legs hit Chris's bed. Off balance, she thudded down on it.

He moved in, blocking her. "What does it take to make you see? If you won't think of yourself, think about what Artemis is doing, what you're fronting for. Their weapon could annihilate a quarter of the world."

"Exactly. The enemy is a *microbe,* not some bad guy you can blow away. You have to face the fact that there's nothing you can do!"

"And surrendering the country will save us?"

"Surrendering? A simple education plan! All it costs is *money.* My God, we're the richest nation on earth. We can afford this."

"What if that doesn't satisfy them?"

She threw up her hands. "We could play 'what if' forever."

"I'm not playing! This demand is probably just their *first*. What if they want a say in every government decision? What if they want to *be* the government? Then who's running the world, Tory?"

"Who's running it now? People who believe the death of millions of women is an acceptable gamble? Well, millions more are going to tell you they don't like those odds. *Women* are going to tell you, Carson. Because that's who's at risk. *I'm* at risk!"

"You think I don't know? I was in that pitiful town, for God's sake! I *saw*!"

He wrenched open his briefcase and pulled out autopsy photographs and held them in front of her, forcing her to look. "This is what Artemis does!"

She gasped at the pictures. Black blood crusted a woman's mouth, matted a girl's hair.

The phone rang, startling them both. Tory pulled it from her pocket, but she had to turn from the pictures before she could speak. "Yes?"

It was Pete Gowan. Tory listened in disbelief, then asked, to clarify, "You mean no detention, no charges at all? I see . . . No . . . Thanks, Pete, we'll talk tomorrow." She closed the phone and looked at Carson, not sure which she felt more—relief or revulsion. She said to him, aware that her voice was far from steady, "You released Jack before you even came home. All this time, while I've been begging you not to hold him, while you've been pumping me for answers, Jack's been free."

She felt sick. He'd hidden Jack's release from her just as he'd hidden Artemis's ultimatum. She felt as if something inside her had died. The faith between them. The trust. Carson had finally killed it.

She was still hiding the campaign, though. So the unbearable question was, Did he break faith, or did I?

At dawn Rachel's Learjet took off from Washington National in a thunderstorm. Jack stared out the window as the plane made its ascent, bucking through the turbulence. Rachel sat an arm's length from him across the narrow aisle, tapping numbers on a calculator. The plane broke through the cloud cover, and the rising sun blazed in his face, but he didn't turn away. To turn would be to look at her, and he couldn't, remembering all that they'd once done together. How he'd tasted her body, sweated with her, entered her— Marisa's murderer. Images collided: Marisa hemorrhaging, calling his name; Rachel climaxing, calling his name.

He closed his eyes, sick with shame.

And opened them, cold with rage.

"Do no harm." The Hippocratic oath. But harm was what he craved to do to her. She had sucked the humanity from him. He hated her most savagely for this, for what she'd made of him. Reduced his existence to a single, primitive drive: vengeance.

So be it.

He'd decided what he had to do first, to stop her: discover how she had programmed her dead man's switch, or gain some clue about the structure of the virus. For any hope of either, he had to approach her calmly, rationally. No threats, just do whatever was necessary to draw her out, even gain her confidence, if he could.

So here, in the calm at fifty thousand feet, alone with her in the hushed cabin, he severed himself from the shame and the rage. He blanked out Marisa's face, and looked at Rachel.

There was only one way to begin. "Why?"

The single word brought her head up. His question hung in the air.

"What do you want to hear, Jack? All about the hole in the ozone as big as Europe? The dying oceans, vacuumed of life? Do you want the catalogue of razed forests, poisoned rivers, species we've slaughtered to extinction? All because there are too many of *us*. It's been said over and over, and no one's listening. The mine canary died years ago. Nobody cares."

"I care. I need to know. Explain to me why you're doing this."

She looked at him as if to size up the likelihood of him understanding. "I'm a very rich woman," she said. "I've reached a point our culture calls the summit. Wealth, status, power on a scale most people can only dream of. So what would you have me do with it? Collect baubles from the jewelry store? Wallow at the spa? Buy young men? Or should I actually *use* my power? I'm one of the few people on earth with both the intellectual and financial capacity to make a change in the world. That's what I'm doing, Jack. Changing the world."

Rage threatened again, burning like vomit in his throat. "You sound as though you think you're some kind of god."

She shrugged. "Depends how you define a god. Superhuman powers? I have them at my lab. An absence of emotional beliefs? I learned long ago to free myself from dogma. Immunity to human laws? I'm counting on that." A slight frown creased her forehead. "For a while, at least."

Immune to laws? Jack thought. It almost seemed she was. The FBI had let them both go. He understood the political and public-relations imperatives that had won them their liberty, but he was still amazed that she was actually going to continue heading up the president's scientific team. As soon as they reached Bar Harbor, they'd begin. What a sick farce.

As for him, while answering Colwell's questions he'd seen the glint of the hunter in the FBI man's eyes. They'd let him go, yes, but he sensed he was still held in Colwell's crosshairs.

He saw that Rachel had turned back to her calculator. *Keep her talking. That's the goal.* "Gods can be merciful," he said. "Surely there's a way to change the world that's more"—he chose the word carefully—"benevolent."

"You don't consider women's education a benevolent solution to overpopulation?"

"Yes, of course. But you're also threatening mass murder."

"It's no more than every nation in history has done, including ours, to fight an enemy. Hiroshima. The firebombing of Dresden—over a hundred thousand German civilians burned to death in that single raid. Were those attacks mass murder, or bold steps to end the war and prevent *more* death? Jack, the enemy now is ourselves, the human race. There've been more people born since World War Two than in the four million years since humans first walked upright. We've overbred to the brink of disaster. We've got to be made to stop."

"But this way? You're a brilliant scientist, you could be using your status and power to bring about change by persuasion."

She smiled bitterly. "You think I haven't tried? Scientists' statements don't get airplay; that's reserved for celebrities. I've tried other ways, too—for years I've donated to population control programs, ecological programs. A drop in the ocean. Anyway, people have become bored with pleas about the environment. The Union of Concerned Scientists recently issued an open petition, called a Warning to Humanity. Signed by over a hundred Nobel prize winners. It warned we may have no more than a decade left to avoid global ecological catastrophe. Didn't even make the evening news."

Jack was suddenly anxious about a new concern. "Won't your activity with those causes raise red flags for the FBI? They'll find your name on lists."

"My donations were anonymous. And I didn't sign the Union petition, only because it reached my office too late. Anyway," she added wryly, "it appears the president's faith in me is boundless. I seem to be above suspicion."

Jack prayed that was true.

Rachel rested her head on the back of the seat. "Homo sapiens," she murmured pensively. "Sapiens, 'wise.' Strange word for a species that never learns. We actually believe we can 'manage' the planet, as if it were some kind of department store. The truth is, we can't even comprehend the ecosystems in a single drop of seawater."

She indicated her calculator with a smile of disdain. "Oh, we're clever at pushing buttons and pulling levers, just miserable when it comes to real thinking, especially thinking ahead. It's not our fault. We've evolved biologically to respond only to short-term dangers: the charging lion, the enemy with a knife, fire. We tune out long-term dangers because we have no personal control over them. So we blithely go on denuding the forests, poisoning the rivers, fouling the air, making dust of fertile land. We're consuming the earth, and we won't stop until there's nothing left."

"But, my God, killing can't solve this."

She shot him a look of scorn. "Platitudes don't suit you, Jack. Of course killing can solve it. Fewer humans cause less damage."

He was too stunned to speak.

She sighed. "Jack, I don't expect ordinary people to understand what I'm doing. It doesn't matter if they do. But surely *you* can. I'm trying to give our species one last chance. Since we aren't programmed to see the danger, I'm forcing us to see it. We've got to *change*."

She gave an impatient shrug. "If we don't, the earth will balance itself by wiping out the surplus humans. It's already begun. Collapse of fisheries, dwindling grain harvests, parched aquifers. It all leads to starvation, mass migrations of refugees, massive die-offs. And that leads to civil wars engulfing whole regions. Tribalism at its most vicious. Too many people fighting over two few resources. Look at Yugoslavia. Look at Zaire. Exactly like Rwanda, where—" She stopped abruptly.

Jack was startled by the change in her. A marked stiffening, a pulling back.

She recovered and said evenly, "So that's your answer, Jack. I'm giving humanity what it is capable of grasping. An immediate danger, and a rational way out."

He thought: such an elaborate intellectual response to the simple question of Why? She hadn't really answered, not with her heart. Some essential piece of this was missing. "I don't believe you," he challenged. "There's more."

A shadow darkened her face. Something like despair, Jack thought. She looked away, murmuring, "Believe what you want."

He leaned closer instinctively to keep his voice low, though there was no one to overhear. "This is what I believe. Whatever drove you to this, you were sure your ultimatum would force the government's hand. When it didn't, you were taken by surprise. Now the security forces are trying to track you down, led by your own son-in-law. And you feel trapped, because he just might get you."

He grasped the arm of her seat. "I'm going to try to win this for you, Rachel. I'm going to do everything in my power to help Tory. Who knows, we just might pull it off. As for the FBI, you know you can trust me, I've just proved that. But face it—at any moment Colwell could bring you in. Whatever your private demons, I can't believe you really want to release a global plague, especially if the campaign looks as if it might succeed. So I'm asking you. Stand down with your dead man's switch. Please. You've got to give me and Tory more time."

She was looking straight ahead, not at him. "It's true that Carson's involvement is worrying." She added quietly, "I may have to force this to a conclusion sooner than I'd hoped."

A barb of dread snagged inside him. "You can't mean that. You've given a deadline, given your word."

Her gaze slid to him in scorn. "Gentlemen's club rules?"

"My God, Rachel, give me at least the time you promised. Let me try to make the campaign work."

She looked into his eyes. "Do, Jack, for everyone's sake. Make it work."

# 11

RACHEL STOOD AT HER DINING-ROOM TABLE, a steaming mug of black coffee between her hands as she looked over spreadsheets from her team's serology reports. No real danger here, she thought; she'd maneuvered the team's efforts well off-track. As for the FBI, her interrogation five days ago, unnerving as it was, seemed far behind her now. Not a word from Carson since. She didn't deceive herself that the lull was anything more than that, but at least it gave her a breather. *For more waiting,* she thought uneasily.

She heard the shower burst on in the bathroom above. Jack, getting ready to come to the lab with her. Five days of enduring him under her roof and at work. The tension was painful. His hatred. But she wouldn't let that pain obscure her focus; this arrangement allowed her to keep an eye on him. Jack was her biggest worry now, that he would see how she was manipulating the lab team. His hostile involvement was a development that, months ago, she could never have anticipated.

Chris ran down the stairs in the hall and launched himself off the last step like an airplane, arms stuck out like wings, cheeks puffed as he mimicked a jet engine's roar. He made his landing, skidding on pajama-smooth knees across the floor, and halted at the dining-room doorway. "Hi, Nana!"

Despite her worries, she had to smile. "Hello, darling." Jays began bickering raucously at Del's feeder outside. Poor Del. Usually she had coffee with him in his room before going to the lab, but this morning he'd woken up with a cold and she'd told him to stay in bed.

This comfortable domestic world, she thought: not my world anymore. It brought a pang, which she quickly mastered. She was beyond remorse. She turned her attention back to the spreadsheets.

Laurel came in, trudging after Chris. Stifling a yawn, she said, "Get the cereal box yourself, will you, kiddo? The milk's in here." When Chris padded off to the kitchen, Laurel flopped into a chair, muttering, "The trouble with morning is it starts so damn early."

Rachel pulled her eyes from the data. "What?"

Laurel slumped lower. "Nothing."

*The waiting,* Rachel thought. It was becoming unbearable. Tory was about to finally unleash the full-blown campaign—prime time this evening. Rachel had invested all her hopes in it. It would take days to have any effect, however, maybe even weeks, right up to the deadline, and meanwhile Carson's manhunt would inevitably close in on her. Months ago, preparing the demonstration, she had done everything possible to cover her tracks, beginning with producing the virus at her Puerto Rico facility. Yet Carson had discovered the perfume vials in Stoney Creek within hours! How long before that trail brought him to her Puerto Rico lab, and from there, straight to her?

And, again, there was Jack. Tory said he'd been brilliant—forceful, charismatic—in the filmed appeals scheduled for broadcast tonight as she opened the campaign floodgates, yet his position as spokesman was the very crux of Rachel's dilemma. In creating the virus, she had engineered a maze to confound any research investigation; and the stroke of fate that had put her in charge of that investigation had given her even further means to prevent discovery. What she hadn't thought of when she'd forced Jack to become the spokesman—and have him remain a credible member of her team—was that her superior position would be jeopardized once he knew the truth. To find the right path through the maze he had only to look to her. And she knew he was bent on finding it. She could sense him watching, assessing, hungering for clues. *Following every move I make.*

Well, she thought, her anger stirred, I'm watching, too. *Don't get too close, Jack, or you'll get burned.*

The small flurry of bravado did little to calm her. Jack was one of the most rigorous scientists she'd ever known. How could she continue, under his scrutiny, to keep the rest of the team scurrying along the path where she wanted them, toward a dead end, without it signaling the right path to him?

Upstairs, his shower stopped.

"Can I eat on the porch?" Chris asked Laurel. He'd returned with a bowl of cereal. Using both hands to lift the pitcher from the table, he sloshed on milk.

Laurel was sleepily pouring orange juice. "Why not?"

Chris left, and Ron, Del's nurse, came in from the hall. "Dr. Lesage, you got a minute?" He was carrying a shopping bag.

"You're going now?" she asked, distracted. He and Doris had planned to go to town to pick up a prescription for Del and do the shopping, but no stores would be open so early.

"No, Doris is getting raspberries from the garden for

breakfast, so I—" He lowered his voice. "I want to ask you something." He was pulling some kind of plastic headgear out of the bag. Rachel was startled to see it was a gas mask.

"For Tina," he said. Their daughter in New York. "See, she can't leave her job at the diner, so it's in case . . . well, you know."

Rachel stared at the mask. "Where did you get this?"

"Doris bought it in Bangor, at the mall. I've seen them in lots of stores. There's people lined up." He gave a nervous laugh. "It's nuts, I know. I told her the damn thing won't do any good, but she won't believe me. Said to ask you. She's pretty upset." He turned the mask in his hands, his face creased with worry. "I know it wouldn't help." He looked at her hopefully. "Would it?"

She said quietly, "No."

Ron stuffed the mask back in the bag. "Course not. I told her, but you know Doris. She'll make me send it to Tina anyway." He offered an unconvincing laugh. "Well, sorry to bother you, Doctor."

Rachel felt a tightness around her heart. Ron had touched that deepest fear: the risk to her *own* daughter. In the event of a pandemic, a certain percentage of females would survive, probably quite large, but there was no way to predict how many, or where, or who. She'd told Ron the truth: there was no guaranteed protection, not even distance. The American cities she had targeted were far from Washington. Far from Tory. Still, the outcome was unknowable.

No question of turning back. The blood of thousands had been shed, a sacrifice on the way to a better world. To stop now would reduce those deaths to plain murder. She must see this through, even if it required further sacrifice. But, could she bear to sacrifice Tory? Facing that dread at the very start, she had overcome it, certain that the president would agree to her demand. Except that hadn't happened.

Then, even as she'd accepted Tory's help, the dread had clawed its way back, with an altered equation whose irony was not lost on Rachel: her worst fear, and her final hope, were both focused on her daughter. Tory's campaign *must* succeed.

"Everybody's so scared," Laurel said gloomily after Ron had left. "Artemis is all anyone's talking about. As if there's anything we can do. My God, gas masks? Like rearranging deck chairs on the *Titanic*." She shivered. "If the plague's coming, it's coming."

Rachel felt a flash of anger. "It doesn't have to be that way. People can act."

"People like you and Jack maybe. But ordinary folks? I can't imagine doing half the stuff you do."

"Why not?"

Laurel made a knowing, wry face. "Don't you watch *Oprah*? Low self-esteem."

"Self-esteem comes with accomplishment. You might try that."

Laurel stiffened at the reprimand and looked away.

Rachel snapped open her briefcase and slid in the spreadsheets. The girl's indolence and lazy fatalism annoyed her. "Can you swim?"

"What? Sure."

"Chris can't. Instead of spending your days watching TV and playing in the dinghy, you might teach him to swim. That would be an accomplishment."

Before Laurel could reply, Rachel noticed Chris standing in the doorway. His eyes were wide and frightened. He pointed behind him and said hesitantly, "Liam."

They found the dog lying at the foot of the verandah steps, drooling, eyes glazed, muzzle matted with blood, his foreleg just above the paw angled sickeningly as though someone had hacked it with a saw. Jagged white bone, shredded muscle, red pulp—a shell exploded in Rachel's brain. *Paul.*

She quelled the memory. "Laurel, get water and towels," she ordered, grabbing a beach towel from the railing. She ran down the steps and spread it over the trembling dog for warmth as he looked up at her with helpless trust. Laurel had frozen.

"Laurel! Water!"

The girl didn't move. Her eyes were locked on the mangled leg.

"Useless!" Rachel said furiously between clenched teeth. She lifted Liam in her arms and struggled up the steps, grunting under his weight.

Chris ran after her. "Open the door, darling," she said. In the kitchen she settled the dog on the table. Catching her breath, she told Chris, "Pat Liam's head and tell him he's a good dog. Yes, you must, darling, he's frightened and he needs you to make him feel better. That's good. Now don't leave him." She hurried to the sink and filled a bowl with water.

"The leg's broken, it needs a splint," Jack said, suddenly walking in. He grabbed a long wooden spoon. "Call the vet. How did it happen?" He was pulling tea towels off a rack and began tying the spoon against Liam's foreleg as a makeshift splint.

Rachel was already punching numbers on the wall phone. "Probably a leg-hold trap," she said with fury. "Trappers set them in the woods." Laurel stood in the doorway, white-faced, then gagged and ran out.

"Sweetheart, you all right?" Jack asked, knocking on her door.

*Oh, God,* she thought, mortified. She'd been sobbing on

her bed. She quickly sat up and swiped away tears. "How's Liam?" she asked as Jack came in.

"Not great, but I've set the break and cleaned the wound and he's stabilized. The vet isn't in yet but Rachel's left a message." He asked again, "You okay?"

"Of course. It just freaked me for a minute."

He sat on the edge of the bed and touched her cheek. "The worst is over. He'll be in good hands with the vet."

"Sure, I know. I'll be fine."

"You don't look it," he said, feeling her forehead.

"I just watched TV too late last night." She shrugged away from his scrutiny and added bitterly, "You know me, that's all I do."

"Are you worried about an outbreak? I've been wondering if you should go away. England, maybe. Stay with the Gardiners."

"No, I don't want to leave you."

"I don't want you to either. Actually, the safest place for you is right here with Ra—" He seemed to catch himself, then checked his watch. "Sorry," he said, getting up, "but I've got to go."

She longed for him to stay, to just *be* with her, but she could see he was itching to get to the lab. "Important work to do, you and Rachel," she said, poking listlessly at the blanket. "You're lucky." The horrible wrongness of the words hit her and she added hastily, "Oh, God, that's not true, after Marisa . . . Oh, I'm sorry."

He nodded sadly. "I know."

"It's just, I wish I could *help* you. But there's nothing I can do. And Rachel can't stand me, and—" Tears welling, she looked away. *Useless.* "I haven't got a clue what to do with my pathetic life."

"Laurel, you've got so much to offer. You'll find your way. It just takes time."

She thought her heart would burst. Jack was the only one who cared.

"Sweetheart, I'm sorry," he said, "but I've *got* to go. You know how it is."

In a moment he was at the door. She hated to see him leave. She blurted, "Can I come to the lab later? Could we have dinner together?"

He hesitated. "Don't see how I can take the time, with—"

"Please?" she begged. "Doris can stay with Chris, and there's another car I can use. Besides, you're working way too hard. You *need* a break."

He looked at her, then relented with a tender smile. "If you say so. Come by around seven?"

She knew he was only doing it for her. She smiled, tears clouding her vision. "I love you."


Jack found Rachel waiting as he came downstairs. "The gatehouse called," she told him curtly. "More reporters today than usual. I'd rather avoid running that gauntlet today. We'll sail to the lab."

They cast off in a strong breeze, and in fifteen minutes reached the middle of the bay, halfway to the lab. As Jack winched in the jib sheet he said carefully, "Maybe you could be a little less rough on Laurel."

"She acts like a child."

"She's got a few problems."

"The whole world has problems."

"Well, since you've got your hands full with the whole world, maybe you could back off with Laurel!"

Stupid to let his temper flare, he told himself. It was being near her, day after day, and appearing to do her bidding—like staying on at Swallow Point instead of a hotel. He'd done it hoping that if he stuck close she might let some vital information slip. She hadn't yet.

He had to be careful, too, about where and how he spoke to her. He knew the FBI was watching him: Colwell's suspicion had been palpable. They'd almost certainly tapped the Swallow Point phones. Probably bugged every room. Glancing back at Rachel's dock, he wondered if they had a surveillance van nearby. In her woods, maybe? With a long-distance parabolic mike? He felt better at her lab. There, she'd assured him, her security systems to prevent corporate espionage were impenetrable. Jack just hoped it was true, because Colwell had to be kept at bay.

*While I stop her myself in the lab.*

It had become clear to him days ago that she wasn't going to let down her guard in private. No, the place to trap her was in the public forum of her own lab, at the helm of this farcically grand research project she was directing. *Misdirecting . . .* that was the reality that Jack alone knew. It gave him his one advantage over Rachel. Her instructions to the team, her approval or dismissal of their various research initiatives, her subtle deceptions to undermine their efforts—that's what he was focusing on now, trying to see through her feints. Every word out of her mouth, every nuance of body language, were ciphers that might help him unscramble the mystery of her creation, if only he could decode them.

The trouble was, the bare facts of that creation were enigmatic enough. The fluid in the red vials had proven to be a true viral soup; analysis was still going on. Tests of the purple vials' contents, on the other hand, revealed only perfume. Jack figured that Rachel had originally tried adding virus right to the perfume, but found that the aromatic oils destabilized her bioengineered pathogen, so she'd separated the elements and devised the mix-your-own gimmick.

As the team spent precious days analyzing the soup, Jack had watched in frustration, more certain every day that

Rachel had dumped these detectable viral agents in as a cover. Nothing here could cause the hemorrhagic devastation he had witnessed, nor explain the extraordinary female-specific pathogenesis. Rachel, naturally, encouraged the broadest investigation, slowing the work. It even occurred to Jack in exasperation that the perfume vials *themselves* might be a ruse, and the real agent was still out there, unfound.

Then, some blood samples from the victims were found to contain antibodies that cross-reacted with swine flu. The team was surprised. No one had suspected mere *influenza*. Jack was skeptical; they'd found it too easily. Yet flu, he had to admit, did open a daunting Pandora's box of possibilities. Every pandemic flu strain consisted of eight genes, and if two strains invaded a single cell, they could mix and match genes to create any of two hundred and fifty-six possible combinations. Could Rachel have accomplished some extraordinary sleight of hand with a common flu bug, which the team had stumbled on by sheer luck? The answers seemed to be yes when, three days ago, the microbiology unit declared a breakthrough. They had identified, within the red vial's soup, a new virus, never seen before. They immediately tried to grow it from victims' tissue, but the agent proved stubborn, tricky to work with, until yesterday. At a crowded, noisy full-team meeting, rumors of success rocketed through the room. Jack stood by the wall, watching. Could this really be a breakthrough despite Rachel's subtle sabotage?

When she stepped forward, everyone hushed. Jack studied her closely. She appeared as always: alert, detached, in control. If she was worried they were getting closer, she was hiding it well.

"We have an isolate," she declared. Her control seemed *too* perfect, Jack thought; she was forcing it. Was she nervous about the discovery after all? He felt a stab of hope, sharp with vengeance.

She brought forward the unit leader, Bill Rensler, on leave from the Yale Microbiology Lab. He announced that polymerase chain reaction analysis had indeed confirmed an influenza virus but had revealed quirks in its genetic sequence different from all others: definitely a new strain. Yes, he added proudly, his people had finally grown it: "We have worms!"

Rachel shook Rensler's hand in congratulation, but again with such an enforced calm that Jack's hope surged. That twitch of tension by her mouth was betraying her. That flicker in her eyes. She *is* nervous!

Rachel offered Rensler the honor of naming the discovery.

"Well, Artemis created it," Rensler replied, flush with his success, "and it's top of the list for gruesomeness. So let's call it A-1."

Rachel hesitated a moment, then declared, "A-1 it is."

Jack suddenly realized that the faint lift at the corners of her lips, the guarded light in her eyes—not nervousness, *satisfaction*. Hope drained from him. Disappointment soured his mouth. She'd *allowed* them to find this. She'd thrown them a goddamn bone.

Applause had broken out for Rensler. He made a theatrical bow, and the people who worked under him congratulated each other exuberantly. Chatter filled the room as everyone joined in the thrill of discovery. Jack's eyes hadn't left Rachel: calm and collected as ever. *Misdirection,* he reminded himself soberly. *Wherever she points, look the other way.*

They docked the boat at the village jetty where Rachel's chauffeur was waiting with the car—probably FBI bugged,

Jack had decided days ago. They drove the mile to the lab in silence. As always, reporters stood milling outside.

"Dr. Lesage," one shouted, running to her as she and Jack marched toward the doors, "do you have a problem working with Dr. Hunt after his statements that the president should give in to the terrorists?"

She answered, "Jack Hunt is one of the most innovative virologists this country has ever produced. He has my complete confidence and trust."

Liar, he thought. You trust me about as much as I trust you. The difference is, I'm going to bring you down.

Reporters swarmed him. A microphone jabbed his jaw, mashing his cheek against his teeth, and he tasted blood. As he shoved the microphone aside, another reporter yelled, "Dr. Hunt, how can you call for appeasing the terrorists when you're also trying to find a cure for their weapon?"

He said hotly, "My sole interest is to prevent more deaths, whether through an agreement to the education plan or a treatment developed by this research team."

Rachel's security guards kept the mob back as she and Jack squeezed into the lobby. About to go their separate ways they exchanged a glance, wordless but bristling with challenge. Jack thought bitterly, *Let the games begin.* He headed for his office.

The halls were crowded with scientists. Many were department chairs or senior researchers seconded from large labs of their own, and they'd all brought extensive support staffs: graduate students, postdoctoral fellows, associate researchers. A dour Brandeis professor of biochemistry brushed by without a greeting. Jack wasn't surprised; he'd encountered some hostility here. "Science and politics don't mix," he'd once overheard one of them grumble. Mostly, though, he'd received sympathy—which rankled him more.

The sympathy of pity. He needed the country to focus on his *message,* not his loss.

The whole team, whatever their feelings about his public statements, seemed baffled about his actual role here. No wonder. Rachel had assigned him only two graduate students as assistants, had restricted his access to lab technicians, and hadn't given him any clear duties. Her presidential-gilded prestige assured the team's compliance, but Jack knew they found the situation odd. Makes sense to me, he thought grimly. She knows I'm gunning for her. Well, let her sweat.

Making his way along the glassed walkway that skirted a ravine, he could see Rachel's jutting corner office, where a glass wall gave her a view of the woods, and an outdoor staircase gave her access to it. It struck him that she seemed to crave closeness to nature. The ravine here, her oceanfront house, the sailing. Even the Pear Tree Inn, twelve years ago. Her idea. Evading the London reporters, he'd driven to the country hotel and found her in a coach house suite where she could walk out into a copse of wilderness carpeted with daffodils. The recollection of their lovemaking brought a fresh wave of loathing. He endured the memory, because the whole *point* now was to not look away, but to study her, observe her, get inside her mind. Her mind had created A-1. Why? Just another ingredient in the soup to confuse them? Or was he getting carried away trying to second-guess her? Could there be more to it? *Careful . . . don't miss anything.*

He took the stairs to his second-floor office, two small cramped rooms. In the outer one, the pair of grad students assigned to him glanced up.

"I'm condensing the PCR analysis for you," Mandy Chang told him, tapping intently at her computer. With her ponytail neatly tied with a red ribbon, and her crisp white blouse and pleated navy skirt, she seemed to Jack more like a guileless schoolgirl than the ambitious Yale doctoral candidate in molecular genetics that she was.

"Lovely morning, Doc," Youssef al-Saadawi said. He lifted his moccasined feet off his desk and lowered the *Playboy* he'd been perusing, tossing it among the Mars bar wrappers around his keyboard. A slight, swarthy young man, he wore a frayed T-shirt and mustard-stained jeans. His black wavy hair always looked as though it hadn't been washed for a week; Jack wryly wondered how he maintained the look every day. Youssef was a biochemist pursuing a doctorate at Johns Hopkins University, top in his class, but as far as Jack could tell his chief aim here, apart from attempting to consume a world record in candy bars, was to proposition every available female. He doubted the kid was having much luck. Mandy, with a drop-dead look, had declined on the first day.

"Don't tax yourself," Jack said. Inside his own cubicle he logged onto the microbiology unit's data. Unsure how to access the newest files, he called in Mandy. Bred in Silicon valley—her American mother was an engineer, her Chinese father a computer programmer—she'd practically been raised in cyberspace.

"How do I bring up Rensler's stats?" he asked her.

Impatiently, she came to his side and tapped at the keyboard. Statistics bloomed on the screen.

He looked up at her. "That's the latest?"

Her almond eyes regarded him frostily. "That's the latest."

He knew she resented being assigned to him. She'd come with Rensler's people from the Yale Microbiology Lab but had been pulled from that elite group to assist Jack. In her estimation it was a dead-end duty and it pissed her off.

He turned back to the screen. "Thanks."

"You're welcome."

A truce, he thought, watching her go.

He heard Youssef murmur to her as she came back to her desk, "Fancy a bite from the caf? I might spring for some Rosie Lee and Holy Ghost."

Cockney rhyme for tea and toast. The Cockney accent had surprised Jack the first day. If there was Bedouin blood in Youssef, it was way back; he was a scrapper from the mean streets of London. Cambridge on scholarship, then a visa to the States to work with the Johns Hopkins select unit of biochemists, whose chief had brought him here. Like Mandy, he'd then been assigned to Jack. As resentful about it as she was, he seemed to accept his lot fatalistically, although at yesterday's meeting to announce A-1 Jack had overheard him grumble enviously, "Nice work. Lucky bastards."

That meeting—what a travesty. The group had settled into their usual cliques after the announcement, and soon the rivalry was thick enough to choke on, because Rachel had immediately invited a discussion about developing a therapy for A-1. Jack wanted to yell, Don't listen to her! He could only watch in exasperation as they'd enthusiastically obliged her, some people advancing ideas, others shooting them down, everyone vociferously defending their pet theories. It was human nature, and the gene jockeys here were far from immune to its workings. Of course, the quarreling was exactly what Rachel wanted. She'd handpicked this bunch of edgy top guns. So easy to fan the rivalry until they fought to deadlock. Then she could step in and lead them where she wanted.

First she'd asked for ideas about the disease's female-specific manifestation, and Larry Silverstein of Yale gave an impassioned plea for focusing on chromosomes, a search for an X-linked susceptibility or a Y-linked resistance. Dwayne Morantz of Duke Medical Center acerbically pointed out,

"Males have the X too." To which Silverstein snapped, "They don't express the same genes from it."

Rachel said, "It's a good idea, Larry. Have your unit start looking at chromosome activity."

*Bingo,* Jack had thought, suddenly alert. She wants a focus on chromosomes, so that has to be a dead end. *Look the other way.*

Reality quickly cooled him. *Which* other way? There were so many other possible female-specific factors: ova production, hormones, immunodeficiency disease susceptibility, to name just a few. One down, fifty to go, he thought grimly.

"Excuse me," Sandra Whitelaw, a Stanford molecular geneticist, had interjected, "the gentlemen's theories would be great if we had years to putter around, but we don't. We need something quick and dirty to abrogate the infection. Now, I've done some preliminary work on designing a ribozyme that would chop up the virus's nucleic acid to prevent it generating its own replication, and I—"

"You're all running off in too many directions," Morantz interrupted. "I suggest a classic approach—tests on animal subjects. Rhesus monkeys would be suitable."

"That would only tell us about A-1 and rhesus monkeys," Whitelaw said disdainfully. "We won't know about A-1 and humans unless it's tested on a human female. That's impossible, so your suggestion is pointless."

"I've heard the scientific method called many things," Morantz sniffed, "but never pointless."

*Oh, please,* Jack thought, disgusted at the sparring.

"There's no time!" Whitelaw shot back. "But perhaps you don't care if a few million victims die, Dr. Morantz. After all, they're only women."

"It seems impossible to me that we can come up with *any-thing* in the allotted time," Morantz replied, keeping his cool with difficulty. "So I suggest we proceed like responsible professionals and do our job properly, even if that takes us past the deadline. We'll get nowhere acting like hysterical amateurs searching for some magic antiserum."

At which Whitelaw really let him have it. Others joined in. It was a free-for-all.

Goddamned prima donnas! Rachel didn't even have to steer them, they steered themselves—babbling and bickering all the way down her primrose path.

"Dwayne," Rachel intervened calmly, "I agree that the logical next step would be tests, but unfortunately Sandra's right. The president needs results. So some processes will have to be cut short. Now, what I suggest—"

Her gaze, for one brief moment, intersected with Jack's, and he caught a flicker, an almost imperceptible loss of composure. Why? he thought, snatching at it. What's bothering her? She quickly turned to give some directive to Silverstein about the chromosome project, and Jack was left wondering if he'd misread the signs again. No, this time her nervousness had been unmistakable. *I know her.*

But she knows me too, he reminded himself. So maybe the nervous glance was a trick to misdirect *me.*

Jesus, am I just getting paranoid? Going in circles.

Only one thing's for sure, he told himself, hanging on to the thought to keep his bearings. *Nothing she approves will lead to a treatment.*

What will? he asked himself now, staring at the data on his office screen. Okay, so she's misdirecting the team with A-1, but misdirecting away from *what?*

He spent the day in his cubicle studying lab reports and poring over electron microscope photos. In the outer office, Mandy threw herself into PCR analysis with a martyr's zeal, her color-coordinated stack of reports growing a few inches higher by the afternoon. Youssef set up a dartboard by the window, took a long lunch in the cafeteria, and napped at his desk.

Late in the day Jack heard them whispering. Then, after a knock on his open door, the two of them walked in purposefully, like a delegation. He turned to them. "What is it?"

Youssef beamed a patronizing smile. "Doc, let's face it, you can't really use us. What say we clear out and stop bothering you? Let you get on with your reading. Say, for the next month?"

Jack was dismayed. "You're quitting?"

Mandy said, "Just the opposite. We'd like you to release us to join Rensler and Silverstein working with A-1."

"Where the action is," Youssef added.

You poor fools, Jack thought, there's nothing there. "Request denied," he said. No way he could make any progress alone.

Youssef's smirk vanished. "Denied?"

"I need you. Both of you."

"Why?" Youssef asked. "To help you with the daily crossword?"

"Dr. Hunt," Mandy pointed out more tactfully, "you have to beg the unit chiefs just to keep you in the picture."

"All the more reason I need your help. No transfer. That's final."

Youssef turned to Mandy. "Dr. Lesage will reassign us. Let's go."

"Don't," Jack warned. "I'm still your superior. You leave this office, you'll leave with my negative report, and I promise you I won't be gentle. My name still means something, and you'll have a hard time explaining my comments to future prospective employers."

They glared at him. We're fighting, like the rest of the team, he realized. Dissension, paralysis. Just what Rachel wants.

The outer door opened and Laurel walked in. Waggling her fingers at Jack, she sat down to wait. Youssef craned around the inner doorway to look at her.

Dinner, Jack remembered with an inward groan. Wrong to have promised her that. Can't possibly take the time, not now with these two little prodigies wanting to mutiny. Everyone's so hot to work on A-1, to follow Rachel blindly as she—

Hold on. What if I really am being paranoid in dismissing A-1? What if it *is* the answer? He thought back to that fleeting anxiety he'd caught in Rachel's eyes. He hadn't imagined it, and it was no trick. She'd been afraid, and it had to do with A-1.

Why would she be nervous, if A-1's a dead end?

Suddenly he thought he saw the answer. He remembered how she'd steered the meeting away from testing A-1 on a monkey; she'd so smoothly let Whitelaw declare it would just waste time. That was it. Everyone wanted to work on A-1—Rachel had practically orchestrated it—but she was anxious to keep that work confined to one channel, and out of another, more dangerous one. She wants us busy with it; oh, yes, fixated on it, but with microscopes, not living beings. *In vitro,* not *in vivo.*

Why? Because the results would give her away. *Because A-1, given to any living creature, won't produce the disease.*

He couldn't hold back his conviction any longer. "Listen to me," he said to Mandy and Youssef. "The team's on completely the wrong track. The agent's not A-1."

Youssef's eyebrows shot up. "Brilliant, Doc. Three hundred geniuses here and they've all made a mistake. Glad I'm not working with *them.*"

Jack restrained an impulse to deck him.

Mandy wasn't sarcastic, just curt. "Of course it's the

agent, Doctor. It's a completely new flu strain, it's in the victims' tissues, and now we've grown it."

"That's not proof enough," Jack said, forcing patience. "Look, it's as if the prime suspect in a murder case confesses, so the investigation stops. But what if the suspect is just crazy—and innocent—and the real killer's still at large? Believe me, a female monkey, even a female human, would not develop the Artemis disease from A-1. Our killer is something else altogether."

"What evidence could possibly lead you to that conclusion?" Mandy asked.

*I know who the killer's creator is!* he wanted to yell. But he couldn't tell them that, or how he knew it. He was stuck with begging, because, damn it, he needed their help; no way could he manage this work on his own. "You've just got to trust me," he said. "I've been around viruses a long time. There are some things you just get to know in your gut." Even as he said it, he despised the lame plea.

They exchanged looks, their patience clearly wearing thin. "Intuition?" Youssef asked derisively.

"Listen, kid," Jack flared, "I was classifying viruses before you could say the word."

The mockery in Youssef's eyes hardened to contempt. "Doc, you've been out of the loop too long, and you're way out of line on this. Okay, I've drawn the straw to baby-sit a star. I can use the time for beauty rest. But I don't have to listen to drivel about gut feelings and trust."

"How can you talk to him like that?" Laurel demanded. She was on her feet. Her face was pale. "This is *Jack Hunt.* A man who's saved thousands of lives, all over the world. He knows more about diseases than you'll *ever* know. If he says this A-1 thing is not the right—"

"Never mind, Laurel," he broke in. He'd lost this round. His assistants thought him incompetent, even neurotic. How could he blame them, when all he could do was plead and look like a fool? It galled him, and his own impotence infuriated him. He needed something concrete to show them. The damn thing was, to find anything concrete he needed *them*. "You're right," he conceded to Youssef. "I'm a has-been. And what are you? A wanna-be. Neither of us is going anywhere fast. So let's work together on this. I'm telling you, A-1 is harmless. It's just flu."

"Well, Doc," Youssef said, coldly humoring him, "if A-1 isn't responsible, what is?"

"That's what we have to find out. The three of us."

"The Three Musketeers?"

Jack bit back rage. You snot-nosed little shit.

"Look," Mandy cut in, "Whitelaw was right. The only way to find out if A-1 is *not* the agent is to inject a human female. Are you prepared to do that?"

"Of course not," Jack said.

"Exactly. Dr. Hunt, I've given you a lot of leeway because I felt sorry for you, but I think grief has seriously clouded your judgment. Now, if you won't release me," she said frostily, "may I at least go back to my hotel for the night? I've been here since dawn."

She was tired, angry. So was Youssef. Better let them calm down. *Me too.* Anyway, he needed time to finish reviewing the A-1 reports if he hoped to find any indication of where the team had gone wrong. Tonight was all he had, because Tory needed him in New York in the morning. "Get some sleep, both of you," he said. "Be here at seven tomorrow, ready to work."

Mandy pushed past Laurel, switched off her computer, and collected her things. As she left, Laurel shot her a murderous look.

Jack gave Laurel a quick hug. "Thanks for sticking up for me," he whispered in her ear. He drew her away, sorry to let her down. "Sweetheart, I've got far more work than I thought. Sorry, but I can't get away for dinner. Go on home. I'll make it up to you, I promise."

As she sighed in disappointment, Youssef sidled over to her. "Dinner?" he asked with a smile. "As it turns out, I'm free."

The waiter in the Thai restaurant interrupted them to serve the spring rolls, then glided away. Laurel looked at Youssef over the rim of her wineglass. He was pouring a small puddle of hot sauce onto his plate while stealing glances at her chest.

She was nervous. *Very* nervous. But I'm doing the right thing, I know it. Jack needs help. He's so tired, working so hard, all alone, and no one's listening to his ideas. She'd asked him quietly before she'd left him at the lab, "You're absolutely sure this A-1 thing is harmless?"

"Never been more sure of anything," Jack had muttered, and turned back to his computer.

The people who *should* be helping him, she thought now, were too conceited or too dim, or both. Like this horny little English-Arab nerd across from her.

She smiled at him and picked up where the waiter had interrupted them. "So, like, the ultraviolet in the level four staging area kills every kind of virus?"

"Yeah, buggers up the viral genetic material," Youssef confirmed. "Course it wouldn't help if the microbe had already got *into* a person." He speared a spring roll with his chopstick, apparently trying to make the action lascivious. Laurel restrained herself from rolling her eyes.

"Scary," she said, pretending excitement. She swallowed the last of her wine, and Youssef quickly refilled her glass, emptying the bottle. He ordered another.

She leaned toward him, curling in the wineglass to nudge

her breast, and asked in an intimate hush, "Is it true some people freak out their first time in those containment suits you have to wear?"

He wrenched his eyes up from her glass and nodded. "I've seen it. Soon as the helmet goes on. Panic in the eyes, sweat breaking out. Some blokes start clawing to get the helmet off. Not a pretty sight." He leaned closer and added huskily, "Unlike what I'm looking at right now."

She fingered a tear of condensation on the cold wineglass, feeling a tumult of emotions, remembering the morning crisis with Liam and how she'd wept on her bed while the voices carried on down in the kitchen. Rachel's, staccato, angry, cursing trappers. Jack's, calm, in charge, asking for help tying the splint. Chris's, high-pitched and eager, assuring the dog, "Good boy, good boy." Hot tears again pricked her eyes. A four-year-old was more helpful!

*Useless.* Rachel's word. It stuck, like hurled mud. Or like the sullen image of her mother; like a bloodstain, it never faded. The sullenness had been stamped on her by life. Teenage pregnancy. Three kids by three different men. Stinking basement apartments and food stamps. Stoned half the time. Too wasted to even lock the front door against intruders. *Useless.*

Almost as useless as her own kid, *me*—should have come home from school, should have kept the killer out.

Laurel's guilty secret, and her most sickening fear, was that she was fated to become just like her mother. Passive. Parasitic. Worthless.

Jack didn't know. *Jack loves me.* His love was the foundation of her life, and of her hope to climb above fate. The first step in doing that, she told herself, was to help him now.

"Wimpy sauce," Youssef said. He was poking the spring roll into his puddle of hot sauce. "I like it sadistic," he added with a grin.

Laurel forced a smile. "Sounds like you've seen a lot. I mean, in level four. Tell me more."

She already had a visitor ID tag from the lab's security desk, authorized by Jack. His coded magnetic keys would do the rest. She'd seen him toss them on his desk before she left, and knew she could palm them—a legacy of her childhood grounding in shoplifting. Youssef said most people would be gone for the night, leaving only a skeleton staff. All she had to do was lift a disposable syringe from the serology department, suit up in the level four antechamber, and locate a flask of A-1.

And then, inject it.

"Level four?" Youssef asked, munching. "Sure. What do you want to know?"

She took a last gulp of wine for courage. *Everything.*

She was going to help Jack by proving he was right. She'd show Rachel she was good for something. Or die trying.

# 12

"SHOW HIM THE TAPE," THE CHIEF OF STAFF TOLD an aide as Carson entered the conference room. The aide slid a cassette into the VCR, and Quincy added sharply, "Sit down, Colwell. Watch this."

Still wondering why he'd been summoned to the White House, Carson glanced at the others around the table. Ed Liota, his immediate superior. FBI Director McAuliffe. Attorney General Julia Manchek. So much for the Bureau's nonpolitical status, he thought grimly, taking a chair.

Quincy asked him, "What do you know about a group called People for a Global Tomorrow?"

Carson hadn't heard of them. "Nothing."

"Jesus," Liota muttered.

The attorney general said dryly, "Maybe you've been inside the command center too long, Mr. Colwell."

"Show him the damn *tape*," Quincy again told the aide, then said to Carson, as the aide hit the play button, "It's a sixty-second TV spot. Watch."

Rear shot of an airline pilot's head, cockpit instruments glowing before him. Sounds of the plane's fuselage tearing. Pilot grips the controls. Somber male announcer—familiar voice, Carson thought, though he couldn't identify it—"Our ecosphere is like an airplane. Just as a plane is held together by rivets, our ecosphere is held together by species, by an interconnected web of animals and plants. Every time we kill off a species—whether in the rain forest, the savannah, or the ocean—the structure of our 'plane' is weakened. It's the burden of too many people consuming too many resources. And if the critical number of rivets is lost, our plane will come apart and crash."

The plane trembles. The pilot shakes his head despairingly. Camera pans around to the cabin crammed with frightened passengers: a mother clutches a child, a businessman stares anxiously out at the darkness, a young woman prays. New shot of the plane from a distance as its lights disappear into night clouds.

Scene shift to a sunlit airstrip in a wheat field. A jetliner sits on the tarmac, with about fifty people at work refitting it, perched on ladders and scaffolds—male and female of all races and ages, laboring with care and pride. Welders finish off rivets. Glaziers check window seals. Children polish the fuselage so it gleams.

A man standing on the tarmac turns to the camera. It's Jack Hunt—*that* was the voice!—and now he says: "We can rebuild. It's not too late. If our government will do the right thing, global population growth can be slowed and the damage to our world can be reversed. Then, the danger ends."

A child slips her hand in his as music swells. A banner unfurls with bold lettering: PEOPLE FOR A GLOBAL TOMORROW. An eight-hundred number flashes. Hunt says: "Join us at PGT. Call this number. Tell your government you don't want a plague. You want a global tomorrow."

Fade to black.

Carson sat back, stunned. When had Hunt made this? Who was behind it? A horrible suspicion stabbed.

Quincy said, "PGT began running this spot nationwide at seven tonight. At seven-twenty the attorney general got a call from Roger Bloom at the *Washington Post* asking—"

"He faxed this for my comment," Julia Manchek interrupted, and read aloud, "The *Washington Post* has learned that Victoria Farr-Colwell, organizer of People for a Global Tomorrow, the grassroots organization that has sprung up calling for an accommodation with the Artemis terrorists, is married to the FBI's counterterrorism chief, Carson J. Colwell, who is leading the investigation. The attorney general, when asked about Mr. Colwell's apparent conflict of interest—" Manchek stopped reading and added tartly, "No comment."

Carson felt as if he'd been kicked in the stomach.

"You knew nothing about this, Mr. Colwell?" Manchek asked incredulously.

*Pressure on the government,* Tory had told him that night in Chris's room. He thought she'd just meant arranging interviews with Hunt. That was bad enough—but this! He answered as calmly as he could, "No, ma'am."

"Unbelievable," Liota said. "It's your goddamn *wife*!"

Carson gritted his teeth. He hadn't been home in over a week.

"Head in the fucking sand," Liota muttered. "Or worse."

Carson flared. "If you're questioning my loyalty—"

"All right, all right," McAuliffe said, raising his hands for peace. "Colwell didn't know. *Nobody* knew."

"Except his wife and Hunt," Quincy pointed out.

Tory and Hunt, Carson thought with a jolt of dread. *Working together.*

"The question is, Mr. Colwell," Manchek said, "*why* didn't

you know? I thought you were watching Hunt. Did you *miss* him running around making television ads?"

His mind was tripping over itself to piece together the timing. "He must have filmed this before his original CNN statement," he said, "or just hours after, because since that evening we've had him under twenty-four-hour surveillance. Days he works until late at the Lesage lab. Nights he's at the house at Swallow Point. He's given interviews from the lab, but he hasn't gone anywhere else."

Questions were ricocheting in his head. How long had Tory been planning this? What else had she organized while he'd been inside the command center? What had she been calculating that night in Chris's room, with her kiss that he'd believed so spontaneous?

"And your wife's involvement?" Manchek pressed.

He stared at her. Involvement in terrorism? Tory? He could still see her by Chris's bed, making her impassioned arguments. The memory brought some relief, though bitter: she'd deceived him because she'd deceived herself. Her *cause*. But Tory knowingly working for Artemis? He didn't for a moment believe it. "We've known from the start that her firm is representing him," he answered. "Nothing unlawful there."

Liota said, "Unless she's connected to Artemis."

Carson heard himself declare, "She's not."

"You *know* that?"

"I'd swear it."

"Good enough for me," the director said.

Carson saw skepticism on all the faces except the director's. It rattled him, but not enough to change his mind. Tory was no terrorist.

It was little comfort. She was also, clearly, not an innocent, duped by Hunt. She'd made herself a player.

"Well obviously, secrecy is one of PGT's tactics," Quincy

said with angry frustration. "First they brought out Hunt alone, with the McIvar bombshell. Then interviews showing him working diligently at the Lesage lab, all wham-bam, in and out, with no face-to-face opposition. Shit, he's got the whole country thinking he's the Lone Ranger, taking just enough time away from his scientific work to denounce the big bad government cover-up. Now Colwell's wife surrounds him with an overnight grassroots organization and tells the country, You're scared? Just sign here and the good doctor will ride into Washington with his silver star of virtue blazing. Jesus, you've got to hand it to them. It's good."

Carson swallowed, his mouth dry. But he'd finally got his mind back on track. Tory had blindsided him for the second time. He wouldn't let it happen again.

Quincy went on grimly, "It's the worst possible timing for us, with Congress about to go ballistic, and Wall Street on the brink of panic, and every—"

"Let's stick to the subject," Manchek said impatiently. "People for a Global Tomorrow and Mr. Colwell's wife." She added with cool firmness, "I'd like to discuss his resignation."

Carson stifled his alarm.

"I can't see any alternative," Manchek went on. "I've got to go out there and answer the media's questions about this god-awful situation with PGT, and about the Bureau's failure to find Artemis. *Mr. Colwell's* failure."

Carson forced calmness into his voice. "You can't remove me."

"Why not?"

"Because we're facing a deadline not even three weeks away. Bringing a replacement up to speed would waste critical time. Moreover, it's vital that we maintain public confidence. Dismissing your lead investigator would cause more panic than any apparent conflict of interest on my part. I assure you that the situation with my . . . with PGT will not compromise my ability to conduct the investigation. Let me find Artemis. Let me stop them."

"Like you found PGT?" Manchek asked acidly.

The director dug in. "Carson Colwell was my choice for this job, and I stand by him. No one can doubt his loyalty."

"The *Washington Post* does," she shot back.

"His resignation is not an option."

"Then maybe *yours* is."

"Absolutely not," Quincy intervened, horrified. "Jesus, if we start eating our own what kind of message does *that* send? Colwell's right, the country's terrified. Flights to Europe are booked solid with women trying to get out before the deadline. We're soon going to see real, ugly panic unless we start fighting back. And I don't mean by shooting *each other.*"

Tense silence.

"Look, we got some good news today," Quincy went on placatingly. "Dr. Lesage announced that her team has isolated the virus. God knows she was a liability at first, but with this breakthrough she's brought us a step closer to a cure. We're getting the news to every media outlet, so that's all to the good. Now let's stop bashing each other and focus on the immediate emergency. People for a Global Tomorrow. If we're going to prevent panic, they've got to be silenced."

Carson felt all their eyes on him. He didn't hesitate. "I agree."

"All right," Quincy said, getting down to business. "First, before a PGT movement gets rolling we need to bring out some heavy guns. But no clear ties to the president—he can't be seen harassing a legal populist group. He's suggested we recruit the Wise Use people, get them to send out their pit bulls."

"What would they want in return?" the attorney general asked.

"What they're always lobbying for—hands off the resource industries. The president's going to promise them we'll gut the clean water bill and drop regulations on clear-cutting. As an immediate gift, how about your office facilitating a few lawsuits Wise Use has pending against environmentalists?"

She nodded. "We can talk."

"Good. We're also enlisting the pro-lifers, warning them PGT's call to control overpopulation is just a euphemism for abortion. That'll bring them out slugging. And they can get mean."

He sat back. "Which brings us to our biggest problem. Jack Hunt. We've done focus groups—people love him. He's a fucking hero." He stabbed his finger at polling sheets on the table. "These numbers are killing us."

Carson warned, "I won't be considering polls if I decide to arrest him."

Quincy said anxiously, "Arrest? I thought you were just watching him, hoping he'd take you to Artemis."

"For the moment."

"Well, we must not appear to be bullying him. People would only sympathize with him more. However," he added emphatically, "we can change their perception of him." He looked at the FBI director. "Get your people on it, Ian. Dig up some dirt on Hunt."

"I'm late for the British ambassador," the attorney general interrupted, getting up. She turned to Carson. "The consensus is that your resignation would be counterproductive, but this conflict of interest with your wife cannot continue. Alter the situation, Mr. Colwell. Persuade her to cut her ties with PGT." She added sternly, "Or cut yours to her."

\* \* \*

"One tomato and basil, one Hawaiian, one Italian sausage with peppers," Eric said, sliding pizza boxes onto the video editing console.

As everyone reached for the food, Tory was about to say "Whoa!" They had to finish cutting Jack's new pitch. But she glanced at her watch. Almost midnight. Everyone was tired and hungry. "Pause it there, Rhonda," she told the editor.

Tory sat back rubbing her stinging eyes. A break was the last thing she wanted. It only let her worries about Carson swarm back. He would have seen the first PGT spot by now. He'd know the worst.

"Hawaiian pizza," Rhonda said, getting up stiffly and stretching. "What is that, an oxymoron?"

"Only to occidental morons," Noah said with a Groucho leer.

Groans all around.

"Oh, and Noah, a message from your wife," Eric added as he dumped soda cans beside the pizzas. "The flights are all booked, so she's putting your kids on a train."

"She can put *my* kids on a train," Vince cracked, flopping back into his chair with a piece of pizza.

The others traded more lame quips, punchy from another grueling night, but Tory saw that Noah had stopped smiling. Was she the only one who'd noticed? Both his children were preteen girls. Was he sending them out of Washington as a precaution?

She sat on the couch beside him as the others went on kidding, and quietly asked him, "Family taking a holiday?"

"Sort of."

"That's nice. Where?"

"The cabin in Connecticut. With Deborah's folks."

"How long?"

He set the wedge of pizza on his knee as if he'd lost his appetite. "I've got obligations, Tory."

Once, he would have confided in me, she thought. Artemis has everyone cowed. She said gently, "No crime in hedging your bets, my friend."

*Obligations,* she thought with a pang. So have I. Why couldn't Carson understand that? She'd been unable to forgive him that night in Chris's room when he'd hidden from her that he'd released Jack. He promised she could talk to him as her husband, but he'd lied. He wasn't her husband first. He was FBI to his core.

But in the last few days, as she'd readied the full campaign, she'd had to face the fact that she had been hiding far more from him. Her duplicity had been worse. Premeditated, calculated, prolonged. By now he'd know it, how deeply she had deceived him. She was ashamed.

Remorse, however, was an emotion she would not indulge. They had *both* broken faith: he'd gone along with the original cover-up, after all, concealing the Artemis danger from her. They'd both done what their jobs demanded. She refused to believe the damage was irreparable, though. They'd been on different sides of issues before, sometimes vehemently, and it had never shaken what was fundamental between them. Their family. *The very reason I'm doing this campaign, if only he'd see.*

Well, she thought, I hardly gave him a chance that night, did I? Ranting about terrorism—his specialty—when I should have shown him what was in my heart: that this is the only way I can be sure I'll still be around for Chris.

I'll call him. Explain calmly. Ask him to try to understand. And to forgive.

She caught Jack's sober face stilled on the large monitor, looking out in midsentence as if to warn her: "This, Carson won't forgive."

I've got to try. As soon as we've done this editing.

She sat beside Rhonda and pointed out the next cuts she wanted. Gradually the others drifted back to work, munching crusts and licking their fingers. "The music should be up when Jack says 'global village not global ghost town,' " she told Rhonda. "And bring the wind FX down as—"

"Tory, we haven't got time for every detail," Vince protested. "There's still tomorrow's rally lineup to revise. Let's move on."

"No, Jack's got to look perfect. The rally can—"

The door flew open and Marcia rushed in, breathless. "FBI!"

Men swarmed in, maybe a dozen federal agents. As Rhonda froze the video, Tory demanded, "What's going on? Who—"

Carson walked in and the words died on Tory's breath.

His men fanned out among her shocked people. One agent announced they'd come with a court order that authorized a search and seizure of evidence, and he outlined their rights. Tory grabbed the phone and called her attorney. As she waited to be connected, voices from her staff in the hall rose in alarm as more agents out there stopped people, opened office doors, began questioning. Carson didn't take his eyes off Tory as she spoke to her lawyer. She returned his stare as she hung up, and instructed the seven people with her, "Answer only the minimum. Gowan's on his way."

Carson gave orders to the agents to take the seven here down the hall to question them. He stood aside as the agents led them out, leaving Tory alone—for him. He shut the door.

In the silence between them, as the commotion in the hall buffeted the editing room, Tory said shakily, "My God, you've brought an army."

His steely expression didn't change. "Who's behind this campaign? Who's paying?"

"My mother donated seed money," she said, startled by his coldness into answering.

"Christ," he said in disgust. Then, "Who else? Jack Hunt? Is he giving the orders?"

She pulled herself together. "You know I don't have to answer your questions. Everything we're doing here is legal."

He jerked his chin toward the door. "We'll find out anyway."

She said flatly, "Do that."

This was all wrong! She knew she should be begging, Please, Carson, this is *us*—let me explain how deeply I believe what I'm doing is right! But the appeals stuck in her throat. He *had never* wanted to know.

For a long moment they stared at one another. He finally blurted a single word—an accusation: "Why?"

She knew he didn't mean the campaign. He meant, *Why did you betray me?* Guilt twisted her heart.

She answered quietly, "I needed the time. Because I knew you'd have to do this."

He shook his head with sadness, the first crack in his icy self-control. "To you, betrayal's just another tactic."

She winced. How he hated her world. Her "dirty" political campaigns, where loyalties shifted, and the only rule was: Win. Carson *lived* by rules: duty, allegiance, obedience to a code. She'd always known it about him. She even admired it. "Carson, this war between us is the last thing I want," she said. "I don't believe you want it either. It's Artemis. It's their poison, and I hate them for it. But never *you*. Please, don't let them split us apart."

She saw turmoil in his eyes. "Walk out of here beside me, right now," he said. "Drop what you're doing. Then they *can't* divide us."

A moan escaped her. "If only."

He seized on her momentary softening. "You could go to Maine tonight, get Chris. I don't want him out there any longer, so close to Hunt. You could pick him up and take him away with you, right now, go someplace far, Hawaii, or New Zealand maybe, until we—"

"Until? Nineteen days, Carson. That's all you have left." She added bleakly, "Oh, yes, escape would be lovely. No responsibility. Except that's not how it is. Chris is the very reason I can't leave this up to you."

"Your responsibility is to stay out of this and get our son and yourself to safety! Away from Hunt! Mine is to find Artemis, *however* long it takes."

Tory was shocked, because although she'd never considered this macabre fact, it seemed starkly clear to him. The deadline existed only for the females of one American city: while those people were dying, he could go on searching. And he would, until he had Artemis. She saw that now. Saw, also, that Jack was the sole target in his sights. Carson was unbending, just as he'd been in concealing the ultimatum from her. It was how he saw his duty. That would never change.

"So," she said, "I hide out in paradise while millions here die? Somehow I don't think I could live with that."

"But you can live with *this*?" Furious, he jerked his chin at the video monitor, at the frozen frame of Jack's face, larger than life. "Giving comfort to the enemy? Treason? Christ, Tory, it's immoral."

"And what do you call following immoral orders?"

"You wouldn't judge it like that if I brought in Artemis tomorrow."

"I have to judge *now*."

"And I have to do my job!"

"You're not *up to it!*"

He slapped her.

She gasped and groped for the monitor for balance. Carson looked as shocked as she was. "Oh, God, Tory. I'm sorry—" He reached out to touch her stinging cheek, but her hand shot up to stop him. She could take his blow, but not his pity. She leaned against the monitor to catch her breath. When she could finally speak, the steadiness in her voice surprised her. "I'm sorry I had to deceive you. But I swear I'd do it again."

He didn't seem to be listening. He was staring at Jack's image on the screen beside her, fury and misery warring in his eyes. "It's Hunt," he said. "Some power he has over you." As if to cut her off from Jack's toxic energy, he grabbed her elbow and pulled her away from the screen.

He didn't let go. Suddenly his arms were around her and he grappled her to him and crushed his mouth on hers. She stood rigid, stunned, locked in his embrace. *He has no right.* But the sensation of being in his arms was so familiar, so powerful. An act she'd welcomed a thousand times. She felt her body respond, felt passion kindle. Her arms slid around his waist, and she pressed against the hardness of his body and opened her mouth to his.

He made a low groan, the sound—desire and need—so familiar too. *There's still love here,* she thought, exulting, grateful, returning his kiss with all the ardor she felt.

As suddenly as he'd grabbed her, Carson froze. Stiffly, he drew her away to arm's length. His breathing was still uneven as he said, shaken, "Christ, how can I be sure you're not playing me? How can I be sure . . . ever again?"

Her breath caught. The insult stung more than his blow.

His hands fell away from her as though weighted with stone. "It's no good, Tory." His voice was bleak. "I've always pictured you walking beside me. From now on I'd have to look over my shoulder to stop you from putting a knife in my back."

She took a rocky step away. She licked her bottom lip and tasted blood. His kiss had cut her. She swallowed the metallic taste, and felt its bitterness seep down to her very soul.

# 13

AT NOON THE NEXT DAY IN NEW YORK, JACK STOOD at a fifteenth-floor window in the Stanhope Hotel across from Central Park. Even at this distance, and through the trees, he could faintly hear the band warming up the crowd on the park's Great Lawn. Behind him, the suite had been turned upside down as PGT's rally headquarters, and Tory's people, over the drone of CNN, were loudly working the phones.

"Within a half hour," one was insisting, "because that's when Dr. Hunt's making an appearance."

Another coaxed, "Tell Representative Donohue that if he wants to be part of the photo op—"

Jack tried to tune out the voices, concentrate. So much depended on this rally. On him. Last night at the lab he'd waded through the A-1 reports until his eyes ached, but he hadn't found a single anomaly to prove his theory to Youssef and Mandy. Nothing to go on but a hunch. Was he completely wrong about A-1? Trying too furiously to second-guess Rachel? Could this really be her lethal agent after all?

Damn her to hell. If he couldn't penetrate her viral mystery, then Tory's campaign was the only hope. Beginning with this rally.

". . . estimate the crowd so far at four hundred thousand," CNN declared. Mike McIvar, the host of "Artemis Watch," was broadcasting live from the park. Ever since his original interview with Jack, his program had presented continuous coverage—experts' commentaries, roundtable discussions, interviews, bulletins—all somberly counting down to the deadline a little more than two weeks away.

Four hundred thousand? Jack thought with some amazement, looking down. It was true: the crowd was huge. People kept streaming in, many carrying placards and banners supplied by Tory's organizers. SAY YES TO SURVIVAL. GLOBAL VILLAGE NOT GLOBAL GHOST TOWN. Almost everyone wore white ribbons in honor of the dead, and most were wearing green clothing—also suggested by the organizers—to symbolize the threatened environment. On Fifth Avenue Jack saw a teenage girl dashing across to join the crowd. Her curly blond hair, bobbing as she ran, reminded him of Laurel. He wished he could have had a word with her before he'd left for Rachel's plane this morning, but she was asleep. He was worried about her. She'd surprised him by coming back to the lab last night after her dinner with Youssef, looking flushed and preoccupied, then disappearing down the hall as Jack had worked on alone. During the drive home she'd been strangely tense and quiet.

"Keep back from the barricade!" a police loudspeaker blared. The NYPD was out in force. Along Fifth Avenue phalanxes of officers stood beside cruisers, and dozens more on horseback were peppered through the crowd.

"No. No response from Jack," Tory snapped to Vince Delvecchio above the noise. "*You* handle the *Times*."

Jack turned from the window. *Damn it, why won't she let*

*me speak for myself?* The front page of the *New York Times* this morning had quoted Randall Quincy, the White House chief of staff, declaring PGT's campaign was dangerously misleading and irresponsible, and warning that Jack's pronouncements as spokesman bordered on criminal subversion. All morning Tory had been fielding media calls asking for Jack's response. Jack was itching to give it, but she hadn't let him. "I don't like it," he said to her now as Delvecchio went back to the phone. "Why shouldn't I talk to them?"

"We don't let them put you on the defensive," she said, watching a fax slither through. "It takes us off message."

"A rebuttal from me would *reinforce* the message."

"Oh? What is the message, Jack?" she said testily.

"That overpopulation is threatening the environment, but that by educating women we can reduce overpopulation."

"Wrong, the message is fear. Pure and simple. And our job is to intensify that fear. That's why you're launching the Daily Memorial. So stick to the speech and don't get all bothered about Quincy." She walked away reading the fax.

Her attitude was what bothered him. He knew better than anyone what the job here was: he had to convince an entire nation. The way to do that was by explaining, not fearmongering. He started after her, but Noah Shapiro reached her first.

"Tory, I've cut the eco-facts like you wanted," he said, holding up the speech he was revising for Jack, "but there's still a hole between the Marisa material and the memorial. How do you want the transition?"

"Marisa?" Jack jumped in, on guard at Shapiro bandying her name. "What are you talking about? The speech is about the environment, then the Daily Memorial."

"That was a preliminary draft," Tory said. "I changed it. This has more punch, the story of you losing Marisa."

Jack glared at her. Trading on Marisa's death—the thought sickened him. He'd deferred to Tory long enough. "Change it back. I won't talk about her."

She was busy writing a long note on the fax, ignoring him.

"Why cut all the important facts anyway?" he demanded.

"Because they're *not* important," she muttered.

She's really losing it, Jack thought. "How the hell can people understand the problem if we don't tell them?"

"Doesn't matter if they understand. It only matters that they act."

"To act they need to hear reasons."

"Not from you," she said, still scribbling.

"So I'm just the voice of doom?"

"For now, yes."

He grabbed the fax from her. "Listen, I know you're a hotshot media manipulator, but we need a hell of a lot more here than sound bites. I'm going to say what has to be said, and I'll say it in my own goddamn way."

She faced him. "This maverick bullshit won't play, Jack. Just do what I tell you."

"Won't play? This isn't some movie script!"

"That's all they *respond* to," she said, pointing to the park. "Can't you get that through your head?"

"Get this through yours. This isn't the movies, it's life and death. I saw the death!"

"Don't give *me* the song and dance about your dead wife!" she shouted. "Give it to the folks out there who—"

She stopped. Everyone was watching. Jack realized he'd been shouting too. Tory bit her lip. Shapiro's eyes flicked between them. A phone rang.

Tory walked briskly toward the bathroom. A staffer across the room called to her, holding the phone, "Jim Joyce at NBC."

"Take a message." She slammed the bathroom door behind her. The frenetic business in the suite resumed.

Jack sat heavily in an armchair and raked his hands through his hair, trying to collect himself. He had to address the crowd in twenty minutes.

"Cut her a little slack," Shapiro said quietly. "She had a rough night."

"Who didn't," Jack growled.

"No, I mean *rough*. The FBI raided our Washington office. And her husband led the raid."

The glass of water slipped from Tory's hand. She flinched as water spewed and glass shattered on the bathroom tiles. She blinked at the shards around her feet hemming her in, trapping her.

Get a grip, she told herself. It's just glass. It's not fucking radioactive.

She knelt to gather up the pieces with trembling hands. How was she going to pull this together? Damn Jack for being so stubborn. Damn the White House. *Damn Artemis.*

And damn Carson for making it unbearable, breaking them apart.

A knock. The door opened. "You okay?" Jack asked, frowning as he saw her on her knees.

"Dropped a glass." The waver in her voice startled her. She caught her reflection in the mirrored wall—even more unnerving: face white, eyes glistening with tears. People out in the suite were anxiously peering her way, and she cringed at having them see her so rattled. "Go," she told Jack, "and close the door."

He stepped inside, then closed it. Mortified under his scrutiny, Tory bent her head and continued collecting shards of glass.

He crouched in front of her. "What did Colwell do?"

"Cleaned out the office."

"Will he shut us down?"

"He can't. We're legal." Fiercely blocking tears, she was picking up even the smallest fragments, cupping them in her hand.

"Don't," Jack said. "You'll cut yourself."

"I broke it, I'll clean it up."

He grabbed her wrist. "Tory. Stop."

She realized, from the warmth of his hand, how icy hers was. She raised her face to his. In the short time she'd known Jack Hunt she'd become used to seeing that shadow of pain in his eyes: now, for the first time, she understood it in her bones. The same shadow had invaded her. It was loss. It was knowing something good was gone forever.

"Carson, wait," she'd said last night, pulling him aside as he and his agents were leaving her office with boxes of evidence. Despite everything, she couldn't hate him. Couldn't even blame him. He was doing what he thought he must to protect his country. Besides, she had to think of what was best for Chris—a boy who adored his father. "This crisis will end, one way or another," she said. "One day it will be over. When it is—if I'm still here, God willing—I want you to know I'm prepared to start again. We'll forget the terrible things we've said. Just wipe them out and try to—"

"Don't you understand?" he'd whispered fiercely. "I can't *trust* you anymore."

"Here," Jack said, dragging over the wastebasket.

She dropped the fragments in, then sat back on her heels, pretending to study her fingertips for grains of glass, but really just trying to hang on. "You think you love someone," she said, faltering. "And it's great, as long as everything's going okay. As long as the love isn't . . . tested. Then something like this happens—"

He said quietly, "Nothing like this ever *has* happened."

She looked at him, needing to speak, to make sense of the loss. "It strips you to your core, both of you. To basic beliefs. Primal allegiances. You find you didn't really know that person at all. Or yourself."

He nodded, and the shadow in his eyes seemed to darken in a silent communion of pain. She felt somehow grateful for his understanding.

"Carson once told me something," she said. "There are terrorist groups who initiate a recruit by ordering them right away to kill. It bloods them. After that, the group owns them forever." She added quietly, "When he brought you in and you stood firm, I thought: Good, Jack's been blooded, he can't turn back. Well, now I've been blooded too."

The CNN drone seeped under the door, along with the hectic voices working the phones. The familiar hustle jolted Tory back to the present. The world was waiting for Jack. She couldn't keep him any longer.

Looking into his troubled eyes, though, she wondered if he really was ready to go out and handle this. And what about the danger he stood in? She'd seen the gleam of vendetta in Carson's eyes; he was bent on catching Jack. Should she warn him? If she did, would it weaken his commitment to the campaign?

Leave it. I've seen him under pressure; he can handle himself with Carson. It's his leadership here that's at stake.

"Jack," she said, "I was way out of line, what I said out there. Forgive me. I know this is agony for you. But it is for everybody. Every one of those people in the park is terrified. You've got to accept that their fear is our raw material. You've got to tell it like it is. Women and girls died hideously, as Marisa did. *More* will die hideously unless the country rallies behind you. Forget the details about over-population and the environment. Let our experts give out that line. *Your* voice, your personal loss, is what people will respond to. Please, do the speech we've written. It's the surest way you can reinforce people's fears, get them to see that only PGT's plan can make them safe, and only—"

There was a knock. "If the pajama party can spare you two," Noah called through the door. "Senator Owen's up next. Then Jack."

Crossing Fifth Avenue with Tory, Jack gripped the speech in his jacket pocket. She was right. Marisa was the most profound image he could invoke. He still hated to do it—but at least, if it works, he thought, her suffering won't have been for nothing.

*Blooded,* he thought bitterly. Me and Tory both. By Rachel. More fuel to heap on his bonfire of hatred. Tory didn't know that the manipulating power behind the demands was her own mother, but she did know she was paying the price in her shattered marriage. Jack had felt her misery. But he'd also realized something new about her, something bracing. He felt for the first time—maybe because of her sacrifice—that she was an ally he could depend on. Tory would stay the course.

The street was a media bazaar. Network video trucks packed the curbs like hucksters' stalls. Roving reporters were hustling interviews. TV crews were perched on balconies and roofs, hawking direct to the world. Over the park's loudspeakers a movie star, speaking from the open stage, was exhorting the crowd to demand action from Congress. Helicopters—police or more media or both—thrummed overhead. Jack heard a faint shout at the park railing. He turned and saw a woman spraying red paint at a cop on horseback. As officers pulled her away to a cruiser, paint dripped off the cop's boot like blood.

Jack and Tory pushed on, skirting the crowd, which was so large that most people, forced to stand far from the stage, were watching giant TV screens instead. Applause erupted as the movie star finished, then introduced Senator Frank Owen, a well-known environmentalist, who began his address.

Tory led Jack to a cordoned-off alley between the rear of the stage and the VIP speakers' trailer, where they stopped to wait. As Senator Owen's voice blared over the sound system, Tory flipped open her cell phone to check in with Delvecchio at the hotel.

"A symbolic setting," the senator boomed. "This great park with its trees and lake and wildlife represents the biological richness of the earth. A richness we should be stewarding, not plundering—"

"How can you *do* this?" a man's voice rasped in Jack's ear.

He turned and found himself face-to-face with a dazed homeless person. Then the bloodshot eyes blinked. *Gerry!* Two weeks scraggly beard, greasy hair, stained T-shirt. Jack barely recognized him. But what a relief to see him. "Christ, Gerry, where have you been? I've been calling every—"

"How can you *do* this? After Marisa and Liz . . . how can you turn it into this fucking circus?"

Jack reached out. "Gerry—"

"Don't touch me, man." He swatted at Jack's arm. "Don't you fucking touch me."

Alarmed, Jack lifted his hands to show he was backing off. Gerry seemed at the breaking point.

Tory closed her phone with a frown. "Who's this?"

Gerry ignored her and stabbed an accusing finger in Jack's face. "You've turned into one of the fucking parasites. How can you even think of caving in to these animals? After what they did? We should be bombing the fuckers, nuking them! But you've turned into one of them."

Jack was stunned. *If only you knew, Gerry. I wish I could kill Rachel myself.*

". . . and act now!" the senator's voice boomed.

Gerry flinched. His red-rimmed eyes lost focus, and he let out a shuddering sigh. "Lord, Jack, I hate this bullshit." He turned and started to wander off.

". . . a hero for our troubled times!" the senator declared.

"Gerry, wait!" Jack started after him, but Tory gripped his elbow. "Jack, you've got to go on."

Go on? He watched Gerry weave aimlessly into the crowd.

". . . a man of uncompromised courage and vision. My friends, I give you Dr. Jack Hunt!"

Tory followed Jack up onstage, afraid this guy Gerry had unhinged him. She'd had to practically shake Jack just to get him to the steps. Now, as he slowly walked forward onstage, she anxiously tucked in behind the celebrity supporters ranged along the back. Jack reached the microphone stand, then stood rock still. Tory glimpsed Gerry in the crowd: a grubby misfit weaving among the people, not even looking at the stage. She knew Jack's eyes were locked on him. Jack didn't move. Watching him, waiting, Tory held her breath.

When she looked out again for Gerry, hoping he was finally gone, releasing Jack from this spell, she spotted a man following him through the crowd. Although he wore a sloppy workshirt and grimy baseball cap, she knew that purposeful stride. Unmistakably FBI. A warning flag popped up in her mind: *They're watching Jack, and watching everyone he talks to.*

Jack still seemed frozen. Tory felt the moments stretch on. All across the Great Lawn people had quieted. There was nervous coughing in the crowd. *The speech, Jack,* she agonized. *Pull out the speech!* But he just stood there, staring out.

She clenched her teeth in the awful silence, then made a quick decision. Abort. Move on to part two. She urgently gestured to the stage manager standing by the trailer. "Bring out the memorial. Now."

The trailer door slammed open, and after a moment's flurry of preparation two teenage girls dressed in white climbed the stage steps carrying poles that held aloft a poster-size photograph of a shyly smiling woman. *Now, Jack, please,* Tory thought, her eyes on him. *Let this snap you out of it.*

And if it doesn't? Then I'll have to present part two myself. Step forward, gently move Jack aside, and launch the Daily Memorial. Her heart pounded with nervousness. Stage fright and worse. Terrible solution. Impossible to take Jack's place. These people had come to see *him.* This rally depended on him. *But how else can I salvage this?*

The girls had walked forward, flanking Jack. The huge photo hovered over him. Come on, Jack, Tory willed him. *Come on.*

He stared up at the poster as though he didn't know what was happening. People in the crowd exchanged confused glances. Tory thought: *He's lost it. Doesn't remember what's happening. It's up to me.* She cleared her dry throat and was about to step forward.

"Lois Tyson," Jack said suddenly into the mike. His voice was low, intense. Tory held her breath.

"Lois was a third-grade teacher in Stoney Creek," Jack said. "Wife of trucker Pete Tyson, and mother of six-year-old Ryan and five-year-old Drew. Lois loved swimming and rafting. A month ago she won first prize in the bathtub derby, a fund-raiser for the county hospital."

Relief washed over Tory. He'd remembered.

Jack stared up at the photo while continuing to speak. "Thirteen days ago Lois prepared a breakfast of pancakes for her family. She saw her husband off on a truck run to California and got her boys onto the school bus. Then she went to work. At lunchtime another teacher brought her home sick. He thought it was flu. Lois began to bleed from her nose and her gums. By the time her boys came home from school, Lois couldn't see them because blood was seeping from her eyes. Then the hemorrhaging began. The same thing was happening to women and girls all over town. Before nightfall, Lois was dead. Her organs had disintegrated, and she'd drowned in her own blood."

The park was silent.

Jack looked out at the faces.

Tory waited for him to go on. He'd delivered basically what she and Noah had written. He was on track.

"I'm afraid," Jack said suddenly.

Tory stiffened. This was out of the blue.

Jack repeated the statement as a bold declaration: "I am afraid. I've seen with my own eyes what this disease does, and *I am afraid.*"

Tory gaped. What the hell is he doing?

"I know you're afraid, too," Jack went on. "You don't want it to happen to you, or to your daughters, your sisters, your mothers, your wives. We wouldn't be human if we weren't afraid. But what gives me hope is that we can also make choices. And the choices we make in the grip of fear are the truest test of our humanity. We can let fear cripple us, or we can let it be a powerful tool for change."

Tory looked in astonishment across the Great Lawn. At the thousands of eyes fixed on Jack. This wasn't the speech—it was better.

"Today we are facing a chance to remake the world," Jack went on, his voice vibrant in the still air. "A chance to overcome the lowest qualities of being human, our greed and rapaciousness. A chance to nurture the *best* quality of being human, our capacity to care. Let's *take* that chance. Together."

He turned. The stage manager was shepherding two little boys up the stage steps. *The finale we planned,* Tory thought, feeling off balance. *What'll Jack do?* The boys hung back shyly, staring at the crowd. Jack took them both by the hand and gently led them forward. He hoisted the smaller one up in his arm while still holding the older boy's hand by his side.

"This is Drew Tyson," Jack said, indicating the child he held. "And this is Ryan. These are Lois's sons."

Tory glimpsed a woman who was close to tears gasp and lay her hand on her heart, glimpsed a man chewing the end of his mustache to maintain a stoic face. Looking back at the motherless boys, Tory felt pierced by pity, too. And more—she saw Chris.

"Today, we honor Lois Tyson," Jack said, his voice ringing powerfully now. "In every day to come we will honor another of the Stoney Creek dead. They will not be forgotten. And we will not be silenced in our demand for change. Our voices will be heard. Remember this, and tell those who must be told: *If we pass through fear, we are made strong.*"

All over the Great Lawn people stood still, electrified.

Tory gazed at Jack, dazzled. He hadn't once glanced at her crafted text. He had taken her precepts and the desolation in his own heart and forged them into something more moving than she had ever imagined.

She remembered Carson's absurd suspicions, and thought: Jack would have to be the most brilliantly creative terrorist of all time. But the opposite was true. He was that rare thing, a very good man.

Suddenly, little Drew Tyson grabbed the white ribbon

pinned to Jack's breast pocket. It came away from the pin, and the boy plopped the ribbon on top of Jack's head—an impossibly silly miniature hat. Jack laughed and hugged him, and the child hugged him back.

A sound swelled through the crowd and erupted. A cheer!

Tory felt hot tears threaten. Jack had brought this stunning moment to life, but the design of it was all hers. She should feel triumph, but felt only a hollow ache. The Daily Memorial concept had come to her that night in Chris's room after Carson had forced her to look at the photographs. Confidential FBI photographs, which he'd quickly taken away. *He should never have let me see. We are going to win.*

Her tears spilled.

Jack could barely move in the crush. People had surged into the cordoned-off area and were reaching out to touch him, calling encouragement, jubilantly trying to stick their ribbons on him as the little boy had done. Tory's organizers pushed through to act as bodyguards, and police began forcing the people back behind the ropes. Jack was as overwhelmed by the response as he'd been by his own eloquence. Where had he summoned those words from? he thought in wonder. He felt a stirring thrill of hope at the result. If all these people would make their voices heard in Washington . . . damn it, this might work!

Tory caught up to him. She yelled to the police who were restraining the reporters, "No, let the press through!" then went up on her toes beside Jack to shout in his ear above the noise, "Over there! Press conference!" Pointing to a spot securely roped off, she guided him to it, and as they waited for the reporters to reach them, she unfastened her own ribbon and pinned it to his lapel to replace his lost one. Straightening the ribbon, she said warmly, "You were incredible." She was slightly breathless from the excitement, and Jack saw that she, too, felt the wild tug of hope. He also noticed the red rims of her eyes. Tears? Tory?

She caught him looking, and seemed to pull back. "But for a minute there," she said, "I was afraid we'd lost you. Who was that guy Gerry? Why did he spook you so badly?"

Same old Tory, Jack thought, doesn't miss a thing. Gerry *had* unnerved him; had shamed away every thought of delivering the part of the speech about Marisa. Yet, oddly, it had worked out for the best. "An old friend," he answered. "Gerry Trowbridge." A friend who's hurt, he thought, as concern flooded back. It wasn't just Gerry's fevered outburst; he'd noticed he was limping. "Tory, I think he needs help. He was with me in Jazida and got shot in the leg. There might be complications, maybe infection. Could you have somebody go after him? He should see a doctor."

"He was with you during the outbreak? Why?"

Jack realized that he'd told Colwell about it but not her. But he had no desire to go into it now. "He and his wife run a film production company. Or . . . ran. They were taping me in Jazida for a documentary when it happened."

Tory stared at him. "This man has video? Of women dying?"

Jack frowned, uncomfortable. "I suppose."

"Video of Marisa?"

"Jesus, is this necessary?"

"Jack, *does he have video?*"

"Yes. No. I don't know." He remembered how Liz had compulsively kept the camera rolling through it all. "He took off when Liz died. God knows if he took the camera with him."

"I can't believe you didn't tell me this."

He said tightly, "I've had a few things on my mind."

"We've got to get that tape."

"Why?"

"Because the public hasn't *seen* this disease. Nobody was allowed into Stoney Creek until the bodies were taken away. All we have is 'before' pictures, so we're stuck with talking about abstracts, statistics. My God, video of real women dying? It could make all the difference to—" She stopped as a new thought struck. "Shit, the FBI. They'll want it too."

"FBI? I don't follow."

"After Gerry talked to you I saw a federal agent trail him. Once they reach him and find out about the video, they'll want it. For evidence, of course, but they'd also be very glad to keep footage like that out of our hands. We've got to get hold of it before they confiscate it."

She grabbed a couple of her assistants helping with crowd control, gave them a description of Gerry, and sent them to search the area. "Where does he live?" she asked Jack.

"SoHo." He gave her the address and phone number. He didn't much like it, but he knew now to trust Tory's instincts. Besides, this way Gerry would get to a doctor.

Tory called Delvecchio in the hotel suite and told him to track down Gerry. "Take charge of this yourself, Vince. Trowbridge may have professional video of women dying in Jazida. The feds will be after it too."

Reporters had pushed through and were moving closer, shouting questions. Closing her phone, Tory said, "Jack, there's something I have to warn you about. Carson's convinced himself you're connected with Artemis. Crazy, I know, but he's—"

"That's my problem. You just concentrate on keeping this campaign in high gear." He said it with more nonchalance than he felt. He couldn't have her probing too near. This family web—Tory, Colwell, Rachel—could trap them all yet.

"Okay. Just be careful."

The reporters were moving in. Tory said, "Talk to these

guys, Jack." Stepping back to give him the limelight, she added with a smile, "Say whatever you think is best."

Her phone rang and she answered it. "Yes? . . . No, he can't, Laurel, he's in the middle of . . . pardon?"

"What is it?" Jack asked.

"She sounds pretty upset." To Laurel she said, "Look, he'll get back to you as soon as—"

He took the phone. "Laurel?"

"Jack! Oh, God, I'm sick. I'm so sick!" She was sobbing, hyperventilating, close to hysteria.

"Calm down, sweetheart. Tell me what's wrong."

"It's the thing! The plague!"

"What?"

Reporters surrounded him, yelling questions.

"Dr. Hunt, do you think PGT riding this wave of support can change the government's position?"

"Dr. Hunt, did you contribute to Dr. Lesage's break-through on growing the virus?"

"Laurel, speak up, I can't hear with—"

"I wanted to *help* you," she wailed. "*They* wouldn't. You told them it was harmless, but they didn't believe you. So I went to the level four lab last night and I . . . I injected some . . . the virus . . . A-1."

The words registered, but his mind balked at understanding. Reporters pressed in, shouting, focusing cameras. He turned his back on them and said to Laurel blankly, "You did what?"

"I wanted to help! To show everybody. You needed to test it, you said. To be sure. So I tested it, but now—"

Panic exploded in his brain. "Jesus Christ!"

"You were *wrong*," she wailed. "It's *in* me! I can feel it. It's going to kill me! Oh, God, Jack, please, *please* come—"

"Who's at the house with you?"

"I'm all alone! Jack, I'm so scared!"

"Calm down. Stay where you are. I'll get help."

He barged through the startled reporters and ran to the trailer. A half-dozen people were inside, cleaning up. "Out!" he shouted.

He slammed the trailer door after them and rammed home the bolt. He dropped the phone, his hands clammy. He stared at it lying on the dirty shag carpeting. Help? Who did he think he was going to call? He stepped over the phone, legs unsteady, and walked down the aisle, going nowhere. *It's happening again.*

*Got to go to her.* He lunged back to the door, but his hand froze on the bolt. Go? It would take over an hour through traffic to reach Rachel's plane. Another hour for the flight. Then the drive to Swallow Point. And when I get there, what can I do for her? I have no cure. Nobody does.

Unless . . .

He scrambled for the phone on the floor, and punched the number and the extension.

"Rachel Lesage," she answered.

He felt his own hot breaths bounce back from the phone.

"Hello?" she said impatiently.

"Rachel, it's me." In forcing control he sounded like an automaton. "Laurel has done something stupid. She's tested A-1 on herself."

There was a pause. "What?"

"She injected it. Last night. An experiment. She just called. She's developed some symptoms, but I—" He heard the panic break through in his voice. "Rachel, you must have *some* idea of a treatment because—" He'd almost blurted, *Because you created it.* The FBI could be listening. "Don't you?" He was pleading, desperate.

Silence from her.

If she'd been standing here he would have killed her with his bare hands.

"Get a doctor to her," he implored. "Tell them to try IV replenishment of electrolytes—it might give her immune system a chance to fight back. Or human interferon. Massive doses, three million units to—" He knew that was useless. "Rachel, I'm begging you. If you can think of any kind of treatment, *anything,* please—"

"I'll handle this. Stay there. Don't do anything." She hung up.

His mouth was dry as dust. Reporters were knocking at the door.

## 14

JACK HARDLY DARED BELIEVE THE EVIDENCE before him. He was sitting on the edge of Laurel's bed, pained at seeing her misery as she groggily woke up, yet unable to stop the exultation coursing through him. *She's alive . . . no symptoms . . . only flu. A-1's harmless. God damn it, I was right!*

Minutes ago he'd been in despair. Crashing up the staircase, he'd burst into her room, and for one heart-stopping moment, seeing her so still, he'd thought she was dead. *I've killed her,* he thought. But Rachel, standing grim watch, told him she'd come from the lab after his call and found Laurel hysterical, so she'd given her a sedative: she was just asleep. A fitful sleep, drugged and feverish, which she was struggling out of now. But alive.

Rachel. She stood rigid beside him, furious. For one sweet vengeful moment Jack savored the victory. *I'm onto you, Rachel. I know.* Then his euphoria evaporated. Her A-1 secret was out, and that changed everything. Caution pricked him. I can't let her fear I'm gaining on her. It might push her over the edge.

Her rage was almost palpable. "Why did you *do* such a stupid thing?" she demanded the moment Laurel opened her eyes.

"Wha . . . ?" Laurel said weakly.

"Nothing, sweetheart," Jack said. "Don't try to talk." Her wretchedness cut him, her red eyelids fluttering as she struggled to focus.

Rachel was merciless. "What made you take such an insane risk?"

Jack couldn't help himself. "Shut up. Can't you see how sick she is?"

He suddenly realized his anguish might actually *work* for him, if it made Rachel think he was shocked to find A-1 harmless.

Her eyes flashed suspicion. She held his gaze for a moment—assessing the danger?—then abruptly turned away.

Laurel had caught his anxious tone. "Jack?" she whispered, terrified. "Am I going to die?"

He couldn't maintain the charade. It was barbaric to let her suffer such fear. "No, you're fine, sweetheart, fine." He squeezed her hand. "Just a low-grade fever. Nothing to worry about." He stroked her damp hair back from her forehead. Her recovery spoke for itself; she alone couldn't believe it. "You were right," he reassured her. "It's only flu."

She sighed in weary relief, then gave him a wobbly smile. "No, *you* were right."

He cursed himself for his lapse. *God, Laurel, don't say any more.* "Shhh, you need to rest. We'll talk later."

Rachel had already turned back. "Right? What do you mean?"

"Let's go," Jack said. "She needs sleep." He grasped

Rachel's elbow to move her out. "And we need to get back to work."

"Oh? Why's that, Jack?" she said, an icy challenge. Again she demanded of Laurel, "Tell me why you *did* this."

Laurel sighed. "For Jack. Okay?"

"Jack? I don't understand."

"Somehow he knew the A-1 virus doesn't cause the Artemis disease. I don't know how he figured it out, but I do know he's brilliant. He said that it—"

"That's enough," Jack cut in. "I don't want you tiring yourself. Rachel and I are leaving now, so—"

"No, I want to hear this. Go on, Laurel."

"Well, last night he tried to tell his assistants it was harmless, but they just said he was nuts. They made me so mad. I wanted to show them he was right. Show everybody. So I did it."

Rachel turned soberly to Jack. "I see."

Despite himself, he felt an exultant rush of satisfaction and reveled in it. *Yes, I've found your weak link, and I'm going to stop you.*

Her concentration was back on Laurel. She was looking at her in wonder. "You trust him so completely?"

"Of course," Laurel said simply. "He's the best." She fidgeted with the blanket, and her expression turned sheepish. "But I see now it was a real dumb thing to do. I mean, everybody else was sure it was the Artemis virus." She suddenly looked up at Rachel with a quizzical expression. "Except you. You knew it wasn't, didn't you? When you found me here. I mean, even *you* couldn't have been that calm if you'd thought I was infected with the plague."

Rachel's eyes flicked to Jack, and he saw she was stuck. *So now I have to save your ass,* he thought grimly. "Laurel," he said, improvising, "Rachel and I are working together on something . . . unusual. It's pretty controversial, what we're trying, so the research has to be kept a secret."

"That's right," Rachel agreed. "A secret." Her eyes met Jack's, and he'd never felt more acutely aware of their bizarre alliance-antagonism. They were bound together, each having to protect the other against anyone else probing the truth, though they remained locked in a life and death struggle.

"So you mustn't tell anyone what you've discovered," Rachel pressed Laurel. "Will you promise us that? It's very important."

Laurel shrugged weakly. "I don't plan to broadcast my idiot move." Her quizzical look at Rachel returned, only more penetrating. "You mean you're not even going to tell the other scientists that they're on the wrong track? Isn't that a little weird?"

Jack had to stop this. "Laurel, leave the thinking to the experts, okay?"

Her confidence crumbled. "Sure. Hey, what do I know?"

Jack felt like a shit for shaming her.

The door creaked open. "Orel?" Chris peeked in, wide-eyed. "Are you throwing up?" He came to the bedside, cradling his stuffed rabbit. "Bunny's throwing up, too."

Laurel offered a trembling smile. "Sorry to hear that, kiddo."

The boy tenderly settled the rabbit beside the pillow, then leaned over to listen to its heart. Watching him, Laurel was suddenly in tears. "Oh, Jack, I've never been so scared. I thought I was going to die. And I was so alone—I thought you wouldn't come." Jack sat again on the bed to comfort her, and she threw her arms around his neck and sobbed on his shoulder. He held her, watching Rachel slowly walk away. "Shhh," he murmured. "I'm not leaving."

*     *     *

Rachel stood at the end of the upstairs hall where the window overlooked the kitchen garden. She stared down at the tall red hollyhocks trained against the wire fence, and tried to regain her inner balance. *Jack knows.* Even before finding that Laurel was all right, he knew. How? Simple deduction because I'd approved research on A-1? If so, that's not so dangerous—it won't take him anywhere.

But what if he's already discovered more? If so, how much more?

*How much closer is he?*

It was hard to think, hard to focus on all that after what she'd just seen. The depth of Laurel's love for him, to do such a reckless thing. The strength of his feeling for her, this spoiled, self-centered girl. How unpredictable, how unfathomable, the wellsprings of love can be, she thought in wonder.

Her eyes fell on the cushioned window seat, Liam's favorite spot. He was recovering at the vet's. Images tumbled in her mind: Liam's mangled leg, the trap in the woods, its iron jaws tearing flesh, *Paul.*

She stared at the hollyhocks crucified against the wire, the blossoms crimson as wounds.

She stumbles to the side of the road as a jeep grinds past spitting gravel at her ankles. Corpses lie in the ditch, swollen by the African sun. Across the road a priest, his cassock ghostly with dust, is sitting on a rock, rubbing his foot. Rachel goes to him, spilling words she has repeated so often she is hoarse. That she is searching for her son, that two weeks ago he fled with other children from the soldiers' machetes, fled into a field and disappeared. Has the priest seen a group of lost children? Hollow-eyed, the priest answers, "Many." Rachel dies again. She has seen them too. Orphans, everywhere, wandering the countryside. But not Paul.

She walks on, glad of the pain from bleeding blisters to keep her brain's primitive core fixated, keep thinking at bay. Crops are rotting in the fields. She comes to a silent village, its huts abandoned. The only movement is wind rustling the eucalyptus leaves, their fresh scent smothered by a lingering reek of death. She spends the night in a dark hut, light-headed with hunger, numb with exhaustion. She forces herself to remember his tough young body, his quick young mind: he could be scavenging, surviving on his wits. But she knows he has no such skills. He has only her.

Next day she reaches the main road where a teacher on a motorbike gives her a lift and shares his stale cheese sandwiches. She wolfs the food, ignoring its lumpen glut in her shrunk stomach; she wants only fuel to go on. Refugees clog the road—human lines miles long. They carry clothes in plastic garbage bags, carry mattresses on their heads. The teacher tells her a quarter of a million have streamed into Tanzania in the last twenty-four hours. When they reach the Kagara River the teacher continues on, but Rachel stays to search. Bodies float downstream. A dead baby bobs in an eddy, light as a cork.

At sundown she stops at a camp in a field crowded with refugees. She sees two boys fight over a bowl of food. One bashes the other on the head with a rock and takes the bowl. During the night, dry coughs of pneumonia and TB echo through the camp. The crying of children never stops. Exhaustion drags her into sleep. She hears Paul's giggle and wakes with a jolt of joy. It's just an old woman childishly babbling in delirium.

At first light she walks on. A Dutch missionary on a rusty bicycle tells her, Yes, he did hear of a group of children. Hiding in a village church about four miles east. "There was talk—yes, I remember thinking, how odd—that one of them is an American boy."

Joy . . . it makes her walk so fast that her body leans, ahead of her feet. Only four miles. An hour and I'll be with him. She almost wishes she believed in a god, just to be able to thank him.

*Four miles. It's nothing.*

FBI agent Rick Barsano felt sweat prickle his back the moment he stepped out of the air-conditioned car. Though trees shaded the paved driveway, the Long Island air felt as thick as pudding. A rotating lawn sprinkler was showering a corner of the east-wing parking area beside the pool, and Barsano could see the asphalt steam. Even Gold Coast stockbrokers don't have enough pull to fix the weather, he thought.

A maid—Hispanic features, crisp uniform—answered the front door to him and his partner. "Special Agents Barsano and Jamail, FBI," he said as they showed their credentials. "Mrs. Cabot is expecting us."

"Yes, this way, please. Mrs. Cabot is in the conservatory."

People still had those? Barsano, under orders, had been checking every cranny of Jack Hunt's past, from the scrubby West Virginia trailer park he'd grown up in to his med school beer hangouts. This was the first *conservatory.*

Vivian Cabot was standing alone in the skylit room. Reaching across a small round supper table—one of seven set with silver and crystal and overarched by glossy ficus trees—she was setting a name card into a mother-of-pearl holder. She wore a green silk blouse and linen skirt. Pure Gold Coast, Barsano thought. Cookie-cutter rich bitch.

"Agent Barsano, right on time," she said, idly casting a final glance over her table setting. The orchid centerpiece trembled in the air-conditioned current, but not a hair on her blond head moved. She dusted nonexistent dust particles from her fingertips. "Is punctuality an FBI virtue?"

Barsano was surprised to find that he instantly liked her voice. It had a real Southern-lady quality. "One of many, ma'am," he answered.

She smiled faintly. Her skin was so Barbie-doll smooth from a face lift, it didn't even pucker. For a woman of fifty-four she was as attractive as money and effort could make her, Barsano figured, but she could never have been a beauty.

"First, let me verify some facts, ma'am," he said. His partner already had out his pad and pencil. "You are the former Mrs. Jack Hunt, correct?"

"I am."

"When was the last time you saw him? Can you recall?"

"Oh, yes." Mrs. Cabot held up a silver knife and examined it intently for spots. The gentle timbre of her voice hardened. "I recall a great deal about the famous Dr. Hunt."

# 15

"CAN WE TALK ABOUT THESE, DOCTOR?" COLWELL held up a clear plastic bag containing the chained red and purple vials.

"Sure, but let's keep it brief, okay?" Jack said. "I'm in the middle of a PCR analysis." He'd answered as coolly as he could, but alarms were going off in his head. *Why is he here?* Paged from his office to Rachel's boardroom, he'd found Colwell waiting. Why? Had he found something? *Has he come for Rachel?*

Take it easy, he told himself, squelching the panic. If he was onto her, would he be bothering with me?

"Shouldn't take long," Colwell said evenly. Jack saw barely disguised suspicion in his eyes. Colwell indicated the vials. "Any idea where Artemis had these filled?"

"No."

"Guess."

"Unscientific, guessing."

It struck him, though, that that's exactly what he'd been reduced to with A-1. Even sweating here in front of Colwell, he felt the unyielding circular enigma drag at his mind: Rachel had bioengineered A-1, but A-1 was virtually harmless, so why had she bothered to create it? He'd reexamined the data on every other element in the vial soup, but nothing there was deadly. So what was? Four days since Laurel's "experiment," yet he was still utterly without answers.

He had to find them before Colwell found Rachel.

"I'd like to ask you about the fluid," Colwell said. "As a scientist."

Jack's dread rushed back. Had Colwell learned about Laurel? That A-1 was only flu? *Stay out of this,* he wanted to warn him. *You don't know what you're fooling with.*

"I'm referring to the binding material that the lethal virus, the A-1, was found in," Colwell went on. "The original CDC analysis lists it as 'nutrient broth.' I understand laboratories use it to grow virus. Is that right?"

"It's called media," Jack said, relaxing a little. Clearly, Colwell still believed A-1 was the agent, as Rachel had publicly announced. He added, still on his guard, "It's used by labs everywhere." Why this line of questioning?

"What's in it?" Colwell asked.

"Vitamins, minerals, animal serum. It's available commercially."

"In these it was calf serum."

"Pretty standard."

"We're checking all purchases made throughout the country in the last year."

Could you trace a batch here? Jack wondered in alarm. Or to another of Rachel's labs? Have you *already* traced it? He said cautiously, "A lot of media is sold."

Colwell regarded him coldly. "Dr. Hunt, why can't I shake the feeling there's something you're hiding?"

Jack finally realized why Colwell was here. The visit was a test. *To pressure me.* To do what? Incriminate myself? Reveal my link with Artemis? He thinks I'm fronting for some terrorist organization, but the truth is something he can't even imagine. Yet. "Look," he answered, "you and I both know we have different goals. I want this crisis resolved by accommodation. That's PGT's position, and mine."

He hadn't mentioned Tory. Didn't have to. She was a presence between them. Something in Colwell's eyes flared, a struggle between the cool professional and the embittered husband. But only for a moment. "Have a seat, Doctor," he said. "I've asked Dr. Lesage to join us."

Sweat slicked Jack's palms. *Has he come for her after all?*

Walking in, Rachel saw them turn to her. She stopped cold. Tension seemed to pulse from both men—dread from Jack, a sharp alertness from her son-in-law. Her own dread surged. *What's Jack told him?*

She caught Jack's eye, and he gave an almost imperceptible shake of his head, as if to reassure her. "Colwell doesn't know." Or did it mean the opposite? A shiver of triumph he couldn't suppress? *Is he here to crow as the FBI takes me away?*

She made her voice cut through her fear. "How can we help you, Carson?"

He held up the vials, and Rachel's heart banged in her chest. *Jack's cracked the puzzle and told him everything.*

Carson dismissively tossed the vials on the table. "With a fresh perspective, I hope."

He'd answered brusquely, squaring his shoulders for business, and Rachel, forcing a brake on her racing heart, took it as his signal that the personal rift between them would be ignored for this higher priority. *Business,* she thought, her breathing coming under control again. The handcuffs would have been on by now if his business was me. Why come at all, then? Why bring in Jack? Jack seemed to be watching with the same confusion she felt. *He doesn't know why Carson's here either,* she realized.

"As an investigator," Carson said to them both, "I look at evidence as a trail. I look backward and ask how does this link back to the perpetrators? I'm hoping you and Dr. Hunt—as scientists—might help me see it from the opposite angle, looking forward. How might Artemis's scientists have done what they did, resulting in this evidence?"

Rachel searched his face for deception but found his somber expression unreadable. As for Jack, he seemed to be warily standing down in relief, taking Carson's statement at face value. *Just business,* Rachel thought again cautiously.

In any case, Carson's tone of authority was unmistakable. *Cooperate, both of you,* it said; *I'm still the law.*

*And I'm supposed to be the good corporate citizen,* Rachel reminded herself. *So play the part.* She took her seat at the head of the conference table, but as she looked up at both men standing watching her, she couldn't block a furious resentment. They were both hunting her—Carson armed with evidence, Jack laying siege in the lab. *Well, I'll keep you both at bay.*

She picked up a bronze paperweight, turning it in her hands. "And what is your evidence?" she asked.

"I'm going to brief you on it," Carson said. "Please, listen carefully—both of you—because any insights you have might be helpful."

He ran through everything the FBI had discovered. That a Pisces Cosmetics Group of Baton Rouge had placed a phone order four months ago for the services of Advantage Direct Mail Merchants in Houston. That the shipment of perfume vials had arrived at Advantage's warehouse by van. That the FBI found no Pisces Cosmetics Group existed, but a shipping clerk at the Advantage warehouse remembered the van because of a gash on the door—a silver Ford Windstar. Rachel listened, appalled. Every detail, every step she'd so laboriously planned to conceal her tracks . . . uncovered.

"We found the van at a rental lot in Miami," Carson was saying. "Bogus ID from the driver, and he paid the rental company cash. We're looking for him, and when we have him we'll learn where he picked up the shipment."

He was watching Jack for a reaction. Jack stonily returned the look. It finally struck Rachel that this was Carson's reason for coming. He's trying to entrap *Jack.*

*No,* she thought. *You can't arrest him. He's got to lead the campaign.*

"We also traced the post office money order that 'Pisces' sent to pay Advantage," Carson went on. "Drawn at an outlet in South Carolina. From the transaction record we lifted a latent print."

Rachel felt a shiver, and set down the paperweight. But there were so many other things here she must have touched recently. A spiral-bound serology report. A stapler. A silver pen. The phone. Her fingerprints were everywhere. She saw by Jack's drawn look that he was thinking the same thing.

"Also, the vials themselves tell us a lot," Carson was saying, "starting with the plastic. Our lab did a differential thermal analysis of the polymer and got a compositional match, and plastics manufacturers tell us this is a new extrusion process, used only since ninety-six, so we should soon locate the manufacturer. The perfume could be an even faster trace. The molecular breakdown shows it contains a compound called oxyphenolon, relatively unusual, so that's narrowed the universe of fragrance manufacturers. Does oxyphenolon have any significance to you?"

Rachel felt unnerved by the mass of evidence and fought to steady her voice. "It's not a compound I'm familiar with."

Carson looked at Jack.

"No."

Carson watched him for a moment. Then, indicating the vials, he said, "Finally, there's the connecting chain. We're analyzing it for characteristics to determine its origin."

"Is that likely?" Rachel asked, pretending disinterest, impatience. "That type of thing must be very common."

"Every metal manufacturing process leaves a mark on the workpiece that's unique to that piece of equipment. In the past we've been able to trace nails, tacks, even paper clips back to the equipment that made them. So, yes, we're hopeful. Also, electron microscopy revealed some microscopic debris on the chain—a paint fleck and some grains of nonindigenous soil. Almost as good as fingerprints."

Rachel struggled to contain her alarm. The question was no longer whether the trail would lead the FBI to her, only how soon.

Carson then gave a rundown of pertinent interviews along the investigation route—comments from plastics manufacturers, perfume producers, direct mail managers—giving locations and dates. Then he said abruptly, "That's about it. Does any of this suggest to either of you how, or where, the Artemis scientists might have operated?"

"No," Jack said, too quickly.

Carson looked at Rachel.

"I can't say that it does."

"Could you explain something to me?" Carson asked. "At the direct mail warehouse, and presumably at other points along the manufacture and delivery route, the personnel is at least half female. There's always some pilfering in these places, plus damage to a certain percentage of post office freight—parcels ruptured and so on. Yet not one woman who handled these virus packages became infected until they were delivered to Stoney Creek. Can you explain that?"

Rachel couldn't suppress a glance at Jack. *He* knew A-1

was harmless. She believed he wouldn't reveal that, for his own purposes, yet she felt little relief, since his purpose was to thwart her himself. And she was at a loss about how to answer Carson. Desperately casting about for some reasonable reply, she heard Jack say, "There might be some resistance factor. Something caused by a particular environment within the delivery routes. Or, conversely, a susceptibility factor among the affected populations."

She thought, amazed, *He's covering for me.* She felt a wild rush of gratitude.

Carson asked him skeptically. "Is that really possible?"

"Not *im*possible," Jack said. Rachel saw that he couldn't maintain the reckless extemporization. "But also not likely," he finally admitted.

Carson regarded him for a moment with barely hidden mistrust. He turned to Rachel. "Something else is bothering me. People in the scientific community are constantly collaborating, sharing information, aren't they? Across the country, even internationally."

"Certainly."

"Yet despite all our interviews with scientists—and I'm talking about thousands of interviews here and abroad—not one of them has given us a single lead to Artemis. I don't get it. I mean, this A-1 that Artemis's scientists created, it would have taken a lot of experimenting to test it, wouldn't it? While they were refining it?"

She was toying with the paperweight to still her trembling hands. His strategy was so obvious now, putting these questions to her and then watching Jack's reactions.

Carson, waiting, prodded, "Rachel?"

"It's reasonable to assume so," she said carefully. "All bioengineered products are tested at various stages."

"Where? I mean, say in a place like your lab here. Lesage Laboratories develops drugs and gene-therapy treatments that use some pretty exotic bioengineering processes, right? Who exactly does that testing here?"

A warning hissed in her head: *It's not a trap, so don't make it one. It's business.* She turned to him. "Here? Well, our vector core laboratory develops the viral systems for a proposed treatment, and they're tested first in our morphology lab. Technicians assess certain factors, such as whether transplanted genes are performing as predicted, and then the animal model core lab tests the safety of the products in pre-clinical stages. Finally, our human applications lab proceeds with clinical trials."

"So these treatments, these products as you call them, they're handled or seen by a lot of people."

"Hundreds."

"That's what I mean. How could Artemis's scientists keep what they were doing secret? Scientists are people, and people talk. With hundreds of people involved, how could there be no leaks?"

She shot a glance at Jack, but knew he couldn't rescue her this time. A cold certainty settled over her. Only one place to hide. In plain sight.

"You're right about the numbers of people involved," she answered. "Every biomedical research project employs large teams, whether in government institutes or private industry. In fact, teams are often multinational. One searching now for a certain breast cancer gene includes over four hundred scientists on three continents. So, the very size of projects leads to compartmentalizing. People work on small pieces of a project at the request of their supervisors, without necessarily knowing what their piece will be used for. Often the biochemists down one corridor won't know what the molecular biologists down another are doing. It happens in every large-scale biomedical endeavor, in every country involved in the industry."

Carson seemed struck by this. "Like Obolensk," he said. "You actually caught the Russians in the act, didn't you?"

Rachel felt her muscles tense. She quickly recovered. "Obolensk is a good example," she replied. "Only a few individuals at the top knew the scope of that operation."

Carson said in mild wonder, "So, conceivably, an army of scientific workers could have been developing A-1 without knowing what it was. Maybe without even knowing about Artemis."

"Conceivably."

"Then Artemis could be just a handful of people?"

"It's possible."

"Even, in theory, just one?"

"Yes."

Carson, clearly gripped by the idea, turned a penetrating look on Jack. "Doctor? Your thoughts?"

Released from the "briefing," Jack strode into the hall. He was breathing hard, as if he'd been trapped underwater and had finally broken the surface—the most tortuous twenty minutes he'd ever been through. If Colwell had hoped to see him crack under pressure, he thought ruefully, he'd almost succeeded, though for reasons Colwell couldn't even fathom. He'd pushed Rachel so close to the edge, without even knowing. So close to disaster.

Despite the awful tension, though, something in Jack had caught fire as he'd watched Rachel sweat. He'd seen her faint panic at Colwell's astute questions, and he had a feeling she'd been cornered into revealing more than she could control. Something buried in her answer about Russia. What had all that been about? What was the connection?

Jesus, did it matter? Was it getting him anywhere, this clutching at straws? Restless, furious, he tramped up the stairs to his office. Feelings, hunches, dead ends—he had *nothing.* Colwell was breathing down his neck, the Central Park rally hadn't brought even a tremor to the White House barricades, the lab team was hypnotized at the mirage of A-1, and his own thinking kept twisting in circles, in knots, the conundrum incessantly nagging: *She created A-1, but A-1's harmless, so why take the trouble to create it?*

He was coming now to a grim decision. He simply couldn't get any further here on his own. He needed his assistants' help, whatever the risk. By the time he reached his office, he was resolved.

Time to rope them in.

In the outer office he found Youssef lounging, feet on his desk, repairing a dart feather. Mandy was setting out her brown-bag lunch beside her computer, lining up plastic containers in a neat row. Watching them, Jack told himself he'd have to manipulate this recruitment carefully. He had to convince them, but without giving any hint of the depth of what he knew. These were very bright kids, but ambitious, too. His plan was simple: a stick, then a carrot.

But first, the proof.

He sat on the edge of Youssef's desk. "Have a nice dinner with Laurel the other night?"

Youssef shrugged. "Yeah, real nice girl." He pulled a box of M&M's from his shirt pocket and shook candy into his palm.

"Told her all about your adventures in level four labs?"

Youssef shot him a butt-out look. "Maybe. Why?"

"Because," Jack said smoothly, "she took your tips and got hold of some A-1 and injected herself."

Youssef's jaw dropped. "What?"

Mandy turned, equally dumbfounded.

"She figured my theory was right," Jack went on, "so she made herself an experimental subject. And you know what?

She only developed flu. Coming around now, though. Just a few sniffles."

They both gaped at him.

Youssef tilted back on his chair's rear legs and whispered, "Holy shit."

Mandy said, appalled, "How could you test it on your own granddaughter? That's sick."

"You heard him," Youssef said. "She wanted to prove he was right. *That's* sick."

It was too much for Jack. He whacked Youssef's feet, knocking them off the desk. The tilted chair slid under him. He tumbled with a yelp and sprawled on the floor, M&M's scattering.

Jack stood over him. "You little shits. People are trying to find a way to save lives, and you two just sit here like slugs. How dare you suggest I'd experiment on Laurel! She may have done a stupid thing, but at least she was trying to help. What the hell good are you two?"

They stared at him, mouths open.

Jack told himself to cool it. He couldn't let anger get the better of him. "We have a responsibility here," he said, "and it's about time you arrogant little geniuses realized it. Laurel understood that, God bless her. However misguided her actions, she's proved my theory right."

Youssef got to his feet, shaken, and Jack demanded like a drill sergeant in his face, *"Hasn't she?"*

"Yeah," he said unsteadily. "Guess she has."

Jack turned on Mandy. "How about you? Any more A-1 doubts I can help you with?"

She swallowed. "None."

Jack decided the stick had done its job. He could put it away. "All right," he said, "let's move on. The first thing we're going to get clear is that discussion about our work does not go beyond this room."

"I don't understand," Mandy said. "This is a crucial breakthrough. We've got to tell Dr. Lesage."

"We won't be telling anyone."

"Why not?" Youssef asked.

"I have my reasons." At all costs he had to keep Rachel from following his efforts. She would certainly try to subvert him, maybe even feel panicked into doing something rash, but he had to keep his fears hidden from these two.

Mandy said, looking uncomfortable, "Listen, Dr. Hunt, I admit I'm impressed that you deduced this before Laurel proved it, but we can't just sit on these results."

"She's right," Youssef said. "This isn't like fudging research numbers on warts. This is world plague time."

"What do you plan to announce?" Jack challenged. "That we conducted an unethical and unapproved experiment, the results of which are completely without documentation or data?"

"Hey, the experiment wasn't *mine*," Youssef protested.

"No, you just gave an unauthorized person the necessary information to enter the level four lab and gain access to the virus. How do you think that'll go down with lab supervisors when you're looking for a job?"

Youssef slumped into his chair.

Mandy was biting her fingernail. "This is *weird*," she muttered.

They were softened up, Jack saw, but still unsure. They needed more. A prod. He quickly thought of one: create an enemy. "There's another reason for keeping quiet," he said. "There might be an Artemis infiltrator here."

They stared at him.

"Think about it," he said. "If you were Artemis, wouldn't you want an operative inside observing the efforts to thwart your work?"

"But Dr. Lesage handpicked this team," Mandy said.

"And they all brought extensive support staff, like you two. An army of postdocs and grad students and technicians. Can you vouch for them all? Can every one of them be immune to bribery from Artemis? If there *is* a spy, the last thing we want is for them to know what we've discovered."

He let this scenario sink in for a moment. "Look, we'll still have access to technicians' help as long as we're careful not to divulge the basis of our research. We can proceed on our own, quietly." He saw they were considering this. Now, he thought, the carrot. "Also, I promise you that anything we discover, I'll give the two of you all the credit. You'll be the first authors listed when we publish."

They exchanged wide-eyed glances. "Sure would be cool to be the ones to crack it," Youssef said.

"And we do have knowledge no one else has," Mandy added. "We have an edge."

Jack almost smiled. They were hooked.

"Let's get started," he said.

They sat down to devise protocols for attacking the research. Mandy and Youssef got excited when Jack pointed out irregularities he'd found last night in the serology group's reports. After a few hours of brainstorming he offered to fetch coffee from the cafeteria, and left them hotly discussing the electron micrographs.

He was making his way down the glassed walkway connecting the two wings when he was stopped by a bottleneck of people. They'd left offices and labs and were gazing outside, the walkway buzzing with nervous chatter. Jack looked out. Beyond the front lawn about a hundred people had converged on the street. Protesters. Lesage security guards and local police were patrolling, though the crowd looked peaceful. Many of the demonstrators were carrying signs. One read: PGT = PAGANS FOR A GODLESS TOMORROW. Another: TER-

RORIST SYMPATHIZERS WORSHIP TREES, SACRIFICE PEOPLE. Another: HUNT + ARTEMIS = DOOM FOR HUMANITY.

A low bang startled everyone. A car backfiring. An old black Chevy slowly drove by, moving like a hungry shark. Effective, Jack thought; the protestors, though kept off the property, were ominously making their presence felt.

He noticed Rachel's public affairs manager and asked him where this group had sprung from, and was told they represented a movement called Wise Use. "It's you they're mad at, Dr. Hunt. Frankly, it's a development we didn't need." He trudged away to resume his job of fending off the press.

"What's Wise Use?" Jack asked Tory on the phone back in his office.

"A lie," she said. "They're a lobby for the natural resource industry's agenda, wise or otherwise. Timber, oil, minerals, range land. They want unregulated access and abolition of environmental laws. It started with the big resource interests protecting their federal subsidies, but lately it's become an even bigger consortium. Agribusiness, the Cattlemen's Association, the National Rifle Association, plus the resource corporations."

"I don't see any corporate types outside here. Just average-looking Joes."

"They've been bussed in," she said. "Forestry workers, miners, oil rig laborers. The poor jerks have been pumped up with scary stories about the green movement taking away their jobs. There's a bunch of them staked out in front of our offices, too. Wise Use organizers are masters at these public harassment tactics. Also at hiring scientists to say threats to the environment are exaggerated."

Jack knew the breed. Hooker Ph.D.s.

"And there's a fresh development, Jack. We're getting flack from a new entity called Concerned Citizens of America. Looks like an umbrella group manufactured by friends of the White House to take on PGT. Wise Use is only part of it. They've got the Christian Right on their side, Wall Street backing, and—well, you get the picture."

"So the people outside are just surrogates for the big interests?"

"Yeah, but they can still bite. And they've been told you're the enemy, as PGT's spokesman. Stay out of their way, Jack. They've been known to get nasty."

"Meaning what?"

"Arson, assaults, even murder. So watch your back."

"I'll add it to my list of things to do."

Tory laughed. Jack knew it was only a release from the tension, but her spontaneity—a reminder that there was a life, at ease, beyond all this—felt oddly comforting.

Then he remembered Colwell. Little comfort for *her*. "Your husband was just here," he said, "asking questions."

He sensed her good humor drain away. "Is he making trouble for you?"

*Other than tracking down your mother any day now?* He gritted his teeth to lie. "Not really."

"Well, as I said, Jack, be careful." He could hear voices behind her, the usual Washington hubbub. "Gotta go," she said. "You all prepped for the Windy City?"

Christ, he'd forgotten the time. She'd scheduled him to give a speech in Chicago and lead a PGT rally there. Only three hours until the flight. He said, "Just on my way to pack."

Tory closed her cell phone as she continued down the crowded corridor of the Longworth House office building. She didn't like it, Carson out in Bar Harbor harassing Jack. Probably hoping to make him buckle, or flush him into the open to contact his "Artemis handlers." Insane. How could he be so wrong about Jack? Anyway, the intimidation was pointless. Jack wasn't the buckling type.

She shouldered through the pack of lobbyists staked out at the closed door of the Ways and Means Committee. Gucci Gulch, the hallway was nicknamed, and it was crowded as usual with well-heeled Chamber of Commerce guys. She joined them, waiting too. The House Speaker, a presidential hopeful, had promised her twenty minutes between meetings. She'd given him a boost last year by shaking serious campaign contributions his way, and it gave her a chit for access, which she was now going to cash. Twenty minutes to pitch PGT, and every minute worth gold if she could swing his support.

Her phone rang. Vince. "I've just left Trowbridge's place," he reported. He'd been trying for days, at Tory's insistence, to get Gerry Trowbridge to see him. "No joy, I'm afraid. He hates our guts. Told me to fuck off."

Damn. "Didn't you explain how important that footage could be?"

"Tory, he'd already given the tape to the feds."

That's that, she thought grimly. Or was it? "Vince, maybe he made dubs. Trowbridge is a pro, they always make copies. Can you go back? Check it out?"

"What if he gave the dubs to the feds too?"

"What if he didn't?"

Vince sighed heavily. "I just got home. First chance I've had to sit, let alone sleep. Can it wait a couple hours?"

She already had a better idea. Jack. He and Trowbridge were friends. Maybe *he* could persuade Trowbridge to part with a copy. She told Vince to get some sleep, then called Jack's office. He'd just left, so she called the Chicago hotel he was booked in and left a message. He'd have to act fast, she thought. Carson wouldn't be long in figuring out how explosive such footage could be in PGT's hands. He'd want every copy destroyed.

The Ways and Means doors opened, revealing Committee staff milling as the meeting broke up. Tory could see the Speaker conferring with an aide, and she started toward him. Her phone rang again. She answered it while threading past people.

"Hi, it's Laurel. Um, sorry to bug you but I thought I'd better call. I mean, I'm sure it's okay but, well, since you hadn't mentioned anything—"

"What is it?"

"Mr. Colwell was just here. He's taken Chris."

Tory stopped, a chill creeping over her heart. "Taken? I don't understand."

"I don't really either. He just told me I wasn't needed anymore to baby-sit, then he packed up Chris's things. I told Chris I'd call him—I really like the little guy, you know?— but Mr. Colwell said not to bother because Chris wasn't going home. They've just left."

The activity in the hall around Tory blurred. She tried to form thoughts that were reasonable, rational. A precaution— he doesn't want Chris around Jack. But all she could hear was a frenzied inner voice, screaming, enraged: *He's kidnapped my son.*

Jack took the stairs two at a time to his bedroom to pack. The house was quiet. He figured Laurel had taken Chris out to the beach.

He threw some clothes into a bag, his mind still dogged by Colwell's words. "Obolensk. You caught the Russians in the act." Rachel had flinched as if he'd touched a nerve. Why?

Carrying his bag downstairs he stopped, torn. Probably

just another dead end, and he had to hustle to catch this flight. But, damn it, he had to find out.

He started down the hall to Rachel's study. Nat King Cole was crooning on the radio in the kitchen where Doris was clattering with pots. The gentle drone of Del's voice drifted from the verandah where he was taping notes. Jack opened Rachel's door. Like the beach house, this room was stamped with her personality. There were bookshelves crammed with volumes of every description from archaeology to poetry. Family photographs. Newspapers: the *London Times, Le Monde*. A computer.

He turned it on. Logging on to the Internet, he did a search for Obolensk. He chose an article, and almost immediately came across Rachel's name. A little over a decade ago she'd led a scientific team to Russia.

During the eighties, the article said, the Russians had established a nationwide biotechnology network called Biopreparat. Plants around the country employed fifteen thousand people. Officially, they were involved in vaccine development and other biomedical research, but when Biopreparat's top scientist, Vladimir Pasechnik, defected to the West, his debriefing by the CIA broke open the Russians' secret. Biopreparat was developing a massive biological warfare program.

Pasechnik's whistle-blowing caused an international diplomatic crisis, and Rachel was asked to lead an Anglo-American scientific delegation to investigate the All-Union Research Institute of Applied Microbiology in Obolensk. The team found that the Russians had been experimenting with tularemia, pneumonic plague, anthrax spores, and Q fever biological agents. They'd stored over three hundred thousand tons of biological and chemical weapons, including sarin, Soman and VX, and they were developing missiles capable of carrying biological agents. Yet, incredibly, of the fifteen thousand scientists employed, only a handful at the top had known what was going on. Given these findings by Rachel's team—and intense pressure from Washington and London—the Russians publicly admitted it all. They signed a decree halting the program, and it was shut down.

Jack read on, quotes from Russian scientists about the debacle. A Doctor Mirzanyanov—one of the few people who'd been in the know—seemed proud of the work he'd done on a new binary weapon based on a phosphorous agent. "Anyone could produce these binary weapons components at civil plants," Mirzanyanov said. "They can be innocent materials, like pesticides or dyes. It only requires mixing two components to produce a devastating weapon."

Jack's heart thudded. Two innocuous components assembled to create something new—and deadly.

*A binary weapon.*

He grabbed the phone, then stopped. FBI wiretaps. He shut off the computer and left.

At the Bar Harbor airport he went to a pay phone and punched the numbers. Youssef answered.

"Youssef, the direct mail samples. We know A-1 is in the red vials, but we've got to look at the other ones, the purple ones."

"The CDC tested them right at the start. It's just perfume."

"I don't think so. Don't ask me why now, but we've got to get one of those samples."

"Dr. Lesage must've been sent a batch. I'll get a requisition and ask her for—"

"No, don't." He could get all he needed from the CDC. He checked his watch. "Look, I'm at the airport. Drop everything and get over here and meet me by the Hertz booth. And put on a decent shirt. You're going to Atlanta."

* * *

Gerry poured himself another shot of scotch and knocked it back. He sat alone, slumped at his desk upstairs in his SoHo loft. For sixteen years the place had been both home and studio for him and Liz. He was listening to Jack's voice feeding into the answering machine in front of him, live.

"It's late and I figure you can't always be out, so maybe you're there now. Are you? Gerry, if you are, pick up the phone. Please."

I'm out, Gerry thought bitterly—*of my skull.* He poured another shot, spilling liquor on the desk. Light from the desk lamp glinted off the amber puddle. Downstairs, the studio lay in darkness.

"No?" Jack said. "Well, then, here's the message. I know you told Vince Delvecchio that you gave your video to the FBI, but we figure you might have made copies, and if you did, you've got to give us one."

Gerry's eyes fell on the wastebasket where Delvecchio's business card lay crumpled. Fat chance.

"Gerry, I'm sorry you feel this way about what I'm doing, but believe me, this PGT campaign is the only way we can prevent more death. If Marisa and Liz . . . I mean, if you and I can . . . Christ, I hate talking to you on a machine." He sighed heavily. "All I can tell you is we need that video desperately. To do the right thing. It could make all the difference. Look, I don't blame you for throwing Delvecchio out, the guy's a bit of a prick."

Gerry almost smiled.

"But, hey, Gerry, this is *me.* You and me, we go way back, and . . . Damn it, are you there?"

Gerry closed his eyes. *Barely.*

Jack sighed again, resigned. "Well, call me. Soon as you get this, okay? By the way, you really should see a doctor about that leg." He gave his Chicago hotel number, his office numbers in Bar Harbor, and e-mail address. "Get in touch, Gerry. Please." He hung up.

Gerry listened to the machine whine and click its way back to a fresh start. Then, silence.

He reached for the bottle. Glenfiddich single malt whiskey. Premium stuff. Jack had brought it over—when was that? Back in the spring, when Liz first brought up the idea of a follow-up documentary. Brazil was his next One World Medics mission, Jack said, and the three of them had sat here eating Gerry's extra-fiery chili and planning the project. Liz put on some wacky new CD. Rumba-fusion or some damn thing. Jack danced with her in the kitchen. She'd boogied like a schoolgirl.

Jesus, it was quiet here. He looked at his night-black windows, and across at the dark warehouse next door. Weekends, the area was crawling with the bridge-and-tunnel people who swarmed in to swill at the bistros and gawk at the gays. On weeknights, though, with the galleries and warehouse studios deserted, it was sometimes so quiet. Odd noises echoed off the old cobblestoned part of the street, noises that seemed to fly in through the loft windows and dart around like bats. Maybe it was just his imagination. Or maybe the half bottle of Jack's Glenfiddich.

He looked at the wastebasket and made a sudden decision. Swiveling his chair around to the computer, he typed a brief e-mail message and sent it off. Done. In the morning the courier could deliver the cassette.

He slumped back in the chair and stared at the phone. Call him? Talk to him after all?

And say what? I'm sending you the dub, Jack, even though I hate this shit, and the thought of showing people what we saw makes me puke, but you tell me you need it and I trust you 'cause you're the best friend I've got since Liz is gone, and I don't know how I'm going to get through

tomorrow let alone the years ahead, so if you really believe
this can do some good, make some sense, help—

A sharp sound made him stiffen. Downstairs. He sat still
and listened.

A crash. Glass shattering. Footsteps.

Fuck, somebody's inside.

He got up almost reluctantly. Too tired for this. If they
want to loot the studio equipment, let them take the shit.
Who needs it?

The footsteps weren't stopping. Solid, assured, coming
straight through. Not thieves. Thieves would be looking
around. Then he heard an odd sound, like water sloshing.

He had no weapon. He grabbed the scotch bottle by the
neck, about to smash the bottom off so he'd have something
sharp, when he caught the smell. Gasoline. He rushed to the
top of the stairs just in time to see a shadowy figure below
reach the door, toss a match, then run. The fire, with a
*whomp*, leaped into a wall of flame.

# 16

"DIRTY PICTURES," YOUSSEF ANNOUNCED, waving glossy eight-by-tens as he walked into Jack's office.

Jack swiveled from his computer, eager to see the electron micrographs Youssef had processed. "Let's have a look."

Youssef made a face at the protesters' din outside. "The natives are restless," he said.

Jack, too, found them irritating—loud even here on the second floor. Their ranks had been growing all morning, and a speaker was now exhorting them over a megaphone, to sporadic cheers. He'd found he could block it out, though. "You get used to it," he muttered, grabbing the micrographs.

They'd been working all night. Youssef had returned with vial samples from Atlanta, and the two of them and Mandy had begun a careful examination of the contents of the purple vial, the one containing only perfume, no A-1. Jack was guessing that Rachel had used the perfume to mask a supernatant fluid: fluid containing virus from cells grown in media, but with the cells removed. He had immediately inoculated a female rhesus monkey, telling Rachel's animal model technicians he was testing a drug. Although he'd been monitoring the monkey every half hour, however, it was showing no sign of distress; if the fluid did contain a virus, it appeared even more harmless than A-1. Still, Jack felt in his bones something was here. Mandy was running assays in the lab, but he hoped these electron microscope images might at least show if he was right about virus being present.

"Trouble is, nothing in them turns me on," Youssef said, looking at the images over Jack's shoulder. "But maybe you're kinkier than me, Doc."

Jack was scanning them carefully.

"Hunt down Hunt!" the protesters began to chant. Jack looked up in surprise. "Hunt down Hunt!" they cried.

Youssef frowned. "*Very* restless."

*Watch your back,* Jack remembered Tory telling him. Mobs, he thought in disgust; the best they could come up with was "shoot the messenger." "They're lucky my name isn't Orzenynski," he muttered, turning back to the micrographs.

Then he saw it. A minute, aberrant, viruslike particle. "There," he said, excited, pointing to the top right corner. "It's got a cone-shaped core. See it?"

Youssef peered at the tiny image. "Holy shit," he whispered. "Is that—"

"We've got RT!" Mandy rushed in, beaming. "I've been fiddling with assay conditions, the pH, buffer, temperature." She flattened her hand on her chest, gulping breaths. "Sorry, ran all the way. Anyway, it took some wangling, but now I'm sure. We've got reverse transcriptase!"

"*Yes!*" Youssef said, exultant.

Jack felt a rush of euphoria. Only one entity on the planet was known to use the reverse transcriptase enzyme: retroviruses. Tiny RNA viruses, they used the enzyme to make mirror-image copies of their RNA genetic material, creating a DNA version of themselves. It gave them the unique ability to insert their own genome into the genetic makeup of cells they infected.

"Good work, Mandy," he said. He meant it. The assay for the reverse transcriptase enzyme was complex, involving substrates that were the nucleotide building blocks for making DNA, at least one of which was radioactive. They could be separated, but it took skill to do it.

"Look," Youssef cracked, "she's glowing."

Mandy laughed. "Yeah, even in the dark." She pushed her hair back from her tired face. "Of course, I can't prove the particle I found it in really *is* a new virus. We'd have to demonstrate biological activity, or get electron microscopy to show the structure, but—"

"Your wish is my command," Youssef said, flourishing the micrographs and pointing out the tiny particle.

Mandy's eyes widened. "My God. There it is."

Youssef gazed over her shoulder at their small piece of evidence. "Smart choice for a terrorist," he said with growing excitement. "Retroviruses are real chameleons. Look at HIV, one of the most mutable microbes around."

"And retroviruses are *hormone* responsive," Mandy added enthusiastically. "Artemis obviously capitalized on that to make this thing female-specific."

"Hunt down Hunt!" the crowd went on chanting.

Mandy seemed to notice it for the first time, glancing at Jack in surprise.

"Never mind them," he said. Eager to move on, he checked his watch. He had to be in New York this evening to appear on *Larry King Live.* "All right," he said, "let's review what we know. In vial number one we have A-1, a brand-new influenza strain, proven by Laurel to be nonlethal. In vial two, masked by the perfume, we have a new retrovirus. I'm going to call it A-2. We also have a female primate inoculated with A-2, who after fourteen hours shows no sign of Artemis disease."

"No shit?" Youssef looked crushed. He and Mandy had been too busy to follow Jack's monitoring of the animal.

"Then A-2 isn't the killer either," Mandy said, equally dejected.

"Not *yet*," Jack said.

"What do you mean? Either it is or it isn't."

"Viruses, like life, aren't that simple," Jack said. The very essence of viruses was their fundamental entanglement with the genetic and metabolic machinery of the host. The tiny structure in the micrograph was so easy to miss, and its cone-cored shape was unlike anything he'd ever seen before, but he was convinced that Rachel had engineered this viruslike particle to combine with her new flu virus and create something lethal. But how? What had she started with? Did one viral element transform the other? What kind of virus could do that?

Then it struck him. "An endogenous retrovirus," he blurted.

Youssef and Mandy looked at him blankly.

Jack's mind was charging ahead. Endogenous retroviruses lay inside cells, latent, inert, a kind of fossil. Little was understood about them, but this much was known: in the DNA of cells in all animals, including humans, lay a complete or partial genome of at least one kind of species-specific retrovirus. Their origin was a mystery. Maybe they had once served some purpose but slowly evolved into the precursors of today's retroviruses. Or maybe they were remnants of ancient infections. Or maybe they were just the evolutionary remains of "junk" DNA. Only rarely were they expressed, and only rarely, or under special laboratory conditions, could they be found to produce complete, freestanding RNA viral particles. Most of the time they seemed to be inactive. However, one theory held that the "turning on" of some endogenous retrovirus was the cause of certain cancers; that their activation encoded disease-causing proteins. In *this* case, Jack thought, what if . . .

He saw from their faces that he was already ahead of Mandy and Youssef. "Look, what can activate an endogenous retrovirus?" he asked, leading them into his thinking.

Youssef shrugged. "Chemical carcinogens. Or radiation. Or another virus." He stopped, the point dawning, and repeated in wonder, "Another virus."

"Exactly," Jack said. "I believe what we have here are the components of a binary biological weapon. Mix A-1 and A-2, relatively benign viral elements, and create A-3, a killer."

Youssef and Mandy exchanged awed glances. They quickly caught up.

"An endogenous retrovirus rendered *ex*ogenous," she said.

"From inside to outside," Youssef agreed in excitement.

"Then sent back inside, to destroy," Jack confirmed. He almost smiled. "And the instructions are printed right on the vials."

Mandy, eyes aglow with amazement, said breathlessly, "Wow. Artemis. We're onto them."

"Yes, my little chickadee," Youssef cried, "we've done it!" He grabbed her and danced a little jive step, then spun her around. In sheer surprise she did a perfect pirouette.

Jack couldn't hold back a laugh. He shared their delight, their giddy awe, and so much more. He'd beaten Rachel. Fought past all her feints and dodges to bar him from her labyrinth. He had stormed her in her stronghold, and this was victory. This was conquest. He felt a surge of dominance as potent as if he'd planted his foot on her chest.

Whoa, he told himself. Reality check. The rough truth was, this was just the *beginning*. He still faced the real challenge: a therapy.

A siren startled them. Mandy and Youssef stopped dancing. Jack went to the window to look. A police cruiser, siren wailing, was inching through the crowd. The protesters—hundreds more than yesterday, Jack now realized—were clogging the entrance to the parking lot and squeezing the traffic in the street. What had Tory called the group behind this? Concerned Citizens of America? Sure enough, among the antigreen slogans there were some bobbing CCA placards. Lots of anti-abortion ones too. One, with a crude drawing of a fetus, read: POPULATION CONTROL MEANS ABORTION ON DEMAND. Another: KILL THE KILLERS NOT THE BABIES. Under the watchful eyes of the police the crowd kept roaring, "Hunt down Hunt! Hunt down Hunt! Hunt down Hunt!"

Unbelievable, he thought; such hysteria, such hate. His anger flared: the one they should be screaming down was Rachel. Now that he'd cracked her puzzle he couldn't help marveling at her Byzantine achievement. Taking a fossil microbe that lay harmlessly inert inside billions of humans and transforming it via her new flu virus into a deadly invasive agent.

He caught himself. Achievement? With this thing she had butchered over a thousand people. Butchered Marisa. Guilt stabbed. He'd been so intent on the combat with Rachel, he hadn't thought of Marisa in days.

"What a breakthrough," Mandy was murmuring. "Incredible."

Jack briskly turned back. "But only a theory," he soberly reminded them, and himself. "We can't be sure until we combine A-1 and A-2 and test the result on an animal."

"Well, let's do it," Youssef urged. "Right now. Let's get—"

Something splatted against the window. Mandy gasped.

Jack went to investigate. The object had fallen, but bloody mucus was dribbling down the glass where bits of gore adhered. Raw liver. Below, the protester who had thrown it was being pulled away by police.

"They've discovered where your office is," Mandy said nervously.

Youssef's lip curled. "Assholes."

"Forget them," Jack said. He was rummaging in his lab coat pockets for his coded keys to the level four lab. "We're going ahead with this right away. We'll combine the two agents and proceed with the second inoculation of the monkey. Mandy, I don't want you anywhere near this stuff when we do the mix. If I'm right, that's when it becomes lethal to females. You get working here on the computer modeling. Youssef, I've got to get to New York, so I'm going to have you do—"

The phone rang. Annoyed, Jack reached across the desk for it. It was Tory. "Have you heard? About Gerry Trowbridge?"

"Gerry? No, what is it?"

"Somebody broke into his loft last night. Torched the place. Jack, he's dead."

He watched the bloody mucus slide down the window.

"I can't prove it," Tory went on bitterly, "but I'd bet money the White House's CCA thugs are behind this. Maybe they didn't know Gerry was home, but I'm sure they went in to keep us from getting copies of his Jazida tape. They dumped gas on all his video stock, all his cassettes. There's nothing left." She added quietly, "Jack, I'm so sorry. I know he was your friend."

Inside, he curled up in pain, then went numb.

*I never got a chance to talk to him, never looked him in the eye and spoke about Liz, about how sorry I am. Now, never again.*

"Hunt down Hunt!" The hate-sharpened chanting pierced his numbness, ripped an opening, and rage invaded him.

He yanked off his lab coat, dumped it on the desk, knocking micrographs to the floor, and stalked out.

"Doc?" Youssef called after him. "Where're you going?"

He strode down the stairs. He was *all* feeling now, filled up with rage, too full to hold it inside. The protesters' clamor got louder as he reached the lobby where lab people were crowded at the glass doors, watching the commotion outside. Jack heard Rachel's voice. She stood outside on the entrance steps, urging the crowd to disperse. They were loudly booing her, drowning her out.

"Please," she called to them, "go home, and let the people inside this laboratory do their work."

"Hunt's doing *terrorist* work!" someone yelled.

Jack shouldered through the lab people toward the doors. He heard Youssef calling behind him, "Doc, I don't think you should go out there."

Jack pushed open the doors.

Rachel didn't notice him come out behind her. "You have every right to your opinions," she declared, trying to be heard above the catcalls and obscene threats, "but so does Dr. Hunt. And if you'd—"

"Shut up, bitch, we want Hunt!"

"Here I am!" Jack yelled. "Talk to *me*!"

As people saw him, raw excitement rippled through the crowd, a collective flurry overwhelming individual voices.

"Talk to me, you cowards!" he shouted. "Or can't you handle that? Oh, you're good at screaming obscenities. You're good at murdering innocent people in their homes! So come on, give *me*—"

"*He's* the murderer," a man called out. "Abortion on demand, that's what he's for!"

"Of course I am. Birth control of every kind. Every child should be a wanted child!"

A roar of boos. A bony woman pushed to the front. Her irate voice piped above the others, but Jack couldn't make out her words. "Let her speak! At least one of you has the guts to face me!"

She declared, "Every human life is sacred."

"Well, you people sure don't act like it is. Most of the world lives in misery, in despair, but all you care—" He stopped, seeing a man charge up the steps, metal flashing in his hand. Jack had only a moment to realize it was a knife. The man lunged at him with a savage underhand thrust.

Rachel cried, "No!" and lurched in front of Jack to shield him. The knife meant for his heart rammed into her throat.

She staggered back. Jack caught her. The man with the knife dashed down the steps and disappeared into the crowd.

Everyone else froze.

"Call an ambulance!" Jack yelled at a lab technician gaping at the blood. "Go!" He eased Rachel to the ground as the technician bolted inside.

Rachel was gasping, clutching her throat. People were crowding around and police were rushing in to move them back. On his knees, Jack pulled away Rachel's bloody hands to see the wound. If the blade had severed a jugular or carotid artery there was nothing he could do. She would bleed to death.

He felt a gust of terror. *Her dead man's switch: if it closes, plague!* It stupefied him, paralyzed his brain.

His hands, on automatic, were obeying a routine from years in the field. By rote, he palpated her throat. Blood oozed over his fingers, masking the wound, but he felt it: pierced trachea.

The discovery—the concreteness of it—jolted his brain back. A single thought consumed him. *Save her.*

He quickly judged the trauma. Her breathing was tortured and her neck was swelling, puffing up. Hematoma: blood collecting in the tissues. Suddenly the skin made a crackling sound under his touch. He could feel no escape of air from the wound. Subcutaneous emphysema: instead of exiting via the wound, air was being forced between the skin and the trachea. If the swelling continued it would close off her airway completely. Even a temporary closure could result in brain damage. Prolonged closure would bring death.

He needed a tube. He looked around. A hollow pen, or plastic straw, or—

He saw Mandy. "A glass tube from the lab," he yelled. "Five centimeters diameter. Hurry!" She disappeared.

Rachel's body was stiff with shock. Her pupils were dilated, fixed on Jack, and her fight for air was desperate. If it reached the high-pitched gasping of stridor it would mean her airway was totally blocked. Jack beat back his panic. "We're going to help you," he told her. "Hold on."

She groped at his chest, clutching a fistful of his shirt. Police were pushing people away.

Mandy was back with the tube. Jack carefully inserted one end into the bleeding wound, terrified he might sink into surrounding tissue and not know it. Blindly, he eased it in. He needed to keep it from slipping. He yelled at a man wearing sneakers, "Give me your shoelaces."

With Mandy's help he lashed the tube in place with the laces, then put his ear to the protruding end, stifling his own ragged breathing to listen. Faint breaths—Rachel was getting air. But for how long? The swelling was increasing.

An ambulance screamed to the entrance. Jack got in with Rachel and sat with her through the race into Bar Harbor. He gripped her hand, told her to hang on, tried to will strength into her, though he felt weak himself, disoriented by the paradox: *I swore to destroy you, but now I've got to keep you alive.* By the time they reached Mount Desert Island Hospital her neck had puffed up ominously. They rushed her into the ER.

Jack stood outside, staring at the closed doors. She'd thrown herself in front of him to protect him, and now she was fighting to survive.

Terror knifed through him. Even if she made it, she could be incapacitated for hours, even days. He didn't know how she'd rigged her dead man's switch, only that she sent an ongoing instruction to keep it open. What? How often? *When did it have to be sent?*

In three hours he was due in New York, to go on live TV.

Tory met him at LaGuardia. Her face was ashen. "How is she?"

Jack heard the monotone of his own voice, devoid of emotion. "Critical. All they can do is keep her under observation. Any invasive procedure could exacerbate the trauma." Doctor-speak. It was all he could manage. Couldn't trust himself with more, not faced with Tory's anguish. If only she knew!

"I just wish I could be with her," she said.

"You couldn't talk to her. She's sedated."

"Jack, will she live?"

"I don't know."

They sat side by side in silence as the airport limousine slipped through the city. Tory stared straight ahead, but Jack felt her hand brush his wrist and rest there. No pressure, just a touch, a reaching out. "They meant to kill you," she said, her voice a horrified murmur. "What have I done?"

He was doing no better himself, images strobing in his brain: Gerry burning, the assassin lunging, Rachel gasping, her switch closing, *plague.*

Larry King's people led them into the warren of network

offices. As they prepped Jack in the makeup room he sat stiffly, watching with a sense of disbelief as chattering staff came and went, milling in collegial chaos. A half-eaten birthday cake sat abandoned on the makeup counter near him, and a young man approaching with a clipboard swiped a fingerful of icing. "We're ready for you, Dr. Hunt," he said. Jack followed, his legs spongy, anxiety roiling inside him.

In the studio he was introduced to King, who greeted him cheerfully from the desk on the set, checking last-minute notes. Jack took the guest's seat and stared out beyond the spill from the halo of lights, chilled by the blithe activity around him. People were moving and murmuring in the studio gloom. Cameras were gliding into position. A young couple flirted at the craft services table. In the glassed control booth, an elevated aerie, the producer, a woman in a purple dress, stood looking down at the set. She said something to the technicians near her at the console, making them laugh. How *can* you? Jack wanted to yell. He was sealed up in a private vacuum of horror, suffocating in his imposed silence. His eyes frantically searched for Tory. On the studio floor, lost in her own thoughts, she leaned back against a wall, her arms crossed, hugging herself.

Jack took it all in, his terror rising. If Rachel had targeted New York, and if she died, within days half the people in this room would be dead. Maybe the switch had already closed. Maybe the virus was being delivered at this moment. Rachel wouldn't have used the perfume-mixing device again: maybe this time it was some airborne vector. Maybe he was looking at women who had only *hours* to live—and Tory was one.

Someone yelled, "Quiet!" and Jack flinched. A red light flashed over the studio doors. The floor director gave a signal.

"It's being called the worst crisis this country has ever faced," Larry King announced gravely to a camera.

Jack swallowed. The show had begun.

"People are scared," King said. "And as the beleaguered FBI tracks a thousand leads in search for the Artemis terrorists, with a frightening deadline looming, many Americans are starting to listen to People for a Global Tomorrow, the grassroots organization that has sprung up in the wake of the Stoney Creek tragedy. PGT's unorthodox message: compromise with Artemis. My guest is Dr. Jack Hunt, humanitarian physician, scientist, and, lately, controversial activist as the spokesman for People for a Global Tomorrow. Tonight our generous sponsors are bringing you this special program with a minimum of commercial messages so that we can take as many of your calls to Dr. Hunt as possible."

Finishing his introduction, King turned to Jack and flung him a direct question, something about "Artemis's paranoia about overpopulation."

Jack found himself answering by rote. Statistics from Tory's office, facts he'd been pounding out with every speech, every interview, for over two weeks: almost six billion people on earth, more than double the number after World War II; ten more born in the time it takes to say the words; in less developed nations forty percent are under the age of fifteen—a global fertility time bomb. He rattled off these facts, his voice hollow, his mind chained to Rachel.

"Doctor, we all agree this is a very serious issue, but let me play devil's advocate for a minute. Many people—and I mean well-educated, serious people—don't agree that overpopulation *is* a problem. I see their point. I mean, I've been to Alaska and some other uninhabited places myself, real pristine wilderness. Most of the earth still hasn't even been settled. Right here in America there's still plenty of room. Even if all the people in China and India lived in the continental United States, this country would still have a smaller population density than England or Holland."

Jack felt dazed. What difference did any of this make? *If Rachel dies there's nothing I can do, nothing anyone can do.*

His lungs felt parched. Hard to breathe. There was no air.

"Doctor? How do you respond to those statistics?"

But she might live. He snatched at the thought, hung on to it. He *had* to hang on, just to breathe. She might live, and if she does there *is* still something I can do. *Got to try. Right now. Convince the country.* "I'd have to say, so what?" he answered with a surge of energy. "Density is irrelevant to the question of overpopulation."

"Oh?" King looked mildly surprised. "Well then, how *do* you measure it?"

"By the number of people in an area relative to its resources. It's called the carrying capacity of the land." Stock replies still, Jack knew, but at least his mind was now in gear, and his voice was strong. "An area is overpopulated when its population can't be maintained without depleting resources. By that standard, almost every nation on earth is grossly overpopulated."

"But countries like England and the Netherlands and Japan have huge populations in small areas, and they're doing very well, thank you."

"Because they go outside their boundaries for resources. That's how rich nations stay rich, by exploiting the resources of others. It's devastating the environment, and if the world's population goes on multiplying, the pressures on ecosystems will eventually lead to environmental collapse." Too intellectual, he realized with a pang. He heard Tory's voice in his head: *Pointy-headed stats, dry, boring. Get to the juice.* But he couldn't think *how* to get to it. How would *she* do it?

"Well, some would say that people aren't the problem at

all, they're the answer," King rejoined. "In fact, people may be the *ultimate* resource, because human ingenuity has created technology, and technology can solve these problems. Just look at the breakthrough you folks on the president's science team have already accomplished. You're close to a cure for the Artemis disease, so right there that's technology to our rescue."

Jack was appalled. "Where did you hear that?"

"*Time* magazine today, cover story."

"They're wrong. Dr. Lesage's lab only announced it has isolated a virus, called A-1. That's a far cry from a treatment. The authorities are hyping these stories because they want the country to believe the situation is under control. It's not. Believe me, there is no cure."

"But there probably will be soon."

"No there won't. There isn't time."

"Look, we, uh, we sure don't want to start a panic here, so—"

"Why not? Maybe panic is what it takes."

"But how can PGT, in all conscience, advocate making deals with terrorists? Look at what they're demanding. They want us to hand over one percent of our gross national product—to send foreign women to school! That's over two hundred billion dollars."

"About the cost of eighty stealth bombers."

"It still comes out of taxes, Doctor. A tax gouge for that would make the money markets quake. All that capital of ours flooding into poor countries would raise their living standards, increasing their productivity—and if you thought foreign competition was bad news now, you ain't seen nothing yet." King stopped his pitch and gave a friendly shrug. "As I said, Doctor, I'm just playing devil's advocate."

Jack felt his fury ignite. *There'll be no money markets at all if half the country's dead.* He was about to speak when

King, responding to a signal from the floor director, turned to the camera. "Well, folks, what do *you* think? Is Artemis's way the right way to deal with the crisis of overpopulation, as PGT insists? Or is caving in to terrorists the worst possible thing we could do? Are too many people on earth the problem, or do people present our best hope? Call and give us your opinion on the most urgent issue we may ever face. Or call with questions for Dr. Hunt. We want to hear from you. Our phone lines are open now, so—"

"Wait, I'm not finished," Jack said.

King gave him an indulgent smile. "Don't get excited, Doctor, you'll get a chance to say all you want to the callers. A free and open exchange of ideas, that's what we're here for."

"No you're not. You're here to create confrontation as entertainment." Anger almost choked him. "This isn't a contest! It's not about who can chalk up more points on some popularity scoreboard. This is life and death!"

"Well, right now, Doctor," King said amiably, "it's about going to a commercial break—"

"Enough!" Jack stood, pushing back his chair so violently it toppled. Furious, he leaned on his knuckles across the desk to King, who shrank back in surprise. "We have a chance to act. Maybe our *last* chance. If we don't, the decision is going to be made for us. The next time the Artemis virus is released it's going to unleash a plague that will make Stoney Creek look like a bad case of measles."

He looked around. People were scurrying beyond the cameras. The producer in the booth was waving her arms, instructing the technicians. Good, Jack thought, I've screwed up your fucking Gong Show. He called out in a challenge to the whole studio, "What are you people doing about it? You think this is just some hot story to milk? You TV people have *power.* Power to tell the public what's really happening. But you abuse it, you fritter it away. You trivialize every damn thing you touch!"

King, obeying some cryptic instruction from the control booth, said, "All right, Doctor, let's hear your ideas. What *should* we in the media be doing? Go ahead, this is good."

Jack suddenly understood. They *wanted* him to act mean. Great theater! People were busy on the studio floor, whispering, moving cameras, every eye hungrily on him, wanting more. His rage almost exploded. *Fools!*

Only, who's giving it to them? he realized with a shock. He saw himself hunched over, red-eyed, snorting indignation, a caricature of fury. *Who's a worse fool than a man who can't control his rage?*

*Who's following who?*

He took a step back, trying to govern his heaving chest, willing self-control. He'd watched third-world demagogues, choleric with arrogance, stirring up confused crowds. It was no way to lead. That's what he had to do here, he realized. Take charge. Of himself, of them. Take command.

Slowly, he righted his chair. But he didn't sit down. He turned to King and spoke calmly.

"Larry, the people watching us are thirsting for the truth. They don't have access to it, so they turn to those who do. People like you and me." He settled his shoulders, more composed now. "They give us their trust. And with the trust comes a responsibility to tell those truths, however hard they are to say, and however hard they are to hear. That's what being a leader is all about."

He hesitated. There was still scurrying and whispering on the studio floor, and it threw him. Was he getting through at all? Then he noticed Tory. She had walked forward. People kept moving around her, but she stood still, alone, listening intently to him. Jack felt her faith arc into him like a spark.

"Leaders have an extra responsibility," he went on with

more vigor, "because we can ask exceptional things of people and they will give them. Leaders in war even ask the ultimate sacrifice—giving one's life. People give what's asked if they know it's *necessary*. But what's being asked of the American people these days? So little, we've become a society of adolescents, fixated on partying, on endless buying sprees. We don't care how many rain forests have to fall, or how choked the atmosphere becomes with our exhaust, or what multitudes of people we force into near slavery to make the cheap goods, just as long as we get our *stuff*. Our leaders tell us that it's okay to stay boozed up and dancing at the party, that if millions are starving at our gates it's their tough luck, and probably their own fault too. Our leaders don't ask that we share, that we strive, that we create. They pander to our most primitive desire, to hoard wealth and feed its growth. Unchecked growth is the credo of the cancer cell. In the frenzy, we've lost sight of what it is to be human."

His lungs felt as cool as water now, his head fresh and clear, as if he were on pure oxygen. Once again, as at the rally, he wondered, Where had these words come from? More than stiff facts, more than Tory's zest, more than his own terror—this was a synergy of it all. All he knew was, he was speaking the truth.

He leaned across the desk on his knuckles again, but this time not to threaten. "We've got to do better than that, Larry, you and me, if we're going to lead. We've got to ask more of people. Because if we tell it like it is, I believe the American people have the courage of heart and mind to understand, and do what has to be done."

He walked around the desk and spoke to the whole studio. All activity had stopped. People were finally listening. "This is how it is," he said. "We've been partying too long at the expense of our fellow man and our common environment.

It's time to wind down the party. Time to live like adults. If we don't, if we cannot begin to make a better world, if we don't act *now*, Artemis will. That young woman standing beside the camera? She'll soon be dead. You up there, Madam Producer, you're going to die, too. You, the cameraman there, I see you're wearing a wedding ring. Well, your wife's going to die. And your mother, sir. And your daughter, Larry. The choice is yours. Together we can prevent this disaster. It's either that, or keep on partying until no one is left dancing."

The studio was silent.

"Hear me," Jack declared, and he heard his voice ring out. *"I am asking."*

Youssef woke up with a crick in his neck. He got up stiffly from the janitor's cot in the small room off the animal model core lab, and checked his watch in surprise. Six A.M. After watching Larry King on the small TV here last night he must have fallen asleep. Not that the Doc's star performance hadn't been a mindblower. Made a bloke think, that was for sure. *Well, Doc, I'm doing my bit.*

He looked toward the connecting storeroom. The door was closed, but inside was the cage with Lucy, the young female rhesus monkey, the object of the experiment. He had taken the janitor's little warren because it had a door he could lock and personally guard; he couldn't risk some female technician straying into the area of infection.

If infection there was. He was beginning to wonder if they'd been wrong about this whole theory of the Doc's. The Three Musketeers, getting carried away. Fourteen hours since he'd combined some A-1 and A-2 and inoculated the animal, but Lucy wasn't chattering in pain—or chattering at all; a lazy little monkey at the best of times, she was still asleep. Not a sound from the storeroom.

Rubbing his stiff shoulder, he got up and unlocked the door. He froze at the sight of the cage. Blood was puddled around Lucy's still form, coagulated in her open, dead eyes. Blood caked her rigid lips, matted her fur. Her corpse looked bony, drained, as though someone had pulled a plug. Youssef's stomach lurched at the smell . . . the agony she must have suffered.

He pulled himself together. Opening his gym bag he took out latex gloves, mask, scalpel, bleach, and the other equipment. The necropsy would have to be quick and dirty: just get samples of tissue, then bundle up the carcass and incinerate it. His fingers were trembling as he began.

Got to hand it to you, Doc. Right again.

"They are ospreys," Del said from his wheelchair. "A common seabird, but lovely nonetheless."

Jack couldn't even summon the will to turn from the verandah railing where he stood looking at the shorebirds in the sunset. Fear about Rachel still wracked him. After a night and day, she remained in intensive care. He sensed Del's anxious presence behind him, where he sat wrapped in a heavy cardigan to ward off the end-of-day chill. He knew Del needed to keep talking as they waited to hear from the hospital, but conversation felt utterly beyond him.

His eyes strayed to Tory. Pacing on the lawn, she was talking on her cell phone, staying just far enough away to keep her calls from upsetting her father. Strategies for hanging on, Jack thought grimly: Del clung to civilized discourse; Tory armored herself in work. And me? In the last hours he'd thought he couldn't endure the tension a moment longer, but he had. No option. All he could do—all any of them could do—was wait. But he alone knew the mind-numbing stakes.

For Del's sake he dragged forth a reply. "Common here,"

he said, turning from the railing, "but I guess a land-locked African might find them exotic."

"True," Del agreed with a faint smile. "And rare sightings are what the birder lives for." He looked out at the water. "I once traveled across to Nova Scotia just to see an American swallow-tailed kite. It's a subtropical hawk normally seen no farther north than Georgia. Black and white plumage, but with an extraordinary, beautiful wine-colored bloom across the shoulders, visible only at extreme close range. Worth the trip. Oddly, the bloom fades after death."

His last word hovered between them.

Del nodded at the remnant of scotch in Jack's glass. "Another?"

Jack shook his head.

"Please," Del said. "I need another. And drinking alone is indecorous."

"I'll get it," Tory said, coming up the steps. She slipped the phone in her jeans pocket and gathered their glasses. She'd been sticking to plain soda herself, Jack had noticed. He watched her go inside, thinking she looked as bone-weary as he felt. She was working at her usual flat-out pace, but he knew she was devastated to think her mother might die. As if her anxiety about Rachel wasn't enough, there was her husband, too. She'd told him that Colwell had taken Chris and was keeping the boy's whereabouts hidden from her. Bastard, Jack thought. Tory was stoical about it, but he knew she was wretched at the rupture from her son. She didn't deserve this. None of it.

He heard her inside dropping ice cubes into the glasses. It made him think of Gerry, who'd always taken his liquor neat, a habit from years of filming in war zones and jungles, where ice was rare. Gerry . . . dead. Because of PGT. *Because of me*. He pushed that anguish to the back of his mind. No room for it. The specter of Rachel's death dwarfed everything else, and made this family vigil seem surreal. Del and Tory, so worried about Rachel, with no inkling of her crimes, nor of the danger she'd rigged looming over them all.

"Jack, you must be absolutely exhausted," Del said as Tory returned with the drinks. "Working at the lab, traveling, making speeches. Tory never lets you rest."

Taking the glass from Tory's hand, Jack said with a rueful smile, "Tory's a force of nature."

"I'm only as strong as my material," she said, returning the smile. "Your favorables jumped sky high after Larry King last night. People adored you. Now, the trick is to turn the bounce we're getting from it into pressure on the White House. Get your millions of admirers off their backsides and badgering Washington. We're working on it."

She never lets up, Jack thought in admiration. If sheer force of will could win this campaign, Tory would do it.

Youssef and Mandy, too; their commitment now was total. The monkey's death left no doubt that they had induced the Artemis disease, and all day they'd been hard at work examining the lethal binary product, A-3.

*If Rachel dies, what's the point of any of it?*

He shut his eyes, overwhelmed by it all. If she hadn't stepped in front of the blade to shield him . . .

"Are you all right?" Del asked.

"That knife was meant for me. She saved my life."

"It shouldn't surprise you. It is true that Rachel has a purely logical mind, but not when her family is threatened."

Jack frowned, uncomfortable. He wasn't family.

"You mean a great deal to her," Del said quietly.

Jack winced inside. Did Del know that he and Rachel had once been lovers? He couldn't help glancing at Tory. Had she heard? She seemed preoccupied, looking out at the sea.

Del shivered. "Perhaps I'll go in. There's an opera broadcast. *The Barber of Seville,* I believe. Frivolous fare, but it keeps the mind occupied." His wheelchair hummed as he went inside.

Jack and Tory, left alone, exchanged a look. Nothing to do but wait. He sat down heavily in one of the cane-back armchairs; she settled on the broad railing between two posts and swung up her legs. Feet on the railing, she rested her back against the post and stared out at the sunset-red ocean. Jack couldn't see her face, but he noticed an uncharacteristic slackness in her shoulders, and when she heaved a troubled sigh, though she tried to subdue it, he knew what was dragging at her thoughts. Chris. God, it was awful to watch how Colwell was breaking her heart.

"You know," she said quietly, "it's true what Dad says about my mother. Family bonds. Losing my brother almost killed her."

Brother? Jack wondered. Then he remembered. The photograph in the beach house, the adopted boy. *He died,* Rachel had said. "What was his name?" he asked Tory.

"Curious George." She looked at him with a smile. "Remember that old children's book? An American nurse at the orphanage in Kigali gave him that nickname because he was into everything, though he was just a baby."

The warmth in her voice, the obvious affection, tugged at something in Jack. Made him want to hear her go on. Besides, he couldn't help feeling intrigued. "Rachel and Del went to Rwanda to adopt?"

"No, she went alone. Not to adopt—I think that just happened."

"Oh?"

Tory ran her finger thoughtfully around the rim of her glass of soda. "She went to Kenya for a conference. Twelve years ago. I was away at university, plowing into law school, wrapped up in my own life, so I didn't get home too much, but I do remember having the feeling at the time that her desire to adopt—her need, I'd call it—germinated months before. Right after she accepted her Nobel prize."

Jack wasn't sure he wanted to hear this after all. Right after Rachel had accepted her Nobel prize she was in England, with him.

"You see," she went on, "after the ceremony in Stockholm and a week's stopover in London, she arrived home to find that Dad had had a stroke. All our lives changed. Theirs the most, of course, but in almost opposite ways, it seemed to me then. Dad's incapacity somehow sharpened my mother's vitality, as though to balance the whole they made. She seemed like a woman suddenly hungry for life."

The picture disturbed Jack. Rachel had given him up for Del's sake, then rechanneled that fierce capacity for love into adopting a child? "Elaborate analysis," he said.

"True," Tory admitted. "Maybe I'd better leave that to the shrinks. What *did* happen was that shortly after Dad's stroke she went to Kenya for a conference and spent some time touring the area, including an orphanage in Rwanda. She called home to tell Dad she wanted to adopt. He agreed. She brought the baby home. To answer your question, his name was Paul."

She pointed to the base of the post beyond her feet. "See those markings?" In the fading light Jack could just make out a series of short horizontal lines running up maybe four feet above the verandah floor. "Dad put those there to mark Paul's height as he was growing." Her expression turned serious. "Wish I *had* made it home more often. I never really got to know him."

She smiled, and cocked her head toward the sea. "I remember he loved the beach. He'd collect all kinds of treasures. Shells, driftwood nuggets, hollowed stones. His pockets used to bulge with the stuff. My mother taught him to swim and to sail, and on his eighth birthday they bought him a Laser dinghy, which he was wild about. Won several club races in his age group. By then I was snowed under with work in D.C., turning away consulting jobs, got home even less, so I only heard about the races from Paul's excited letters. He was a natural sailor, absolutely fearless. Like my mother." She added with a self-deprecating grin, "Unlike me."

Jack couldn't actually see the grin—could only see her shape in the dusk—but he heard it in her voice. He realized, with mild surprise, what a calming pleasure it gave him to hear her talk. With all the chaos roiling inside him, he found comfort in her equilibrium, her fine balance of heart and brains. Her voice made a small pool of peace around him. He just wanted her to go on.

Her tone suddenly changed. "Then, about a year later," she said, the smile in her voice gone, "they heard from the orphanage in Rwanda. Paul's mother, a Tutsi woman, had turned up and wanted him back. I came home to discuss it. Told Mother and Dad the request was ridiculous: Paul had grown up in our family, and the adoption had been perfectly legal. They agreed—they had no intention of giving him up." She stared into her glass. "But my mother felt it was only right for Paul to at least meet his natural mother, and for the woman to see that her child was happy and loved."

A light switched on inside the house, casting her in a burnished glow. Jack saw sadness on her face. "They flew to Kigali on April sixth, my mother and Paul. The next day the Rwandan president's plane was shot down over the presidential palace and plunged into the palace gardens. The whole world watched what followed. Hutu gangs swarmed the capital, massacring Tutsis. My mother and Paul fled their hotel. Somewhere in the hills they were separated. Then—"

The phone in the house rang. Jack froze. Tory swung her legs off the railing, riveting her attention on the door, waiting, like him, for the news. Jack found himself trying not to think, trying not to hear the terrifying voice in his head: *They're calling to say she's dead.*

The wind chime above Tory jangled in a gust. She reached up to still it with her fingers. The gentle silence of dusk returned. No one came to the door; the phone call, apparently, was something else. Watching Tory, his emotions stretched so tight, Jack shivered in a kind of release, as though her fingers on the chime were also stilling him.

A curlew cried in the distance. The story of Paul hung in the air. Jack realized that he wanted to know the end. "What happened?"

Tory seemed to shake off her own trepidation about the phone call. "She spent weeks searching for him. God only knows what she went through. The country was in total anarchy. No one could help her. She was alone. We heard no news. Dad was frantic." She looked up at the wind chime, which stirred with a faint tinkle, as though from her breath. "Then she heard about some children hiding in a village church a few miles away. She walked. When she reached the village—"

"Jack," Del said from the doorway. His face was like chalk. "It's the hospital. They say Rachel is asking for you."

# 17

"THIS WAY, PLEASE." THE EDGY NURSE AT THE third-floor reception desk started down the corridor. Jack followed, dread cramping his chest. Was Rachel dying? Dead? When the nurse stopped at a private room and opened the door, relief flooded him. Rachel was sitting at the foot of the bed, dressed, signing a form on a clipboard.

The relief lasted only a moment. What if her dead man's switch had *already* closed?

Three doctors stood around her, all talking.

"... can't be held responsible for any complications if you go."

"... return to that punishing pace of work, you'll collapse."

"... stay another day, at least."

Rachel was struggling to get up, but the effort appeared too much and she sat back. Jack thought desperately: If it's too late, she couldn't be so composed, could she? She suddenly noticed him and begged him with her eyes to help her, indicating her bandaged throat where purple bruising spread beyond the dressing. He rushed forward, pushing between the doctors, and leaned down to bring his ear to her mouth.

"Tell them," she whispered hoarsely. "I *must* leave."

The switch. "How much time?" he blurted. She shook her head, wincing. *How long before it closes?* he wanted to yell. *Hours? Minutes?* He had to get her out of here. Grabbing her elbow, he yanked her up. "*I'll* be responsible," he told the doctors, and pulled Rachel to a waiting wheelchair. She sat, closing her eyes in pain.

Jack pushed the wheelchair out, ignoring the nurse protesting, "Sir, let me, it's hospital policy—" He rushed Rachel down the corridor. As they reached the elevator two nurses went by, chattering: Jack barely waited until they'd passed. "How much time do we have?" he asked under his breath, jabbing the elevator button.

Rachel said nothing.

He felt a knife of new dread, cold steel in his gut. "You *are* going to stop it?"

She jabbed the button herself. "Tory hasn't succeeded with the campaign."

"Christ, she's doing everything humanly possible. We all are."

"Not enough," she said in a fierce whisper.

He wanted to scream at her, shake her senseless. *What more can we do?* The elevator doors opened and an orderly stepped out pushing a gurney. A janitor standing in the elevator corner with his mop and bucket asked, "Going down?" Jack maneuvered Rachel's wheelchair in, desperation eating him, and they rode down in silence.

The ground floor was busier—a stream of night-shift staff arriving—and he was forced to slow down. Rachel suddenly pushed out of the chair. She started walking quickly down the hall. Jack caught up, grabbed her arm, and pinned her to the wall beside a pay phone. "What are you going to do?"

"Let me go. There's no time for this."

So she *was* going to stop it. No, he thought wildly, this might be just another of her feints, a ruse to throw me off. But what if it isn't? No time . . . Jesus, I have no choice. I have to trust her.

The moment he released her she started for the lobby doors. Jack kept by her side. Halfway there she faltered, in pain, and groped for him. He shot his arm around her waist to support her. Almost dragging her, terrified she might pass out, he got her to the doors where they hurried past a yawning security officer.

Jack helped her into the car. As he rushed around to take the wheel she sat hugging herself, conserving energy. He butted recklessly into the northbound traffic, heading for the lab. Car horns around them blared.

"No," Rachel said. "Take me home."

He shot her a look of suspicion. What was she trying to pull?

"The lab's too far," she insisted hoarsely. "There isn't time. I can send the instruction from home."

He made a squealing U-turn and raced to Swallow Point.

As he roared down the laneway the headlights caught Del on the verandah. "Rachel, are you all right?" he asked as she and Jack hurried up the steps. "Should you be up if—"

"I'm fine," she said blankly, brushing a kiss on his cheek. Jack followed her inside.

Tory rushed down the stairs. "Mother! Are you—"

"I'm fine," she said again, not stopping, not looking. She went down the hall to her study and closed the door. Jack heard her lock it. He stood in the hall, waiting, his heart hammering as he strained to hear how she was sending her command. A phone call? Fax? E-mail? He still wasn't sure—had to lean against the door to steady himself at the thought—if it was a command to stop the switch from closing, or to activate it.

As sudden as the knife stab that had begun this terror yesterday morning, it was over.

About an hour after he'd stood outside Rachel's door, the evening sky outside her jet was darkening. But for Jack, night had turned into day. That's how it felt. The dread, the despair consuming him for two days, it had all lifted like fog in the sun. He was sitting alone with Tory, flying to Washington to plan tomorrow's press conference. She was upbeat, her relief at Rachel's recovery almost as great as his own. Finally, Jack allowed himself to relax. He knew Rachel had stopped the switch, and more: she would wait out the campaign. Tory, thank God, had convinced her.

Buoyant as soon as she'd seen that her mother was out of danger, Tory had enthusiastically told her all about the Larry King interview. A knockout, she'd called it, giving the highlights almost verbatim. She'd confidently explained to Rachel her strategy for capitalizing on the huge "bounce" it had given PGT, starting with Jack's press conference tomorrow. "His coronation," she'd predicted with a grin. "So you get some rest, Mother, and leave this to us. Me and Jack, we're on a roll." Rachel, listening, had reevaluated. Jack had seen it in her eyes—an instant command decision to wait out the campaign.

It was all Tory's doing. Jack could have kissed her.

As he rested his head on the seat-back and glanced at her beside him working busily on her notes under a small spotlight, he felt her ebullience, her confidence, flow through him too. It made him almost light-headed. They *were* on a roll. Their hard work, their commitment, were paying off just as she'd planned. Grateful for her, that's what he felt. A gratitude that was profound, because she'd carried on despite the pain about Colwell and her son, which Jack knew she was suffering, yet she'd never wavered.

She caught him looking at her. "What?"

He shook his head. "You deserve a medal."

"Hey, I'd settle for four hours' sleep."

"Outrageous request. Hand back the medal."

They both chuckled.

"Jack," she said, resting her head back too, her voice an intimate murmur in the hushed jet cabin, "I don't know if you realize what an amazing thing you've accomplished. True, we're not out of the woods quite yet. But, oh, boy, it's looking awfully sunny beyond those last few trees. I've never seen anything like this. People truly love you. I could run you for president and give new meaning to the word landslide."

"I'd settle for hearing this president sign off on what we want."

"Amen to that. Believe me, I'm not usually one to encourage the counting of unhatched chickens, but I'm telling you, we are *this* close. Gives me goose bumps." She grinned. "Chickens, geese—I'm so excited my language is getting fowl."

"Love it when you talk dirty."

They looked at each other and burst out laughing. God, it felt good, Jack thought. Laughter. Silliness. Sheer damn happiness. He'd forgotten all of that was possible.

The limo whisked them through the capital to Tory's building. In her office—her war room, Jack called it—her top gang of ten were working late. Their paperwork was spread out among a litter of still pungent take-out leftovers, and CNN, as always, was droning under their talk. As he and Tory walked in the whole group turned and cheered him.

Jack was taken aback. As they gathered round him clapping, he noticed himself on CNN—a replayed clip of his King interview. Ouch, had he really looked that mad?

"Dr. Kick-Ass!" Noah Shapiro quipped. "Outstanding!"

Vince Delvecchio theatrically unfurled a T-shirt emblazoned with Jack's stern face above the slogan, *I'm asking!*

Jack felt an unaccustomed blush. The others laughed. Tory's communications director, a strapping Whoopi Goldberg look-alike, threw her arms around his neck like a swooning heroine and sighed, "My hero." Jack had to laugh. Catching their mood, he raised his fist in a mock revolutionary salute. It cracked them up.

Tory, her eyes smiling at him, said, "Okay, knock it off, children. Work to do. *I'm* asking."

The others settled down. Delvecchio handed Tory a briefing paper. Jack, still chuckling, noticed fresh coffee on the sideboard and decided he could use some. Shapiro moved to the TV and switched the channel, saying to no one in particular, "Roger Bloom called, said to catch *Hard Copy*."

Tory got them started discussing strategy for the morning press conference. Jack was helping himself to coffee, with people moving around him getting cream and sugar and picking up briefing notes, when he heard, ". . . with the shocking truth about Dr. Jack Hunt."

His head snapped up to the TV.

"Tonight, *Hard Copy* brings you an exclusive interview with Mrs. Vivian Cabot, the former wife of Jack Hunt, the outspoken humanitarian doctor."

Jack froze. There was Vivian, coifed and composed among her orchids. He had a threatening trapdoor feeling at the bottom of his stomach.

"We visited Mrs. Cabot, now married to a New York investment executive, at her home on Long Island. What she told us about the saintly Dr. Hunt will surprise you, and possibly disgust you."

Jack felt the trapdoor tremble.

"Jack and I were both very young when we got married, only twenty," Vivian said to the unseen interviewer, "and perhaps that was part of the problem."

"Who's this?" Delvecchio asked across the room.

"Shhh!" Shapiro said, watching.

". . . could tell that Jack was a very determined young man. Very ambitious. He grew up rather disadvantaged, you see, whereas my family—" She offered a modest smile. "Well, as people in my day used to say, Jack married well."

Pictures flashed on screen: a trailer park, arid, trash-strewn. Jack groaned inside. Home.

The announcer: "Jack Hunt was a poor kid from the wrong side of the tracks. Wealthy Vivian was his ticket out."

Delvecchio snorted, "No cliché unturned."

"Shhh!" Shapiro hissed.

The interviewer asked, "Were you happy, at first?"

"Not unhappy. But Jack didn't seem satisfied. He had a problem with . . . well, with fidelity. I'm old-fashioned, I know, but I've always believed that wedding vows really mean what they say."

Jack felt all eyes in the room snap toward him. His palms were suddenly damp. Maybe she'll stop there, he thought with sudden wild hope. Maybe she'll be satisfied with drawing this blood. *Stop short of Diane.* Please, Vivian. Stop.

"You said Jack Hunt was ambitious," the announcer was saying. "How did that ambition present itself?"

"Oh, you know, we always had to have the biggest house, the fanciest cars, give the most lavish dinners, for the most important people. And, of course, he was very keen to excel at his work. He was—is—a brilliant clinical virologist. He rose very high at the CDC, as you know. I wouldn't want to take any of that away from Jack. He's a fine doctor."

Shots of his former home in Atlanta. The plantation-style columns, palm trees, pool, tennis court. Jack could only watch, helpless, as Tory's people drifted in closer to the TV. They were going to hear it all. He knew that now, saw it in Vivian's eyes, going for the kill. *Diane.* He tasted the metallic bite of fear, imagining people all across the country drawing closer to their sets. *Everyone* was going to hear. There was nothing he could do to stop it.

Above ominous music the announcer continued. "It was at this gracious home in Atlanta, the house bought with Vivian's money while her ambitious husband pursued his private affairs, that events occurred that would shatter this family forever."

A school photograph filled the screen—a sullen teenage face. The trapdoor in Jack's stomach dropped, and he pitched into the abyss.

The announcer: "This was Diane Hunt, Jack and Vivian's only child."

"Even at fourteen Diane had problems," Vivian said. "She didn't fit in at school. She got in trouble with the police for . . . well, for drugs. Marijuana. Jack smoothed things over with the police, but he was very angry with Diane. He hated the image she was giving of our family. He cared very much about position, about what his CDC superiors thought. And then . . ."

The announcer took over. "Then, at age fifteen, Diane got pregnant. It was the last straw for the social-climbing young doctor. Furious, he ordered his daughter out of his house. His wife remembers it all."

"It was a terrible scene," she said. "They both shouted things they shouldn't have. Diane ran out. That very night, quite late . . ." She paused as if the memory was too difficult, and touched a straying lock of hair. "I'll never forget it. It was after midnight. Diane was outside banging on our front door. I could faintly hear her crying, saying she was sorry, that she had nowhere to go, asking her father to forgive her. Her pleas were quite pitiful. Jack got out of bed and went downstairs. Diane begged him to let her in. She sounded like a little girl, crying. But Jack turned out the porch light, leaving her in darkness. He walked back up to bed."

Jack, in limbo, was skidding on nightmare ice, no control, just praying it would stop in time.

"So the troubled teenager was forced to leave the safety of her home," the announcer intoned, "driven out by her unforgiving father. Her parents heard nothing more from her for years. Their marriage, torn by Jack Hunt's infidelities and ruthless personality, soon foundered and ended in divorce. And then . . ."

A sudden scene shift: jerky shots of a snowy slum street. Detroit. Jack had only time to think, Dear God, no.

"Ten years after that fateful night, on a gray, cold February afternoon, the Detroit Police Department answered a 911 call about a young mother in a downtown tenement who had gone berserk. They hurried to the squalid basement apartment. These police file photos show the grisly scene they discovered."

In the self-torture of the damned, Jack stared at the pictures: the youthful couple and the two small children sprawled in pools of blood. The announcer intoned, "The young mother had shot her common-law husband and her two youngest children, then turned the gun on herself. Diane Hunt, the troubled teen driven from home, destitute and drug-addled, had finally ended the pain."

Even in his misery, Jack heard the muffled gasps of shock in the room around him.

"But there was one survivor of Diane's gruesome killing spree," the announcer went on. "Her oldest child, the baby for which she had been thrown into the street by her heartless father. Her name was Laurel. Now eighteen, she lives in Boston. We've been unable to locate her for her comments."

On screen, a grinning photo of Laurel as a gap-toothed eight-year-old ambushed Jack. A machine-gun barrage of emotions riddled him. Love, grief, shame, fury at this public confiscation of his life, but most of all a craving to have Laurel understand. He grabbed a phone and hurriedly dialed Swallow Point. *If I can just talk to her before she hears about it.* Del answered. Jack asked him to put Laurel on. *Break it to her slowly, gently—*

"Liar!" she shouted the moment she came on the line. "She shot them! She shot herself! You *lied* to me!"

The blood seemed to drain from his heart. "Laurel—"

"It was on TV." She was crying, sobbing. "I saw the pictures. Everybody's seen. The whole world's found out what you're *really* like. You threw her out. We lived like rats because of *you*. She snapped and she killed them *because of you*."

"Laurel, listen to me—" The words clogged in his throat. What could he say?

"You told me they'd been murdered! Some crazy junkie did it, you said, and I *believed* you." Her sobs were uncontrollable. "I always believed I might have stopped it if I'd just come home from school, just got there in time. You *let* me believe it! How *could* you—"

Three phones were loudly ringing near Jack. The sound knifed into a separate part of his mind, a separate torture: the press, smelling blood.

"They're onto you," Laurel cried. "Oh, and *I'm* going to be real popular now too," she added savagely. "Every fucking reporter in the world's going to want to talk to me. Did your grandfather mistreat you too, Miss Hunt? Was it hard having a teenage addict for a mother, Miss Hunt? What's it like, Miss Hunt, living with the man who drove your mother to murder and suicide?"

"Jack," Tory cut in across the room. "We need to talk."

Laurel screamed, "Bastard! You go around acting like a saint but you're a hypocritical lying *bastard*." She slammed down the phone.

Jack's hands were shaking. They were watching him, everyone in the office. On TV an inane commercial droned. Someone snapped it off. The faces here were a blur to him as Laurel's words burned into his brain.

Phones were ringing madly. Reporters, Jack was sure, and PGT field-workers wanting answers, just like everyone here. Delvecchio was already on his cell phone: ". . . fucking lynch mob. *Of course* he'll give a statement, as soon as—" Shapiro sat at Tory's desk, chewing the end of his pen. Tory sat tensely on the desk edge. They were all watching him, waiting.

"Jack," Tory said firmly, "we've got to know how much of this is true."

He couldn't bear to meet her eyes. Stiffly, he walked to the half-moon window overlooking K Street and stared out.

Shapiro took his silence as an answer. "We're fucked," he groaned, and dropped his head on his arms on the desk.

Tory said, "Stop it, Noah. It's bad, but—"

"It's *disastrous*," her pollster said, and began to pace.

"*If* it's true," Tory said. "Only Jack can tell us that."

He felt all their eyes bore into his back. Down on the street a skinny black teenager with a filthy sleeping bag slung over his shoulders like a shawl wandered into the traffic. Horns blasted. Jack felt a disorienting union with the kid: nowhere to go, nowhere to hide.

Tory turned to the others. "Henry, line up your focus

groups. And call Dean Forsythe, I need his advice." She called across the room, "Is that Pete Gowan? I'll talk to him." She grabbed the phone to speak to the lawyer.

"Won't help," Shapiro said, lifting his head from the desk. "Can't put Humpty together again. It's over."

"Not if the story's a crock," Delvecchio said, closing his phone.

Jack sensed them all turn to him again. He was frozen to the spot. *It's over.*

Shapiro challenged Delvecchio: "So you're saying they made this up? That's crazy."

"Oh, right," Delvecchio said sourly. "*Hard Copy* is so scrupulous in checking their facts."

"You saw the bodies," Shapiro snapped. "You think the Detroit PD computer-generated those pictures?"

*Bodies*—my flesh and blood. Jack tasted the old horror like vomit in his mouth.

"I just think we shouldn't be snowed," Delvecchio countered. "Quincy's CCA gang orchestrated this, you can be sure. And the FBI must have dug up the ex-wife. Who knows how they pressured her?"

"To do *what*? Spin this out of thin air? There was a pregnant fifteen-year-old, Vince, and there were *corpses*!"

*The baby's chest shredded by the bullet.*

"All I'm saying," Delvecchio replied, "is that we all know Jack pretty well now, and this isn't ... well, it just isn't *him*."

Jack saw his own face reflected in the night-dark window. He shut his eyes. In that darker blackness he saw Laurel screaming, betrayed. He suddenly felt very cold. She would never forgive him. How could she, when he'd never forgiven himself?

"Mortally wounded," the pollster was saying as Tory finished on the phone. "Our biggest favorables were with women twenty-five to fifty, and that group always reacts with the strongest negatives to family scandal. We'll plummet thirty points overnight. Noah's right. We're fucked."

"We can recover overnight, too," Tory said sternly. "We've done it before."

Jack opened his eyes. Was she serious? He caught the window reflection of her face watching him and couldn't bear it, her scrutiny. He ducked his head. Of all the eyes in the room, hers were the ones he craved to avoid.

"My people are going nuts," the field coordinator said, slamming down a phone. "We've already got cancellations for fund-raisers in Minneapolis and Denver. Major donors are soon going to be stampeding away if—"

"We know the *problem*," Tory said sharply to the whole room. "I want *solutions*!"

The campaign, Jack thought. Rachel. An icy drop of panic dripped in a dark corner of his consciousness, and then was still. The well of his terror about Rachel had gone dry. Too much had pumped through him for too long. He was numb to it.

But not to the merciless shame.

Another phone rang and Eric answered it. "Dick Shannon, *Wall Street Journal*, for Dr. Hunt."

Tory shook her head. "Not available."

"He's got to give a statement sooner or later," the communications director warned.

*"Later."*

Tory's steady voice made Jack shudder. Can't she see it's over?

"Tory, we've taken too hard a hit," Shapiro said. "We have to consider cooling Jack and bringing forward Senator Owen as spokesman."

"Not an option," Tory said. "Nothing would look weaker.

If we abandon Jack, we abandon all credibility. No, we've got to hit back."

*Tory,* Jack groaned inside, *give it up.*

"Hit back with what?" Shapiro demanded. "Jack saying he's *sorry* he destroyed his teenage daughter? This moral crusader who's telling everybody in the country they have to clean up *their* act? They'll eat him alive."

"No. No apologies," Tory insisted. "We have to fight."

"How, if this shit is *true?*"

Jack heard the room fall silent except for the hysterically ringing phones. They were all waiting for his answer.

He couldn't force himself to turn around. Not to Tory. He could face the others if he had to, but not her. She'd put everything on the line for this. Put her trust in him, her faith. She'd *believed* in him.

"Jack," she said. "Talk to us."

Tory watched his back as he stood frozen at her window. She'd never felt such fury. Damn you, Jack Hunt, what have you done? *If you've killed this campaign—*

Suddenly he twisted around. Their eyes met, and he went as rigid as a buck stunned by headlights. He ducked his head, his stiff hand shielding his face from the stares. The gesture was so unlike Jack—so furtive, so pathetic—Tory knew right then: *The story's true.* Her fury was swallowed up by shock.

As she took in his contorted face, shock gave way to pity. This might not be the Jack she knew, but this was a man in pain.

He suddenly made for the door.

"Hey, we've got to bang out some answers!" Noah yelled. "Come back!"

"Shut up, Noah," she said, snatching her shoulder bag to go after Jack. "He isn't a politician, he's a human being."

Out in the hall, seeing him head for the elevator, she said to him, "Not down to the lobby. Reporters."

He turned on his heel and took the stairs. Tory followed. The facts behind the story she had to accept, so if she was going to salvage anything here she needed more. The story behind the facts. As Jack pushed out through a fire exit and started up the street, she said, "Where are we going?"

He stared ahead, iron-faced, and kept on. She had to work to keep pace with his stride. In the sultry night heat her T-shirt was already sticking to her back. Jack banged shoulders with a kid strolling by with a ghetto blaster. "Motherfucker," the kid sneered.

Jack struck out across the street. Tory was right behind, but got cut off by an ambulance strobing past, siren screaming. She called, "Jack, wait." But he didn't.

Running, she finally caught up. Still he wouldn't look at her. A pair of well-dressed women approaching watched him wide-eyed, obviously recognizing him, and whispered to one another as they neared. Jack barged past them, stepping up his pace.

Just before the intersection he stopped cold. He stood uncertain, fists bunched at his sides, face taut, as though he longed to keep going, to escape, only where? Tory's heart lurched. *He has nowhere to go.*

She stepped to the curb and hailed a cab. "Too many curious eyes out here, Jack," she said. "Come on, I'll take you to a nice quiet spot. Private."

"Not your place," he said, eyes fixed on the ground. "Colwell."

"He doesn't come home these days." She opened the cab door for him. "Don't worry, we're not going there. Get in."

The key, as always, was on the grimy lintel above the door outside the third-floor walk-up apartment.

"Go on in," Tory said, replacing the key. "My friend's out of town."

The small place was stuffy, with a faint trapped scent of curry. Plucking at her sticking shirt, Tory moved the dusty cactus off the windowsill and lifted the window to let in some air. She glanced at the flood-lit capitol dome in the distance. It glowed as if in arrogant triumph, and she shivered, despite the heat. "Mortally wounded," her pollster had said, and the coldness in the pit of her stomach told her it was true. But she needed to hear Jack's side first. If she could just get him to talk.

"Have a seat," she said.

He was looking around, frowning. She saw the problem: there *was* no seat. The threadbare sofa was stacked with books. The single easy chair held a jumble of greasy bicycle parts nested in a wad of newspaper. Of the two wooden chairs at the Formica kitchen table, one was piled with dirty laundry and the other was missing a leg. She noticed him glance at the man's ten-speed bike leaning against the wall. True, Jack, you can't sit there.

"Here," she said, moving an armload of books off the sofa. "How about a drink?" She opened the cupboard above the fridge. There wasn't much. "Bourbon all right?" she asked, reaching for it.

Without a word he took the bottle from her and sat on the sofa. She brought him a glass. He poured a large shot and downed it. She hoped the liquor would soften him, lead him to open up.

She called Eric at the office and gave him the number without saying where they were; as long as he didn't know, reporters couldn't pry it out of him. He told her the phones had gone ballistic, and the media were staking out the lobby for Jack. What was he supposed to tell people? "He's unavailable until I say otherwise," Tory said. "And don't call here unless it's an emergency."

"What do you call this?" Eric said, and hung up.

Jack muttered in disgust, "Plague threatens and all they want to talk about is me."

Tory turned to him with hope. He'd finally spoken. "People aren't interested in mankind," she said, "only in folks they know."

"They don't know me," he said darkly, and poured another shot.

Tory felt despair. Had she totally misjudged this man? Had she fallen into the most common trap in the business: believing her own propaganda? She moved the mess of bicycle parts off the easy chair, kicked off her shoes, and sat, waiting for the room to cool down. Waiting for Jack. And beginning to wonder if she really wanted to hear this after all.

Slumped on the sofa, Jack held the open bottle propped on one knee, the glass on the other, and gazed at the faded carpet between his feet. From somewhere through the walls came a thread of orchestral music. Tory recognized the plaintive theme. Aaron Copland—"Appalachian Spring." A springtime memory stabbed: Chris flying a kite at Swallow Point with his father. Oh, why did beautiful music have such power to torment? Still she had no idea where Carson was keeping their son. He hadn't returned any of her calls. None of their friends she'd called knew anything either. She took some small comfort in knowing he would have arranged for Chris to be well taken care of—a housekeeper at a hotel, maybe. But to cut her off from all contact? She'd never thought she could feel such a thing, but she truly hated Carson for this. She would never forgive him. And she would fight him.

That wasn't the crisis to deal with now. She pushed her

concentration past that private ache, past the music, and focused on Jack. She watched as the liquor began to loosen the tension in his face, his shoulders, his hands. "Talk to me, Jack," she said. "I'm on your side."

He glanced at her with a look that said: For how long? Then he let out a deep, angry sigh of resignation, and Tory thought: He knows he's cornered.

Staring again at the thin carpet, he spoke. "My mother wore washed-out dresses donated to the church. My dad picked through ashtrays in truck stops for butts. I was ashamed of them for their failure, their weakness. I went after Vivian to escape their infection. Poverty."

"You pursued her?"

"Very successfully. Got her pregnant." He smiled bitterly. "Like the man said, she was my ticket out." He shook his head at the folly. "Twenty years old we were."

The plaintive orchestral music stopped abruptly. Upbeat Latin dance music took its place. The shift seemed to break Jack's tenuous concentration, and Tory silently cursed it. "Did you love her when you married her?" she asked to push him back on track.

He looked at her with weary scorn. "I loved her money. It got me into med school. Got me big houses and fancy cars. Got me respect." He snorted in self-disgust. "From country club waiters and bank managers, the only kind of respect Vivian understood. And me too, for too long. When I finished med school I went on loving her money, because it let me do the research I wanted and still live like a prince. I figured I had it all."

He stared into his drink. "The work was all I really cared about. So hot to make a name for myself. God, but it was exciting in those days. Postdoc research at Yale Arbovirus Lab. Fieldwork with Lassa fever in Liberia in seventy-two. The first Ebola outbreak in seventy-six. Cutting-edge stuff. Vivian wasn't interested. She spent half the year in Palm Beach. I didn't care, as long as she signed the checks."

This wasn't so bad, Tory thought cautiously. The picture at least gibed with the Jack she knew: the exceptional medical man, driven but dedicated. And the socialite wife leaving a hardworking husband for long periods on his own wasn't a character to stir sympathy.

As if reading her thoughts, he said flatly, "Yes, I saw other women. I'm no monk. I wasn't straight with you when you asked about that." He shrugged in distaste. "Our marriage was a fraud." His gaze drifted and he added wonderingly, "But I had no idea she still hated me this much."

He suddenly fixed hard eyes on her. "You want to know if the rest of what she said is true? No. The truth is worse."

Tory felt a shiver. His failed marriage wasn't the point, never had been. It was the rest that chilled her. The daughter.

Jack poured another drink. Tory waited.

"Diane wasn't wanted," he said flatly. "I was too busy, and Vivian never wanted children in the first place. Kids know it, always do. We both ignored the warning signs. The calls from the school, the drugs. Diane was fifteen when she got pregnant. At breakfast one day she blurted it out. Vivian was furious. Her standing in the community, her good name, blah, blah. She ordered Diane to get an abortion. Diane refused. They screamed at each other. Diane stormed out. I didn't say anything—I'd heard their screaming matches before. I just went to work. I was up for a big promotion at the CDC, been working hard for it, and there was an interview scheduled that morning I didn't want to blow. I still wasn't bringing in anything like the money Vivian had in her own name. Anyway, I figured Diane would soon realize she'd have to have the abortion. What else could a fifteen-year-old do?"

His fingers tightened around his glass. "That night, she came knocking on our door. I got out of bed to go downstairs and let her in. Vivian stopped me. She'd had all she could take with Diane, she said, this was the last straw. Yeah, yeah, I said, and started to go. 'I mean it, Jack,' she said. 'You let her in, I walk out.' I saw she was serious. She was giving me an ultimatum, making me choose. Diane or her."

Tory found she was holding her breath—in disgust at such a hard-hearted bitch, and in dread at what Jack was going to say next.

He stared into the liquor, his face like stone. "I was an addict, hooked on the life my rich wife supplied. So I did what she wanted. As she said, I went down and turned off the porch light. Never saw my daughter alive again."

Even though she'd braced herself to hear it, Tory was shocked. To abandon your own child—how *could* he?

Jack knocked back the rest of the drink, but he was no longer holding the bottle steadily. "When I did it, I figured I could patch things up between the two of them later. I was wrong. Vivian had been itching to burn the bridge, and Diane didn't want to be found. I hired someone to look for her, but . . . not a trace."

He took a deep, steadying breath. "Jump to ten years later. I was a big shot at the CDC by then, chief of Special Pathogens, and Vivian and I were long divorced. It was a February morning, cold for Atlanta. Diane called me from Detroit. 'Daddy, help me, please.' God forgive me, that's what she said, after ten years' silence. I left right away, but there was a blizzard in Detroit. Planes backed up, only one runway open. It was dark when I got to the address she'd given. A basement room, smelled like a sewer. I found her. Too late. She'd shot the man she was with and two of her kids, then herself. I found the gun under her hip. She'd fallen on it." He paused. When he spoke again his voice was ragged from trying so long to keep it controlled. "Might as well have pulled the trigger myself. Ten years before, I'd condemned her to that life. Her children too. This was just the execution."

Tory could almost smell the horror in that basement room. The indictment Jack had leveled on himself seemed just. How had he dared, all these years, to pass himself off as a great humanitarian?

Then she caught herself. Heaven help me, who am I to judge? Who latched on to his superman image, no questions asked, right at the start? Who packaged him for public adoration, this hero who was going to save us all?

The Latin music through the wall swelled in lighthearted abandon. It rattled Tory, but it couldn't break the pall of this tragic story. She sensed she hadn't yet heard it all. "What about Laurel?" she asked quietly.

Jack stared at the carpet. "She was there when I arrived. She'd found the bodies but hadn't seen the gun, so she didn't realize how it happened. I didn't think she could take that extra burden. She was eight, a dirty-faced, confused street kid. First time I'd laid eyes on her. So I lied, told her some addict had broken in. When the police came I told them what happened and asked them to keep Laurel in the dark, if they could. They questioned her, but once they'd confirmed Diane's fingerprints on the gun, they had no reason to talk to Laurel further. She never knew. Right after, I took her away to Europe for a year. Left the CDC cold, never went back. Volunteered for One World Medics in Brussels. After that, it was just the two of us, Laurel and me."

He took a deep breath, and Tory heard the shudder in it. When he spoke again, his voice was shaky. "I could build myself anew because of her. Because in her eyes I was a great guy, not the obscene failure I knew I was. I finally saw I was on this earth to protect her."

Tory felt a quiver run through her. She was looking hard at him—at *him*, she realized, not the newsreel hero she'd created for the public, not the depraved criminal *he'd* decided he was, just the man before her. She thought of her parting shot to Noah. *"He's not a politician, he's a human being."* Why had she never seen it before?

Jack rubbed his forearm harshly across his face. His eyes were bloodshot. "Now she's found out and she hates—" He didn't finish.

Tory couldn't bear to see him suffer. "Jack, it was your wife's fault. If she hadn't—"

*"My* fault!" he said with sudden ferocity. Then again, quietly, "My fault." He raised his glass in a bitter mock toast. "So this's the hero you picked to save the world. You sure picked wrong. The guy's a shit. Fooled everybody."

He poured another drink, sloshing some onto his pant leg. Tory saw his exhaustion, felt he was near a breaking point. She gently eased the bottle and glass away from him, then got him on his feet and into the bedroom. He sat heavily on the bed. "Lie down," she said. "You need to sleep."

He lay back in a sprawl. When she reached to take off his shoes, he snatched her hand and pulled her down to her knees on the floor beside him. His bloodshot eyes, losing focus, searched her face. "Forgive me." She wasn't sure if he was speaking to her or someone in his mind. His grip slackened. His eyelids drooped. The bourbon, and exhaustion, were pulling him under, into sleep.

She didn't let go of his hand. Seeing him this way, as if for the first time, she was filled with awe to think of all he'd endured in the past three weeks. He'd watched his wife die. Taken a massive public campaign on his shoulders—and the overwhelming responsibility. Lost his friend to arsonist thugs. Now, smeared on national TV, he feared he'd lost the affection of the person he loved most, Laurel. He'd taken everything that had been thrown at him, but this was tearing him apart.

She felt ashamed to realize that she'd never looked beneath his facade. He wore his fame and stature so effortlessly, she hadn't suspected the inner demons that tormented him, nor his compulsion to maintain his image. Now she understood. He'd built that image on the ruins of a terrible personal failure. How had he put it? *"Built himself anew."* Jack never called himself a hero, but he loved having the world call him that. It had given his life purpose. She realized that this public unmasking was the one blow he could not take, and Laurel's love the one loss he could not bear.

Reluctantly, she let go of his hand. Too much was at stake here to get sidetracked. She settled in an armchair across from the bed and watched him, trying to focus on how to salvage his credibility. How to play this. How to spin.

Her hand tingled from the anguish of his grip, and try as she might to think of Jack the spokesman, she kept being drawn back to Jack the man.

He had once been greedy, ambitious, even ruthless. And a bad father. But his daughter's death, and Laurel's need, had made him turn his life around. To atone, of course; that had obviously been the impetus. Still, no one could deny the astonishing results. The unfeeling father had become the most tender of guardians. The greedy young doctor had become a courageous humanitarian, risking his life again and again to save others.

*You're too hard on yourself, Jack. Not a hero? You're the only kind that's real. One who made a choice.*

A normal man. He made mistakes, but he's doing good to

make up for them. Isn't that exactly what the whole country has to do?

My God. My own feelings about him—is *that* the spin?

Jack awoke because of the heat. Glaring sun pinned him to the bed where he lay still dressed, his clothes bunched up uncomfortably. He sat up, thirsty, head throbbing.

The apartment was quiet. He went to the other room. Tory was gone. Her absence hit him like a loss. But how could he blame her? He'd lied about himself. Lied by pretending.

Where was he to go from here? The shock of last night's exposé was behind him now—a swamp he'd crawled out of, stinking but alive. Ahead lay a desert, uncharted, unknown. He would no longer have Tory as his guide, while Rachel remained, all-powerful, on the far side.

On the sofa, sunlight glinted off a piece of metal. An earring. He picked it up. A simple gold hoop, the kind Tory always wore. She must have slept here, he thought, noticing the sofa was cleared of books. Or maybe she'd left the earring behind some other time. He glanced at the man's bike by the wall. A friend, she'd said.

His hand closed around the earring. She was a friend to me last night. Defended me. Got me away from the staring eyes, hid me, listened to me. And passed no judgment.

But she has to judge, that's her job.

And so, she's gone.

Can't keep dwelling on her, he commanded himself. Can't let emotion get in the way. He sat on the sofa arm, thumbing the earring like a worry bead, and tried to think.

His participation in the campaign was finished, that was a given. His credibility couldn't survive the scandal. Tory wouldn't give up, of course. She'd regroup, move Senator Owen forward as spokesman, and fight on, however desperate the odds. But without him.

That's what was gnawing him. Rachel would hold off only as long as she was convinced there was a chance the campaign could succeed, and right from the start she'd accepted Tory's caveat that success depended on the public's love affair with him. *Now that I've been disgraced, will Rachel bother to wait for the deadline?*

Call Colwell? Is that the only way out now? Tell him everything? Can I trust the FBI not to charge in on her with SWAT teams, guns blazing, and trip her switch? Assuming they even *believe* my story. *Assuming they don't lock me up.* No, he realized, that route's impossible. No FBI.

A key scraped in the lock. The door opened. Tory.

*She came back.*

Hugging a paper bag of groceries, she gave him a quick psychic audit with her eyes. Then she briskly moved to the kitchen counter and started to unpack food. "Feeling better?"

He didn't know how to begin. He realized he was still holding her earring. He came to her, palm open. "You dropped this."

"Oh, good," she said, touching her ear self-consciously through her hair. "Thought I'd lost it." She usually wore her hair tied back, but Jack noticed it was loose today. She still wore the jeans and white T-shirt she'd had on last night.

"Tory, I want to thank you."

"For letting you have the bed?" she said with a small smile.

"For standing by me through all that, last night. For not leaving."

Their eyes met. "I'm not going anywhere," she said.

A rush of happiness—that's what he felt. A sensation he knew he had no right to. But he held on to it.

She put the earring on the counter. "I got orange juice and blueberry muffins and coffee," she said, opening a cupboard for a plate. As she set the muffins on it she noticed the plate's chipped edge. "My friend's not the best little home-maker."

Bizarre, Jack thought, the two of us here. Hiding away, playing house, trying to avoid mentioning the crippled campaign, the crisis. A crisis her mother created.

"He doesn't get home much," Tory added, moving laundry off the kitchen chair for him.

Jack sat down, as willing as she was to avoid what had to be said. To hang on to this breathing space. "What's he do?"

"Kevin? Runs a little group that helps ex-cons get back on their feet. I do pro bono legal work for them." She glanced at him. "Don't look so surprised. You thought I didn't have a heart?"

"I thought you'd be too busy."

She gave him a knowing look. "Same thing."

She was pouring orange juice into two glasses. "Weird, isn't it? Carson hauls the bad guys off the streets. I help get them back on." She added quietly, "Guess some things weren't meant to be."

She drank her juice, still standing. "Anyway, I usually meet Kevin and his people here. His clients don't like the dress requirements on K Street."

Jack tried to imagine her sitting among the dirty laundry and bicycle parts, explaining parole procedure to a nervous felon too broke to buy a tie. No power lunches, no media hype, no fees. A new picture of her. He couldn't help wondering if the guy who lived here was the inducement. Wouldn't surprise him if she'd responded to affection from another quarter. It was clear that Colwell didn't value her. "This Kevin must be a very good friend," he said.

"Since Mrs. Lee's third grade." She added with a grin, "Ever since he looked up under my skirt in the lunchroom."

She'd finished setting out everything for him, and she

picked up the earring from the counter. He watched her toss back her hair and tilt her head as she fitted the gold hoop back in place. Her beauty stirred him—the fall of her hair curving over her shoulder, her bent arm gently squeezing her breast as she eased the earring into her lobe, her slim hip braced casually against the counter. All the allure Rachel had when they'd first met, but with a warmth of spirit Rachel never—

He stopped himself, shocked. Revolted. How could he think of Tory like that, or dishonor her with such a comparison? She was *in no way* like the woman who'd murdered thousands.

"Well, I've got to get back to the office," she said, straightening. "I've been thinking. You need some time off. How about you catch your breath here today, with nobody bugging you, while I get things sorted out at—"

"No."

"Jack—"

"I'm going back to the lab, Tory. Right away. You know, and I know, that I've become a liability to the campaign."

"That's not true. I just need some time for damage control and—"

"There *is* no time."

"Jack, listen to me, I thought about it all night. You're a good man, a *real* man, not a superhuman god. You took charge of your life and changed yourself, and that's exactly what the whole country has to—"

"I've been thinking, too," he cut in, getting to his feet. He came to her. "Here's the deal. I'll give any public statement you want, make any speech, give any interview—however you want to play it. I'll support Senator Owen as the new spokesman if that's what you want, or I'll grovel with apologies on national TV if that's what you want." The last thought made his skin crawl, but he had to do everything possible to keep Rachel believing the campaign was still viable. "I'll comply with whatever you think is best. I ask only one thing. That you keep my appearances to an absolute minimum. I'm going to spend every available moment from here on in at the lab. All right?"

"I would never ask you to apologize."

He blessed her for that. Still, he had to be sure she understood his priorities. "Tory, the lab is where I may still have some hope of turning this nightmare around. The only place I still have a chance. So unless you call me out, that's going to be my home, night and day. You understand?"

She didn't take her eyes off his. He could almost hear the gears of her mind whirring. Finally she said, "I can live with that."

# 18

CARSON SCANNED THE CROWDED WHITE HOUSE drawing room, looking for FBI Director McAuliffe. He hadn't been able to reach Liota, and this couldn't wait.

President Lowell was finishing a jovial speech to the gathering of staffers. It was his anniversary. "And since the first twenty-five years have been pretty good," he quipped, "we've decided to go for another twenty-five!" Beaming, he put his arm around the First Lady's shoulders. She smiled.

Laughter and applause from the staffers. Cameras flashed. A champagne cork popped. The president joked with mock impatience, "*Now* can I eat my cake?" More laughter.

Carson found it disturbing, this cheerful disregard of the Artemis threat—and the staffers' unquestioning trust that the president would overcome it. Obviously, the party was being staged for this effect; photographers almost outnumbered the guests. The First Lady was setting the blithe tone. Still, Carson couldn't help being impressed by Mrs. Lowell's loyalty. Despite the personal risk of remaining in the capital instead of going to Camp David or the family retreat in Colorado, she was standing by her husband. Bitterly, he recalled the surveillance report on Hunt yesterday morning.

"At 22:10 he entered a low-rise apartment on Walmer Road. He spent the night there."

"Alone?"

"No, sir."

"Well? Who was with him?"

A pause. "Your wife, sir."

"Now go enjoy yourselves!" the president called out. He and the First Lady moved apart to mingle, and the jazz trio seamlessly slid into a *Porgy and Bess* medley.

Carson shouldered into the crowd, looking for McAuliffe. He noticed that the president had joined Quincy in a corner, and he moved toward them thinking Quincy might point him to the director.

"No word? Nothing?" the president was asking in controlled fury. His bluff good humor had vanished.

Quincy shook his head. "Nothing."

"That cocksucker. How—" The president stopped, seeing Carson, and Quincy anxiously asked, "Colwell, have you heard from McAuliffe?"

Carson was surprised. "No. I'm here to find him."

"Christ," the president growled. "Tell him."

Quincy said tightly to Carson, "He's bailed."

"What?"

"Forty-five minutes ago I got a call from Akim Faludi at CBS News. Their video crew at National caught McAuliffe and his wife rushing for a British Airways flight to London. I guess McAuliffe tried to keep his wife quiet, but she talked to the video crew anyway. Said she was terrified of the plague and was getting out of the country. They both got on the flight. McAuliffe's gone." He shook his head at the enormity of the disaster. "Just when the president's making a national address in less than two hours. Jesus."

Carson was appalled. Ian McAuliffe had been his mentor, and one of President Lowell's oldest friends.

Quincy gave a snort of dismay. "Here I thought we'd blown PGT out of the water with the exposé of Hunt. *He's* fucked, sure, but their message is still sucking them in, people are so scared. And *our* message? 'No need to fear, folks, everything's under control.' After this? After the world sees the FBI director jumping ship on the six o'clock news?" He added savagely, "Fucking coward."

"Shut up, Randy," Lowell said wearily. "What do you know? You're not even married." He glanced at Carson with a look that said, What man can predict how he'll act where his wife is concerned?

My wife left me no alternative, Carson thought bitterly. Tory chose to stand with the enemy—and apparently to sleep with the enemy. Worst of all, she put my son in harm's way at Swallow Point with Hunt. That was unforgivable. Poor Chris—naturally he couldn't understand being taken away to a strange place. This morning, when Carson had called the Maryland hotel where an agent had been with the boy for almost a week, Chris had asked plaintively, as he did every day, "When is Mommy coming? When can I go home?" It only deepened Carson's anger. Chris's anxiety was a direct result of Tory's own destructive actions. She had damaged their family beyond repair.

The president asked Quincy with sudden cold-blooded resolve, "All right, who the fuck do we put in Ian's place?"

"Ed Liota?"

"That jerk-off?"

"He's on top of this," Quincy said.

"*Acting* director, then. Effective immediately."

Stifling his distaste at the decision, Carson checked his

watch. Time to move. "Mr. President, in the absence of the director, I'd like to inform you of a decision I've made regarding Jack Hunt."

"Not a player anymore," Quincy said dismissively. "His credibility's shot to hell."

"Agreed," Carson said, "but my concern is that the situation may have put him in an unstable frame of mind. I don't want to risk it pushing him over the edge, maybe to effect an early release of the virus."

Did he also want something else? To wrench Hunt away from Tory? He'd had to face that question before he came. Had this become too personal—a jealous husband's vendetta? The answer had come easily: no. Tory had made her own bed, and Carson felt more disgust than vengeance. What he felt most strongly, however, was that his responsibility in this crisis transcended *all* personal considerations.

"What do you want to do?" the president asked him.

"Arrest him, sir."

"I thought you wanted him to guide you to the Artemis leaders."

"I now believe he may be one."

"No shit?" Quincy asked, excited.

Carson hesitated. The evidence was thin, but he was running out of time; he had to go now on instinct. He hated being pushed into that, but on one level at least, his instinct about Hunt had already proved right: look how the man, years ago, had treated his own family. As for the Artemis connection, he was certain of this much: Hunt was hiding something huge. The conclusion seemed obvious. Hunt was right at the center.

"In that case," the president said, "do whatever—"

"Colwell," Quincy jumped in, "how soon can you make this arrest?"

"The Boston SAC is ready to move on the Lesage lab at

my signal. I'm leaving now. Barring irregularities, we'll have Hunt within two hours."

"Then you can announce it in your address, Mr. President," Quincy said eagerly. "Artemis suspect captured. It's perfect. We deflect focus from McAuliffe's desertion, *and* annihilate PGT."

Lowell nodded gravely. "I can't announce anything, though, until we hear from Colwell that he's got Hunt in custody. Can we postpone the address until then?"

Quincy looked pained. "Another hour, tops. We have to get out there with it before CBS runs the story on McAuliffe."

The president turned to Carson. "Mr. Colwell, you've got until the six o'clock news."

Rachel sat in the easy chair by Del's desk in his study, feeling imprisoned. Fussing over her, he had tucked a blanket around her and insisted she sit quietly for at least an hour while he worked on his book. "If you won't obey the doctors, obey me," he'd told her firmly. "I won't have you drive yourself into the ground."

Although she craved to get up, get out, she also craved rest. Her throat still felt on fire, and the headaches were almost unbearable. But it was nothing compared to her agony about Jack. The exposé two days ago disgracing him had jeopardized the whole campaign. *Another* crisis she hadn't foreseen. There'd been too many. And still he persisted in his work at the lab. Was he gaining on her?

She winced at the throbbing pain in her jaw. A low-grade infection. The antibiotics seemed useless. What if the infection got worse, incapacitated her? *I cannot allow it,* she wanted to shout. *None of it.*

"What is it?" Del asked, his forehead creased in concern.

"Nothing," she said, still hoarse. Impatiently, she waved him back to work. He'd been writing notes in his meticulous left-handed script; he still used the gold fountain pen she'd given him twenty years ago. Instead of taking up the pen again, though, he opened a drawer and lifted out a yellow binder. Rachel felt a prick of alarm.

She remembered the binder. One of Tory's old ones from high school, exuberantly graffitied with designs—Del never threw anything out. Rachel remembered it because it held an early draft of Del's manuscript, one she'd helped him organize over two years ago. But the book had gone through radical editing in several drafts since then, so why had he kept this old version, the only one that presented a threat to her? And how had she missed it herself? She thought she'd destroyed every shred of evidence. "That's obsolete material, surely," she said, more edgily than she'd intended. After all, the risk here, she reminded herself, was minimal. "You should throw it away."

He murmured, "Hmmm," and nodded vaguely, absorbed as he leafed through pages, apparently looking for something. Rachel's nervousness became acute.

*Too many worries.* It was getting hard to sort them all, prioritize. Her mind felt fevered from the nagging infection. Walking wounded, she thought bitterly; a houseful of us—me, poor Del, Laurel. The girl had been acting like a zombie ever since the tabloid TV program, one moment blindly packing to return to her apartment in Boston, the next moment giving up, whining that the media mob at the gates would only swarm her, follow her. Her indecision irritated Rachel beyond reason. *Why are people so incapable of action?*

The thought tripped her. Have I become incapable too? Is direct action the only answer now? Release the virus early, before Jack discovers how to stop me at the lab?

There was no perfume device this time; she'd done that only for the demonstration, separating the two benign viruses to prevent an outbreak until the shipments reached the remote targeted sites, and then to ensure confinement of the epidemic there. This time the elements were already mixed. The lethal virus was in shipments of water bottles—free samples labeled as a promotion for a well-known charity. Couriers would deliver them to selected outlets in malls, airports, and hotels.

Del suddenly looked up at her. "You're quite right," he said. "I'm too much of a pack rat. Must toss this rubbish away."

Rachel gave him a ghost of a smile. One minuscule worry less.

Gigantic ones remained.

"So the field hospital you were running was under constant shelling?"

"Night and day," Jack said, his eyes on the computer. He was sitting with Tory in his office, his concentration split between her questions about his time in Bosnia and the virus modeling data on the screen. A discrepancy in the data was nagging him. For two days he'd been holed up with Youssef and Mandy, living on cafeteria sandwiches and caffeine, refusing all calls but Tory's, trying to force the computer modeling to reveal a route toward a treatment. "Explosion every few minutes," he went on absently, shifting the mouse to speed up the scrolling. "Bullets through ward windows. Part of the roof blown off."

"But you kept on operating, delivering babies, tending patients?"

"Sure."

"Thousands wouldn't," she said wryly, jotting a note.

He looked at her. The negative response to the news that he'd abandoned his daughter had been instant and vitriolic, even from the woman's groups and environmental groups who'd been most favorable to PGT, but Tory still kept slogging. Yesterday she'd flown a video crew here for him to make a public statement, and wrote his script herself, crafting it to be neither groveling nor arrogant, and ending with a challenge to the government to address the crisis at hand. Jack had given it his best shot, but PGT's numbers had continued to plummet. With only eight days left.

If Rachel waited that long.

Watching Tory write, he could only think with a shudder: She's at risk. He couldn't conceive of Rachel jeopardizing her own daughter by targeting Washington. But she'd already done so much that was inconceivable. Laurel, too, was at risk. Laurel, who wasn't talking to him, taking none of his calls.

"So I guess, to you, this is nothing," she said.

"What?"

She nodded at the window where the faint chanting of the protesters outside could be heard: *"Hunt down Hunt!"*

"Oh, them. The police keep them in line now." He barely noticed them anymore. Protesters were the least of his worries. "Mandy," he shouted at the outer office, "did you check these numbers on the bacteriophages?"

"Not since you added the data on the DNA sequencing," she called.

"Well, damn it, get *on* it!"

She shot back angrily, "Before or after I analyze the proviral integration into the chromosomal DNA?"

He clamped down his frustration. No good yelling at Mandy. "Keep at the analysis," he called back, "I'll check this myself." As he reached for a spreadsheet on his littered desk he told Tory, "That's all the time I can give you. Sorry. You see how it is."

"Well, you've given me lots of ammunition." She closed her notebook. "Your One World Medics work is definitely our new focus. This morning we taped a testimonial from the organization's director in New York. He can't praise you enough. And we got another from a Zambian immigrant, a teacher, who swears you saved his life and thousands of others by turning the tide of a cholera epidemic in his refugee camp. The world can't dismiss all the good you've done."

He looked at her skeptically. "Whatever you say."

Packing away her notes, she shook her head in angry frustration. "If we only had the Brazil video, or—"

"Or?"

"Or Laurel. Jack, won't you reconsider?"

He'd forbidden Tory to call her. He was adamant about protecting Laurel from a media feeding frenzy. Already she was a virtual prisoner at Swallow Point, under siege by hordes of journalists at the gates intimidating her from returning to Boston as she wanted. "Leave her out of it," he said. "She's been through enough."

"A statement from her in your defense would mean so much."

"She's not interested in defending me."

"How do you know? Camping here, you haven't seen her since that scumbag program aired. It caught her off guard, that's all. Now she's had a couple of days to think. If you'd just let me talk to her—"

"Drop it," he said, then immediately regretted his harshness. "Tory, just leave her alone, please."

She slammed her briefcase shut. "I can't stand by and watch them crucify you."

He couldn't help thinking how much he liked having her in his corner. Colwell was a fool. "Don't worry," he said, "I'm still kicking."

Outside, the chanting swelled ominously. *"Hunt down Hunt!"* Tory flashed a murderous look at the window. "Bastards." She quickly pulled herself together. "Well, I'd better go if I'm going to catch my flight." She stood.

"Tory," he said, getting up with her, "couldn't you run the campaign from somewhere else? Europe, maybe? I mean, with all the technology it's possible, isn't it?"

"Trying to get rid of me?"

*At risk.* "Yes."

"Bit of a downer for troop morale though, don't you think? Commander sneaking off the battlefield? Go on, get back to work. I'm calling a cab." She reached for his phone.

"Your keys, Doc."

"What?" Jack turned. Youssef stood in the doorway looking Tory up and down. "Keys." He tapped his watch for Jack's benefit. "Five o'clock, remember? CDC?"

"Oh, right." Jack had called the CDC to request fresh serum samples. They were being hand-delivered to the airport and he'd asked Youssef to take his car to pick them up. He flipped back his lab coat to rummage in his pants pocket for the car keys. "Sure you're okay to leave?" he asked as he tossed over the key chain. Youssef was running a delicate experiment in level four.

"Don't fret, Doc. I've got an A-3 cake in the oven but it'll be a couple of hours before I can ice it."

Tory hung up. "Jack, I'll call you from D.C. after the president's address." She started for the door.

"Tory, wait. Cancel the cab. Youssef's going to the airport. He can drive you."

"Okay. Thanks, Youssef."

Youssef eyed her appreciatively. "Pleasure's mine."

Hands off, kid, Jack almost said. Instead, he grumbled to Tory as he turned back to work, "Make sure he behaves himself."

As they left, Mandy excused herself to go to the washroom, and Jack, alone, started scrolling through the data again from the top and refocusing his thoughts. The tasks he'd set for Youssef and Mandy and himself were huge. He'd directed their research on two fronts. One was a bacteriophage interference theory, but it depended on manipulating an intracellular separation of the binary virus, a process that still eluded them. The second involved an attempt to circumvent the virus's ability to replicate. With retroviruses, this process was not infallible, and "mistakes" sometimes led to inactive, dead virus. He was trying to find ways to boost those mistakes in A-3 by attacking its protective structural proteins.

Both, he reminded himself, were only hypotheses.

He was jotting notes when an explosion rocked the room. His pen scrawled wildly down the page, his head boomed, the window rattled. Grabbing the desk edge he knocked over a cup of cold coffee that flooded his notes and splashed his thigh. "Mandy, you okay?" he yelled, then remembered she'd gone.

All was quiet again. Whatever it was had lasted for just one shattering moment.

Then he heard screams. He rushed to the window and saw people running toward the parking lot where his car was.

*Youssef and Tory!*

He tore down the stairs. People were pouring out of offices and filling the halls. In the lobby the open glass doors reflected an orange glow outside. Jack ran out with the others. Over people's heads he saw the top of the oak tree on fire at the corner of the lot. His parking spot was under that tree. Through a break in the people he saw his car. His heart ballooned in him, then seized. The car was an orange ball of flame.

# 19

"JESUS!" THE HELICOPTER PILOT HISSED. THE EXPLOSION on the ground forced him to veer, aborting his landing on the Lesage Laboratories roof. Beside him, Carson was craning down at the parking lot, while behind him the Bangor agent yelled, despite the helmet mike, "What the hell is that?" They all stared at the billowing orange blaze.

The pilot was lifting the helicopter in a wide arc, moving away. "No, down! Over there!" Carson ordered, pointing to a company lawn across the street. He grabbed the handheld radio. He could see Bureau cars racing down the Lesage driveway as scheduled, with Boston SAC Art Strentz in the lead. Maine was his territory and he was coordinating this mission to apprehend Hunt. "Strentz, what's happening?" Carson yelled into the radio. "Are you under fire?"

"Can't tell . . . stand by!" Strentz's voice crackled over the radio, the static not masking his alarm. Though the importance of the mission dictated they arrive in force, no one had anticipated serious resistance, Carson least of all. Christ, had he underestimated the extent of Hunt's organization?

Strentz said, "Looks like a car bomb," and the Bangor agent in the rear clamped Carson's shoulder and said, pointing down, "Demonstrators. Might be their doing." Carson could see them running around the blaze. A bomb at the very moment of his arrival?

The pilot landed on the lawn across the street, and Carson jumped out, yelling into the radio as he ran, "Strentz, talk to me!"

Over static: ". . . trouble breaking through the crowd . . ."

Carson raced across the street toward the Lesage parking lot. Chaos. Protesters and lab personnel swarmed the lot. Victims of the bomb cried out above the shouting. Local police on-site, confused by the explosion and the sudden arrival of the unmarked Bureau cars, made things worse as they tried to halt the plainclothes federal agents as well as the civilians. Through the crowd Carson glimpsed the blazing wreck, a tree beside it on fire. He pushed through toward Strentz, who stood by his car overseeing the FBI team's frustrated advance, while also trying to assess the situation, including the possibility of further attack.

Strentz yelled at several agents in succession, "How many fatalities? Get some people to the roof. Are the medics—" He stopped as Carson reached him. "It's Hunt's parking space," he reported, "and we're pretty sure it's his vehicle."

Hunt dead? Carson thought wildly, *No! He's mine.* "You sure he's in it?" he demanded.

"Somebody is," Strentz said grimly. He turned and yelled to an agent, "Ray, clear these people out of here!"

"Sir," another agent called to Strentz. He was leading forward a uniformed, balding man, very agitated. "This man's a Lesage security guard. Says he saw Hunt after the detonation."

Carson pushed through to the guard. "You saw Jack Hunt out here? *After?*"

"Yes, sir. Running out of the building. Running right in front of me."

Carson tried to scan the area around the lab's front doors for Hunt, but the crowd was too dense. He turned back to the guard. The man wore glasses. Thick lenses. "You're positive it was Dr. Hunt you saw?"

The guard scratched his head, confused. "Looked like him."

Carson groaned. "Strentz, get some people to—"

"Sir!" An agent was leading a young Asian woman toward them. She stumbled, looking over her shoulder in horror at the blazing wreck. "Mandy Chang," the agent reported.

Strentz quickly clarified to Carson, "Yale postdoctoral student, works with Hunt. We've been watching her."

"Miss Chang," Carson said, "we've got to know if Dr. Hunt is in that car."

She couldn't tear her eyes from the fire. "Youssef," she mumbled. "Oh, God."

"Al-Saadawi?" Strentz asked her. "He's in the car?"

She nodded, stunned. "Yes."

Strentz told Carson, "Youssef al-Saadawi, John Hopkins doctoral candidate, also working with Hunt."

Carson said impatiently to the girl, "Did *Dr. Hunt* get in the car with him?"

"No."

"You're positive?"

She nodded shakily. "Just Youssef and that woman."

"Woman?"

"From Washington. PGT."

*Tory.* Carson spun around to the fire, aghast. No one could have survived that.

*  *  *

She was struggling to her feet, dazed, dizzy from the explosion. She'd stopped in the lobby to make a call. Coming out and approaching the car, she'd seen Youssef open the driver's door, then a giant fist of energy slammed into her, her vision went black, and she'd found herself on her back on the asphalt, gasping for breath.

She crooked her arm in front of her face to block the searing heat, and squinted at the flames in horror. *Youssef!* She staggered forward to look for him. Smoke clogged her throat. People were running around, mouths open as though they were shouting, but she couldn't hear, not anything—as if her skull were packed with wool. Suddenly her legs buckled and she fell to the pavement on her hands and knees, trembling, disoriented. She touched the top of her head. A clump of her hair was wet. She lowered her hand: her palm glistened with blood. Blood dripped from her head onto the pavement.

Someone jerked her arm and it sprang up, weightless, like a puppet's arm. She twisted her head to look. Jack, pulling her up from her knees. His distraught face was lurid in the orange glow. His mouth was moving, but she couldn't hear.

Throwing his arm around her waist, he flipped her on her back, catching her head before it hit the ground, then picked her up and ran with her in his arms. She felt the heat diminish from the burning car, the burning tree.

"No, Jack!" She pointed back. "Youssef."

He shouldered around people, reached the lawn, and set her down on the grass. She struggled to sit up. "No!" she cried, pointing. "Youssef's—"

He grabbed her hands, restraining her. He was on his knees beside her, frantically saying something. She couldn't *hear.* She clutched his lab coat. "We've got to go back for him!"

Face creased in anguish, he looked at the car. Tory saw it was only a skeleton as flames consumed it. She knew now what Jack was saying. Youssef could not have survived.

"Oh, Jack!" She threw her arms around him. He held her so tightly she felt the breaths ripping into his lungs, felt their hearts pounding together. He pulled her away and searched her face as if to assure himself she was really alive. He suddenly looked appalled, seeing the blood on the side of her head—she felt its warmth dribbling through her hair and into her ear. She was about to tell him she couldn't hear, when she glimpsed a form moving through the crowd. Carson? She blinked. Gone. Must have imagined him?

Jack's head jerked toward the lot as if he'd heard a shout. Tory turned. A man was crawling beneath the burning tree. Jack ran toward him, but a flaming branch from the tree pitched down and crashed onto the crawling man's legs, and his mouth stretched in a scream. Jack reached him and kicked the branch off, but the man's pant leg was on fire. Jack ripped off his lab coat to beat out the flames, then dragged the man by his arms to the lawn beside Tory.

Again, through a break in the crowd, she saw Carson. Only a glimpse, but no hallucination. He was here. She started to get up. "Jack. Look."

He tried to restrain her, gesturing that she must sit down, but she struggled to her feet. "I can't hear you, but look!" She pointed. "It's Carson." He was moving purposefully through the crowd, searching, with two men at his side. Fellow agents. "Jack, he's come for you. You've got to get out of here."

He shook his head, protesting, and gently placed his hands on either side of her head to calm her, his face tight with worry about her.

Damn it, hadn't he seen Carson? "Listen to me." She grabbed his hands to stop him—to hang on to him. She knew her words must be slurred because she couldn't even hear herself. "I know Carson. He's suspected you from the start. And I know how the White House operates. They're desperate. They need an arrest and you're *it*. Look around, for God's sake. Carson's brought a squad."

He still didn't believe her, just kept talking. It was terrifying, the impotence, the disorientation—*deafness*. She was holding on to him for balance, for strength, but she had to let go, had to get him away. Out of danger. "Jack, please—"

Red lights strobed over them. An ambulance snaked through the crowd. Jack waved wildly to beckon it.

She wrenched his head back to face her. "You can't let Carson take you. If he locks you up I can't do anything for you. Look, if I'm wrong you won't have done anything illegal by going, and PGT can carry on. But if I'm right and he arrests you—if you're their trophy—it will snap the last thread of hope for the campaign. You've got to run."

With a pained look he pointed at the building, talking frantically. She couldn't hear a word, but she realized why he was still resisting. His lab work.

"Jack, if they take you into custody, even without charges they can keep you for days, weeks. You can't do any good inside prison." She was pushing him away. "Go! Now!"

Carson shoved aside a police officer, trying to get to her. Thank God, she was alive. Two medics were lowering her onto a stretcher on the grass. They'd wound a bandage around her head, but a wet stain of blood had already wept through, her clothes were splattered with blood, and she looked as if she was in shock. Or worse? Reaching her, he called, "Tory!"

She stared straight ahead as though nothing registered. Concussion, he thought. How bad was it?

"Move aside, sir," one of the medics said.

"Is she badly hurt?"

"Are you a relative?"

"She's my wife."

"Call the hospital later. Now move aside, sir, *please.*"

"Sir," an agent yelled, running to him. "It's Hunt." He pointed to the far edge of the parking lot.

Carson twisted around. Hunt was running out of the lot. But not toward the street.

He looked back at Tory. If her injuries were critical, how could he leave? *But if I stay with her, Hunt escapes.* He wouldn't entrust this to Strentz's men—he had to take Hunt himself. For a moment he stood paralyzed. "She's my wife," he'd just said. Three weeks ago their family had been intact. But she had moved herself outside their family, beyond his protection, and he no longer felt she *was* his wife, or any essential part of his life. He cared, of course—wanted her to live—but she'd be in good hands at the hospital. The truth was, he wanted Hunt more.

He looked back. Too late: he'd lost Hunt in the crowd. But he'd seen the direction he was going. "Strentz!" he called into his radio. "Hunt may be headed back into the lab. Have your people cover all exits and proceed as planned."

"Haven't got the manpower," Strentz replied. "We're spread too thin with these casualties, plus deploying among the demonstrators, because I can't assume this bomb is the last."

"Hunt's the priority!" Carson yelled back. "Get your—" He stopped. The medics were lifting Tory on the stretcher. She was looking straight at him, her face white, eyes hard. She knew. Carson felt no remorse. The chasm between them had become too wide to bridge. He didn't even want to.

As the medics carried her to the ambulance he lifted his radio and broke into a run. "Just get those exits covered!" he told Strentz. "I'm going in."

*   *   *

Rachel stood staring at the flames rippling like liquid over the hulk of the car. Jack's parking spot. Jack's car. A horror like ice tightened her spine. *Jack's dead.*

Coming from home, her chauffeur had stopped at the entrance, and she'd just stepped out when the explosion made her stagger on the spot. Now, in the chaotic swirl around her—people swarming, a fire truck pushing through, an officer barking orders at a radio—she was the only still point, frozen, her eyes on the burning car.

"Rachel!" She turned and saw Carson running toward her.

From the corner of her eye she noticed a man walking quickly into the building. The movement caught her attention only because everyone else was moving in the opposite direction. It was Jack.

Carson grabbed her elbow and forced her to move along with him. "Rachel, I need your help. Hunt's headed into the lab. I've got a warrant for his arrest. I can't explain now. Just show me the layout inside."

Jack tore down the hall, rage constricting his chest. *They killed Youssef.*

And almost killed Tory—her blood still streaked his hands. He'd left her with agonized reluctance, hardly believing her frantic warnings, until he'd glimpsed Colwell himself. For a moment, in fury, he'd considered a confrontation. The bastard had no evidence to hold him! But Tory was right: You can't do anything from prison.

He'd felt his only hope of getting out was to go in; Colwell would have blocked off the street. He would position agents at all the lab's exits, too, but there was a chance that the thick crowd would keep them from reaching the rear of the east extension for a few minutes. All the lead Jack needed.

He ran down the empty hall, hearing only his pounding footsteps and his own breaths strident with rage. *They murdered Gerry. Now they've murdered Youssef. And if Tory's concussion—*

A door swung open and a young technician burst out. Jack lurched around him. The kid took off in the opposite direction. Jack ran on.

He was passing an open staircase when he heard voices ahead. Colwell—with Rachel. Sprinting up the steps to avoid them, he'd made it only halfway when they reached the spot beneath him. He stopped. Any sound would make them look up. Through the steps' open slats he could see their heads. He tried to hold back his sawing breaths.

"What about your special lab, level four?" Colwell was asking her. "Does he have keys?"

"Yes, but it has only one entrance. If he went in he'd be trapped."

"Maybe he went for something in his office. Where is it?"

"Second floor, west wing."

Jack's heart thudded. Was she actually helping Colwell search? Logical, he told himself. His usefulness to the campaign was finished. She could afford to sacrifice him.

Two agents reached Colwell, their radios crackling. One reported, "Sir, we have the west and north exits sealed."

Rachel said, "Carson, I must see about the people hurt outside. It's my responsibility. Jack's office is 2D, that way. If he's anywhere inside he can't get away." She left.

"You're with me," Colwell ordered the two agents. They took off down the hall.

Jack scrambled down the stairs and ran onto the east extension and reached Rachel's door. Crossing her office, he realized he was horribly exposed: two whole walls were glass. But her rear door led to the steel staircase he'd seen

her climbing that first day he'd arrived. She'd been returning from the ravine. The ravine was what he'd come for.

At the glass wall he scanned the grassy area below. No
one in sight. The wooded ravine lay just a long stone's throw
away. He knew he had only moments before Colwell's men
outside made it around to this private exit. Then he would be
trapped.

He checked the door handle. Not locked. He pushed it
open.

"I thought you might try this."

He twisted back. Rachel stood in the doorway to the hall.
Was Colwell right behind her?

She hurried to her desk, snatched a scrap of paper and a
pen, and scribbled something. "He's come to arrest you."
Moving to him, she stuffed the paper in his shirt pocket.
"Go."

He bolted down the steel staircase. In thirty seconds he
was inside the woods.

He couldn't help leaving deep tracks in the spongy
ground. He struggled through the thick trees, descending
over uneven ground down to a stream, and splashed into the
water. Keeping to the gravel edge where the water was ankle
deep, he ran along the stream. He had no idea where it led—
his only thought was to put distance between himself and
the FBI. When he judged the stream was shallow enough, he
waded across it and left it by the opposite bank, wet to his
thighs.

He started up the opposite slope of the ravine. Soon his
mud-caked shoes were heavy clubs. Near the top of the
slope he lost his footing and fell, his knee hitting a sharp
rock. Pain flared up his leg. He labored onto the summit,
then struck out through dense bush, his knee throbbing.

He saw more sky through the branches, and heard traffic:

a road was near. Breathing hard, he looked over his shoulder. Colwell's men wouldn't be far behind.

One gear of his mind was still locked on Rachel: What had she written? He pulled the paper from his pocket and read it. His fist closed around it.

*Have to get out of here.*

He pushed on toward the sounds of the road, through a stretch of brambles, thorns catching at his muddy pants. The brambles gave way to unkempt grass at the verge of the road. A sixteen-wheeler roared by, belching diesel exhaust.

He paused for breath, and to think. *Can't get far on foot. Hitchhike? No, police bulletins out soon. My face is too well known. Got to find a vehicle.*

A police cruiser sped by, siren screaming. He bent over as if collecting beer empties in the grass. The siren faded.

He looked across the road and saw a Sipco gas station and a strip mall with a half-dozen shabby stores, including a corner 7-Eleven. A lone pickup truck, its cab in shadow, was parked in front of the 7-Eleven. Oily exhaust drifted from the tailpipe . . . *It's running.*

He waited for a break in the traffic and crossed the asphalt toward the truck—then noticed the driver in the cab studying a newspaper. *Damn.* He turned to the gas station instead. No cars there at all, but inside the cashier's booth a middle-aged man and woman wearing matching blue windbreakers stood poring over a map with the teenage attendant. Outside sat their vehicles: identical gleaming blue Honda Goldwing motorcycles. On the seat of one lay a silver full-face helmet.

Jack judged by the helmet's size it was the man's. He approached the bike. No key in the ignition. *The guy must have taken it with him into the booth.* He looked back across the road, expecting through every break in the traffic to see federal agents streaming out of the bush. Two more wailing cruisers raced by, heading toward the lab.

Then he saw, on the other bike, a blue Pisces decal dangling on a key chain from the ignition.

He glanced back at the booth. The man was engrossed in talking to the attendant, apparently arguing over directions, each pointing a different way. The woman was busy applying lipstick, stretching her lips before the booth's darkened glass. None of them noticed Jack as he slid the helmet off the man's seat, stepped back to the other bike, and straddled it. He jammed the helmet on his head, twisted the key, punched the starter, and pulled out into the traffic.

# 20

THE SUN WAS SETTING WITH ORANGE-GOLD BRILLIANCE behind the small town of Ryeport as Jack turned the Goldwing onto the quiet main street. He'd been riding fast for hours; in town now he'd slowed, going as unobtrusively as possible. Still, the expensive motorcycle turned heads. A woman outside the Laundromat, stuffing a garbage bag of clothes into a station wagon, looked at him and frowned. A little boy leaving the drugstore with a Popsicle stared at the mysterious, helmeted head. Two teenagers lounging at the Shell station eyed the bike covetously.

Leaving town, Jack passed a few straggling outskirts businesses—a used car lot, a peeling clapboard motel, a deserted roadside fruit stand—and pulled into a lonely self-serve station where he filled up and checked the road map. Only about ten miles to go.

The station had a small general store where he picked up bread and cheese, bottled water, a flashlight, a knife, and matches. At the last moment he grabbed a sweatshirt; he figured he'd be sleeping rough. He paid with cash, didn't stop to talk to the chatty young woman at the register, crammed the stuff in the bike's saddlebag, and drove off.

Back on the highway again, the going was smooth. The hours of riding—the wind, the speed—suffused him with a raw energy that was both bracing and soothing. Sheer momentum. He was on the move, alone, all complicating options left behind, all baggage of remorse cast off. The mind-set felt familiar. How many third-world roads had he barreled along, concentration grimly but calmly focused on potholes, mines, and snipers, and the simple, urgent goal of reaching the next village where suffering people were counting on him? Even more familiar was the absence of fear. A sense that over the years, he'd faced—and fought through—worse. Now, people were depending on him as never before. Maybe the whole world. So, was this self-assurance an illusion? He was being hunted. His chances were slim. The stakes were immeasurable. Yet, at this moment, on the move, stripped to nothing but the creed that had defined him for a decade, he felt on solid, self-chosen ground.

After a few miles, following a sign, he turned off on a dirt road that skirted a woods. He slowed, scanning the edge of the trees. The cover was thick. He hated to part with the bike, but it made him too easy to track, and this was a good place to ditch it. He gunned it into the woods. He couldn't get far in the dense underbrush; when the tires spun in the loam he stopped and turned off the engine. Silence, except for a woodpecker madly drilling deep inside the woods.

With some effort he pushed the big machine over and set to cutting pine branches, covering the bike with them, then throwing dead leaves and dirt on top. After fifteen minutes he'd only managed to bury two-thirds of the gleaming metal, but at least what wasn't covered was dulled by the film of debris. It would have to do. He had to get moving.

He didn't know the country—wasn't sure how far he'd have to walk—and the sun would soon be gone.

Grabbing his bag of provisions, he headed back to the dirt road. As he stepped out of the woods he heard the whomp of helicopter rotors and ducked back under the foliage canopy. Had they tracked him so fast? He listened, his heartbeat thumping like the rotors. As the overhead sound faded he decided that they hadn't spotted him. He started quickly down the road, constantly checking the sky.

After about half a mile the road curved around a wooded hill. He could make out a large house sitting alone at the top above a thick collar of pines. He was startled to see, through a huge picture window, a fire blazing, orange flames leaping out of control, a form writhing in the flames—Youssef.

The hallucination lasted only a heartbeat: the blaze was just the orange sunset reflected in the glass. For one wild moment he hoped Youssef's death itself might be just a delusion. No such luck, of course; and no such balm for his sorrow.

The mirage of the fire persisted. He realized it was because the rest of the house lay in darkness, with no other light as a reference.

The helicopter sounded again in the distance. Coming back? He couldn't risk staying in the open any longer. He decided to try the house: no lights on probably meant no one was home. Besides, it was near where he needed to be.

Walking quickly up the gravel drive, he saw this was a home on a grand scale. Or had been, once. His hallucination hadn't been completely unfounded: fire had ravaged the place, though some time ago. Must have been some millionaire's fantasy retreat, he thought. The sweeping facade of marble and steel was an arrogant snub to the humble landscape of scrub pine and rock. Now, though, it was just a scarred hulk, its doors and shattered windows boarded up with plywood, a section of the roof caved in, the lawn a tangle of weeds. He found a side door where porcupines had eaten away a corner of the plywood panel; he wrenched off the rest and went in.

The cavernous, charred living room was barren of furniture, and squirrel droppings littered the ivory broadloom. A huge painting took up half a wall: a nude walking into the sea, her back to the artist, raven hair swinging between white shoulder blades. Jack thought of Tory, deafened by the bomb, blood dribbling through her hair. How he'd longed to hold her, stay with her. He turned away from the painting. No room for worry about her condition. The ER staff would do all they could. Out of his hands.

He walked briskly through to the back and came out on a deck overlooking the ocean. Adjoining it was a squat round tower, its door hanging on one hinge. Inside, Jack went up three broad steps to a marble platform. He saw that the whole tower was a lavish hot tub room, its circular walls and domed ceiling brilliant with turquoise ceramic tiles, though the drained tub was just a hole. There had once been a curved picture window, but it too was a gaping hole; its glass lay in shards in the tub's cracked bottom and over the surrounding floor. Bird dung streaked a section of the turquoise walls, and a nest bristled in the crook of a mahogany beam.

Jack walked to the window hole, shoes crunching on the glass, and looked out on the cove below. The tower made a good observation post, just as he'd hoped. He glanced again at the darkening sky for helicopters. Nothing. His eyes swept the expanse of water. Nothing. His ear strained to hear racing FBI cars crunching up the gravel drive behind him. Only silence. But he knew they were up there, out there, all around. It was only a matter of time.

He'd taken his stand.

He set down his bag of provisions. He still had many hours to wait.

At eight the next morning Tory scanned the bleary group slumped around her conference-room table, and thought everyone looked as beat-up as she felt. Her head still throbbed from the wound sutured with staples last night in the Bar Harbor ER. Attractive, the shaved spot with those staples: Bride of Frankenstein. At least, thank God, her hearing had returned—although she would almost have preferred deafness, given the two-hour grilling by FBI agents she'd endured at the hospital. They'd only let her go when they seemed convinced she didn't know where Jack was, which was true—a worry that had hovered in her mind all night, above a heavy lingering sadness about Youssef. The uneasy sleep she'd finally snatched on the dawn flight back to Washington had brought little relief.

"All right, any other thoughts?" she asked the group.

There'd been precious few in the last twelve hours. Her staff had been stunned last night by the attorney general's televised declaration that Jack was wanted by the FBI in connection with Artemis. Their shock, she'd told herself, had been natural: every one of them had been through political campaigns where, at one crushing blow to their candidate, all had been lost. But they'd been through just as many where they'd rallied by the next press deadline, and turned catastrophe into victory. The roller-coaster ride was part of the all-midway ticket. The outcome here was infinitely more significant, of course—but all the more reason, it was clear to Tory, to blast away with all the firepower of their experience. For most of this campaign, they had. No, what was unnatural, what was worrying her now—and beginning to make her angry—was that twelve hours later they were *still* in shock. Noah had been standing at the window for fifteen minutes, hands in his pockets, looking out. Her pollster, Henry D'Aquila, sat obsessively picking invisible lint from his sleeve. Others just stared ahead blankly. Tory had been doing all the talking. No one had answered her last question. She thought in exasperation: What if they simply don't move?

"Then I'm going with the harassment concept," she said brusquely. "Persecution of an innocent man. White House using the FBI hammer to silence a dissenting voice. Eric, line up the VidVox people for a production meeting. Where's Vince?" As Eric trudged out she turned to her communications director. "Janice, let's get this persecution angle out to the friendly media first."

"Sure, all two of them," someone muttered in despair.

"Almost impossible to play," Janice agreed shakily.

"Tory, this spin is hopeless," her field coordinator, Fletcher Brown, said.

She counted to five to master her irritation, then said, "That's a word I don't use."

"For God's sake," he yelled, slamming his palms on the table, "the FBI's calling him Public Enemy Number One!"

Tory was taken aback by his aggression. Until this moment, Fletcher had been the quietest. "That's just to deflect the focus from McAuliffe," she said. She'd already explained this White House tactic. Why couldn't they grasp it? "Don't you see? His desertion has made them desperate."

"And we're not?" he shot back.

His wrath surprised her. Flustered, she dug in her pocket for the painkillers from the ER nurse and popped back two with a mouthful of lukewarm tea. She needed them, but she also needed the cover. The best policy was to ignore Fletcher's comment. She couldn't let these dramatics get out of hand. *She* hadn't lost sight of the stakes here, even if they had. The fate of millions—maybe of humanity itself—depended on the fragile hope that this campaign would succeed. Fragile, but still very real; her every instinct, her every reading of the public pulse, told her that. Clear thinking was needed now as never before. She turned to her pollster. "Henry, how soon can you get me some numbers?"

Wearily, he pushed his glasses to the top of his head and massaged the inner corners of his eyes. "Which focus? Stifling dissent or persecution?"

"Persecution. Innocent man hounded."

He shrugged, exhausted. "Maybe some preliminaries by tonight."

"Get on it," she said. "Noah, I'll need a statement prepared within an hour."

Noah, at the window, didn't turn. "Is he?" he asked.

"What?"

"Innocent."

She felt the eyes of the others slide to her, and felt dread hovering like a raptor. Her mouth went dry. In the silence, a phone in the reception area bleated over and over. Someone finally answered it.

Noah turned. "Where's he hiding, Tory?"

She made herself swallow. "I don't know."

"He hasn't even contacted you, has he." It was a statement, not a question.

She pretended to look at her notes. "Where the hell is Vince?"

"Time to face facts," Noah said. "Hunt's been using us."

Tory shuddered. Two weeks ago Carson had said the same thing. She'd rejected it wholesale, blocked it out. Now she had to face the horrible thought. *Was Jack part of Artemis?*

Amazingly, the moment she met the threat eye-to-eye, it dissolved. The Jack she had come to know—know almost as intimately as a lover—could never be part of such a thing. She said to Noah firmly, "That's not true."

"Damn it, Tory, he *ran*. If he's not guilty why did he run?"

"I told him to! And I'm telling *you*, Noah, this isn't a campaign you can just bow out of because you're not comfortable with the candidate's position. None of us can. This *matters*."

"You're fucking right it matters!" Fletcher burst out. "Jesus, Tory, I've got a wife and daughter here in D.C. and a mother and sister in Minneapolis. Artemis could target either place. *Any* place. Jack Hunt's nothing. You've hung this whole campaign on him and it was a rotten decision. You want to talk about persecution? Fuck Jack Hunt, let's talk about the thousands of innocent women who are going to die. The millions. *That's* persecution!"

Stunned, Tory was groping for a response when Eric rushed back in looking stricken, holding up a photograph. "This was just couriered from Dallas," he said. "Ken says it's happening all over the South." The photo showed a PGT billboard of Jack, his face spray-painted over with huge red letters: KILLER! "I called VidVox," he added shakily. "They say they won't work with us anymore."

"Christ," Fletcher moaned, "it's hopeless. The FBI's got an army looking for Hunt. They'll get him. The campaign's finished. Without it the White House won't negotiate. Hopeless. Christ, a plague."

Janice burst into tears. "I can't take this!"

"Stop it. Everybody," Tory said. "We've got—"

"No, *you* stop," Noah told her. "You've completely lost sight of the *real* campaign here. It's not about Hunt! We should have changed tack the minute we heard about what he did to his family, but you're so smitten with him you can't see he's—"

"That's enough!"

"Yeah," he said coldly, "I guess it is. I've had it, Tory. I'm out of here. And I'm going to try to get my family out of the country, too, while there's still time."

Alone in her office she shut the door, then had to lean against it to collect herself. She'd pulled the rest of them together after Noah had stalked out, but only by demanding assignments to keep them frantically busy. How long could she keep their panic at bay? How many more would desert with Noah?

*The only hope is to show them we're not dead. Show everyone.* There was still one person who could do that. She grabbed the phone and called Swallow Point. "Doris, I need to talk to Laurel."

When Laurel came on the line she sounded as though she'd been crying. *She's heard from Jack,* Tory thought, hope and worry colliding. She longed to ask, but she had to assume that Carson had tapped the Swallow Point phones, so she said quickly, "Laurel, if you've heard from him, don't say anything, just—"

"I haven't," Laurel snapped, "and I hope I *don't.* Ever again." She sounded about twelve years old, Tory thought, and very hurt. Was she still nursing her private wounds, even in this crisis? Incredible.

"Why can't everybody just leave me alone?" Laurel complained. "You're as bad as the FBI. 'Any secret place he might have spoken about?' Like I told them, he doesn't tell me his secrets. Only lies."

*Oh, please,* Tory thought, gritting her teeth. Wasn't anyone going to stand up for Jack? Mustn't upset her, though; got to get her on our side. Try a different tack. "I'm sorry about the FBI. Have they been harassing you?"

"They still are. Crawling all over the place."

Tory thought of Chris, glad for the first time that he wasn't there any longer, with armed agents now in the house. The realization made her feel slightly sick. Had Carson been justified in taking him away?

No. If the house had become dangerous for a child, that was Carson's doing. Chris had never been in danger from Jack.

"Laurel," she said firmly, "I need your help. To make a public testimonial in Jack's defense. It could make all the difference to what we're doing here. And to Jack. I know it's asking a lot, that you've been through a lot. But, well, you hurt him too, and—"

"I hurt *him*? What about what he did to *me*?"

This was too much. "What's he ever done but take care of you and give you everything you want and love you unconditionally? What more *should* he do?"

"How about telling the truth! It took my grandmother to do that!"

"Oh? And where's *she* been all these years? Sounds to me like she didn't knock herself out to find your mother, or even to contact you after the killings. Am I right? Did she ever visit you? Call you? Even write to you?"

Frosty silence. Then: "No. I never saw her in my life till that program."

"But since Jack found you he's *always* been there for you. He's done everything for you a loving parent could, and he's done it all alone. Laurel, you must not hurt the people who love you. It's the only sin there is."

"*He* hurt people. He treated my mother like shit. He lied to me! He let me go on believing those deaths were my fault. He's *evil*."

"That's a very stupid thing to say."

"Yeah, well, I'm a stupid kid, right? Isn't that what you all think of me?"

"I think you're immature and self-centered, but for some reason Jack loves you. Now, when he most needs your support, you desert him? It's time you took some responsibility for your own life and recognize how much you owe him."

"God, you're a witch," Laurel sputtered. "No wonder your husband left you!" She slammed down the phone.

Tory realized her hand was trembling. *What the hell am I doing, haranguing a mixed-up adolescent? How is that going to save this campaign?* For years she'd cautioned her staff: *"It's not personal, it's politics."* The stakes here went horrifically beyond politics, yet she couldn't seem to move past the personal—Jack. Noah's accusation still echoed. *"You're smitten."* God help me, she thought, closing her eyes, it's true. The world's crashing down around me, and I'm falling in love with the man who's pulled it all down.

By seven that evening the bread and cheese were gone and he was rationing the water. He sat cross-legged in the hot tub tower, rearranging shards of glass on the marble floor.

He hadn't been outside all day. Last night he'd slept in the charred living room, his sleep fitful on the musty carpet as he listened to mice scrabbling in the walls. About midday he'd heard rotors again, and the bone-tingling vibrations told him the helicopter was passing directing overhead.

It was almost time. He was waiting. And working.

He'd had to pick the spot by the wall carefully because shattered glass lay everywhere. He'd found a use for the glass. He had lined up the shards as proxy molecules, each one selected for a resemblance to a specific molecular shape. He'd been working with them for hours.

He had blanked out all other thoughts. About Tory, maybe lying right now beneath a neurosurgeon's knife. About the death blow he had delivered her campaign. About Colwell tracking him. About whether Rachel would stick to the deadline. All these horrors he refused to examine. Marisa,

Gerry, Youssef—he allowed none of those pitiful specters to intrude. Not even the hated image of Rachel herself. He had no idea how much time he had before the FBI would find him. He focused his mind on the work, because his mind was all he had.

Over and over he'd been realigning the shards in various configurations, trying to put himself inside the micro-universe of Rachel's viral creation. To overcome it, he needed to enter its world.

The setting sun turned bloody as he worked. Moving the glass around, he conjured up the visuals of Mandy's computer modeling, pondered the essence of endogenous retroviruses, pictured the sequence of viral DNA reproduction.

Molecular weight of the retrovirus envelope: 160,000; glycoprotein 160.

Matrix proteins.

Macrophage tropism.

Data and formulae stretched into thin abstractions of energy that flitted through his mind like the bats darting outside in the dusk. Insubstantial, but real.

Something—some answer—felt close, just beyond the reach of his mind.

Daylight faded as he stared out the window hole, waiting for the last of the light to die, and thinking . . . thinking.

"Persecution of an innocent man, it's all I ask!" Tory slammed down a badly written press release draft. "Come on, people, this isn't rocket science!"

Henry, her pollster, glared at her, one of the remaining few of her team spread thinly around the conference table. Tory knew she was bluffing with this indignant act, bluffing herself, unwilling to face the fact that everything was falling apart. Janice and Fletcher had quit around noon, and two more hadn't showed up for this late meeting. Tory and the four who remained were trying to juggle video, print, and radio themselves—and Tory had her doubts about the pollster. And where the hell was Vince? "Damn it," she said, snatching the draft, "I'll edit it myself."

"Excuse me," Marcia interrupted from the door, "there's someone here to—"

"Who is it?" Tory snapped.

"Laurel Hunt."

The moment they were alone in her office Tory almost pounced with, "You've heard from him?"

Laurel shook her head. Tory slumped in disappointment. Her back ached, her head throbbed, and her whole body longed to sink into the sofa, curl up, sleep. "Then what is it?" she said, more harshly than she'd intended. She had no time for more tantrums.

Laurel looked uncertain. Tory crossed her arms, impatient, waiting. In the hole of silence between them, the evening traffic on K Street was a faint, disinterested roar.

"That car bomb," Laurel said hesitantly. "I still can't believe it. Youssef took me out to dinner once." She added with a sad smile, "Quite a little operator." The smile vanished. "He didn't deserve to die."

Did anyone ever deserve to die? Tory wondered bitterly. The millions threatened by Artemis? Despair was claiming its perch, hunkering down on her shoulders. She'd been trying to maintain the strength to shake it off, and the last thing she needed was the extra weight of Laurel's angst. "Listen, Laurel, I'm very busy. Was there something you came for?"

A struggle was going on in Laurel's eyes. "Funny," she said quietly, "how a person gets mad when they're really just scared to death. Me, that is. I don't mean about Artemis. That's out of my control. I mean, scared about *myself.* I think maybe I've always known, deep down, the truth about what my mother did. And always been terrified that"—her voice wavered, thin as a child's—"that sooner or later I'd become just like her." Tears welled. She looked down in shame.

Tory's anger melted. *Life goes on,* she thought, struck by the paradox Laurel personified: a girl trying to get her own life straight even as catastrophe loomed. Self-centeredness is at the core of everything people have screwed up on our benighted planet, Tory thought, yet this self-engrossed struggle of Laurel's—to change oneself, to rise above—is exactly the human spirit that's worth fighting to preserve.

She came to Laurel and cupped her chin and lifted her head. "You're not your mother," she said gently. "You've just proved that by facing your demons. But," she added, "there's a lot of Jack in you."

Laurel smiled through her tears. "Thank you," she whispered. She looked down at the desk where press photos of Jack were scattered, and fingered one. "He's been working so hard. Your campaign, the lab. Now he's on the run, all alone—and I've been such a bitch."

She looked Tory in the eye and said suddenly, decisively, "I came to help him. What do you want me to do?"

"Scrap the persecution angle," Tory announced, striding back into the conference room with Jack's photo. She'd never felt so energized. Laurel was right behind her. "We're going to show Jack Hunt for what he is. A hero. A leader. The only one brave enough to act. His granddaughter is going to tell that to the nation."

They looked at her, dazed.

Tory suffered a flicker of doubt. Was it too late to turn them around? She met Laurel's smiling eyes, and confidence surged back. I'll bring in a whole new team if I have to, she thought. Mercenaries, if that's what it takes. I will get this *done.*

"Rod and Eric," she plowed on, "you come with Laurel and me into the studio. To hell with VidVox, we'll tape her statement ourselves, right now. We'll work on the script while we set up. Magda, go find that guy Jack saved from the fire in the lab parking lot. He's likely still in the hospital. Take a camera and get a testimonial. I'll tape one too, about how Jack rescued me. Don, pull the best file pictures from One World Medics showing Jack saving lives abroad. Of kids, if you can. We're going to give the public a good look at the man the FBI wants to throw in prison."

A couple of her people sat up straighter, but everyone still looked hesitant. Tory realized she'd blasted ahead too fast. She had to slow down, let them catch up, let them feel the hope, the urgency, the *necessity*, of her plan.

"Listen to me," she said, "we're not talking about winning or losing anymore, we're talking about survival. That's why this campaign *is* about Jack. Artemis is poised to attack." She grabbed a front page *Times* photo of President Lowell and held it up to them. "The president is willing to take acceptable losses." She held up Jack's photo beside it. "Jack Hunt isn't. Ask yourself, Which man will you follow?"

She didn't wait for an answer. "On your feet, everybody," she commanded as she walked out. "And somebody find Vince."

A far-off splash. Jack straightened with a jolt. It was dark. He'd barely noticed the loss of light, so lost in his thoughts, chasing formulae, drifting with data.

He depressed the light dial on his watch. Not yet ten. Frustrated by the interruption, he went to the window and strained to see what lay out in the darkness. The cove was a black desert. Above, no stars, just a sliver of moon. His mind was tugged back to the black hole of his thinking. That nagging *something* felt so near—a core of light, masked, lurking, as though at the far end of a wormhole, its attainment just beyond his grasp. He felt if he could just stop pushing, just float, let his mind go on ahead . . .

Then he saw it. A low, lone star slowly moving through the watery desert, coming directly toward him.

A masthead light.

He swiftly gathered the garbage of food wrappers and water bottles, crammed them into the bag they'd come in, then yanked on the sweatshirt. Grabbing the bag, he glanced around to make sure he'd collected everything he'd come with. No one would know he had been here.

He scrambled down the slope, virtually blind in the darkness. Couldn't risk using the flashlight in the open. When he reached the cove's sandy shore he could no longer see the masthead light. He stared out at the black void. Lapping water probed his feet. Frogs chorused. Had he only imagined the light?

He cursed the false alarm for severing the thread of his thinking. He'd felt so close.

His eyes caught a pinprick of yellow. This new light, smaller, lower, was bobbing over the water toward him, as though the moving star before dying had spawned a tiny offspring. He signaled three times with the flashlight—all he could risk.

Minutes later the inflatable dinghy with its small yellow light on the gunwale whispered onto the wet sand near him. Rachel switched off the light. "Get in."

He tossed the bag aboard and hopped over the gunwale. "I'll take the oars, he said.

Rachel made room. Jack rowed. Yesterday, he'd burned her note: *Kingfisher Cove, seven miles south of Ryeport, 22:00 hours tomorrow. Meet me*. If the FBI caught him, he couldn't have them find this message from Rachel on him.

She guided him out through the darkness; she knew where the cove's rocks were. They reached her boat and climbed aboard. Jack hauled up the anchor as Rachel took the helm. Within minutes they were leaving the cove under sail. The wind was rising.

# 21

"A PRIVATE AIRSTRIP CUT INTO THE BUSH?" Carson suggested, standing at the wall map.

"FAA says there's nothing in a thirty-mile radius."

"Helicopter?"

"Unlikely. It's all backwoods where he was headed. If one met him in a populated area, we'd have heard."

"Well, we haven't heard anything about the damn motorcycle for twenty-eight hours either. Question is, what does that *mean*?" Carson immediately regretted raising his voice to Stan Kendrew, his deputy. At least no one else noticed, given the din in the command center. It was almost midnight. An agent nearby was irritably demanding clarification on stats from a red-eyed researcher. Phones were ringing. Someone slammed shut a filing drawer. The smell of burned coffee lingered in the air.

"He's *got* to have been picked up," Carson insisted, eyes again on the map. "You sure the people at Machias are on top of this?" He jabbed the spot indicating the Machias municipal airport fifty miles west of Bar Harbor.

"We've had guys crawling over it since dawn. All roadblocks are operational."

"Dawn, hell, the witnesses saw him pass the Ryeport Laundromat at seven-fifteen last night, and Machias is just another twenty miles. He could be having breakfast in Baghdad by now."

"Or he could still be out there right under our noses," Kendrew shot back. "Look, the choppers'll be up again at first light. We can't assume we've lost him."

"I'm not assuming anything. Keep your guys looking, sure, but think about what Hunt is *doing*."

"Keeping his head down, if he's gone to ground."

"He isn't a man to sit and wait."

"Unless he had orders to."

"That's not how we've seen him operate. He has to be *doing*."

"Well, shit, he only has to sit tight for six days. Less, if Artemis shoots before the deadline."

Carson didn't miss the desperation in Kendrew's voice, but his own concentration was already elsewhere. On Rachel. He was thinking of her deduction that Artemis, like the Russians' Biopreparat operation, might comprise only a handful of individuals. Conceivably, just one.

Of course, that was just from a scientist's point of view; she'd been thinking of the virus. At the time, Carson had felt that the sophisticated organization of Artemis's attacks required a network. Yet in three weeks he hadn't uncovered a single link to it, not even an informer. A multitude of crank calls aside, not one authenticated individual had come forward spurred by remorse, or fear, or even greed for a reward. Artemis's network was either the best trained army in history, or nonexistent.

So now he was thinking, What if Hunt *alone* is Artemis?

If so, he'd have to be operational to release the virus by the deadline. Strentz's people had established, as nearly as they could, that Hunt had escaped from the lab with nothing, not even a cell phone, so to activate the release he'd have to *get* somewhere. Carson turned back to the map. Three weeks ago he'd considered Hunt only an opportunistic mouthpiece of the terrorists. Then, almost immediately, as one of their operatives. Recently, as one of their leaders. Now, the sole leader?

"He isn't in hiding," he said to Kendrew. "He's on the move." On the map he ran his finger along the coastline around Ryeport. For miles it was raggedly indented with bays and coves and inlets. Literally hundreds of them. And each one led to the open sea.

There was only one answer. A boat.

Jack saw a jagged pine horizon burst out of the night off their port bow. As Rachel quickly tacked, Jack winched in the jib sheet, and the island's rocky coast slipped past, a mere two boat-lengths from their hull. Minutes later, to resume their course, they had to tack again. For a nerve-wracking hour they'd been beating into the wind this way, zigzagging toward open water. He knew Rachel's whole concentration was on navigating through the maze of small islands, with only a slice of moon to light their way, and the strain showed on her face. Jack, too, when he wasn't grinding the winch after their tacks, was peering out for rock hazards. They had barely spoken, except, as soon as they'd left Kingfisher Cove, he'd anxiously asked, "How's Tory?"

"She's fine, back at work."

Thank God, he thought.

"Keep a lookout, Jack. Other boats can't see us to avoid

us." With the running lights off, they were ghosting through the night.

Finally they cleared the bay and headed south, and Rachel bore off onto a swift beam reach. Jack could almost feel the boat settle into a groove, black water combing past the leeward deck. Despite the darkness, he could sense the wider sea room, too. It felt good to be moving fast and free again after his night and day huddled in the burned house. But he reminded himself that both the speed and the freedom were illusions. "Where are we going?" he asked warily.

"Home."

*Home?* "They'll be looking for me there."

"They already have. They're still there. If we can maintain this speed and make it back before dawn, I'll put you ashore in the dark at our point. You can hide in the beach house. They checked it once. I doubt they will again."

Hide. The thought galled him. Is she shutting me down, or protecting me? Why bother? With the campaign in its death throes, why not let them capture me? She knows I can't betray her.

She seemed to read his face. "I don't believe you'd talk willingly, but they do have sodium pentathol."

Drugs to elicit truth. A sobering thought.

"Besides," Rachel added, "it's important to me you remain available to communicate with Tory. You may still have some small influence with the public. There's still a chance, however slight . . ." Her voice drifted, and Jack thought: She knows it's hopeless.

"If I'm wrong," she said flatly, "I'm prepared to accept the alternative."

Jesus. Release of the virus.

"You can contact Tory from the beach house," she went on as if they were merely talking business. "Not by phone, of course—I'm sure our lines are tapped. But there's e-mail.

My company Internet domain name covers thousands of employees' computers at my labs here and abroad. It would be virtually impossible for the FBI to trace a message sent from the beach house computer."

"What about you? If they're at the house didn't they see you sail away?"

"They saw me sail to the lab. I told my assistant I'd be busy with an experiment all night and wasn't to be disturbed. After I drop you off I'll sail back, then use the ravine to get back inside."

As if she'd never left, he thought. Very neat. She'll be free to act; I'll be a prisoner in the beach house. What can I do from there?

Christ, what had he expected? A flight to Paris on her jet and free use of the Pasteur Institute? Obviously the FBI would have the roads and airports covered. He looked up at the Milky Way glittering coldly above, and suddenly felt like the desperate fugitive he was. Powerless. His fate in her hands. The deaths of innocent friends in his wake. The deaths of millions looming.

The black night seemed to blot him out, make his irrelevance absolute. It struck him, with a whole new sickening perspective, that in the last hours he'd been reduced to obsessively shuffling glass shards, as if they might yield up some magic. There was no magic, he saw now, only reality. And the reality was that he had failed, in every way. Failed to convince the country. Failed to discover a treatment. Failed Gerry and Youssef. Failed Tory. Failed Marisa.

He felt cold to his bones. Rachel was going to win her dark victory, and there was nothing he could do to stop her. *I can't even kill her.*

Never had he known such despair.

He watched her. Her eyes were feverish in the starlight, her breathing shallow, and she was shivering slightly, though the night was warm. The purple bruising around the bandaged sutures on her throat looked inflamed. Was infection from her wound making her fevered? Was she unhinged after the weeks of tension? Or just plain insane? He remembered Del's words: *"She has a purely logical mind, but not when her family is threatened."* And Tory's statement: *"Losing my brother almost killed her."* Was that what had triggered this madness? Rwanda? The lost boy?

The thought gave him the faintest jolt of hope. Could he use that? *Disable her with kindness?* "Curious George," he said suddenly.

Rachel gave a small gasp and stared at him. Turning way abruptly, she concentrated again on the helm. But Jack saw that she was fighting for composure. He'd exposed a traumatized nerve.

"Tory told me," he said cautiously. "How you took him to Kigali, then got separated in the war." Careful, he told himself. Probe the wound but don't induce pain. He sensed the partly severed nerve would yield an answer, if he could delicately reconnect it. "What happened?" he asked gently. "Didn't you ever find him?"

She said, as if he hadn't spoken, "There's a bell buoy around here marking a channel entrance. Watch for it."

"Rachel, tell me about Paul. Please."

"Why?"

"Because I want to understand."

Her eyes flicked to him, betraying a spark of trust. She said in a hollow voice, "I found him." Her gaze slid back to the darkness.

Jack waited. Finally, she spoke.

"I came to a village. Full of hope, because a missionary told me he'd heard there were children hiding there and one was American. But I heard no children's voices when I walked in. No voices at all. The place was deserted. Soldiers had been camping, I could see that, but they'd gone. An orange brick church dominated the square, the Church of Our Lady. Inside, more soldiers' litter. Apparently they'd stayed for some time. I sat in a pew, sick with disappointment. I'd been searching for weeks."

A bell tolled mournfully in the distance as a wave stirred the channel buoy.

"Then I heard a snuffling sound. I hurried past the altar. A hall led back to the church offices and kitchen. A dog was tearing open garbage under the kitchen sink. But there was a smell—an awful smell—farther down the hall. I reached the room—the library. Easy chairs. A portrait of the pope. And on the floor, corpses of naked children. Twenty or so. They'd been beaten, tortured, starved . . ."

She looked up at the barren sky. "I found him in an alcove. Curled up as if asleep. Wrists tied behind his back with wire. Leg chained to a spike in the floor. The shackle on his ankle had scraped his skin raw. He'd been sodomized, burned with cigarettes . . ." Her voice broke. "Every agony you'd rather suffer a thousand times yourself than have your child go through."

She closed her eyes, unable to go on.

Watching her, Jack felt the mountain of his hatred erode under a trickle of pity.

When Rachel could speak again she seemed to shunt her mind forcibly onto a different track, to leave the place of misery and move on. She said flatly, "Rwanda is one of the most densely populated places on earth, and the result was the most barbarous civil war in memory. People dismiss the cause as tribalism, but that's too shallow. All humans are tribal. No, the Rwandan chaos stemmed from something worse, from—"

"Too many people fighting over too few resources," he said, finally piecing it all together.

She nodded. "People clawing each other for the last bone. Rwanda, Yugoslavia, the Congo. It's what lies in store for the whole planet. Hundreds of millions will die."

He saw now what must have happened after Rwanda. Rachel was not a woman to weep, or whine, or even rage. She had rechanneled the energy of her grief by learning the tragedy's root cause. These last weeks, he'd been trying to inhabit her mind, and knew that was how her mind worked: for every phenomenon, a cause. For every problem, a solution.

"So," he said carefully, "you're doing this to prevent the death of hundreds of millions."

"Triage, Jack. Sacrificing some so the majority may survive. It's a technical decision, not a moral one. You know that. As a physician you've practiced triage every working day of your life."

He thought of Somalia, of the Mogadishu hospital overflowing with the sick while hundreds of wounded and dying camped in the street. He'd personally walked among them taping numbered squares of paper on their foreheads: a "one" for the cases where intervention could be lifesaving, a "two" for those to be hospitalized and treated later, a "three" for those whose injuries required too many resources and must be left to die. "All the time" he admitted. "But—"

"But this is too many deaths? Well, tell me, what's the magic number? In a refugee camp you'll sacrifice hundreds to save thousands, and you're called a hero. Yet you won't grant me that same standard on a global scale?"

"No one gave you the authority. You aren't God."

She smiled with profound sadness. "I've learned the humility of being a god. When Paul and I were first separated, when he ran from the soldiers' guns, I screamed at them, 'He's not one of you!' How wrong I was. They are us, and we are them. We will all live together, or we'll die together."

"Paul. That's what all of this is about, isn't it? Because you failed to protect him."

Her eyes searched his. "You understand. I know you do. Because you failed, too, with your daughter. You've been trying to atone ever since by committing yourself to saving others, one at a time."

"This isn't about me."

"Yes, it is. You think your way of saving the world is better than mine. It's not, because it's not enough. You change nothing."

He'd been following, sticking with her arguments, edging closer to her reasoning, and finding he couldn't help but agree with most of it. Her logic, unassailable, had almost seduced him. But finally his mind balked. Logic could not mask the fundamental evil of her actions. No amount of brilliant dialectic could change her in his eyes into anything less than Marisa's murderer. He said harshly, "Global murder cannot be the answer."

"That's not my choice!" she shot back. "I'm offering a humane solution, but they—" She coughed, and Jack saw again that she was shivering. He stood and pulled off his sweatshirt for her. "Here."

"I'm all right."

"There's hours of hard sailing ahead, right? Take it."

She relented. As she slipped the sweatshirt on she raised her eyes to his. They were standing face-to-face.

"Rachel," he said quietly, "you can still stop this. Give it up. Right now."

She shook her head. "Too late."

Dread clutched him. "There's still six days before—"

"The campaign has self-destructed. The country's paralyzed. Nothing but hysteria and viciousness. Car bombs and homicidal protests and billions of dollars spent on a mad scramble of security forces instead of on the solution. People don't change even when it's blatantly in their interest. Humans cannot see beyond tomorrow."

Her doom-laden voice infuriated him. "Christ, if you think we're such a worthless species, why not just let the ecological disaster you're so sure is coming wipe us out, get it over with? Why go through this psychotic exercise?"

She looked surprised. "Worthless? I thought you understood. I'm doing this because I have hope."

"Hope?" After her nihilistic statements the word made no sense.

"Of course. I believe humankind has dazzling potential."

He felt unbalanced. "You say the whole problem is that we can't change."

"No, I say it's rare. Our history is mostly a story of mediocrity. Greed and misuse of power and willful ignorance. But it's also a story studded with individuals who've pushed us onto higher planes. Forgiving one's enemy. Sharing wealth. Dreaming of going to the moon, and doing it. These are the spheres of true humanity, and they are within our collective reach."

"I've always believed that."

"I know. You're the finest example of what humans can be. You're the paradigm I'm talking about."

He couldn't speak.

"Unlike you," she went on darkly, "the rest of humanity presently shows no *will* to change. Well, the virus has no such obstinacy. Maybe, in its aftermath, this stubborn species will finally learn. That's what I'm trying to do, Jack. Give the human race a chance to get it right."

He looked out into the darkness. Wind sighed over the sails. Water whispered past the hull. Stars glinted in the high black sky and in the low black ripples. The night was wildly beautiful. He stared at it, his thoughts in free fall as they sailed on, alone on the ocean—he and the woman who was prepared to destroy perhaps a third of the world's people. For all the right reasons.

"The wind's dropping," she said.

Jack pulled his mind back from the void.

In the faint electronic glow of the compasses he could see Rachel checking her watch, then the readout on the GPS, which gave their position. She seemed to be calculating odds. "We've got to get back before it's light," she said.

She turned on the engine. It kicked in with a brutal roar, shattering the still night. As she slid the throttle forward, the hull plowed into the low waves.

They were a ghost boat no longer. Now, they could be heard.

"He's out there," Carson said under his breath, staring at the map's blue expanse.

"Coast Guard's reporting every hour," Kendrew reminded him.

"I want *our* people on it, checking every craft along this coast. Tankers, trawlers, power yachts, sailboats, even dinghies if they've got an outboard. There's been good weather for thirty hours, so even a small boat with enough fuel could have covered a couple hundred miles by now. If he made a rendezvous at sea with an oceangoing vessel—"

"Then he could be halfway down to Cuba or up to Newfoundland."

They exchanged glances. Carson knew it, but didn't say it: a boat at sea would be all but impossible to trace.

"Sir, we found the motorcycle!" It was Strentz's liaison man, shouldering past people to get to Carson. "Hunt ditched it in the woods about six miles south of Ryeport."

"Good, let's lay out a grid," Carson said. He was moving to a table map when he noticed Shelby Sanger, the FBI lab's materials analysis chief, pushing in through the glass doors and heading his way.

"What have you got?" he asked as Sanger reached him.

"Something real interesting," the chief reported in his soft Georgia drawl. "Those traces of soil on some of the vials? We found a microorganism in them that Chem/Tox reports is rare. In fact, only found on a few islands in the Caribbean." He handed Carson a list.

Carson snatched it. Seven islands of the Greater Antilles. It brought him closer. Damn it, not close enough.

Sanger was smiling. "I also did a little checking. Did you know that Uncle Sam gives a mighty generous tax subsidy to U.S. corporations doing business in Puerto Rico? Section Nine three six of the Internal Revenue Code. Costs the America taxpayer a bundle, but I guess the windfall of jobs keeps the islanders from getting uppity and heading north. And you know what the biggest business sector in Puerto Rico is? Pharmaceuticals. Why, just about every drug corporation on the Fortune 500's there. Whole flock of 'em, soaking up the Caribbean sun."

Carson felt a fierce adrenaline rush. Finally, the breakthrough he'd been waiting for.

The wind had been dropping all night. The sails were almost useless now, but the engine kept the boat's speed up. The autohelm, which Rachel had programmed with coordinates hours ago, was steering a straight course. She was resting in the cabin below. Jack was alone on deck.

He sat in the cockpit, his back against the cold fiberglass, his spine deadened by the engine's vibrations, his mind numb. He'd seen no boats, heard no sounds above the engine drone. For hours there'd been nothing for him to do. When the realization had swept him that there was nothing more he *could* do to stop Rachel, he had finally surrendered.

To the truth. To the exhaustion of weeks of trying. To the inevitable. He'd let go, emptied his mind. Emptied himself into the nothingness around him.

The submission had been oddly liberating: a kind of relief to no longer exist.

His eyes burned from staring so long into the darkness. He closed them, and when he opened them again he noticed that the cover of the lazarette—a seat locker by the tiller—was raised about a finger's width, propped open by a protruding loop of dock line. When Rachel had lifted out the autohelm she must have tugged the line with it.

Absently, Jack raised the cover to stuff the line away. Inside, a plastic bucket held a jumble of junk: broken shackles, a cracked block, some frayed nylon line. He crammed the dock line in and was about to close the cover when he noticed an object on top of the junk. A sphere of dulled metal about the size of his fist. Its surface was badly corroded, gouged in craters, some so deep that they exposed—which was what had attracted him—the starkly white core, white as an apple's flesh.

A memory tugged. They'd been sitting over lunch at Swallow Point that day he and Laurel had arrived, and Del had spoken about the boat's recent repairs, including a new sacrificial anode. He'd explained about corrosion in underwater metals caused by current due to the difference in electrical potential. "If a zinc anode is mounted near the metal you want to preserve, like the bronze propeller, the zinc corrodes first, protecting the bronze. It's sacrificed."

This half-eaten object must be the discarded anode, Jack thought. He lifted it from the bucket, its pitted surface rough against his palm, and studied it, oddly attracted by its poignancy. Maybe it was the hours of inactivity, so alien to him. Or maybe the sense of his own insignificance. Whatever the reason, he let his mind drift into unexplored channels. Like words. *Sacrifice*—a word so potent with meaning. *Attract*—the corrosion had attracted him. *Protect—the zinc is sacrificed to protect the bronze.*

Suddenly, in his mind's eye, a glass shard glittered. A shard in the hot tub tower. He'd used it to represent the molecule called CD5. It was present on the surface of cells related to macrophages, and he and Mandy and Youssef had identified it as the principal cell receptor for the A-3 virus.

He felt a tingling at the back of his neck, like a mild electrical current. What if *free* CD5 molecules could be introduced into the bloodstream? This purified CD5 might compete with the CD5 on cell surfaces for binding with the virus. In theory, it would attract the virus, blocking its binding to the cell. Eventually, the complex of free CD5 and virus would simply degrade. The free molecules would be "sacrificed," preserving the cell. The chemical equivalent of a sacrificial anode.

A molecular decoy.

Cool air chilled his wide-open eyes. He realized he was holding his breath.

A sound startled him, a faint electronic beeping inside the cabin. It stopped, and Rachel came up on deck holding the portable GPS. Jack remembered she'd programmed it to signal when they reached a critical waypoint. He quickly slipped the zinc anode into his pocket.

"We're approaching the channel to our bay," she said.

He peered into the gloom and could just make out the mainland in the distance. Still far off, though, and the house at Swallow Point was hidden, tucked into its bay. He knew the FBI was there, watching.

Rachel switched off the engine. "From here on we can't risk the noise."

The moment the motor cut out, they slowed, and Jack felt the wind on his face die. Silence shrouded the boat.

Rachel eased out the limp sails. They were running downwind—what little wind there was, really no more than a breath—but were barely gliding through the placid water. Dawn was beginning to glimmer.

Rachel tried sailing wing and wing. They worked together, Jack pushing the boom out as far as he could over the port side, while she coaxed the languid jib sheet as far as possible to starboard. They inched along, the sails luffing sluggishly, the boat hardly leaving a wake.

They crept through the channel and into the bay. In the predawn murkiness the wooded shore stretched out on either side. Jack watched it slide by, feeling their exposure. They still had to limp around the point. Would Colwell's agents be on the dock, waiting? He recalled that a rocky spit hid the beach house from the dock. Unless they were posted there too.

He heard birdsong on the shore, the faintest liquid warble from deep within the woods. The sun would soon be up. He slid his hand into his pocket to feel the anode's pitted surface, needing to hang on to the sensation, the thrill of the inspiration. Already it was slipping away. Even if he did make it ashore without being seen, he was going to have to hide in the beach house, alone, cut off from the lab. What good would inspiration be then?

Tory told Rhonda, the video editor, "Again," and watched while Rhonda, with a weary sigh, recued the final section of Laurel's taped testimonial, then hit the start button.

". . . ask you a very important question," the off-camera interviewer said somberly to Laurel. "Are you absolutely convinced, in your heart, that Dr. Hunt is not in any way connected to the terrorists?"

"Absolutely," Laurel declared. "It's not possible. It's a terrible mistake. He's just not capable of hurting people like that. I mean, look at the lives he's saved around the world. Now he's trying to save us *all*, from Artemis. He had the courage to stand up to the government, and now he's paying for his courage." She looked at the camera. "I think what all Americans have to do is tell the government they think he was right. Tell them *now*. Before it's too late. I guess it's not safe for my grandfather to come out and say that himself, so I'm saying it for him—"

"Cut after 'too late,'" Tory said, "and lower the FX of—"

"Ms. Farr-Colwell?" a hesitant voice said over the intercom. Yesterday, Marcia, her receptionist of five years, had jumped on a flight to Mexico. Over three-quarters of Tory's staff had quit after Noah. This was the voice of a young male intern: no wife, no daughters. He said, "I know you said not to disturb—"

"But?"

"Um, your father's here. Should I send him to the screening room?"

Dad? *Mother . . . a relapse.* "No, my office." She hurried down the quiet hall. A phone was ringing in an empty cubicle.

At first, opening her office door, she saw only the broad back of Ron Norsky, her father's nurse, standing behind the wheelchair, masking him.

"Dad, what's happened? Is it Mother?" She reached his side and stopped, shocked by the pallor of his face. *He* was ill.

"Ron," Del said shakily, "would you please wait outside?"

Alone with him, Tory knelt by the wheelchair. "Dad, what's wrong? Are you sick?"

He fluttered his hand erratically, dismissing the question. About to speak, his distorted mouth became more twisted than usual. Tory wondered if she should call a doctor.

"Last night," Del began rockily, "I was consulting an early draft of my manuscript. She said, the other day . . . told me I should throw it out, but—" His voice drifted. "You know my tendency to hoard."

What's he talking about? Tory wondered.

"I wanted to corroborate some facts," Del went on, "on the relation between water table depletion and infant mortality in sub-Saharan Africa. I had compiled the population statistics several years ago, you see, and—"

Tory groaned and stood up. "Dad, I've got stats from a whole stable of population experts, and U.N. demographic charts ad infinitum. I don't need more." She moved to her desk where a scatter of faxes lay, and picked up one. McIvar at CNN. "Is that all you came for?"

"No!" His ferocity surprised her. "No," he repeated softly. "It's because I came across a footnote in the manuscript. A surprisingly detailed note, yet I had forgotten all about it."

Tory knew he wanted to help, but she had no time for this. Her eyes went back to the fax.

"The footnote was a reference to Artemis."

She looked up.

Del swallowed and went on. "Artemis was a goddess to whom the ancients assigned several spheres of power, one of them quite special—she was considered the protector of all young things, both human and animal."

He moved his wheelchair to her. "Tory, when Paul was killed your mother was stricken. People did not see it in her because she kept on at her work so steadily, so conscientiously. But I saw it. I tried to do what I could to ease her grief, encouraged her to help me with my demographic research, just to focus her mind elsewhere. She did, indeed, become engrossed in the work, organizing large parts of my manuscript, at least the early draft I just spoke of. But meanwhile her own work, her *scientific* work, was moving, I now believe, into paths . . . of darkness. I am only now discovering how dark."

She started at him.

"Tory, in asking her to help me I may have set in motion a dreadful thing."

"What are you saying?"

"That Rachel . . . that I believe . . . Rachel is Artemis."

Her brain made the leap, but her consciousness refused to follow. The thought hovered, unclaimed, unbearable.

*Her mother had begged for her political advice. Her mother had provided the campaign funding. Her mother had talked Jack into becoming the spokesman . . .*

Del made a small sound of despair. "You see it, don't you? Who else has the genius? The financial and technical capability? The will?"

She heard an echo of Carson's voice, the FBI man sounding the litany of criteria for a crime: *motive, means, and opportunity.* The echo became a bludgeon. Her mind shrank back in pain. The edges of her vision blackened.

Someone knocked at the door. Tory flinched.

Her father grabbed her wrist. "I have said nothing to your mother. I wouldn't know how. And informing on her is something I cannot do. But you——" His cold fingers dug into her like claws. "Tory, I don't know what she has planned if the president refuses her ultimatum, but I do know she will somehow enact what she threatens. I've come to ask you— beg you—you *must* make the government heed your appeals. Whatever it takes to convince them. You must. And Jack Hunt—don't listen to him anymore. He and Rachel, they . . . knew each other, years ago. People told me. Tory, I fear he may be in this as deep as——"

"Ms. Farr-Colwell?" Vince's assistant had opened the door. "Got a minute?"

Tory could not move. Sound would not come to her throat, nor breath. The very valves of her heart had locked.

The assistant took a few steps in. "Sorry, but I noticed this package in Mr. Delvecchio's office. It was couriered a few days ago but I guess in all the craziness he missed it, so I thought I'd better open it. It's a video from Gerry Trowbridge's distribution agent. The Brazil footage." He approached her desk with it, looking anxious. "I called the agent. Turns out he had dubs. Trowbridge, the night he died, had just sent an e-mail authorizing him to send one here." He set the videocassette on the desk as if relieved to put some distance between it and himself. "It's disturbing. I thought you'd want to check it out."

Tory's eyes fixed on the black cassette. She feared her mind had broken and she was going mad, because she thought she could see inside the box, and all she saw was blood.

# 22

You're a genius! I'm starting with the CD5 on T4
lymphocytes. Want me to keep investigating steps
in virus penetration after the binding to CD5? Also,
should we be considering potential resistance to the
therapy?

JACK CONSIDERED THE MESSAGE on the computer screen.
The moment Rachel had dropped him off at the beach house
yesterday he'd contacted Mandy by e-mail, almost blessing
Rachel for pointing out how untraceable it would be from her
computer here. He'd told Mandy he was in hiding, and
broached his molecular decoy theory. Working all yesterday
and most of last night through a flurry of messages, they'd
been hacking at the problems inherent in the hypothesis.
Now she had to do the actual tests herself. Jack typed a reply:

No to both queries because,
1. I doubt there would be effective inhibition at an
advanced level.

2. Resistance would indicate that A-3 had mutated to a form that no longer causes the Artemis disease.

3. There's no time.

Can you start in vitro tests immediately?

After a frustrating few hours of silence he got a reply:

Will do. Sorry about the holdup, but I was in town at the memorial service for Youssef. Hard to jump back into work. I'm on it now. By the way, the FBI have finally taken their damn army out, though there's still a few left patrolling the halls. I don't know what's going on, but I know they must be wrong about you. Wherever you are, be careful.

*Youssef.* I should have been there. And what am I getting Mandy into? She's a brilliant kid, but is she up to this? With the FBI breathing down her neck? *You* be careful, Mandy.

It was hot, the room stuffy, the linen curtains closed. The noon sun baking the beach house found pinholes in the curtains' weave and probed the room with needle-thin beams. Jack's shirt was plastered to his back. Restless, he pushed away from the computer. E-mail was a maddeningly constrained way to work. He needed to be *there*. And how long before the FBI agents up at the house decided to patrol this far down the beach? Could he give Mandy enough guidance to make progress on her own before they found him?

And why hadn't he heard from Tory? In his e-mail to her he hadn't said where he was—more for her safety than his—but he had broached an idea: Could she strike a bargain with the FBI? After all, Colwell didn't have a shred of evidence against him. If Tory went to the media telling them Jack would turn himself in, ready to cooperate with the FBI's inquiries on the condition they wouldn't arrest him, might that leverage gain him his liberty, and access to the lab? For that he would bargain anything. He needed Tory to swing such a delicate deal. He needed to hear from her.

*Before* a federal agent kicked in the door.

He glanced at the mute TV tuned to CNN. He was keeping the picture on, turning up the sound only for "Artemis Watch" bulletins. Nothing now; just two politicians in hard hats in a factory. Outside the beach house the sound of waves washing monotonously over the shore whispered through the open window, though no breeze stirred the curtains. Far out, a seabird shrieked.

Jack rubbed the stiffness in the back of his neck. In a dark moment last night he'd again considered telling the FBI everything. Colwell was a professional. If the peril of Rachel's dead man's switch was made clear to him, surely he would proceed against her with extreme caution. But that would take precious hours, maybe days, and Jack's biggest hurdle now was the clock. He'd seen Rachel's precarious state of mind on the boat. If she sensed the smallest change in the FBI's movements, it could push her over the brink.

No, nothing to do but wait for Tory.

And Mandy.

He prowled the room, frustrated, hot. He pulled open the fridge, grabbed a can of soda, and ripped off the tab, thinking uncomfortably that he couldn't touch a single object here that hadn't been touched by Rachel. The food she'd left him. The scattered books and newspapers. Her collection of driftwood over the fireplace. Her bed.

He winced at the memory, and turning, saw the desk photograph of Paul in his Superman bathing suit and orange life jacket, giggling at the helm of his dinghy. Looking at the sweet face, Jack took a swig of soda. A breeze drifted in, picking up a smell of cold ashes from the grate. He swallowed the soda, tasting ash. He heard buzzing. A bee was trapped between the window and the curtain. He could hear it bumping against the glass, frantic for release.

A fighter jet roared overhead and Tory shuddered at the noise. It died as quickly as it had erupted, and she was left with the monstrous silence of her living room.

She was standing at the sliding-glass door that overlooked the patio and yard. A mangy squirrel crouched in a crook of the magnolia tree, staring up as though dazed by the noonday heat. Even with the glass door closed, and above the whisper of the air-conditioning, Tory could hear the high-pitched keening of cicadas in the trees. Like hearing the heat.

She was alone. She'd disconnected the phone. Hadn't turned on CNN. Hadn't called the office. Hadn't even got dressed; she still wore the long shirt she'd slept in, except she'd barely slept. She had sat in the dark in misery. Around three she'd curled up on top of the bed and drifted into a wretched semiconsciousness. Dawn had found her bleary, her stomach rocky.

The printed e-mail Jack had sent yesterday lay on the table, waiting for an answer. Gerry Trowbridge's videocassette waited, too, jutting from the VCR. She felt it like a living presence—the tortured ghosts of Jazida's dead watching her, waiting for her decision. A judgment about their murderer. *My mother.*

The tomblike silence of the house was agony. She craved to get out. Escape.

She slid open the glass door and stepped onto the patio flagstones, blinking in the sun. The steambath noonday heat of Washington wilted over her. In moments her shirt was damp under her arms, and a bead of sweat trickled between her breasts. The flagstones, broiled by the sun, hurt her bare soles.

A shriek of female laughter burst through the neighbor's foliage. A party. Tory imagined it, hosted by the stockbroker's wife—Bloody Marys, a swim, lunch, bridge—these women, like so many others, obsessively ignoring the crisis. She thought of stories she'd heard about London during the Blitz, when teenagers at jitterbug clubs kept on dancing while the bombs fell. Next door, the inane laughter crescendoed, sounding eerily like screams. Tory imagined them all cut down by the virus, dead in a pool of sunlit blood.

She stumbled inside and wrenched the door shut.

Jack's message again caught her eye, and the questions that had hissed at her all night began again. Did Jack know the truth about her mother? Was he a partner in this horrifying plot? It seemed inconceivable. Yet her father's suspicion haunted her: *"They knew each other, years ago."* From the start Tory had sensed some dark current flowing between Jack and her mother. What was behind that? She couldn't think . . . didn't want to imagine.

She clutched at the idea that Rachel had somehow *coerced* him. She remembered meeting him at Swallow Point, and his initial adamant refusal to lead the campaign until her mother spoke to him alone. The change in him had been dramatic, both his sudden agreement and his shaken composure. Could it be that he'd suspected Rachel was Artemis? Or maybe she had even revealed it to him? Yet, if he knew, why hadn't he turned her in? Why had he silently submitted, and allowed the FBI's suspicions to fall on *him*? It only made sense if her mother had some hold over him, something forcing his compliance. But what? Tory couldn't disentangle it.

Unless there was nothing to disentangle. A simple answer. The one Carson had seen right at the start. That Jack was a conscious, active agent.

Her mother's partner in mass murder.

It made her ill to think any further. Her mind recoiled from even trying.

Only one thing was clear: Tory herself had been acting in total ignorance. She felt a flash of rage, realizing how her mother had used her. *I've been her pawn.*

Oh, no, she thought grimly, catching herself, I can't let myself so easily off the hook. I willfully defied all Carson's warnings, leaped into the campaign, certain that I understood the stakes better than he did, that no approach was right but mine. I'm no pawn.

For the hundredth time she tortured herself with the most fundamental question of all: Could her father simply be wrong? Was this only a panicked, ailing man's delusion? She had so desperately tried to assure herself of that during her night-long vigil, minutely examining the events of the past weeks, dissecting her mother's actions, her mother's words, her mother's character. But every conclusion convinced her that her father's suspicion was right. Every piece fit, and every instinct about her mother confirmed it. She'd grown up knowing—proud!—that her mother was capable of doing things ordinary people could not. Brilliant, unconventional, freethinking, Rachel was an exalted person, with extraordinary power at her fingertips. A power to use for good . . . or evil.

*My mother is Artemis.*

Must I, therefore, turn her in? Do I have a duty, just as Carson said from the beginning? A duty to my country? To humanity?

But don't I have some duty to my mother, if she's gone insane?

Besides, would humanity really be served by her capture? The crimes she'd committed were unspeakable, yet Tory simply could not believe her plan was to release the virus on a city, unleashing a pandemic. No, her weapon was merely the *threat* of that terror. Amazingly, it had brought America to the brink of something extraordinary: a chance to act like a truly great nation. Without the threat, the chance would be lost. Her mother knew that, had commissioned the campaign knowing it. *So perhaps she's not insane at all.*

Dear God, what am I talking myself into? All those people in Stoney Creek and Pakistan and Brazil.

She looked at the VCR with its protruding black cassette. The hidden, writhing ghosts. She would not view the tape again. Once had been torture enough. In a normal world she would destroy the thing.

But this was no longer a normal world, and she was no longer sure of anything. Except one fact: she had to make a decision.

Confront Rachel? Try to talk her out of this madness, call off the threat? The thought was barely formed before Tory knew that route was hopeless. She'd seen her mother's fervor that first day in her office, almost a fantacism. No mere argument would break such steely resolve.

That leaves only two choices, she realized. Make a last stand, or betray my mother.

I can send the video to the networks. One call to my office would do it.

Or I can turn my mother in. One call to Carson.

Her legs trembled, suddenly weak. She groped for the curtain, but it was too flimsy to steady her and she sank to her knees beside the glass door. The squirrel in the magnolia tree sat holding its paws before its chest as if in fright, and stared into the room, either not seeing her or too alarmed to move. Tory stared back into its glassy, vacant eyes.

*If I send out the video I'll be giving the campaign one last chance.*

*But if the campaign succeeds, I'll have let my mother get away with mass murder.*

She watched the squirrel's paws shiver almost imperceptibly to the pulse of its racing heart.

She got to her feet. The squirrel darted for cover. Before she could change her mind, she went straight to the phone.

The noise level at the command center was frantic. Carson, briefing a group of agents, saw his phone line flashing. How long had it been ringing?

He lunged across the desk for it. He'd take anything. The Puerto Rico lead was too little, too late, and Hunt seemed to have evaporated from the surface of the sea. He snatched the phone. "Colwell."

"Perez, sir. We're in the—"

The Puerto Rico connection was so bad, the San Juan SAC sounded as if he were drowning in a mine shaft. "Say again, Perez. The line's terrible."

"Creative Containers," Perez shouted, excited. "It's a small operation here in a San Juan suburb. They buy cheap cosmetics in bulk, and package them in containers they make. That's where the trace of soil on the vials originated, some packer's grubby fingers. Prints analysis just confirmed it. Plus, they regularly buy perfume from one of the scent manufacturers on our list. We don't know yet whether they also received product from a pharmaceutical lab here, because their records are a mess, but we're going through them now."

Carson tried to rein in his excitement. "But you believe they put the Artemis material in the vials?"

"They may not have known what it was, sir. We're talking to their people now, and we'll have a better idea once we get through their files. Trouble is, well, we're not set up down here for an operation of this scale. We could use some help, particularly ops specialists, because—"

"I'll pull the team together myself," Carson said quickly. His eyes snapped to the clock. Eight minutes before noon. A Bureau jet could have him and the team in San Juan in a few hours. Kendrew could take over here. Cradling the receiver against his shoulder, he snatched his jacket off the chair. "Perez, we're on our way."

At dusk Jack was entering a detailed message to Mandy, the glow of the computer screen and TV the only illumination in the beach house, when he heard a thud outside. Footsteps on the wooden stairs. They became louder, moving along the deck. FBI? Stiffening, Jack stood to face the door.

Rachel opened it. "I didn't want to knock in case they're watching." She quickly stepped in and shut the door.

Jack's relief turned to apprehension. "What's happened?"

"Nothing."

"You shouldn't come here."

"It's all right, I told them I was going for a swim." She lifted a straw bag with a beach towel on top. "I've brought you clean clothes." She looked around. "Are you all right? Enough food?"

Her eyes brushed over the computer screen beside him, and he realized: *Mandy's message!* He hit a key and iconized the text, making it disappear.

She came beside him and looked at the blank screen. Did she suspect he was communicating with Mandy, getting closer? "Have you heard from Tory?" she asked.

"No."

"But you have e-mailed her?"

"Several times. She must be too busy to check."

He moved away from her. While the worst of the day's heat had faded, the evening was still sultry. He wished he could rip open the curtains, let in the last of the light, feel some space. He wished Rachel would leave.

She was looking now at the mute TV, her face unguarded, and he saw again the feverish gleam in her eyes that he'd noticed on the boat, intensified now in the harsh electronic light.

"Jack," she murmured. "It's you."

He followed her gaze to the TV. It was him, in Brazil. With Marisa.

Stepping out of the church, holding hands. Waltzing at her uncle's house, confetti brightening her hair and the shoulder of his suit. Hurrying across the tarmac to her uncle's plane. Joking with Liz Trowbridge as she hefted video gear aboard.

Jack realized with a shock: Gerry took this video.

Rachel turned up the sound. An announcer gravely intoned: "Jack and Marisa Hunt never reached their honeymoon paradise. When the pilot received a call concerning a sick woman in a mining settlement, Jack insisted on a detour to take the woman to the hospital. They landed in the remote shantytown of Jazida. What was supposed to be a short stopover turned into Jack Hunt's longest day, and Marisa's last."

There he was, striding through the shantytown. Mudcaked miners, scabby-mouthed children, skinny dogs. The pink-painted brothel at the edge of town. Inside the brothel, shot after shot of women in agony. They lay on beds, some on bare mattresses on the floor, mumbling in fevered incoherence. Sixteen-year-old Pia, her eyes ruby-red. Pregnant Teresinha, hemorrhaging between her legs. Jack, trying to care for them, his hands and shirt streaked with blood.

He stared, with Rachel, at Liz's record of the horror, realizing this was the video that the White House's friends had been so bent on suppressing they had torched Gerry's loft.

"Jack Hunt was the only doctor in town," the announcer

went on, "and every female was stricken by the deadly disease. They screamed. They suffered brain damage. They bled uncontrollably. They began to die. Jack worked on, trying to ease their suffering, and so did Marisa." Shots of Marisa wiping bloody vomit from the mouth of a woman in convulsions.

Rachel gave a small gasp and clamped her hand to her mouth.

On screen, Teresinha's baby was born into Jack's hands. The child wasn't breathing. Jack lifted it and pressed its small mouth against his in gentle, mouth-to-mouth resuscitation. The baby's blood smeared his face.

"Jack Hunt did not know then that the disease spared men," the announcer declared. "For all he knew, he was now infected with death. But he was a doctor. He saw only the chance to give life." The baby gasped, breathing on its own, and Jack spat out blood with a laugh of desperate elation. The mother lay dead, sprawled in a swamp of blood.

Rachel strangled a cry at the back of her throat, and turned away.

Jack felt hatred boil up. "You didn't know it was like this, did you?" He grabbed her shoulders and brutally twisted her around to the TV. Her hand shot up to cover her eyes. Jack yanked it away. *"Look!"*

"His efforts could not stem the tide of horror," the announcer went on in a hush. "Because now, Marisa had been struck." On screen, Jack knelt beside Marisa, who lay on the floor, mumbling, bleeding from her nose and gums, crying red tears. "Jack," she moaned.

Rachel's legs gave way. She slid from Jack's grip, to her knees.

Marisa lay sprawled in blood. Jack ripped off his shirt to stanch her hemorrhaging. Then she was dead. He knelt by her, panting, blood glinting on his skin.

Rachel gagged. She staggered to her feet and tried to make it to the bathroom, but only got to the door before she began to retch. She collapsed onto her hands and knees and vomited.

Jack felt something alien overtake him, something seething, vicious. He craved to witness her pain. He stood over her, taking in every spasm of her suffering, wanting more. As her body jerked in dry heaves, he said with savage satisfaction, "Good. Good!" He grabbed a fistful of her hair, and her arm, and pulling both, dragged her across the floor back to the TV. "*You* did this. You *look*!"

The video became jerky as the camera panned erratically across the brothel carnage, until finally the scene was just a series of freeze-frame images: snapshots of hell.

Rachel moaned. On her knees between Jack's legs she groped blindly for his leg to steady herself. He saw that she was broken. Looking down at her, he felt the alien sadism drain out of him as quickly as it had overwhelmed him.

He lifted her to her feet. She swayed against him. He led her to the bed and told her to sit. "Lower your head," he said. "Take deep breaths."

She sat with her face in her hands, shivering.

Jack soaked a towel in the sink, then filled a glass with water and brought them both to her. "Here. Drink." He held the towel against her clammy forehead as she sipped the water.

Jack looked back to the TV. Mike McIvar was now reporting from the CNN studio, sounding excited.

"... harrowing video document first broadcast just six hours ago. Since then, in the interest of public awareness, CNN and other networks have been replaying it continuously. The impact on the country seems to be nothing less than staggering. Calls are clogging the White House lines. In cities across the nation, people have taken to the streets in

spontaneous demonstrations against the government's hard-
line stand."

The picture flashed to crowds of people jamming streets
in one city after another. There were many men, but the vast
majority marching were female. Young mothers helped their
little girls hold up signs and banners. Elderly women walked
with determined steps, arms linked with friends or sisters.
Teenage girls jabbed fists in the air. All of America was represented here, young and old, black and white, rich and
poor. Jack saw that one thing united them all: fear. Tory was
right, he thought in awe. It takes terror to get them to move.

Abruptly, the picture shifted to a harried reporter standing
in the White House press briefing room. "Mike, yes, we're
here. Uh, we've been advised that the president will be arriving momentarily to make an address. We're just waiting."
Around him reporters were rushing to take chairs, while others were locked in whispered, frantic discussions. Suddenly,
the president walked in. The press room hushed.

Taking the podium, Lowell looked out over the tangle of
cameras and cables, lights and faces. He appeared solemn
but confident.

"My fellow Americans," he began, "in the past weeks I
have watched with tremendous pride as citizens all across
this great nation have remained calm and resolute in the face
of terrible tragedy and strain. I have talked to many of you
personally about your hopes and fears, and I have discussed
the situation in great depth with scientific experts and with
your representatives in Congress. I want to assure you now
that I have listened very carefully to everything I have
heard, to all the varying points of view. I have considered
and weighed the merits of each argument. I have listened
with my mind, and with my heart.

"In the end, it is my responsibility to make the difficult
decisions for this nation. Today I am announcing a decision

I hope will ease the fears so many of you have expressed, one that will insure the bright and secure future to which all Americans have a right. America's future is inextricably linked with the future of the rest of the world, and with the health of our shared environment. That is the inescapable reality of today's global village."

Jack stood staring at the screen, hardly daring to hope, unable not to.

"Two facts have become clear during the last weeks," the president went on. "Clear to me and, I know, to many of you. First, that our shared global environment is threatened by the planet's burgeoning human population, and second, that, as study after study has proved, the key to reducing runaway population growth lies in raising the living standards of poor women, a goal best accomplished through basic education. Therefore, I am herewith establishing, immediately, the Global Educational Assistance Endowment, a program to be funded by a new, modest federal tax which will raise revenues equaling one percent of the nation's gross national product."

There were gasps from the reporters. Jack felt the same gasp fill his own lungs. This was incredible!

The president ignored the audible shock wave. "The Global Education Assistance Endowment will provide schools, teachers, learning materials, and education administrators to developing nations, with the goal of eventually assuring that girls and women worldwide receive the minimum of a primary school education. With this farsighted step, America will be playing a vital role in . . ."

His words were drowned by the sudden roar from reporters shouting questions—at the president, at each other. A few jumped up to yell for quiet. A woman at the back cheered. People rushed forward with cameras. Secret Service agents lurched to block them. It was mayhem.

Jack was stunned. He thudded down on the edge of the bed beside Rachel. "My God," he whispered. "It's over." Absorbing the shock, he felt elation begin to burble inside him. They'd done it, he and Tory. Done the impossible.

The elation quickly fizzled. It was over, yes, but at what cost? Marisa's image on the screen had barely faded.

"Over?" Rachel said dully, as if she could scarcely believe it. Jack looked back at the TV. The president seemed to make a sudden decision that, given the hopelessness of restoring order, his best policy was to leave before he appeared ineffectual. He strode off the podium, a door was opened for him, and he was gone. A flustered spokesman rushed to the lectern to field the onslaught of questions.

Jack turned back to Rachel. Her face was ashen, as though she could not comprehend what was happening. He grabbed her shoulders. "Rachel, don't you see? They're doing exactly what you want. The survival tax. The fund. All of it. You've *won*."

Suddenly, she seemed to believe it, accept it. Color flushed over her cheeks. "Over. Oh, Jack, is it?"

Her pager beeped.


Tory was packing a suitcase. She had watched the president's address and knew the broadcast of the video had worked the miracle she'd hoped for. But she felt no jubilation. She was sick to her soul. She had just talked to Carson.

She dropped clothes into the suitcase automatically, barely thinking of what she was choosing. Trying, in fact, to block memories of the last time she'd packed for the tropics. It had been the first holiday she and Carson had taken—the honeymoon they'd both been too busy for when they'd got married two years before—and she had picked her clothes with languid pleasure. Gauzy dresses, sarongs, bikinis. Perfect for the seaside guest house at Luquillo, with its secluded beach. Carson always said later he was sure that the beach was where Chris had been conceived.

She zipped the suitcase shut and stood for a moment in the awful silence of her bedroom, willing the strength to carry this out.

She'd called the FBI command center and told Stan Kendrew it was urgent that she speak to Carson; it was about the case. "He's in Puerto Rico, Tory, but I'll relay your message," Stan said. *Puerto Rico,* she'd thought in horror. Her mother had a lab in San Juan. Had Carson already discovered the truth? Impossible, she decided: If he knew, his agents would already have us both in custody. Yet, some evidence must have taken him there, so how much time did she have?

Within fifteen minutes Carson had called her back.

"So, Puerto Rico," she'd said, trying to sound at ease. She needed to open a channel, offer a truce. "Remember Luquillo? Last time we were there Chris was just a gleam in your eye."

Silence. Then he said witheringly, "I'm busy, Tory. What is it?"

She cringed inside. She had hoped the invocation of their son might soften him, but it had only antagonized him. Still, she plowed on. "Carson, there's no more deadline. You can relax a little."

"Not until I have Artemis."

She felt a gust pass through her heart. He was implacable.

Her mother's life lay in her hands. She would have to match his hardness.

"That's what I called about," she said. "What if Artemis were to surrender?" She stated it flatly, the opening salvo of a negotiation.

She could almost hear him trying to control his excitement: she knew he was thinking of Jack. He said carefully, "What makes you think that's possible?"

"Everything's changed now that the president has agreed to the fund. Artemis might be persuaded."

"By you?"

"Yes. I have a proposition. But I'll present it only to you, and only face-to-face."

Her plan was this: a plea bargain. Surrender, in return for a guarantee that Artemis would be spared the death penalty. On the phone, she'd given Carson no indication of what was in her mind; however, he had agreed to meet her. Oh, yes, he was eager. It sickened her how easily he'd believed she was acting in betrayal. How quickly he'd concluded she was turning in Jack.

They would meet in just a few hours. If all went well, it might take only a moment for her to strike the deal, and save her mother from the electric chair.

She was booked on a dawn flight out of National. After a short stop in Atlanta to change planes, she would be on her way to San Juan. She had no idea if either part of her plan was possible: whether she could persuade her mother now to turn herself in, or whether Carson even had the authority to make such a bargain. She only knew she had to try.

## 23

"THE PRESIDENT IS WAITING FOR YOU, DR. LESAGE."

Rachel, clipping on an ID badge at the White House security desk, looked up at the young aide. "This way," the girl said, smiling. "They're in the solarium."

Rachel followed her over the plush carpeting of the west wing. At three A.M. the brightly lit corridors were bustling with staffers. Rachel found she had to concentrate on walking, like someone intoxicated. It wasn't trepidation at the summons; she was confident she could discuss whatever follow-up agenda the president had in mind for her lab team. No, this was sheer euphoria. *It's over.* Like a pardoned prisoner, she was light-headed with joy.

"It's wonderful, isn't it?" the aide whispered conspiratorially as they stepped into the elevator. "Like waking up after a nightmare and finding you're safe. I can't stop smiling."

It's infectious, Rachel thought, unable to stop smiling herself.

They emerged on the third floor of the Executive Mansion. "The solarium is the president's favorite room," the girl told her with the blithe assurance of an insider. She opened a door and gestured for her to enter.

Rachel stepped into a spacious sun parlor, a private aerie on top of the White House, though at the moment the electric night-glow of Washington was an anemic surrogate for the sun. About a dozen people glanced at her, some standing, carrying on hushed conversations, some sitting hunched over a coffee table messy with papers, half-eaten sandwiches, coffee cups, and juice bottles. Hank Vorhees, the CDC director, shot her a harried look. President Lowell, wearing a gray sweatshirt and shorts, stood apart at the night-black bay of windows. He held a can of Coke, snapping off the tab as he turned to Rachel. He did not smile.

Something's wrong, she thought.

Randall Quincy, the White House chief of staff, beckoned her in, and she slipped into a chair beside Vorhees. Her eye was caught by a photocopied message on the coffee table in front of him. "Yes, it came in right after the president's address," Vorhees said in a whisper, handing it to her. "The Artemis signature icon is the same as on the original warning, so they've accepted it's authentic."

Reading it, she kept her face immobile. "Regarding the immediate implementation of the Global Education Assistance Fund: this is acceptable." After taking the president's call at home, she'd just had time to fire off this e-mail, anonymized by her Internet server, before heading for her plane. Vorhees added, "So they're satisfied the terrorists are standing down."

No one seemed to be celebrating, Rachel thought uneasily. Or even relaxing. The mood was more like a war-party strategy session. What was going on?

A cell phone rang and a stocky man answered it. Rachel

recognized him from newscasts, Ed Liota, the new FBI director. "What's he *doing*?" Liota shouted into the phone. "Well, Christ, tell him to call me. No, I'm with the president *now*. He's *waiting*."

Rachel leaned over to replace the Artemis message on the table as Liota, closing the cell phone, said loudly to the whole room, "Okay, the San Juan SAC says Colwell's been at the Creative Container offices all evening, and that's definitely where the vials were filled."

*San Juan!* Her hand jerked back, knocking an open bottle of orange juice. It splashed Vorhees's pant leg and flooded the corner of the table, and he grabbed some napkins to sop it up and dabbed at the stain on his leg.

*Carson in San Juan.* Now she knew: *they* knew. She hadn't been called to a meeting, she'd walked into an ambush.

Yet the atmosphere made no sense. No one was even looking at her. They were all still focused on Liota. "Mr. President," he said, moving toward Lowell, "I'm sorry about this delay, but we're getting very close now, and the moment Colwell has *anything* he'll—"

"Yeah, yeah," Lowell muttered tightly.

Rachel's mind lurched again. Carson *doesn't* know?

Lowell guzzled the last of his Coke, then rolled the can between his hands. His eyes fell again on Rachel. "Tell her," he said to Quincy.

Quincy cleared his throat.

This is it, Rachel thought, stiffening. *You're under arrest.*

"Dr. Lesage, we're very grateful for the service you've performed," Quincy began. "However, the situation has changed dramatically, and the president has decided to consolidate the scientific effort within existing government institutions. That is, within the CDC, NIH, and USAMRIID. Dr. Vorhees of the CDC will be coordinating that mission from now on, and we would appreciate your cooperation in managing a swift and efficient transition."

Rachel blinked at him. *What's going on?* "Am I to understand—"

"You're fired," Lowell said with sudden venom.

People instantly looked at their notes, or nervously stared at Vorhees wiping up the last of the spilled juice. Rachel alone met the president's gaze, her heart pounding. It was clear to her now. Lowell wanted to distance himself from her before her arrest. A ferocious instinct welled up in her— she would not go meekly, silenced for his purposes! "Mr. President," she said, "if not for your political—"

"Oh, it's not politics," he cut in acidly, "it's personal. You had to cross me at the very beginning, didn't you? Right after that first meeting, you had to undermine my position. Then you leaked the declaration, and bankrolled PGT. At first they told me I couldn't touch you—bad PR—so I let you have your say. Free country. But now, Doctor, everything's changed." He crushed the Coke can in his hand. "For the endgame here, I need people I can trust."

He turned back to the window, done with her.

Rachel felt she'd been dragged to the edge of a cliff and left teetering on the brink. *Is that all?* She knew enough to shut her mouth.

"Dr. Lesage, your team will be reassigned to the CDC," Quincy went on smoothly. "Dr. Vorhees will arrange with you the transfer of your lab's data. He's already been briefed, so perhaps you two could get together to discuss the details now? Outside?" He gave her a perfunctory smile of dismissal. "Dr. Lesage, Dr. Vorhees, thank you both for coming."

Vorhees gathered his notes. The others resumed their conversations. Quincy buzzed the steward for more coffee. Rachel was forgotten. Swallowing in relief, she stepped back from the cliff edge. But this was far from over, she knew. Carson would very soon discover the truth. This reprieve, this foothold, was only a narrow ledge above the chasm. It would not support her long.

She had to get out of here. She was moving to the door when she heard Quincy saying grimly to his aide, ". . . need some heavy spin for the president to bounce back from these unfavorables."

The aide muttered, "Crazy thing is, agreeing to the fund would have given us room for that, if we'd just announced it at the start."

*"We?"* the president bellowed. He pitched the Coke can at the aide's back with a vicious overhand. *"Fuck* your hindsight!" He turned to Quincy and yelled, "Get him out of here!"

Quincy pulled the stunned aide to his feet and hustled him out of the room. Rachel watched Lowell, amazed at his outburst.

"Who does that little cocksucker think he is?" Lowell raged. *"I'm* the one who had to go out there and spew that global village crap. *I'm* the one who had to roll over like some little bitch pissing itself. I bent over and let Artemis screw me in front of the whole country, *the whole fucking world!* So don't give me your bullshit about spin and bouncing back. My chance of a second term is about as viable as your dead grandma's cunt!"

His face suddenly creased, his emotions beyond his control. Tears welled and his voice wobbled. "I did it because I love this country, God damn it. I did it because it's my job to save American lives. I'd do it again if I had to. But, by Christ, if you people had done *your* job I could have gone out there like a man!"

He took a deep, steadying breath, and stabbed a threatening finger in Liota's face. "You find me my counterpart in

Artemis," he said with quiet menace. "Hunt, or Saddam, or *whoever* the fuck it is. You deliver him up to me, you hear? Because, by God, before I go I'm going to rip the bastard's balls off and make him *eat* them."

No one moved. People were looking down. Rachel alone stared Lowell in the face, repelled.

Quincy whispered to the president. "Sir . . ." He nodded toward Rachel and Vorhees as if to say, *Don't let the outsiders see this.*

Lowell lifted his head high, mastering himself, then abruptly turned his back and began talking to an advisor, the incident closed.

Quincy quickly escorted Rachel and Vorhees to the door, murmuring, "I've buzzed downstairs—someone will meet you and show you out."

She and Vorhees stepped into the corridor and the door closed behind them. Rachel felt slightly dizzy. *The president out of control, and Carson so close.*

"Real helpful way to behave," Vorhees scoffed as they approached the elevator. "These political people, they just don't get it, do they—the public health time bomb we're dealing with. But how can I tell the president of the United States what to do? I mean, even if we *do* have something with this breakthrough, Artemis might already have—"

"Breakthrough?" she asked.

"Didn't you get my memo?"

"No."

"Well, there's a possibility of developing a DNA chain terminator." He repeated grimly, "A *possibility* . . . shit." Distracted, he ran a hand over his hair. "I never thought I'd hear myself say this, but you were right, Rachel, from the start. The president should have agreed to the demand immediately."

They'd reached the elevator, and Rachel jabbed the button. "He's agreed now," she said. "That's what matters."

"Ha," he grunted. "Smoke screen."

She looked at him. "What?"

He glanced around to make sure no one was listening, though no one was in the corridor except a Secret Service agent far behind them. Vorhees whispered, "I heard them talking. They have absolutely no intention of honoring the education fund pledge."

An icicle entered her heart. "But . . . the president's address."

"Smoke screen, to give the FBI time. They're so damn sure they're just about to catch Artemis."

*"It's over."*

Nothing was over.

From her jet's darkened cabin she stared out in fury at the blackness above New England. A new moon glimmered like a scythe, and moon-silvered clouds ghosted by.

*"No intention of honoring the pledge."*

*Twice* now she had misjudged her adversary. At the outset she'd so naively assumed that the demonstrations would make them agree to her demand, a demand so benign, so logically in the best interest of all humanity. But she'd just been graphically reminded by Lowell that human beings, far from logical, routinely acted against their own best interests. *"I'm the one who had to roll over like some little bitch pissing itself!"* Ego superseded even self-interest.

They would not do the right thing, though the facts stared them in the face. Exponential population growth made global environmental catastrophe inevitable. In the misery of mass migrations and mass famine that would follow, desperate populations would savagely turn on one another for the last scraps, and the madness that had descended on Rwanda would consume the world.

The people in power could prevent this, but they refused. They were prepared to leave their children—all the earth's children—a planet on the brink of an abyss. In the face of her threat, they were willing to gamble. Their arrogance enraged her!

Well, she thought, they're going to lose that gamble.

I win by doing absolutely nothing.

Shipments of virus-contaminated bottled water were waiting in storage facilities in three major American cities, as well as in Rio, Frankfurt, Nairobi, and Shanghai. They were labeled as free samples in a promotion for a respected worldwide charity. The moment she stopped sending the regular computer command, faxes would automatically go to couriers, ordering pickup of the water and its delivery to selected outlets in public places: shopping malls, airports, hotels. The operation would be complete within a day. Worldwide plague would follow, and the goal would be accomplished. A partial cull of humans. Swift, limited, precise.

Possibly including me.

She looked out at the darkness, and hesitated. She did not fear death; she had died long ago. What made her waver now was anger, a bitter fury at herself, because this failure was hers as much as Lowell's. She'd been too timid in her demonstration. The two foreign villages had held people Americans cared nothing about, and the target at home, Stoney Creek, was small enough for the government to write off. If she had made the demonstration overwhelming—devastated San Francisco, say—it would have brought Lowell to his knees at the start. And now? she asked herself. Must the entire world suffer because my lapse has empowered a vain and ignorant president? Am I letting my rage, *my* ego, push me into a decision as bad as his?

That wasn't all. She could forfeit her own life . . . but forfeit Tory?

*Step back.* The Artemis Declaration was specific: noncompliance would result in the virus being released in one American city to begin. *Just as I should have done three weeks ago. One meaningful strategic target. A demonstration of power so staggering, it will shock the enemy to its senses. A Hiroshima.*

The deadline was still five days away, but she didn't have five days. Carson would trace the viral material to her San Juan lab within hours, a day at most. If the FBI incapacitated her, *all* the virus shipments would be delivered automatically. *As long as I control the dead man's switch, I maintain my option to limit the targets. The moment Carson captures me, I lose that. I must act now.*

One phone call to temporarily modify the computer command would do it. Delivery would be made by midmorning. The target city would be infected by nightfall.

One more call would be necessary—to the FBI. To keep the disease from spreading, the infection must be contained. An anonymous tip about the impending outbreak would compel the FBI to seal off the target city—its roads, its airports. She would make that call the moment she was satisfied that delivery had been accomplished.

She was becoming calm. The wild ups and downs of the past weeks—the nerve-wracking live chess match with Jack, the hope for Tory's campaign, the anxiety of watching Carson close in, the elation at Lowell's announcement, the rage at learning he'd lied—it was all behind her now. She would allow no more distracting emotions.

Now it came down to which city. She considered the trio of preselected targets. San Francisco, Minneapolis, and Atlanta. The choice, she realized, was clear. The president was transferring the scientific program to the CDC's purview, and that threatened her control; Vorhees had said they were trying to develop a DNA chain terminator. The CDC's headquarters were in Atlanta, so Atlanta would be the target.

The only obstacle left would be Jack.

At the Bar Harbor airport she found the terminal almost deserted. A yawning caretaker mopped the floor. The air held faint, competing smells of cigarette butts and bleach.

At a pay phone outside the darkened snack bar she lifted the receiver, cold in her hand. The caretaker, shuffling by her with mop and pail, nodded deferentially. She paused, staring at the metallic numbered squares in front of her, waiting until he'd passed. Her hand faintly trembling, she depressed the squares, and issued her command.

# 24

IN THE MORNING SUN TORY WALKED DOWN THE corridor of Atlanta's busy terminal, heading for the departure lounge. Her connecting flight to Puerto Rico left in twenty minutes. She was so engrossed in her tortured thoughts over how she would begin the negotiation with Carson that she didn't at first tune in to the announcement over the public address system.

". . . is due to severe electrical storms in the area," the disembodied voice declared. "Again, we repeat, all flights are indefinitely delayed."

Delayed? Tory thought in alarm. *All* flights? She looked outside the wall of windows at blue sky and blinding sunshine. Storms? What was going on?

She rushed to the departure lounge. Angry travelers were swarming the harried airline agents at the desk. One agent announced over a handheld microphone that all passengers would be issued hotel vouchers for the length of the delay, or reimbursed if they preferred to arrange overnight accommodation on their own. *Overnight?* Tory thought in dismay. It was barely ten A.M.

She managed to push through to an agent, who confessed they were getting conflicting information from management about the cause of the delay. "Now they're saying it's a foul-up with the air traffic control computers. Ten minutes ago it was because of storms. It's weird." He gave an exasperated shrug. "Anyway, a long delay *is* definite. No flights in or out until tonight, maybe even tomorrow." He thrust a hotel voucher at her and turned to the next protesting passenger.

Tory couldn't wait until tomorrow. Or even a few hours. Carson was getting too close to her mother's lab, and the moment he made that connection, the chance to negotiate would be lost. She pulled out her phone, her mouth dry, and called the San Juan number he'd given her. Told he wasn't available, she clamped down her panic and left a message. It was extremely urgent, she said, explaining that her flight had been delayed and it was imperative that Carson call her. Glancing at the voucher, she gave the hotel number, adding she'd be there in half an hour. Her skin was clammy at the thought of plea bargaining with Carson on the phone, but she had no more options.

The taxi rank was crowded with irate travelers. Tory finally got a cab. As the driver sped through the spaghetti of freeway junctions that rimmed Atlanta's downtown, Tory looked out at the bright sunshine glittering off the skyscrapers. The storm that wasn't a storm. She thought of the summer her mother had taught her to sail. She must have been eleven or twelve, and definitely not a natural sailor. One day the sunny afternoon deteriorated into heavy weather with high winds, choppy seas, the sails and rigging howling. Tory, at the helm, was terrified. She got disoriented after a tack, and wrenched the tiller over so far she lost all control of steering. She panicked. "What do I *do*?" she screamed.

Rachel said calmly, "Let go."

"What?" Tory gasped in terror, frantically struggling with the tiller.

"Lift both hands. Just let go."

It seemed like suicide, but she did it because her mother said so. They didn't capsize. The boat, unhelmed, simply rounded up into the wind, slowed, and settled. "There's a balance," her mother explained, gently placing Tory's hand back on the tiller and helping her to begin again, in control. "To move ahead you have to work *with* the wind and water, not fight them."

How she wished she could lift her hands now and have everything settle, at peace. She feared that the storm closing in around her this time had unleashed forces more terrible than she could manage.

Her mind strayed to Jack. Ensnared with all her other fears, thoughts of him had troubled her all night. Following those hours of uncertainty about him, she'd finally reached a conclusion as her plane took off from D.C. It had come to her suddenly, a welling-up of conviction so absolute it felt like the only thing she'd ever been sure of in her life: no way on earth was Jack a partner in this horror. It was remembering the video of Jazida that did it—seeing him desperately trying to help those suffering people and save his wife. He'd kept on despite inhuman conditions, despite his own exhaustion and despair, working past the point when hope was gone. Jack was the most heroic man she'd ever known. His every action since Jazida confirmed it. How could she have doubted him?

Where was he now? she wondered sadly. She hadn't replied to his e-mail, though from the sound of it he was safe, at least; she knew Jack could take care of himself. She wished he were at her side now, to act, as he had through every crisis in the past weeks, as her exacting conscience:

arguing, questioning her tactics, forcing her to reexamine, clarify, refine. How she'd come to rely on his steadiness, his nerve. On an impulse she grabbed her phone again and called his office. His voice-mail recording answered as she'd expected, and she realized how tightly wound she was—and how hopelessly deep her feelings for him—that she could draw such comfort just from the sound of his voice.

She doubted he was checking his messages, but she longed to sustain this connection with him, even if it was only in her mind. So she just talked. Told him she was stuck in Atlanta, that she'd be staying at the Hyatt Regency, and that she was about to attempt the most terrifying gamble she'd ever undertaken.

"I need some of your bravery now, Jack," she said, gazing out uneasily at the Caribbean-blue sky. "Or at least a little of your pigheadedness. Wish me luck."

# 25

AT THE BEACH HOUSE, JACK HAD SLEPT LATE. A profound, empty, renewing sleep. He didn't know what the call was that had made Rachel leave so abruptly last night, and he hardly cared. It was enough that she knew she'd won, and could stop. The moment she had gone, his body seemed to decide that he too, after weeks of strain, could finally stop. He sank onto the bed and was asleep almost the moment his head hit the pillow.

When he awoke to the squawk of a beachcombing gull, it was after ten. The first thing he checked was his e-mail.

Hold on to your hat! The computer modeling shows the purified CD5 inhibiting entry of virus to macrophages and T4 lymphocytes! Of course, the in vitro results won't be conclusive for another twelve hours, but I really believe this is IT! Kind of anticlimactic, isn't it, considering the president's speech? Anyway, I'll keep you posted. P.S. Tory

left a message for you. She's in Atlanta at the Hyatt
Regency and wants you to wish her luck. Didn't
say why.
P.P.S. Can you come back now?

Why Atlanta? Jack wondered. Whatever had taken Tory
there, he was glad she'd called. It was going to be a joy con-
gratulating her on what she'd accomplished. The CD5 results were equally satisfying, anticlimax or not; the most
welcome ending to the last month's troubled events.
*Events?* Marisa. Gerry. Youssef. Those had been *lives,*
and the remembrance of their deaths was still an open
wound in his soul. But now, at least, there would be no
more.

The nightmare was over.

He thought of Laurel. Cut off from the world for three
days, he didn't know if she was still up at the house or had
gone back to Boston. These last weeks, he'd wanted her to
stay, figuring the safest place for her was with Rachel. Now,
he hoped she'd gone home; he wanted her to get back to a
normal life. He had caught the last bit of a TV testimonial
she had done, supporting him. That had to have been Tory's
work, and it filled Jack with gladness. What wonders Tory
could do. It gave him hope that, one day, Laurel would talk
to him again.

The nightmare was over, but the waiting was not. He
would still have to face Colwell. Terrible crimes had been
committed, and he remained the FBI's prime suspect. That
meeting with Colwell was going to be tricky. Best to have
Tory broker it, with her attorneys present. Before coming
out of hiding he needed to confer with her. No phones yet;
the FBI would still be listening.

Tricky? he thought. It was going to be hell. He didn't
know if it was finally time to tell Colwell about Rachel. Her

lethal viral material was still out there. Was it really safe to divulge everything before he was sure she had recalled all her virus "bombs"?

Yet, if he kept silent what did that make him? Her accomplice.

One step at a time, he told himself. Wait for Tory to reply to his e-mail.

Damn it, though, he hated being penned up here any longer.

He'd give it another few hours. If she hadn't contacted him by then he'd walk out and deal with the FBI himself, however the hell that might play out. He wasn't going to spend another day prowling this prison cell. Not now, when it was all over.

Three hours later he checked his mail and found a message from Mandy.

> I don't know what to do. The CDC just posted an e-mail bulletin. They caution it's only a preliminary report, but they say a lot of women in Atlanta are coming in for ER services and presenting what look like Artemis symptoms. The FBI's closed Atlanta's airports and roads. Is it an outbreak? What's going on? Please tell me what to do. I'm so scared.

Jack stared at the words. They seemed to scream at him. Outbreak! Artemis!

*What has Rachel done?*

One word shrieked above the others. *Atlanta.*

He snatched the phone. The Hyatt Regency, Mandy had said. From Information he got the number. Busy. He punched the redial. *Busy.* He finally got through and asked for her room. His pulse drubbed in his throat as he waited.

Her phone rang and rang. The clerk came back, sounding frantic. Over a dozen women in the hotel had been taken to Grady Memorial Hospital, he said, and it was simply impossible to—

"Was Tory Colwell one?" Jack cut in. The clerk said he'd check the list but it was getting hard to keep track of every . . . oh, dear, there were so many other calls, he was sorry, he *had* to go . . . wait, yes, a Victoria Farr-Colwell was on the list. Was that the same—?

Jack hung up. His heart banged so hard he couldn't breathe.

Have to get to Atlanta!

*And do what? Watch her die?*

His legs weakened. The room hissed in his ears. Objects around him blurred. *Has Rachel struck other cities too?* The screen sucked back his attention. He zeroed in on the e-mail address: mchang@lesage.com. *The lab.*

Purified CD5. Could it work? It did in theory. *Christ, in theory?* Millions of people are going to die! Tory . . . Laurel. He beat down the panic. Theory was all he had. *Have to try.*

How much CD5? How purified? Is enough available? Is there *time*?

*Think!*

The data. Get the data.

He pulled open the door and charged down the beach. When he reached the path that led up to the house, he stopped, breathing hard, unsure. Can't go for the car. FBI in the house. Can't let them stop me.

He looked to the dock. Rachel's inflatable dinghy was tethered at the far end. He ran down the dock, loosened the bowline, and scrambled to the stern. As he yanked the motor's cord it roared to life, and he sped across the bay to the town jetty. Twenty minutes later he was crashing through the underbrush in the ravine. He raced across the clearing to the back of the lab and bounded up the steel staircase.

Rachel's office was empty.

He crossed it and opened the door to the hall. People were hurrying past. He could almost smell their fear at the news of the outbreak. He walked out among them, his chest heaving after the race from the jetty and through the ravine. He tried to conceal it, tried to force himself to walk slowly. Mustn't draw attention. Mandy said the FBI was still here. Can't let them stop me. Unable to hold himself back he bounded up the stairs to his office.

Mandy was at her computer. As Jack closed the door she turned in surprise.

"Pull up the CD5 data," he ordered.

Her face was white.

"Mandy, the data! Now!"

She stammered, "It's gone."

"What?"

"Five minutes ago. The files just began to disappear. I get nothing but this." She gestured at the screen, blank except for the words: UNABLE TO FIND FILE. PLEASE VERIFY THAT THE CORRECT PATH AND FILENAME ARE GIVEN. "A virus invaded the directory," she said in shock.

Jack shoved her aside and took over at the keyboard. He typed command after command, everything he could think of to retrieve the files. He and Mandy and Youssef had input a massive amount of data in over two hundred files, but each one he opened displayed the same disclaimer: UNABLE TO FIND FILE. PLEASE VERIFY THAT THE CORRECT PATH AND FILENAME ARE GIVEN.

"Christ, what did you do?"

"Nothing! I'd just come back from Dr. Lesage's office and I—"

"You went to *her*?"

"Of course. We might have the only viable concept for a treatment."

Rachel. She'd trashed the files. Wiped out the entire directory.

He grabbed Mandy's arm. "Did you back it up?"

She winced at his grip. "Of course, it's automatic. But when I tried to retrieve the backup, I found it was erased too. I was just going to call the systems administrator. Everything in the lab's computers is backed up to an off-site server, so maybe he can—"

Jack didn't listen to the rest. Rachel would have trashed that backup, too. He was listening instead to a cold voice inside him: Think like *she* thinks . . . what would she have done—*you know her.*

*And she knows me.* That was it. She'd known he was doing this research. She'd been hacking into it all along. At the very beginning, to prevent that, Jack had encrypted the data, but clearly he hadn't known the full extent of Rachel's security systems. Now he realized: she'd previously input a decrypting command, system-wide. He'd believed his data was hidden, but everything he and Mandy and Youssef had been doing, Rachel had been following.

She would never destroy such vital information, though. She would secure it, transfer it to some safe place. Then she could study it herself, test the theories, manipulate them. If the CD5 treatment proved effective she could counter it, maybe by creating a resistant strain.

What if she's *already* created one? Stop—one step at a time. She's only had the same number of hours I did. She's probably still working on it. And she can only do that if she has my data.

He was already at the door.

He dashed downstairs to the first floor and moved along the hall scanning faces like a predator. He wanted only

Rachel. People stepped back, out of his way. She couldn't have gone far. Mandy had just talked to her.

Then he saw her, walking quickly, her back to him, heading for her office. She hadn't seen him. Silently, he fell in behind her.

She reached her door and opened it, and he shoved her inside. She gasped in surprise and stumbled. Grabbing her, he kicked the door shut and forced her up against the wall. Rachel met his eyes levelly, unrepentant.

He wanted to smash her face.

"Have you released it worldwide?"

"One city. To make the president see."

Just Atlanta. Laurel was safe, so far. But not Tory.

"Where's the data?" he demanded.

"Gone."

"You're lying! You've transferred it somewhere. Where?"

She said nothing.

He gripped her throat and pressed his thumbs on her windpipe. *"Where?"*

Her stitched wound turned livid. She coughed and tried to pull his hands away. "Jack, believe me, you can't get it back." She strained to breathe. "There's nothing you can do." She clawed at his hands.

Fury overwhelmed him. "There's a chance!" He pulled her around, forced her backward across the room, and pushed her down on the desk on her back. He bent over her, gripping her shoulders, and shook her viciously. "Where is it?"

Her hands flailed, knocking things to the floor—books, papers, disks. Enraged, Jack shoved her farther along the desk. The computer keyboard crashed to the floor, and the side of Rachel's head thudded against the monitor. She gasped in pain, blood trickling from her ear. She groped across the desk for something. Whatever it was, Jack wrenched her away from it.

"You've got to tell me," he cried. "For Tory. She's there!"

Even in her pain she was immovable. "That trick won't work, Jack. Tory's in Washington."

"I'm telling you, she went to Atlanta! I don't know why, but she's *there*."

She blinked at him. "No, she's at her office. She's been at home since—"

"I just called her hotel in Atlanta. She's been sent to Grady Hospital. *You put her there*."

Rachel froze.

"I won't let you kill her," he yelled, and grappled her throat again.

Suddenly he felt a tremor course through her, a surge of power. "Release me," she said, a disembodied voice, a threat. Jack heard a scrape of metal, glimpsed the flash of a brass letter opener . . . and then she stabbed.

Pain flamed through his thigh. He staggered back. Clutching behind him at the letter opener, he wrenched the blade out of his thigh. Pain seared up to his groin.

Rachel stumbled to her feet and hurried past him to the adjoining room, her private lab. He limped after her, his leg on fire, blood soaking his pant leg. He found her beside the stainless-steel counter, pulling open a wall safe. Pulling out a gun.

"Stop there!" she said, aiming the gun at him.

He didn't. He couldn't. He wanted to crack open her skull and force the data out. He stalked toward her, the bloody letter opener still in his fist.

She turned the gun and held it at her own temple.

Jack stopped. Her fevered eyes told him she might actually do it. Then there'd be no hope for Tory. If the switch released a global outbreak, there'd be no hope for millions.

With the gun trained again on him, Rachel grabbed a hard-sided briefcase and opened it on the counter. She snatched bound wads of cash from the safe and threw them in. He couldn't believe it. Escape? Was that her mad plan? She opened the door of a refrigeration unit and lifted out a stoppered test tube half-filled with blue liquid. As she carefully fitted it into the briefcase, cushioning it inside the wadded money, the truth of what she was doing slammed into Jack: *"Logical mind except when her family is threatened."*

"My God," he whispered. "It's CD5."

Her face was immobile. She snapped the briefcase shut. Blood still trickled from her ear. She glanced at the doorway behind him. "Step aside, Jack."

She was leaving to go to Tory.

If she didn't die first herself.

"Rachel, let me come with you." He lifted his hands in surrender. He stepped closer, blocking her path. *If she goes there and dies, it's all over.* "You're not well enough," he urged gently. "Let me help you do this."

She scoffed. "Why would you?"

"Because it's Tory."

It was from his heart, and she saw it.

She hesitated. "If I could believe—"

The office door slammed open. Three FBI agents pounded in, weapons raised, taking in the scene: Rachel's bloody ear, the bloody letter opener in Jack's hand. "Drop the knife!" one yelled.

Jack realized what she'd been groping at earlier on the desk: the security alarm.

The agent shouted again to drop the knife, step back, raise his hands, and make no sudden moves. Jack heard the click of the safety catch released. *"Do it now!"*

With a maddened groan he dropped the letter opener. Two

agents grabbed his arms and dragged him away from Rachel. She slipped her gun in her pocket. Carrying the briefcase, she headed for the door while the FBI man told Jack, "Don't move!"

Handcuffs clamped his wrists.

Rachel was gone.

It took him over half an hour just to get them to listen.

They marched him outside, handcuffed, surrounded by a throng of more agents, and excited local police, and a hastily conscripted doctor to dress his bleeding wound. They shoved him into a car to transport him to Bangor, ignoring his protests amid their flurry of activity and calls on car phones and radios, asking for instructions from superiors. Not until they were speeding along Route 1A, with Jack wedged between two of them in the back, did he flatly declare, like the madman they thought he was, that virus bombs were about to detonate in cities across the country and around the world, that global plague was imminent, and that only he could stop it. They finally gave him their stunned attention.

"I've got to speak to Carson Colwell," he ordered. The agent to his right held a phone. Jack, wrists cuffed behind him, thrust his chin toward it. "Get him on the line."

"Mr. Colwell left San Juan as soon as he knew we'd apprehended you," the agent said nervously. "He's on his way."

"Then patch me through to his plane, God damn it!"

The agent seemed frozen by doubt.

Jack's bloody knee shot up, knocking the phone from the man's hand. *Do it now!*

# 26

THE LEARJET SCREAMED DOWN THE RUNWAY. Rachel was on her feet before it taxied to a stop. She opened the clamshell door and warm evening air rushed into the air-conditioned cabin.

*Warm as the Rwandan rain, warm as blood.*

The suburban Atlanta flying club—no air traffic control—looked like any modest municipal airport on any normal evening. A low, rambling terminal. A few parked cars and service trucks. Chain-link fencing. Neon-lit fast-food outlets on the street beyond, wafting a faint odor of frying oil. No sign that the city twelve miles away was in the throes of panic.

*Tory, I'm coming.*

She picked up the briefcase and stepped off the plane. As she walked across the tarmac she could faintly hear car horns blaring far in the distance. Inside the club terminal a knot of employees, a half-dozen men, stood silently around a TV. Passing behind them, Rachel glimpsed the screen: a man in military fatigues making an announcement.

At the taxi rank only one cab sat waiting, a dented green Buick, the driver nowhere in sight.

She went back inside. "Is there a cabdriver?"

The men looked at her, dazed.

"That's me, ma'am." A burly black man with grizzled gray hair.

"You're available?"

"Guess so."

They went out to the green Buick. "Where to?" he asked as he opened his door.

"Downtown." She slid into the backseat, careful to keep the briefcase upright.

He flopped behind the wheel, frowning. "Maybe you ain't heard, ma'am. They got bad sickness there. Real bad."

"Yes. I'm a doctor."

"That so?" He turned to look at her. "So you got some special—what they call it?—immunity, I guess?"

She tightened her grip on the briefcase. *My blood for my daughter's blood.* "Go," she said. "Please."

The driver shook his head. "Sorry. Army's put up road-blocks."

"There must be some way. I'll make it worth your while."

He studied her. "Wasn't easy gettin' out. Be plenty hard gettin' back *in.*"

She handed him a thick wad of cash. "Is five thousand dollars enough?"

His eyes widened. He took the money and examined it. On the car radio a clipped, male, military voice was giving instructions on staying indoors and keeping windows and doors closed, and announcing emergency numbers for po-lice and ambulance services. The quarantine was being strictly enforced, he warned. Persons found out-of-doors would be taken into custody.

"Man, that's bad," the driver murmured, shaking his head while he counted the cash. "It don't bother *me,* on account of this bug don't hurt men. But you . . . You sure 'bout this, ma'am?"

"Just go."

He shrugged. "Long as you know what you're doin'." He tucked away the cash and started the car, adding with grim satisfaction, "My wife and kids're in Disney World."

As he pulled away from the curb, he turned up the radio. The announcer was listing roads that were closed. "Folks is so scared," the driver said, "they all been tryin' to get out. Few hours ago, you couldn't hardly move on them roads. But the army come in, cleaned things up some."

"I'm not familiar with Atlanta," Rachel said. "Do you know Grady Hospital?"

He nodded. "See that blue dome yonder? Up top the Hyatt Regency? Grady's just a hop skip away."

She looked at the lights of the skyline where a bubble of deep royal blue on the hotel roof glowed like a beacon in the dark.

*I'm coming.*

The driver was frowning at her in the rearview mirror. "Them GI's are mighty jumpy. They clap eyes on you, a woman, they'll haul you out for sure, doctor or no."

"Stop," she said. "I'll get in the trunk."

As she climbed into the dank space that smelled of gasoline and mildew, the driver said, "Don't you fret, ma'am." He gave her a sly look. "I know me a way or two them good ol' boys *don't* know."

# 27

GRADY MEMORIAL HOSPITAL WAS UNDER SIEGE.

At first, looking out from the FBI car, Jack could see only a hatching of crisscrossed headlight beams as the car crawled in among the snarl of vehicles in front of the twenty-one-story medical complex on Butler Street. Police cruisers, ambulances, fire trucks, FBI cars, armored military vans. It was almost impossible to move. On the flight from Maine, Jack's escort, Agent Heaslip, had been giving him updates as they came in.

First bulletin: Rachel had taken over the hospital's sixth floor at gunpoint, sending the staff out, and now she had the authorities in a standoff. Heaslip had been astounded by her action; it was suicide. Jack was not. He knew exactly what she was doing. Trying to save Tory. His despair and hope fused—one relentless impulse to reach them both in time.

Second bulletin: Grady and every other hospital in the city were overflowing with victims.

Third: the dying had begun.

As their car was squeezed to a halt, Jack looked up at the floodlit building's facade. The windows were dark squares in the illumination of the searchlights. Tory was in there, suffering.

He pushed open the door and plunged into the swarm of people. Pain stabbed from the wound in his thigh. Heaslip was right behind him, yelling, "Doctor, slow down!"

There were soldiers, SWAT teams, officers in riot gear, FBI, reporters restrained far back behind barricades. All the faces were male. Helicopters thrummed overhead. All around was a din of barked commands, voices crackling on two-way radios, and the clatter of weapons being prepared.

Jack and Heaslip were pushing through toward the FBI command post when Jack spotted Colwell. He'd never seen a man age so much in mere hours. Over the phone to Colwell's plane, when Jack had finally told him everything—about Rachel, her dead man's switch, the hidden data—he had heard, inside the awful silence, Colwell's thundering realization of his failure: his obstructive obsession with Jack, his fatal blindness about Rachel. Jack now saw it etched in his face.

Colwell was still proceeding like the calm professional, though. He stood conferring with a circle of about twenty FBI agents in riot gear, all equipped with submachine guns and night-vision apparatus. "FBI Hostage Rescue Team," Heaslip told Jack as they moved closer. "Elite SWAT guys."

Colwell, giving last-minute instructions to the HRT commander, turned Jack's way. Their eyes met, acknowledging all they shared: an admission of despair, a refusal to accept it, and pain over the woman in both their minds, Tory.

Jack was thinking of Laurel, too. Of the millions who would die if Rachel died. The FBI was at work alerting couriers across the country and around the world, but there were so many: large corporations, small companies, independents, unlicensed fly-by-nights, individuals even. No one knew what kind of containers to look for this time, or what alias Rachel had used in consigning the shipments to the storage companies.

As the HRT commander moved off with his team, Jack, limping, pushed through to Colwell. "Are they going in?" he asked anxiously. "Do they know Rachel must not be harmed?"

"They know," Colwell said, and Jack heard the edge of rage beneath the steely voice. "She's armed, with patients as hostages, and she's threatened to kill them if we interfere."

Unnerved, Heaslip said, "The virus'll kill them anyway."

"Including her, right, Doctor?" Colwell asked.

Jack nodded. "Yes. I don't believe she has enough CD5 for herself." He didn't utter the myriad other fears tearing at him: maybe not even enough for Tory . . . if it even works . . . and then, all the others here, millions more if the switch closes. *Too little, too late.*

Colwell said evenly, "So we've got to find out two things fast. Where she's stored your therapy data, and how she's rigged her dead man's switch. Our computer systems analysts in D.C. are standing by. All they need are her codes." He looked Jack in the eye. "She used to consider you her friend, Doctor. If I get you inside, you think you can talk to her?"

Jack looked up at the dark windows. Her friend? No one could hate her more.

"Get me in," he said. "I'll try."

Jack watched as the HRT commander took half his team inside. The moment their point man reported to Colwell from position on the sixth floor, Colwell radioed the Atlanta SWAT team to confirm they'd secured the exits. Then, drawing his own side arm, he turned to Jack. "Ready?"

Jack took a deep breath. "Let's go."

He moved inside with Colwell and the rest of the HRT force. In the deserted lobby his nostrils stung at the smell of death. As the group swarmed up to the sixth floor, Jack ran with them. On the sixth floor the team took up position in the main corridor, and Jack and Colwell stopped with them. The advance team were still moving patients from this section of the corridor to safety, so they had to wait until the space was cleared. Watching the agents work, Jack stood catching his breath, wiping his sweating palms on his pants. He could hear women's voices, crying, moaning. The sounds were terrible, but at least they covered the team's movements. The HRT commander, ahead, was giving hand signals. Jack looked frantically back at Colwell: what did the signals mean? Then he understood—they were establishing that Rachel was in the hallway around the corner. The pit of his stomach cramped. In a moment, this would all be up to him.

He saw Colwell motion to the half-dozen sharpshooters to stand by. Then Colwell lifted a megaphone. For a moment he froze, and Jack could almost smell the man's dread. None of Colwell's experience in negotiating with desperate criminals, none of his training, not even his imagination, could have prepared him for this. Nor mine, Jack thought with a sickening stab of doubt.

"Rachel," Colwell finally called to her, "this is Carson Colwell. Can you hear me? I'd like to talk to you."

"Don't come any closer!" she called. "Don't let your men interfere with me, Carson. Virus deliveries are ready in other cities, and if I'm killed they'll be activated."

He said with calmness, real or pretended, "We need to talk about that."

"No more talking. It's over. If I see your men come this way I will kill *myself*."

Jack made a gesture to catch Colwell's eye. Colwell turned his head and Jack nodded vigorously to tell him, Yes, she'd do it!

"No one's coming, Rachel," Colwell said, a new flintiness in his voice. "You have my word. But there's someone who wants to see you. It's Jack Hunt. Will you let him come?"

Silence. Jack waited in agony. Why should she give in now?

Then: "Jack's here?"

"Right beside me. He wants very much to meet with you. Can I send him to you?"

Silence. Jack clenched his teeth, regretting every brutal word he'd ever said to her, every act that had poisoned her trust in him. *Please, Rachel, just one last time!*

Then: "Yes. Only Jack."

His heart almost sprang into his throat. Colwell swiveled to him and whispered fiercely, "Get her codes! *Go!*"

Moving down the silent corridor, Jack could hardly hear his own footsteps above the rasping pulse in his ears. As he neared the corner, his fingers felt for the small microphone the HRT technician had fitted in his breast pocket. He turned the corner into the hallway, and was immediately among a jumble of gurneys. Women lay on them moaning. Bloody dressings littered the floor. Jack blocked it all out. His target was Rachel.

He saw her standing at the far end of the hall near a fire door. On a trolley beside her lay her gun, a syringe, and the stoppered test tube with the blue fluid. Where was Tory? Hadn't Rachel found her? Was she on some other floor, writhing in terror and pain, alone?

*Get the codes,* his brain commanded. *It's all over—for Tory, for all of them—if you can't get the codes.*

He kept on toward Rachel, sidestepping the moaning women as obstacles in his path. Rachel watched him come.

Then he saw Tory lying on a gurney behind Rachel. His heart cracked. Her head was lolling on the bloodstained sheet. Her lips had split. Her gums were bleeding. Blood trickled from her nose. A sob like a saw blade ripped his throat. "Tory!"

He couldn't stop himself. He ran to her and took her by the shoulders and pulled her into his arms. She was so weak, her head flopped onto his shoulder. Frantically, he looked toward the test tube on the trolley. The blue fluid was almost gone. "Isn't it working?" he asked Rachel in despair.

"I don't know if it's enough. It's all I had."

Jack pressed Tory against him, helplessly willing his strength into her.

"Jack," Rachel said, clutching his arm. "Carson is going to stop me, and when he does you must give her—" She coughed, and pointed to the syringe. "Give the last injection. In twenty minutes. She's had two. Three's the minimum—at least an hour apart." She coughed again. "Twenty minutes. Do you understand?"

*Oh, God, if only it would work.*

"Do you understand?" she demanded hoarsely.

He noticed a bright bead of blood oozing from a crack in Rachel's lower lip. Her eyes were losing focus. The first visible symptoms. She was going to die in agony, like the rest of her victims. But Tory? "Yes," he said shakily, "I understand."

Tory suddenly moaned, "Why?"

Jack released his embrace enough to look at her face. Was she rallying?

Tory whispered, her eyes on Rachel. "Why did you do it? You were always . . . my idol," Blood dribbled from the corner of her mouth. "Why, Mother? When there was no need? We'd won."

Rachel seemed to rock on her feet. Jack saw this was breaking her heart. "The president lied," she said. "I had to act." She shook her head and looked at Jack as though supremely puzzled. "He could have chosen life, Jack. Why wouldn't he do that?"

The president lied? Jack had no answer.

Rachel suddenly winced in pain and reached out to brace herself against Tory's gurney. Jack knew there was no more time. He was holding Tory so tightly against him she was covering the mike. To do what he must, he had to let her go. He gently laid her down, then stood face to face with Rachel.

"You don't have much longer," he said. "When you're gone, the switch will close." He took hold of her arms. "I don't believe you want that. Not in the deepest, best part of you. I know you, Rachel, the way you used to be. Your brilliance. Your genius. Your soul. Don't let this be your legacy. Don't let this be the way you change the world. Let me stop it. Let me do it *for* you. Please, Rachel, tell me your codes."

A sharp noise clicked down the corridor. Rachel flinched. "Yes, you know me. And I know you. And if I tell . . . ?" She hesitated, then suddenly clamped her hands on his shoulders and locked her eyes on his. "Listen to me, Jack."

Her sudden focus caught him like an electrode in the chest. *She's going to tell me.*

"The switch," she said. "You keep it from closing by calling a number. At the prompt, you input a numeric code. The call has to be made by eleven. The numbers—" She grabbed the edge of Tory's gurney for balance, her strength ebbing. "A pencil?"

Jack groped in his pocket for a pen, then grabbed a doctor's abandoned clipboard from the floor. He scribbled the numbers Rachel dictated.

"Your therapy data," she went on quickly. "It's safe, but encrypted. You can access it through my Internet address and decrypt it with a simple alpha code—a name." Blood trickled from the crack in her lip. "My son's name."

*Paul!* Jack scribbled it, then stiffened as he heard the faint crackle of a radio down the hall. Colwell. He would have heard all of this over the mike. He had the codes now too.

"The Pear Tree Inn," Rachel said quietly.

Jack's eyes snapped back to her. She was watching his face intently. "Remember, Jack?" she whispered. "The daffodils?"

He stared at her, shaken. Their hotel outside London. Caution pricked his scalp. Something was wrong here.

A sudden deafening tramp of boots. Sharpshooters storming the hall. Jack froze, thinking wildly, *Colwell, no. You gave her your word.* He saw Colwell running with them. More commandos burst through the fire door near Rachel, shouting, flashing lights to stun her.

Rachel stood in shock, her back braced against Tory's gurney.

Colwell raised his weapon, aiming at her.

Jack cried, "No!" He threw himself against Rachel, pushing her down on top of Tory, shielding them both with his body.

"Hold your fire," Colwell shouted.

The sharpshooters halted, weapons still poised.

Rachel squirmed out from under Jack. She groped for the trolley, for the syringe. "Jack, remember!" she gasped. "The third injec—"

"She's going for the gun!" someone yelled.

Colwell fired twice. Her head and her heart.

Jack caught her in his arms. No! *No!*

*   *   *

"Jack? Are you there?"

His fingers trembled as he injected the last of the blue fluid into Tory's arm. Her eyelids fluttered as she hovered in and out of delirium. "It's all right," he said, using his sleeve to wipe blood from her mouth. He squeezed her hand. "You're going to be fine." He had no idea if it was true.

His eyes flicked to Colwell across the hall, standing with a few of his men, all on phones, working to dismantle Rachel's system. Jack could hear their ragged voices, see their tension, and he sensed again, with a slippery feeling in his stomach, that something was very wrong.

He was sitting on a chair in an abandoned room, alone with Tory. He'd pushed her gurney here, far from Rachel's body. Through the open door he was watching the cluster of Colwell and his men. One of them, a phone jammed between chin and shoulder, was relaying the code for the data to FBI computer specialists in Washington. On another phone, Colwell himself was making the call to halt the dead man's switch. Jack could see there was a problem. Uneasy, he went to the doorway.

Colwell, lowering the cell phone, saw him. "Woke up some old man," he said shakily. He hit the numbers again, verified the number with the person who answered, then closed the phone again, white-faced. Slowly, meticulously, he tried the number again. Again, he listened briefly, then lowered the phone. Jack saw his look of horror. And felt the horror himself. The number was no good.

"Sir," the agent on the other phone blurted, "you did say the code for the encrypted data was 'Paul,' correct?"

"Yes."

"The computer team is reporting that code doesn't get them in."

Jack felt a claw of fear. "My son's name," she had said.

But "Paul" was wrong. And the phone number Colwell had tried was wrong. *All the information she'd given was wrong.*

In fifteen minutes the dead man's switch would close.

Colwell was now in a frantic discussion with the other agents. Jack looked toward Rachel's body down the corridor. Two agents were lifting her onto a gurney, covering her with a bloodied sheet. And suddenly it struck him what was wrong. What she'd done.

"The Pear Tree Inn," she'd said. The English country hotel where he had come to her in the coach house surrounded by daffodils. The night before, in London, she'd told him the inn's phone number as they stood encircled by reporters, then had whispered as she passed him, "Deduct one numeral."

She had guessed Colwell was listening so she'd given the codes—in code. A message only Jack would understand.

*She handed me her power.* To carry on? For a moment, the enormity of it stunned him.

Tory moaned. The military din outside on the street reached him. All around him, the city was dying.

It wrenched him back. He ran across the hall. "Colwell."

Jack quickly explained. He dictated the altered digits, which Colwell furiously scribbled down. Jack watched him grab the phone and, very carefully, press the numbers. This time Colwell seemed to get through: no words, so probably a computer had answered. Colwell proceeded gingerly to enter the command, the reconfigured numeric code.

The other agent, who'd immediately relayed to the D.C. specialists the new rendering of "Paul" to unlock the therapy data, now called to Colwell in a panicky voice, "They're saying that doesn't work either."

Jack thought: Another of Rachel's tricks?

Colwell, desperation in his eyes, turned to Jack. Desperate himself, Jack saw nowhere else to go.

Then a feeble voice behind him said, "Not Paul."

Jack twisted around. Tory was staggering toward him, bracing herself against the wall as she came. Jack ran to her. Her face was chalky, her lips blue. "Not Paul," she said, clutching his arm, her voice a thread. "His nickname . . . she loved it." She stopped, coughing a mist of blood.

Jack twisted back to Colwell. "Curious George! Try it!"

Colwell wrenched the phone from the agent and shouted it over the line to D.C. Tory swayed on her feet. Her eyes rolled up in their sockets. *"Tory!"* Jack cried. He caught her in his arms as she collapsed.

# 28

WINTER STUBBORNLY PERSISTED IN POCKETS of the Maine woods. Driving from the Bar Harbor airport, Jack passed through countryside filigreed with spring buds in the youngest, freshest colors of green, where birds with nest twigs in their beaks were darting among the branches. When he turned onto the private road to Swallow Point, however, the deeper into the woods he went the more residue of winter he saw. Clumps of snow clung in hollows in the shade of trees. Melting knobs of ice, trapped under matted fallen leaves, dripped slowly down to their cores.

Some cores of sadness, Jack thought, would never melt.

The gate stood open, unattended, security no longer a priority here, and he drove through under the foliage canopy. It had been six months since he had passed these birches and maples and beeches, but the woods had endured unchanged. Nothing around him spoke of the chaos that had shaken the world outside. Nothing registered the human tragedy. Noth-

ing marked the final passing in the home at the end of this
road, but it was the reason Jack had come. Del Farr had died.

He wasn't sure who would be here for the memorial gathering—as he emerged from the woods he saw about two
dozen cars parked in front of the house—but there was one
person he wanted very much to see. When he'd got her note
about her father's death, the contact from her, after so many
months of solitude, had shafted through his darkness like
sunlight through a forest.

The old house, he saw as he pulled up, looked as unchanged as the woods. The government had confiscated
Rachel's corporate assets, but Swallow Point, which had
been in Del's name, they could not touch. It felt strange to
be back, Jack thought as he climbed the verandah steps.

In the living room about forty people stood around awk-
wardly, holding coffee cups. Men in suits, women in
dresses, a few kids scrubbed for the event and fidgeting.
Conversation was muted.

Jack spotted Tory across the room. In the six months since
he'd seen her, sorrow had sculpted its claim on her. Her face
was thinner, her eyes more watchful, her air more subdued.
The effect only intensified her beauty, he thought. Turning
her head, she met his gaze, and a faint smile lighted her
eyes. He started to go to her, but an anxious-looking older
couple drew her into conversation. Jack held back.

"Oh, Dr. Hunt," Doris, the housekeeper, greeted him, "it's
so good of you to come. We saw you the other day on TV.
The president giving you that medal."

"How are you, Doris?"

She shrugged sadly. "Getting by." She leaned closer and
said in a conspiratorial whisper, "Don't look now, but half
these people want your autograph."

"They'll get over it."

The president's invitation to accept a special humanitarian award had reached him in Italy three weeks ago, yet as he'd looked out his hotel window at the glacial beauty of Lake Como, he'd felt only a profound melancholy. Twenty-two thousand women and girls in Atlanta had died.

Tory had been right about the nickname that night at Grady Hospital. "Curious George" had accessed the stored data. And the decoded phone number had halted the dead man's switch. With Colwell organizing FBI and military support, Jack had coordinated a nationwide operation to mass-produce the CD5 therapy. Within hours, labs across the country were preparing the antidote. The army flew it into the quarantine city and the CDC managed an inoculation blitz. The treatment had saved the lives of hundreds of thousands of stricken victims, and prevented the spread of the disease beyond Atlanta. Jack had been hailed as a national hero. Yet over twenty-two thousand had died.

Afterward, in Washington, there were months of hearings and inquiries. Jack gave reports, answered endless questions from committees, told everything he knew. But he'd shunned the mobs of reporters. Colwell, after tracking the virus containers in other cities here and abroad and having them destroyed, had been promoted, and now headed up the FBI's National Security Division. Jack could only approve. Under hellish conditions, the man had done his job.

Tory, as soon as she'd recovered, had been obliged to give public testimony too, about PGT, although the FBI laid no charges once they were satisfied she had played no part in her mother's crimes. Jack had watched in admiration as she'd handled herself in the hearings with dignity and restraint while the media trumpeted her mother as evil incarnate. He had seen Tory's private suffering, though, so he'd stayed away to give her space. That was hard. In those awful hours when he'd known she might die, he had realized all that she meant to him. While working round the clock on the treatment program in the following days, he'd continually checked with the doctors about her, drawing relief from the news of her steady recovery.

Laurel had been his lifesaver. He'd called her after that night in Grady, so grateful she hadn't been harmed. She'd cried and apologized for the way she'd treated him; he told her none of that mattered, he was just happy to hear her voice. Later, during the Washington hearings, she'd come to stay with him for several days, her presence a comfort, just like the old days, until the start of classes took her back to Boston. Jack had been glad to see her get back to a normal life. His own life felt on hold.

A month before, while Tory was still recuperating in the hospital, he'd gone to visit her, flowers in hand. He'd stopped at the doorway when he saw Colwell sitting on her bed. They were quietly talking; their little boy stood beside Colwell. The intimacy of the scene made Jack back away, and made him face a hard truth. He had no rights here. She was Colwell's wife.

When the inquiries were done, he left the country. Went to Scotland first and hiked for long days in the rainy highlands. Went on to Italy, where his host in Milan, a friend on the university's medical faculty, didn't ask questions about his days spent mountain climbing, or walking alone by the lake, or wandering in galleries and gazing at sculpture. There, on a chilly hill above Lake Como, he said his final, silent good-bye to Marisa. A lovely woman he'd barely known.

Three weeks ago he'd received President Lowell's invitation, so he'd come straight home. A few days later he got Tory's note about Del.

Finally, when it was clear that no more guests were going to straggle in, a white-haired man introduced himself to the gathering as Del's brother, Arthur, then cleared his throat and began solemnly, "I want to thank you all for coming."

Jack looked over at Tory. She was listening gravely to her uncle's eulogy, another male relative's arm around her shoulders. Jack suddenly felt out of place. He'd come to honor Del, and in his heart he did, but he wasn't part of this group. He wasn't family.

He quietly made his way out the door.

Standing on the dock in the raw spring wind, he gazed out at the unsettled ocean, thinking of Rachel. Like some vengeful sea goddess who'd risen from the deep to send a whirlwind against humanity, she had, in the end, been swallowed into its vortex. She could not be more alien to him now, or more dead. He shivered.

"Cold?"

He turned. It was Tory, coming down the lawn, the grass a rippling palette of shadows around her as sunshine fought through racing clouds. "Just thinking," he said as she reached him.

They stood together, looking out at the energy-charged world of sea and sky. Jack felt as turbulent as the scene. How was he to begin?

"You did a fine job, organizing this," he said. "Del would have been pleased."

She nodded. "So many friends, his colleagues, old students. Poor Ron got pretty choked up. He'd been with my father for eleven years and he told me, 'Half these folks I don't even know, but they've been telling me stories about him like he was their best pal.'"

"Doesn't surprise me," Jack said. "Del was a good man."

"The best. Tolerant, always ready to see good in people. A truly wise man." She crossed her arms, hugging herself in the chilly wind. "It broke him, that she was gone. One morning I was bringing him tea and he just sort of turned himself off for good. I saw it in his eyes—like a switch. Next day, another stroke. He never recovered. And yet, not long before that, he'd looked at me with an odd smile and said, 'Isn't this world extraordinary?' Imagine. After all he'd suffered, in knowing about her."

Jack listened gravely. He doubted that Tory could ever forgive Rachel, but he felt that Del probably had.

She looked at him. "You, too. All those weeks, knowing about her, unable to turn her in. It must have been horrible living with that truth."

Truth, he thought, steeling himself. She deserved to know it all. "Tory, there's something I need to tell you. About Rachel and me. Once, we—"

"I know."

He was taken aback.

"At least, I guessed," she said. "I had a hint, and"—she looked down—"and I remember the way she looked at you."

He waited to see some kind of door shut between them. He'd prepared himself for it, and he certainly wouldn't blame her. Instead she said simply, somberly, "Jack, when my mother wanted something, *nobody* could say no."

He watched her in wonder. Clear-eyed, forgiving—she was her father's daughter.

"So," she said, briskly changing the subject, "what's up with you? Climbed enough mountains yet?"

"Maybe too many."

"Does that mean you're ready to come back to earth?"

He nodded. "I've been in touch with One World Medics. Their cholera camp in Sierra Leone needs some straightening out. I leave tomorrow." He'd be glad to get back to work.

"Mr. Fix-It," she said, smiling.

Mr. Tongue-Tied at the moment, he thought. She'd spoken of everyone but herself, and he longed to know. "Tory," he said gently, "how are *you*?"

"Busy. I've been in touch with some people, environmental groups, hashing out some ideas. I'm considering launching an organization to target congressional seats, exact a direct political price for bad environmental policies. Sort of a new improved People for a Global Tomorrow."

Jack couldn't hide his surprise.

"The wrongness of her crimes doesn't change what's right," Tory said quietly. "During the campaign I learned a lot about the sorry state of the world. I want to carry on. But I know people are uncomfortable with my . . . pedigree." She turned to him. "I could use your help, Jack. On the board of directors. You're an international hero again, presidential medal and all. You could help attract some serious attention."

He shook his head in awe. "You're amazing."

"Does that mean you'll join me?"

"Tory, I hope you know I'll always be there to help you, but—"

"But?"

"I'd like to do more." For weeks he'd felt an inchoate nagging that the One World Medics work wasn't enough. "I don't even know what yet. Hell, I don't even know what I'm talking about. Are you sure I'm the man you want for this?"

She said warmly, "Very sure."

The verandah wind chime far behind them sounded faintly in a gust. Tory looked up at the house. The sea-resonant tinkling seemed to hold her focus. "People are telling me to sell Swallow Point, move away from the terrible associations. To me, though, the memories aren't terrible. I can't hate this place. Can't even hate my mother. At first, yes, in the awful days after Atlanta. She murdered thousands, almost murdered me. But somehow, inside that fog of evil, I don't see my mother's *face*. It's as though someone else committed those atrocities, someone wild, deranged. I can't feel any connection there with the inspiring woman I grew up with in this house. The memories remain pure."

She turned back to him. "I only hope it won't hurt Chris."

"Chris'll be fine wherever *you* are."

"I live for the weeks I get to be with him."

"Isn't he with you now?"

"With Carson this week. You didn't know we'd got a divorce?"

"No." He hoped the thrill he felt didn't show on his face.

"We've worked out joint custody. It's the only civilized arrangement. Best for Chris."

Jack looked out at the sea. He told himself he had no right to hope. He was too old for her. It was too weird, his past affair with her mother. Besides, she'd been through such hell. Yet hope he did.

"I came out here to tell you something," Tory said. Her businesslike tone was suddenly vibrant, as though suppressing excitement. "About two months ago I got a statement from the Credite Suisse Bank in Zurich—an annual statement on a numbered account in my name. Except that I've never in my life opened an account there. The depositor is anonymous, and of course there's no way to trace their identity. Jack, the balance is just over three hundred million dollars. A life-blood infusion for PGT, out of the blue."

He felt a shiver between his shoulder blades. "Rachel."

She nodded. "I had no idea until I got the statement. A year ago, apparently, she was worth over six hundred million dollars, but when the government confiscated her estate there was only half that left. From what I've been able to find out, she'd liquidated most of her offshore assets and deposited that whole amount in Switzerland for me. And she did it a month before she set her terrible plan in motion. She knew, Jack. Knew she wasn't going to make it."

A benevolent final blessing? he wondered. Or the implacable grip of the dead? Did it matter which? He'd never believed money was intrinsically good or evil; people gave it that power in how they used it. He was sure Tory would put this legacy to the most dynamic and positive use. He suddenly realized: that's what Rachel intended.

"You're the only person I've told," she said. "There's no one else I'd trust with the location of three hundred million the government still wants."

He was moved that she would confide it to him.

"You're wondering why tell you at all?" she asked. "Because I'm hoping you'll come on the board of the new PGT."

"I told you, I'll always be around to help you."

"Well, actually," she said with a sly smile, "I'm talking about you being around a *lot*. In D.C. In fact, right on the Hill."

He didn't follow. "The Hill?"

"Yesterday I received a letter from Senator Owen. Remember him?"

Of course. Good man. Frank Owen had been one of the campaign's staunchest supporters.

"He's resigning his seat," Tory said. "Quincy and his CCA pit bulls didn't succeed in digging up any dirt on the poor guy during the crisis, but he was shaken by their harassment and I guess he's had enough. He heard you were out of the country, so he wrote me asking if I thought you'd consider running for his seat. He'd like to endorse you, Jack. He says you won't let the CCA types of this world get away with their shit." She smiled. "That's a paraphrase, but it's his general sentiment. And I agree. You're a man who won't be beholden to any special interests. Even if your character didn't ensure that, this legacy will. You can be truly independent, and work for real change right from the heart of the system. What do you say?"

He was surprised. Very surprised. But he liked the idea. Somehow it felt natural, as though this was the challenge he'd been wanting but didn't know it until she'd made it concrete.

Challenge? No, it went deeper than that. "Tory," he said, needing to share this with her, "for a moment, that night in Atlanta, when I realized what she'd done in giving me the codes, I was stunned by the capability she'd put in my hands. Her global threat to do right. She'd handed me her power, and for a moment I actually craved to run with it."

"Only for a moment."

"But how powerful the feeling was."

"Don't kid yourself, Jack. You'd make a lousy terrorist."

"True enough," he said, glad to have that bubble burst. "But there's another reason. We shouldn't need some godlike intervention to bring us to our senses about how to live on this planet without destroying it. If that's what it takes, maybe we don't deserve to prevail. We've got to clean up our mess and it's time we began, here and now."

"Damn straight," she said with a grin. "And you're the guy to tell the country. From Congress."

Jack nodded, excited. He was up for this. Then reality gave him a slap: he'd have to get elected first. "Frank Owen's a class act to follow. You think I'd have a chance?"

"A chance? I think the voters will eat you with a spoon!"

God, he loved that smile of hers. "You'll manage the campaign, I hope?"

"I'll be handing out free spoons."

He laughed. It felt so great—to laugh again. He wanted to do a lot more of that, and with her. He didn't feel old. He didn't feel wrong. He'd have six weeks in Sierra Leone, and he was already counting the days until he could see her again.

They started up to his car, Tory explaining the intricate machinery of the Senate to him. He was watching the breeze play with her hair like a lover.

He stopped. He took her face in his hands, gently, longingly. It was not the gesture of a candidate to his campaign manager, and Tory blushed. He didn't think he'd ever seen her blush before.

Then she smiled. A big, dazzling smile. "Jack, I thought you'd never ask."

Suddenly, the world was his home again.